I0592621

THE THUNDEREGG SPEAKS

K MCVERE

An Imprint of K McVere LLC Publisher
Cover Design by Red Couch Creative, inc.

K McVere LLC.
P.O. Box 50262
Boise, ID 83705

ISBN: 978-0-692-14133-5

Cover design by Red Couch Creative, inc.
Interior design by K McVere LLC

Chapter One

In the Owyhee Mountains there is a place where thundereggs sleep. The coyote passes over them. The whistle pig sleeps beside them. The roots of the sage stretch to meet them. In ugly misshapen shells that hide their beauty, their white hearts intersect in rays of opal and they wait—impervious to the elements, although naked and vulnerable to the collector's eye. Daniel believed he had such an eye, more powerful than Superman's x-ray vision.

Experience had taught him to trust in his instincts. He could pick up an egg resembling nothing more than a dried concrete ball, rough to the touch with bumps on the surface like boils and just know whether something special hid inside. Today his search had uncovered two samples of petrified wood, as large as his hand, and a bit of picture jasper. No thunderegg though. There were discarded eggs on the ground behind him, split in half, but nothing worth taking home.

He sat on the hillside with his elbows on his knees and his hands pressing into his cheeks. He stared at the ground between his legs. There was life going on here in this bit of earth: cheatgrass, a new born shoot that might one-day bloom into sagebrush, bits of crushed rock sprinkled over sand and dirt, an ant making its way home, and a monarch resting between flights. He hadn't moved for so long his legs were almost numb and a throbbing of drums inside his head begun to play along his temples. He had to blink away the whiteness of the heat radiating off the ground. He could no longer stand the stillness or the sweat dripping from his forehead into his eyes. He wiped the sweat with the back of his hand. The monarch flew away. He shifted position. The ant picked up speed.

He and the ant had become acquainted. He'd watched the ant make his way home. Daniel stood up slow—careful, careful of the ant. He compared his journey home to the ant's journey and decided the ant had less distance to cover; yet, Daniel would be home before him. He wanted the ant to be a boy, a boy like him. We could be friends, he thought. We could play together on the hillside. We could share secrets and laugh at the spider.

—

Maggie Treloar watched the man make his way down the hillside moving like a goat, a two-legged goat, fat and furry. He did not come down like most folks, direct slipping and sliding in the loose soil, sending rocks and dirt tumbling to the bottom, but rather he traveled south for a bit following the cow's path than north and downward and once again back to his original desire the Anderson Pass which was between the Old Anderson farm and the newly built Eagle Gateway Boarding School.

On his way, he stepped carefully around sagebrush and over rocks and made a wide swath to avoid burrows. At the bottom of the hillside, he turned to face east and proceeded to walk along the side of the road. Even though he had trespassed on her favorite spot, Maggie appreciated the careful way the man maneuvered through the desert. She supposed he must be one of the local geologists from the university, what with his backpack slung over his shoulder and the binoculars riding on his neck.

—

Vera paused in her work to watch the man come down from the hill beyond her house. He walked carefully as if walking in a mine field. Once he descended the steep slope he picked up speed, his tennis shoes kicking up dust behind him and his green backpack thumping against his broad shoulder. He cut across Vera's property, her fallow ten acres of land which came with the farmhouse was the quickest way to Jump Creek Road. She could not see his face, only the odd way he moved as if he had to force his arms and legs to obey him. She watched him become a smaller and smaller figure in the distance, until a clump of taller sagebrush, what the locals called mahogany, hid him from view.

All morning Vera had been pulling weeds and neglected dried up husks which had once been plants from the garden growing along the east side of her house. Once the shade had made the work bearable but now the sun had moved, and the light burned through the back of her cotton shirt. Her plan had been to remove all the plants, the tenacious bulbs, and the stubborn rhubarb with its glossy purple-green blades.

Someday she would plant Prickly Pear or as her mother liked to call them Elephant Ear Cactus, yucca also, and Mexican Stonecrop, as well as many other succulents. Potentially in a few years' time, she hoped to xeriscaping the entire front face of the property. The old farmhouse would have a blanket of flowering plants come next May from cactus and yucca to the white perfumed flowers of the catalpa trees. She might even keep a few of the roses, the floribundas perhaps and two of the larger ornamental plants;

though most of her landscaping would be drought resistant shrubs and succulents.

Vera sat back on her heels and wiped the sweat off her brow. The truth came to her slowly. The man she had seen was a type of person who made some people uncomfortable. She recognized him as belonging to a group of people the world referred to as disabled or special or back in her mother's day, the pejorative term retarded which was still used sometimes; although, she was confident social pressure would eradicate the term. She'd seen people like him on buses and occasionally in movies or on television but never up close, never as a neighbor.

It was 1985. The school for the blind and deaf in Gooding, Idaho had been around since the early1900s and she was sure there would be many more. Times were changing, the Rehabilitation Act of 1973 meant people with disabilities could not be discriminated against with respect to access and employment from federal agencies. The act wasn't sweeping reform; but someday, people with disabilities would have equal opportunity in housing and health care. Although, people were still afraid of what they didn't understand; gradually, she was confident more people would become accustomed to the need to treat people with disabilities with respect.

Yet when would the time come for her people, she wondered? Human nature decreed that there would always be someone or some group the insecure, the ignorant, or the nasty could punish for not being more like them. She had few illusions about people now. She'd seen her share of good and bad. The truly nasty specimens always find a way to make themselves feel good no matter how many social changes occur. For them, in order to feel superior, there has to be someone at the bottom of the ladder, a group who they can blame for the ills of the world.

The sight of the young man enjoying himself on a beautiful sunny day in May reminded her that a break from gardening was in order. She rose to her feet and made her way inside the cool house. After drinking a nice cold glass of lemonade and eating a few cookies, Vera spotted her fiddle on the kitchen window seat. The window seat looked out upon the backyard which she carefully avoided because she already knew there was a whole hell of a lot of work to be done there.

She sat down on her brand-new cushion which she'd made for the window seat specifically, the colorful material for the cushion chosen over several visits to a sweet little fabric shop in Boise. She had measured and cut and sewn with much swearing and hair

3

pulling. But once she'd finished the project, she had been very pleased with the result; the cushion looked marvelous and its bright blue and yellow flowers with the gold thread weaved among them made her kitchen so cozy and modern.

Feeling good for the first time in a long time, she put her fiddle on her shoulder and began to play *The Queen of the May* just the way her mother had taught her. She sang along and when she couldn't remember all the lyrics she hummed, "Bring flowers of the fairest. Bring flowers of the rarest, from garden and forest, no, woodland, hum, hum."

She gave up on singing the verse and just played the tune as she remembered her Nonnie, her sweet great-grandmother used to play it when Vera was a child. In 1884, her Nonnie had immigrated to America from Scotland. She'd been sixteen and with her had come her older brother. There was no one in their family left back home. Only now did Vera appreciate her great-grandmother's incredible courage and toughness.

As the story goes her Nonnie not only traveled the vast ocean between countries in a cramped dark hold set aside for third class passengers, once she got to America she traveled the backroads and highways, buried a husband along the way and finally met the love of her life at the age of forty-six. When she met him, she was a childless-widow. Cawley Allaway was ten years younger than her. It was 1914; he had joined up to fight the Germans in Europe a week before meeting her great-grandmother.

They parted never expecting to meet again; and fifteen months later, Cawley returned to the states with bad lungs and a missing eye. It took him six months to find Nonnie. Once he did, he discovered he had a daughter called Sorcha. He found her, and the Lee clan camped a few miles beyond the orchards of Orange County, California. There were camps set up all along the route to the orchards with many groups claiming certain locations. Back then, according to Vera's mother fruit pickers didn't have the luxury of indoor plumbing and soft beds. They had to fend for themselves for a cool place to put up their tents.

Over the years, the Lee clan moved from job to job, picking fruit, planting seeds, harvesting wheat, milking cows, and tending the young. Struana Lee Ferguson Caumlo and Cawley Aidan Allaway never married. They had one child Sorcha. Vera's grandmother Sorcha had four children with her husband Cam and three of them survived: Vera's mother Analetta, her Aunt Vista, and her Uncle Aidan.

Vera's great-grandparents were together for thirty more years. Nonnie managed to live to the age of ninety-four. Vera didn't want to think about that terrible day in 1962. She had been the eldest and responsible for her siblings. She had been 13. Their mother had been left behind in Texas to have her fourth child. After Nonnie's brother died, Uncle Patrick Lee became the head of the clan. Out of respect for Nonnie's age and infirmity, the Lee family wintered in Florida. No one knew that Analetta's baby had died and she nearly died with him. When Analetta returned to the family, she discovered her grandmother was dead and her children separated and sent to foster homes.

As the last of her line, Vera's traveling days were over. The desire to set down roots started the day she watched her Nonnie die, the same day the police raided the camp and rounded up anyone under the age of eighteen and sent them to foster homes. Vera's conviction grew stronger when her mother, after recovering from her illness, retrieved Vera and the others, and returned to the same nomadic life with the expectation that everything would return to normal.

Nothing was normal anymore for Vera. The older members of the family were clueless. It was 1964. The world was a different place. Travelers like the Lee Family had always lived on the fringes of society; but now, they could no longer be assured the police and civil servants would look the other way. Laws were being passed and enforced: child labor laws, the Civil Rights Act, the fight for a decent wage and the formation of the United Farm Workers. It was all changing.

At sixteen, after having lived her whole life on the road, Vera was enraged by the hippies and their communes and their obsession with freedom. Freedom was an illusion. Did they honestly think that running around naked and smoking pot and living off the land was freedom?

No.

It was not.

It took more backbreaking work to set up and tear down a campsite every week, sometimes every morning, to find and fetch water, to preserve food than it would have been to find a job, buy a refrigerator, and pay for water to be pumped into your house. After having this epiphany, Vera left them all behind: the Lee clan, her mother, and her younger siblings. She lied about her age and found a job working as a cashier in a grocery store. If Nonnie could do it, Vera reasoned she could do it too.

And here she was eighteen years later living in a house – which she owned – which she paid taxes to keep – which did not move. Would she regret her decision to buy this farm and settle down in this community again? Was her reasoning based on revenge? Arthur Vlasky her former husband had taken away her trust in her instincts and what she had grown to love the most – the ranch. Now she had her own home which he could not take away. As long as she paid her mortgage and her taxes, the house belonged to her. She would make her new home beautiful. She would work hard and create a warm, cozy, safe haven. Someday, she would have the finest garden in all of Owyhee County.

It would be a long time before Vera felt as much joy as she felt that sunny beautiful afternoon in May.

—

Andrew Treloar driving on Jump Creek Road spotted Daniel Harden walking on the shoulder of the road. Before Daniel turned up the drive toward his home, he noticed Treloar' Jeep Laredo and paused to wave. Andrew waved back. Despite the petty cruelties Daniel had endured over the years, he was still more even-tempered than most grownups. Every time Andrew saw Daniel he was reminded of Daniel's father Michael Harden. Michael had been years older than Andrew in 1973, old enough to marry and have a kid and a good job in town while Andrew was on the point of finishing his senior year at Marsing High. For some inexplicable reason Michael had joined the Marines, even though the war had become unpopular and he had already done his two years straight out of high school.

It was a shame what had happened. Why was it always the poor who ended up suffering for old men's dreams of glory? Michael had become a statistic, an MIA, his family, and friends unable to mourn him because they still had hope. Constance Harden, his wife, had no trouble forgetting Michael. A year after he had been reported missing in action, Constance left Idaho and moved to California.

Maybe Michael's sudden decision to join the Marines had been out of shame for what he had produced? At least that's what some mean-spirited people said about him. Andrew didn't remember Michael being mean-spirited. He'd been a jock, a wrestler for the high school and street smart too. He collected antique guns and thundereggs. He hunted. He fished. His heroes had been godfathers, gangsters, and cowboys who could outwit the law. Michael's son Daniel, as Andrew recalled had been a six-year-old skinny kid who walked with a brace on his right leg and cultivated a prepared wariness on his round face. No longer was he that skinny

6

kid. From the back Andrew could see Michael's wide shoulders, muscled arms, and heavy legs. Socially, Daniel was stuck at around ten or eleven years of age, while the body continued to grow into manhood. Now Daniel resembled Hollywood's version of Doctor Frankenstein's creation; and children ever the cruelest of what humanity could produce enjoyed reminding Daniel of that fact.

He and Daniel were about the same height and there the difference ended. Daniel was six feet three inches tall and weighed about two hundred and fifty pounds now – a big guy. Nobody he would want to tangle with anywhere or at any time. If life had turned out differently, Daniel might have been a wrestler like his father. What a shame. When he recalled the numerous times, he had watched Daniel talking about his favorite subject – rock collecting, Daniel looked as serene as a Buddha. Andrew wanted to believe Daniel's father would be happy that Daniel had found a hobby he loved. There had been nothing idle about Michael Harden and that was equally true of his son Daniel.

Once Andrew cleared the outskirts of Marsing Idaho, he continued down I55 until he came to the intersection where he could turn left onto US 95 which pristine highway wound through the Owyhee Mountain Range like a ribbon of black silk from the overlook to McBride Road and on to Jordan Valley, Oregon. Owyhee County covered over 7,600 square miles and was a favorite spot for hunters, hikers, rock-hounds, and tourists. If a traveler wanted he could turn onto US 95 and head for McBride Road then wind his way to Succor Creek National Park or in the other direction to the red sandstone cathedral spires of Leslie Gulch where he could end up at the Owyhee Reservoir; and if he'd planned his trip carefully, he could have his fishing pole in one of the many creeks and rivers along the entire county before ten a.m.

On such a beautiful spring day the idea was tempting. He had his nephew Kit's fishing pole in the truck cab and the tackle box in the truck's toolbox; and maybe, he could find himself a nice spot along the Snake River to do a bit of fishing and napping. Or, instead, he could continue down US 95 and keep going until he hit Winnemucca, Nevada and do a bit of gambling.

Unfortunately, those options had to be put on hold today; Andrew's job was to head to his family's farm in Mintlaw, Idaho. The farming community chose the name Mintlaw because a few of the major families happened to be of Scottish ancestry and only five families showed up for the christening of the town's name at the Anderson farmhouse in 1935. The Owyhee Project had been a big draw for these families who had immigrated to Idaho with the hopes of making a living farming and ranching. A few of the families had come from Mintlaw in Aberdeenshire, Scotland and remembered it fondly. Perhaps because the area consists mostly of mountains and canyons rather than smooth flat places, Mintlaw seemed like a good name at the time.

The tiny town of Mintlaw sits between the bigger towns of Marsing and Homedale. Mintlaw has about 700 to 800 people in any given census year. As Andrew neared the town of Mintlaw he obeyed the posted speed of twenty-five miles an hour and crawled through the town passing Lucy's Diner strategically situated at the gateway to the town and directly across the street from the Mintlaw Police Station. Next to the diner was Peterson's Grocery. Beatrice Peterson was standing on the sidewalk in front of the parking lot hammering a sign into the tiny wedge of lawn bordering the store.

He'd forgotten about the upcoming Mintlaw Spring Founder's Day celebration which would be next week. Before he could get by without Beatrice noticing, she looked up and saw him and waved her hammer as if it was the opening of the Olympics and she was the torchbearer then lowered the hammer to tap the head of it on the sign emphasizing the date for his benefit. He nodded and smiled and luckily for him the light changed to green before she had a chance to run up to the truck (and as she liked to call it) chew-the-cud with him.

Jarvis Hardware was next to the grocery store and on the other side of Jump Creek Road was O'Reilly's Ice Cream Shack where several cars were queueing up to the drive-through- window for their orders while a group of teens sat at the picnic tables eating ice cream cones for breakfast. School wasn't due to be out for six weeks yet. Then he remembered it was Friday. Ghee, for a second he wondered if he was getting senile; maybe he needed a break from the studio.

Once he reached the three-storied Victorian which had been converted into the Mintlaw City Hall where the Mayor, two councilmen, and the clerk were housed, he pulled over to the curb and parked with the engine still running letting an impatient tailgater pass. The Victorian was in the 2nd Empire Style with a mansard roof. He was familiar with the style because for a brief but exhilarating year he had lived in Paris spending most of his time trying to imitate the great masters. When Andrew was young this particular Victorian had been Mintlaw's haunted house.

Mr. Steel, the last remaining descendent of the family was a hoarder and spent all his time digging through trash or old deposits left by prospectors. He had collected piles and piles of junk: old glass, rusty cans, and most everything not nailed down that caught his eye. He would even go all the way up to War Eagle Mountain or Walter's Ferry or Sandpoint to find something to bring home. The city allowed Mr. Steel to remain in his house once he donated the Victorian to the town. After many contentious quarrels between the farmers and the city officials, the Victorian was finally renovated. Its blue shingled siding with the mansard roof was too grand for their little town, but as the Mayor liked to say, "It's a great tourist attraction."

Yes, Andrew thought, not just because it was grand but because a rich eccentric hoarder had lived in it for seventy years.

While Andrew waited for the traffic to dissipate, he glanced over at the other side of the street where the Mintlaw Post Office stood, a small one story red brick building. The post office had a planter and a trellis by the glass doors where Mrs. Danvers, the postmaster's wife made it her business to fill the planter with seasonal flowers and holiday decorations. He had no idea what the flowers were but the way she had arranged them looked colorful and small town sweet. Maybe the purple ones were pansies? But he wasn't really interested in the pansies he was appreciating the object that stood next to them.

He looked at the bench with a critical eye. It had been several months since he'd finished this latest commission. Even after studying it closely he could see no fault with it. He relaxed. Sometimes during the fever of creation, he overlooked tiny flaws and would itch to fix the defect. Because Mintlaw was his town, he wanted to be sure the bench was perfect. It had taken him months of thinking and drafting and mostly burning bad ideas in his woodstove before he came up with a worthwhile design.

To the back of the bench he'd welded a long winding river of black iron which represented the Snake River. Behind the Snake were the peaks of the Owyhee Mountains. In the middle between two peaks was Jump Creek Falls and flying above the mountain peaks in the sky were birds of prey. On the seat of the bench, his first attempt had been to try to represent Mintlaw with farmhouses and fields where horses and cows grazed. He didn't like it. In frustration one day, he drew the word Mintlaw on the seat. It looked great. And the letters, the way he'd arranged them on the seat were so good no one's butt would fall between them.

Originally, he'd wanted to create something dramatic and abstract. He realized soon enough, an avant-garde piece wouldn't work in Mintlaw. The people here were extremely conservative, and they wouldn't appreciate his creative nonconformity. Otherwise, he was happy with the bench. It suited the town and the dignity of the post office.

Once he left the town of Mintlaw, he put his foot on the accelerator and made his way down Jump Creek Road toward the Treloar Farm. But before he could get to the farm, he had to pass several new developments. Today instead of being in his studio working on his most recent consignment he was delivering a new irrigation pump for Kit. The houses along the road became fewer and farther between until Prairie Star Estates where a few cookie cutter homes had been built. The rest of the development remained vacant with plumbing underground and electrical boxes surrounded by dirt representing future homes. A plumber had told him once that you could cut your way inside one of the Prairie Star homes with a box cutter knife the walls were that flimsy.

In contrast, Eagle Gateway School next to Prairie Star had been built with charitable donations from some very wealthy patrons who wished to remain anonymous and Ms. Matthews, the director of the school, stubbornly protected. It was considered one of the premier schools for the deaf and blind that were lucky enough to have rich and/or famous parents. Unlike the school in Gooding which had been the only school for the deaf and blind in Idaho since the early 1900s, Eagle Gateway's benefactors maintained their school as a private boarding school permitting only a few select low-income students to attend.

The school was four stories tall and made of red brick. The occupants of the school were protected by a fancy black wrought iron fence which encompassed the entire five acres. At the front, just off Jump Creek Road was an imposing electric gate. The place reminded him of pictures he'd seen of fancy English boarding schools. In the high desert of Owyhee County, it was a startling sight to see so much greenery, as much greenery as the United Kingdom perhaps.

Beyond Eagle Gateway School there were mostly farms like his family farm and across the road the Old Anderson Farm. Andrew had heard Carl and Annie had sold what was left of their property, the farmhouse and about ten acres. When Andrew was a kid, the Andersons had had the biggest farm in Owyhee County; now what had once been acres of potato fields and corn had become Eagle Gateway Boarding School and Prairie Star Estates. The little that was left of the farm had been the most difficult to sell. The old farmhouse had been built right up against a popular hillside where hunters and hikers trespassed knowing as they did so that it was the shortest route to the Owyhee Canyonlands.

He'd heard from his nephew Kit that the new owner of the Anderson Farm had made a deal with Andrew's father to lease ten acres for planting. His father had already planted his mint on his own fields this season with help from local labor before he had his stroke. Now Andrew's nephew Kit had stepped in to manage the property until Murray recovered enough to take over. Kit's wife Rachel had doubts Murray would ever recover from his stroke. Murray was nearly ninety.

Andrew supposed he should feel guilty for uprooting his nephew and his nephew's family from their home in Minnesota because he refused to take over for his father. When Andrew was younger, he and Murray had had some hellacious arguments about the fate of the farm. Andrew wanted nothing to do with farming. Luckily for Andrew his nephew Kit who was only a year older seemed eager to learn about managing a farm. Or at least he pretended to for Murray's sake. Kit had been an adjunct at the University of Minnesota and his wife a teacher at a local high school when Murray had his stroke. Because Kit's job had ended, he chose to come out to Idaho first. Rachel finished her school year in Minnesota and followed him out with their youngest daughter Margaret. Their twin sons Cody and Cameron were attending the University of Minnesota as freshman. Rachel still had hopes of returning to teaching once Murray was back on his feet.

As Andrew slowed down to turn into the drive leading to his father's farmhouse, his thoughts shifted to the new occupant of the Anderson property across the road. He was pleasantly surprised when he saw a thick mahogany sign set near the entrance to the graveled drive. It had been hung between two cedar posts and on the wood the engraver had carved the logo – Rock Wren House. Andrew slowed down long enough to figure out the drawing below the logo. It was a bird with a stick in its peak. The artist in Andrew appreciated the attention to detail. It was simple but elegant. So busy examining the artwork of his newest neighbor, Andrew nearly missed his father's drive. As he looked away, from the corner of his eye, he saw a woman standing up with a bundle of weeds and plants in her arms. In his rearview mirror, he could see the backside of her, her hips swaying slightly as she moved. She walked naturally with firm unhurried steps. Her thick curly black hair had been braided and tied back into a ponytail and the ponytail swung down behind her back directing the eye toward her slim hips and firm buttocks.

Andrew watched with appreciation as she bent to pick up a fallen weed. It was only when he climbed out of the truck and called to his nephew to help him unload the new irrigation pump that he had an excuse to take a closer look at the woman and the farm. Kit was busy watching the irrigation water spill down the rows of mint, as usual worrying himself sick that he might fail to keep the mint alive.

Andrew was patient. He had all the time in the world.

It was a beautiful day, the mint smelled sweet and the sun was shining. At first, he pretended to be interested in Hunter's Hill behind the farmhouse. Over the years, the hill had become a contentious bit of politics for the community especially between the farmers and the day trippers. It had taken the Andersons twenty years before they received permission from the Bureau of Land Management to dump a barricade of large rocks along the ledge of the hill to prevent dirt bikers, four-wheel drivers, and snowmobilers from cutting across the Anderson property to get to the top.

These days there was a steady migration of people moving to Idaho and the new residents were curious about the country. It seemed as if Hunter's Hill attracted more hikers and rock hounds than ever before. They continued to ignore the posted signs especially when the ten acres was fallow. Finally, the Andersons gave up and paid for a graveled hiking trail to be built from Jump Creek Road to the top of the hill. They christened the trail Anderson Pass. Some people in town called it Anderson's Folly. It didn't take long for hikers, mountain bikers, and rock hounds to learn about the shortcut into the Owyhee Mountains. Unfortunately, there were plenty of tourists who thought they could manage the Owyhees without adequate supplies and ended up having to be rescued from their own stupidity.

Murray had been especially cantankerous about the influx of people from California. When the Andersons sent him a letter and told him they'd sold their farmhouse and the acreage around it to some stranger in Vegas, Murray had ranted and raved for weeks. It was inevitable that the pressure of the changing times and the heavy workload would aggravate his father's health. Andrew didn't blame the new owner. Murray just didn't know how to relax. His body had other plans for Murray and made the decision for him.

Andrew leaned back against the gate of his truck pretending to be interested in the foothills and watched as the woman moved about the property picking up tools and black trash bags full of weeds. He assumed she was the wife of the new owner. There was something familiar about her though. He tried to recall where he had seen her before. He had known her. He was sure of it. He searched through his memory of other women he had known – dark haired and petite like her. Although her name eluded him he knew he had known her at some time in his recent past. He straightened feeling an unexpected impulse to walk over and introduce himself. He was too late; before he could take two steps, she had already disappeared inside the farmhouse. He stared at the ground sifting through old memories hoping to find her likeness in some forgotten file.

—

That same day, Saturday before dusk, Daniel returned to his favorite hunting ground, his mission urgent. He had to get there before dark. He had to find his treasure before someone else took it. In his desperation to find his lost rocks, he ran up Hunter's Hill. When he got to the top he had to pause to catch his breath. He puffed and gasped until his heart steadied, and his vision cleared. He rested his hands on his legs to stop them trembling and waited for the spots to clear from his eyes. He straightened and looked about trying to remember where he had put the other ones. He stood on top of the hill with rocky cliffs on either side of him. The top was as wide as Boise State University's football field, only the ground wasn't covered in blue.

Daniel stood on the old road which was no more than grooves cut in the desert floor by several generations of ATVs, Jeeps and trucks traveling south. On either side of the grooves the desert floor was overgrown with sagebrush both big and small along with wild grasses. A few plants grew in the middle of the road and the occasional rut or washout reminded him that hunters of animals and hunters of rock had been here before him. It was his place now.

He slipped between two of the seven walrus rocks barricading the old road tapping their rough hides for good luck. Seven was a lucky number. The smooth parts of the rock indicated that others also liked to rub the rocks for good luck. He liked the barricade because kids couldn't scar up the hillside on their dirt bikes anymore and snowmobilers had to haul their vehicles in their trucks on US 95 to Poison Creek Road to get to the Owyhee Mountains. Sometimes people thought they could take the little-known dirt road off the highway just after the Weigh Station and discovered how nasty the backroad was to Hunter's Hill on tailpipes and the under carriage of their cars. Sometimes they got stuck trying to turn around. The boulder barricade on top of the hill forced the Sunday drivers to go back to I55 and find themselves another spot to litter. Few people came up here anymore, except for him.

It would be dark soon. Daniel hurried down the road searching the chaparral of sagebrush for the pile of rocks he had left behind. The road followed alongside a solid mass of red rock cliff which towered over his head and when he came around the corner onto level ground, he made himself go faster watching his feet, so he wouldn't trip on obstacles in the road. When he lifted his head for a moment to make sure he was close to the place where he'd left his treasure, he saw the vehicle parked near the cattle guard. To reach his rocks, he had to make a wide swath around a red van with a white bunny painted on the side. The sight of the van made him mad. There were signs everywhere telling people No Vehicles Allowed.

In the haze before dusk, the sandy ground and the tips of the sagebrush seemed to glow an ugly shade of yellow, even his shoes looked sickly. He took his green backpack off and unzipped it, then started shoving his broken thundereggs inside. When he heard a car door open and someone grunting, he stood up and peered around the tall woody sagebrush. The sun had dipped behind the cliffs and all he could see was a dark shape shoving a chair with wheels out of the van. There was a human in the chair. Its head kept moving back and forth and from side to side like those little toys, the word was on the tip of his tongue – oh yeah, a bobble head. Then the human inside the van jumped down to the ground and grunting and swearing pushed and pulled the chair into its upright position. He watched as the stranger yanked and pushed and pulled the chair over the rocky ground toward the gully. When they were nearly at the edge of the gully, the litterer began to untie the bobble head from the chair.

All sorts of humans thought they could dump their garbage in the gully. He was getting madder and madder and thinking about going over and telling him to stop littering, when he hesitated to wonder if the litterer might see him and want to pick a fight or take his rocks. He decided to stay put for a bit. He crouched down and started quickly shoving the rest of his treasure in his backpack. Absently he heard a crash and thud as a large object hit the brush and rocks in the gully below.

By the time he threw his backpack over his shoulder and stood up ready to hurry home, he saw the human dragging the empty chair back to the van. He threw the chair inside with a crash. When Daniel saw the human go back to the driver's door and open it, he decided to wait assuming the jerk was getting ready to leave. The thought made him very happy. Minutes went by and the guy didn't leave. He heard the human digging around inside the back of the van and wanted to go and punch him. He was going to throw more garbage into the gully. Daniel worried about being seen. Some humans were as mean as badgers. The guy reappeared dragging something else out of the van and started walking toward the gully.

Daniel couldn't stand it any longer; he dropped his backpack behind the sagebrush and rushed out to the road, "You're trespassing. Go on. Get. Get or I'll call the cops."

The guy dropped the pile of blankets on the ground and started running toward the van, then spun around and stopped to face Daniel. It was so dark now; Daniel had trouble seeing his stupid jerky face, just the short round body with the wide shoulders. It dawned upon him the litterer wasn't so big. The guy just stood by the van without saying a word. Daniel thought he'd scared him enough and turned to walk back to his rocks. A screechy voice screamed and cursed him.

He twisted around in shocked surprise and something hard and sharp hit him in the head near his left eye. More objects flew through the air, some landing on the ground near him, others flying over his head. Ping. Crack. Ping. A small rock hit him in the stomach. He ducked protecting his face from the rain of stones striking him on the head and shoulders. He fought back with words he'd heard his stepfather use. He used all the bad words he could sum up from memory to frighten the jerk away. His words had no power here. Daniel moved out of the range of flying stones and wondered what he'd done to make this stranger mad at him. He grabbed his backpack and ran down the road toward the ledge near the Anderson farm. There was a crevice large enough for him to squeeze into and once secure, he waited hoping the crazy person wouldn't find him.

He heard the crazy human shouting the words echoing off the cliff sides, "I know you're there. Come on, Vera, let's talk. I won't hurt you. I heard you sneaking around and I know where you live, you nosy bitch. Come out and let's talk. I won't bite. I promise."

Daniel closed his eyes and tried to hold his breath.

"Fine, you dirty gyp. If you tell anyone, I'll hurt you so bad you won't be able to walk for a month."

He heard an engine turn over and with relief knew the crazy human was leaving. Once the air no longer smelled of gasoline and he could hear the crickets, he climbed out from his hiding place and started walking down the narrow path behind the old Anderson farm. He heard a child crying and stopped. He didn't want to go back. He was afraid of the evil spirit. The child cried again.

Annoyed, he turned around and headed back up the hill to the ledge where he had been hiding. When he could hear nothing more, he thought maybe he'd been mistaken and it had been a cat crying. Cats sounded just like kids. He moved past the ledge and stood by the rock barricade. It was difficult to see what was on the old road. He peered into the shadows. He heard something coming toward him. Frightened that the evil spirit was after him, Daniel ran down the path faster than he should have, and the steep slope propelled him faster and faster. He couldn't stop. He fell forward, tried to stop his fall with his right arm, and hit the ground with the full force of his weight, sliding for a few feet further on the gravel. He heard something snap. He made himself get up and stand still listening. When he was sure the evil was gone, he held his hurt arm to his chest and ran across the meadow toward Jump Creek Road terrified the ghost would get him.

—

Saturday evening, shortly after a late supper, Maggie's parents set out for the D & B Supply store in the hopes of reaching the store before it closed. Maggie noticed by the clock above the fireplace that it was nearly eight thirty. Her parents had promised to be home before nine and then her father would take her to Amy's house for the overnight pajama party. Maggie sat in her favorite rocking chair and when she glanced through the bay window, she noticed the same geologist back on the hilltop. He was just standing there looking around. Maggie had not expected to see him again.

Maggie sprang off the rocking chair and moved about the room impatient for her parents to return. She rested a knee on the window seat and stared out at the road in front of the house. To herself she willed her parents to come home quickly. After a few minutes, Maggie shifted into a more comfortable position to ease a cramp in her leg and heard the wheels of Murray's wheelchair bumping across the uneven hardwood floor of the hall. He was headed her way. Maggie watched him maneuver through the entryway into the living room. His gray eyes looked up briefly in her direction. "Wha ya doen idin in ere?" he asked her.

Great Grandpa Murray and her father were soft spoken men. Maggie loved to listen to her father speak. He knew so many things and he loved to talk about them. Murray didn't talk much and when he did he sounded mad all the time, even when he asked for a cup of coffee or a piece of toast. Maggie was tired of babysitting Murray. She had already missed the swimming party at Lucky Peak. The drive to Lucky Peak sitting beside Jeremy would have made up for all the boredom of being stuck in the house all day. Even helping her father irrigate the fields would have been more fun than sitting in the house listening to Murray grumble.

"Mom should be home from the store soon Grandpa," she said unable to think of anything else to say. Murray's right-hand shook. Maggie could see blue veins trying to erupt through the skin of his bony hand. His left hand lay lifeless in his lap. He'd had a stroke last year. Sometimes she could barely understand him. It took her a minute or two to realize what he'd asked her when he came in the room – *What are you doing hiding in here?* That had been his question, the usual grouching. He had a knack for insulting people. When Maggie's chicken pox erupted all over her body, Murray had said, "He's oo ol for icken ox." Her mother had told him that some people if not exposed at an early age contracted chicken pox much later. Maggie would be fifteen in a few months.

Murray ignored her and headed for the radio in the corner of the room. He switched it on and listened to the farm report. Maggie couldn't concentrate on her reading when the radio was on. She was debating whether to slip up to her bedroom to read; then changed her mind. Her maneuver would be too obvious. Murray, trying to reach for the newspaper on the coffee table without success forced Maggie into motion.

Maggie slipped off the window seat and handed the paper to him. He accepted the paper from her without looking at her or so much as saying thank you. Typical, she thought, the old grouch. Maggie returned to her seat and pretended to read her book. A few minutes passed. Maggie thought she was being watched and looked up. Murray turned away from her to stare out the window. Maggie tried not to smile. He was always doing that, staring at her as if he wondered what egg she'd hatched from.

Something had caught his eye. His body was practically vibrating he was so excited. Maggie leaned forward and looked in the direction he was looking. Murray was watching the geologist climbing down the hillside. His body stiffened. He reminded Maggie of Agnus, the black barn cat spotting a potential prey in the distance, body all tense, head reared forward, ready to spring.

"You know that man, Grandpa?"

Murray just glanced at her for a moment, then back to the view outside the window.

"I think he's a geologist from the university," Maggie said, uncomfortable with the silence between them.

Murray's body convulsed for a moment in a spasm of rage and he said with an effort. "Ees no amn olo'ist! Ees a oron."

"What did you say?" Maggie asked realizing that she really wanted to know this time. He reached for the notebook on the coffee table. Maggie handed him her ballpoint pen. Maggie took the

17

notebook from Murray before he dropped it and tried to decipher his scribbling: *Daniel Harden. Retarded boy. Eagle School.*

Maggie slipped her bookmark between the pages and dropped the book on the seat beside her. "Grandpa," she said to him and when he didn't respond, she shouted his name. "Murray!" He looked in her direction and with the setting sun's light from the big window close to burning a hole through the glass; Murray's cloudy gray eyes looked almost yellow. When she was sure she had his attention, she asked, "What happened to Grandpa Stewart? How'd he die?"

"A moron ot im!"

"Who? What's his name?"

He sighed. "On't no."

"Then why'd you say a moron shot him if you don't know who shot him?"

"Ause anyody at ot my boy ust ee a oron."

"What do you think moron means?"

Murray threw down his newspaper and propelled himself across the room toward the door. Maggie had never seen him so angry. Years of working in the sun and wind had turned his skin a copper color, but his stroke and old age had turned what was once a healthy tan into something that resembled her favorite rocks – those bluish gray rocks with the red stains on them. His forehead and cheeks were turning purple. Maggie's heart skipped a beat and for a moment she thought he was having another stroke. Her parents would blame her for upsetting him.

Maggie ran toward him and placed her hand on his shoulder. "I'm sorry Murray. I'm sorry if I hurt your feelings. I didn't mean to be fresh with you." Maggie remembered that "fresh" was his word for talking back to someone.

He paused in the hall near the kitchen. She heard him gasping for air. Maggie squeezed between his chair and the wall and ran for a glass of water. "Please Grandpa. Don't be mad," she said offering him the glass. Sweat beaded his forehead. She helped him lift the glass to his lips. He took a sip and then shook his head.

"No or," he said. For some strange reason, hearing Murray talk like a two-year-old and seeing the fatigue in his body made Maggie want to cry. She would never grow so old and helpless. She would die first.

Maggie pushed his wheelchair into the kitchen. This had been the first room her mother had restored and redecorated. It had always been a warm and friendly room. Now it had a modern look with copper pots and a fancy new ivory colored refrigerator and stove. The floor had been an old 3/8" oak – scuffed, scratched, and marked with cigarette burns. Now the floor was covered in white vinyl flooring with matching vinyl kitchen cabinets and a herringbone pattern of red brick surrounding the stove. Her mom had even put a wall of mirrors in the dark hallway with track lightening so that no one tripped or bumped into the cellar door. The room no longer reminded Maggie of old black and white movies or poverty or dirtiness. The room belonged to her parents now. It had become everybody's favorite place to sit and talk.

—

Contrary to Maggie's opinion of the remodeled room, Murray resented the upheaval to his home. The family acted as if he'd already passed on to his ancestors. Well they were in for a surprise. He was going to hang on as long as possible just to annoy the hell out of them all. He had survived nearly ninety years because no slick fast-talking con artist was going to manipulate him into running off to another country to get himself killed. Besides, his father wouldn't let him go. Paul Treloar needed him on the farm. Nebraska was going to be their promised land.

They had been farmers since immigrating to America in 1827. So, Murray stayed behind while the rest of his friends went to war. Over the years, Murray ignored the bullshit speeches and because he did, he survived. But his sons, every last damned one, thought they knew better. He stared at the floor as if the fancy new vinyl had the answer to the question that had tormented him since 1974.Three of his sons had died; two of them on foreign soil, one of them right here in Mintlaw Idaho. Stewart managed to survive the Korean War only to get himself killed by some lowlife piece of dunghill on Poison Creek Road. Nobody had ever found out who had killed Stewart. The not knowing made Murray madder than a badger in a pit viper's jaws.

Those hungry years, those years when Murray was a kid in Nebraska with season after season of dust and drought and no work to be found – those years were embedded in Murray's memory forever. Sometimes Murray woke from the nightmare of dust piled up against the farmhouse door unable to escape the relentless shrieking of the wind. And when the wind stopped blowing, he struggled to open windows caked with dust, unable to see outside, all the while wondering if the house would be his tomb with the storm stripping the paint right off the shingles.

Even today there were times when he woke up and found himself unable to suppress the urge to run to the window to look out at his fields imagining himself back home in Nebraska. Murray tried to wipe away the image of his father on his knees in the dirt. He didn't want to remember his father that way.

Murray heard a voice calling to him. He lifted his head and saw the girl standing by the table watching him anxiously. She reminded him of Stewart with her long neck and brown eyes. She had long legs too and a stubborn glint which reminded him of his own beautiful bonnie Kate. She would push and push and drive them all crazy until she was satisfied with the answers. It had nothing to do with her, Stewart's murder. It's none of her business. He knew who was to blame.

—

Vera Lee dreamed of the hilltop north of her property where lava rocks covered the slope and spilled down the side black against the tan earth. Interspersed among the rocks grew tough sagebrush. The leaves of the desert flowers of spring, once yellow, were now dried stalks crackling in the wind. Vera heard the flowers shiver against each other in syncopation to the sound of a car door slamming shut. Vera saw Aunt Vista running madly around her green Buick slamming all the car doors that dared to open without her permission. As Aunt Vista shut them, she cursed them. Once the doors remained obedient to Aunt Vista's will, Vera heard the wheels of a chair bumping across the rocks.

She remembered that chair, Uncle Frank's favorite chair made of black plastic, designed to resemble a Victorian leather wingback chair. Uncle Frank pushed the chair along the lava rocks toward the shelf's lip. Her aunt watched her husband without expression as he stood with his bare toes gripping the ledge like the claws of a hawk. Her aunt's angry contemplation of a world without order and Uncle Frank's intense fascination with the macabre frightened Vera. She wanted to think about something else, something other than Aunt Vista and Uncle Frank.

Her mind obliged. She turned over and sank back into sleep.

The cowboy peeked through the crack in the door. Vera could see the hallway behind him, the doors on each side, shut, everyone either asleep in their beds or out for the night trawling for sex. She could see the faded gray carpet of the hall and the cowboy's leather boots standing on the loose fold of the carpet by their apartment door. The stink of beer on his breath weaved around her head and once touched her face when he leaned in close to talk to her through the crack. She listened politely to him with the feeble chain her only defense.

"She's not here. I don't know where they went."

"Let me in, Vera, now."

Vera let him in. He was Lisa's husband. Her mom had warned her if he came to the apartment to tell him nothing. Vera had promised, yet, he was an adult and she knew him, and he could probably break the feeble little chain without much effort. He pushed past her and weaved his way toward the living room. He moved without conscious thought, hit his head on the door jam and swore. "Son of a bitch."

Vera returned to her position on the floor in front of the television set. She stared at the black and white screen with sightless eyes. She heard him wander into the bathroom, then out again. He opened both bedroom doors. She stared at the screen and saw nothing but white flickering lights and shadows and voices making no sense. He came back to the living room and knelt by her side. He had to hold onto her knee to catch his balance.

"Where are they Vera? I wanna know. Where are they? What's she done with Emmie, huh? Where's Emmie?"

Vera stared at the screen. "I don't know. I don't know where mom and Lisa are. They just left. They didn't say where they were going. I don't know where Emmie is."

"You swear you're telling the truth?" he demanded poking his big finger into the flesh of her shoulder.

Vera stared at the screen and pretended to be nowhere, no one. "I swear," she said. From the corner of her eye she watched him struggle to his feet. She returned her eyes to the television screen as if the television meant life or death. It did. It meant she didn't have to face him or look him in the eye. The television was as unreal as the now, as unreal as the man standing in her mother's apartment.

She breathed in and out, in and out, and time stretched on forever. Sweat trickled down her neck, down between her training-bra. Sweat trickled down her armpits and stopped at her pants. She could feel moisture on her upper lip. She waited and waited for him to go away so she could wipe the sweat off her lip. She stared at the screen, the heat from the screen making her even hotter.

The cowboy turned and marched toward the kitchen. A chair flew against the wall and a picture fell. She heard him yank the kitchen door open. She jumped up when she heard the door whack the wall. Vera peeked around the refrigerator and saw his long legs moving down the hallway every so often he would smash a neighbor's door. She ran to their apartment door and shut it and locked it and picked up the chair he had thrown and set the chair under the doorknob.

Then and only then did she wipe the sweat off her upper lip. She heard the clock ticking the time. It had only been thirty minutes, yes, only thirty minutes but she would never forget what had happened. She would never forget. The cowboy she feared and hated. Her mother, she was beginning to hate her mother too. Mama is a coward Vera thought to herself, she's a damn coward. I hate her guts.

Vera wandered toward the dark hall and opened the bedroom door. This door led to the room Vera shared with her mother. The other three kids slept in the room across the hall. Vera was the only one in the house save one other person. She tiptoed toward the twin beds and stood at the foot of the bed closest to the window. She looked down at Emmie wrapped tight in a pink blanket on the floor between the beds. Emmie was still asleep. Her brown eyes were shut against the dark. Her baby cheeks were flushed. Emmie was safe.

Finally, struggling up from the depths of her dream, Vera opened her eyes. Two bad dreams in one night, her mother would call that an omen. It was still the middle of the night and the moonlight streaming through the lace curtains seemed cold and angry. She'd left the window open. She could hear the creaking of chains. The chains were rubbing on rusty metal posts. Her bedroom faced her backyard.

Had she been sleepwalking again? It had been years since she woke feeling tired and guilty her legs trembling as if she'd left her bed and run a marathon – not since Vlasky. She didn't want to think about her deceased husband. Not tonight. Or was it today?

The man beside her shifted in his sleep and sighed. His broad tanned back blocked her view of the window. For a moment Vera couldn't remember his name. Then it came to her. Joshua Adams. How could she forget Joshua? But Joshua at meetings and Joshua in her bed were two different people. The public Joshua she had known for two years now, someone she talked to on the other side of the table, someone who contributed to the conversations with enthusiasm. He had a powerful voice, a compelling personality. Everyone liked Joshua. But now, he was the other Joshua, the one sleeping in her bed, the one she had allowed into her private world.

Vera slipped out of bed naked and walked to the window. The air was still heavy with the previous day's heat. Her wind chimes remained motionless. From her position at the window, the wooden pipes resembled sticks thrown in the air by a petulant child-god. Vera glanced over her shoulder at the sleeping male in her bed. At first Joshua's eager friendliness had annoyed her until he noticed her book on the table near her coffee cup and said, "*Of Love and Other Demons*—I haven't read that one yet. Is it as good as his earlier fictions?" Vera, over the years, had grown accustomed to the fact she had no one to talk to about her favorite books, outside of a college classroom, which she couldn't afford anyway; so, she was startled and pleasantly surprised to meet a man who read good literature.

Without hesitation, she invited him to sit at her table. Then she launched into a stream-of-consciousness monologue, more intense than she liked due to the misery of being suppressed for so long. Most men would have flipped their wigs and boogied out the back door or thought up some lamebrain excuse to ditch her. In retrospect, a female babbling about biblical metaphors and histories repeated in *One Hundred Years of Solitude* did seem kind of nuts, but Joshua had stuck around and listened as if he were honestly interested in what she had to say.

Remembering that pleasant moment, Vera turned to face the man sleeping so peacefully in her bed. It had been nearly two years now since a man had slept beside her. She had met Joshua at an AA meeting. She thought she knew him well enough to trust him. Yet in the night surrounded by the dark and quiet of this new place, she realized she knew nothing about him. She should be concerned.

The chill in the air had more to do with her Roma superstitions than the weather. Today promised to be as hot as yesterday, perhaps peaking at 105 degrees again. Her shiver was generated by an unknown future and a desire to forget the past. The two warred with each other and would not let her sleep. As the creaking persisted, Vera got angry. She grabbed her robe and hurried through the house to the patio door. She stood a moment on the porch listening to the sound of chains rubbing on metal. After a minute or so, she realized where the creaking originated.

The irritating noise belonged to the day, not the night. Vera stepped off the porch and onto loose paving stones and gravel, material long since ground into the dirt, but hurting the soles of her bare feet when she moved too fast. She circled the house moving toward the backyard where the foothills met her tipsy fence. The sparse lawn began to ascend and abruptly turned into sharp blades of dying grass and prickly weeds. The moonlight illuminated the yard as if Vera stood before a dimly lit stage. She saw the props and the actor only a few feet away.

The willow tree to her right and the stubborn trumpet vine climbing the back fence to her left might have been citadels surrounding and protecting the figure below them. Vera moved toward the trespasser sitting on the seat of the middle swing with legs pumping and body soaring higher and higher in the night air. Vera considered her options. This was no ghost from the past. Vera understood enough to know that she had no more reality than the willow or the trumpet vine to this little person. Yet to go back to bed without trying to do something was unthinkable.

Vera walked the few steps to the swing and inched closer until she became a wall between the air and the sky. The girl's small feet hit Vera in the stomach, once, twice, and a third time before the momentum of her swing slowed enough for Vera to catch her in her arms. The thin small body hung limp in her arms making it difficult to hold her. Vera marched toward the porch with the child clutched to her chest. The sliding glass door had been left partway open. The girl grunted and slapped Vera's face and kept on slapping her. She ignored the stinging slaps and entered the kitchen with the child wriggling to be free.

For a moment Vera hesitated, unable to think what she should do next. The child used Vera's uncertainty to wiggle out of Vera's arms and onto the floor. Vera managed to chase the child down before she ran out the front door. She held on tight to the wild creature and managed to make her way down the hall to the guest bedroom without dropping her. The silent struggle between them was an ugly moment Vera wished never to repeat. Even though the struggle repulsed her sensibilities, she knew she couldn't let go for fear the child would do herself an injury.

Vera set the child on the guest bed and with her hands firmly holding the thin pale shoulders lowered the child toward the bed urging her to lie down. At first the child refused to obey, imperiously brushing off Vera's hands and struggling to sit up. Each time she brushed Vera off and attempted to sit up, the child would make a soft grunting sound like a panting bear cub.

"Oh, no you don't. It's time for bed," Vera told her firmly. She could be just as stubborn. The struggle seemed to go on forever but couldn't have lasted too long because the stinging slaps the child welded were getting weaker and weaker and barely raised a red rash on Vera's naked arms.

By the end of the ordeal, Vera felt as if she'd run a marathon. The nastiness of the episode confirmed her opinion that children were designed by the universal creator/joker as a form of punishment for adults, proving once again that life is a combat between opposing wills and has nothing to do with aesthetics or philosophy or theology. Close proximity to children reminded Vera of her childhood and how her rebelliousness had been harvested by

24

her own family. A momentary pity for her mother and Nonnie rose to the surface of her consciousness and just as swiftly was extinguished by less pleasant memories. They knew better. She hadn't been asked to be born.

Eventually the child lay back on the pillow and remained still and watchful. The moon's light through the window glass made the child's large blue eyes glow red the way a cat's eyes could change colors at night. Having this strange child in her house with a strange man in her bed and herself unsure of her own reality made this entire episode seem like a bad dream after a heavy meal. The child wasn't a child but a feral creature of fantasy. And this little she-devil was attempting to cast a magical curse on her new home. Vera thought about how the little girl's blonde hair had shone in the moonlight like tinsel on a Christmas tree. Nothing felt right about this night. Even the house sounded and smelled foreign. It creaked and snapped and groaned; yet, there was no outside natural force creating the noise. The air smelled of sage and dust motes and the energy around the child made Vera feel alien even to herself.

When she was confident the child would not bounce up off the bed, Vera slipped out of the room and turned on the hall light. She stood in the hall and peeked through the crack in the door. The light from the hall spilled into the room and onto the child. The cot was the only piece of furniture in the room. It had been Vera's bed once, until she could afford to buy a big comfortable queen size bed. The child's body was in shadow until Vera stepped inside and the light from the hall shone down upon the cot and its occupant. The child's hair was so fine and thin that Vera could see her pink ghostly scalp. This little ghost was a figment of her imagination. She must be dreaming. And then the child with her eyes squeezed tightly shut began to grunt and toss feverishly from side to side. Vera wished she could read minds. Right now, reading this little girl's mind would answer so many questions.

Resigned to a sleepless night, Vera opened the guest bedroom door and stepped inside. She sat down on the edge of the bed and waited until she heard the child's breathing change from gasps of angry frustration to shallow whistles. Eventually the little girl relaxed. Vera waited another ten minutes until she was certain the child slept, then crept out of the room and closed the door. She considered her options.

Calling the police would mean waking Joshua and having to wait around the rest of the night until a police officer appeared at the door. Vera wanted Joshua away before the police arrived. She decided to wait until morning. Even if the little girl belonged to someone in the new subdivision, they were probably still asleep and unaware that their child was missing. At least Vera managed to convince herself that her postponement made sense. In the light of day, she would soon realize how foolish she'd been to wait.

She glanced out the window.

Beyond her property and the fallow fields stretched miles of high desert where roots grew deep and cheat-grass spread like a relentless enemy, its seeds once carried by travelers across the desert, now carried by the wind. In the distance she could see the foothills leading to the Owyhee Mountains and a farmhouse about three miles from her property. Stubben's subdivision was on the other side of Eagle Gateway Boarding School. Carl Anderson had sold most of his land to the boarding school and to Stubben. He'd mentioned that Treloar who owned the farm across the road also owned property on the other side of Stubben's subdivision and refused to sell to him which prevented any further expansion of Prairie Star Estates. It amused Vera to know progress could be postponed by one man. Yet, Treloar's stubbornness would be a temporary impediment for developers, eventually money would win out.

When Vera returned to her bedroom, she found Joshua still asleep. He had slept through the child's grunts and the bedsprings creaking. Vera wandered through the old farm house checking windows and relocking locked doors. She supposed she should report the missing child to the police. She should do so right away. She rubbed her throbbing temples as she wandered through the dark house trying to make up her mind. When she realized she'd circled the kitchen table three times, she forced herself to stop. Outside the sliding glass door, she could see the swing set. No. She had two good reasons not to call the police: her privacy would be invaded, and the police would ask a lot of uncomfortable questions. Yes, she'd wait. She'd wait because Joshua would be inconvenienced, and the child needed her sleep.

Before slipping back into bed, Vera went into the bathroom and washed the dirt and grass off her feet. Joshua mumbled something she couldn't understand and turned over on his side facing her. Vera dried her feet and tiptoed to the bed, carefully slipping under the covers. Joshua never woke. Vera prone beside him examined his sleeping face with new interest. There was something rather attractive about a man smiling while he slept. His dreams gave him pleasure. Vera wished that she could fall asleep so easily and dream pleasant dreams.

—

Andrew lay beside Debra in the dark, his head resting on his crossed arms. He stared at the ceiling and watched as the headlights from a passing car traveled across the ceiling. Debra snored in her sleep. Contrary to Kit's assessment of Debra, the woman had turned out to be pleasantly intelligent, funny, and athletic. Debra was the most recent of a series of women of similar physical perfection, similar savvy, and agreeable disposition. Andrew thought about the qualities that attracted him most and began to wonder whether Kit might be right. Maybe he is shallow?

Andrew ticked off his shallow traits. If shallow meant what he thought it meant – someone who only thought about appearances, Andrew could disagree. Yes, he chose women for their physical attractiveness. And no, in every other respect, designer clothes, fancy cars, money in the bank did not concern him. He was the opposite of shallow, he was deep, a deep, deep guy. He worked with underprivileged kids at the Center in Nampa. He was a big brother. Rogelio called him El Hombre and all the kids at the Rec Center respected him. He must be doing something right if Rogelio had chosen to finish high school.

In fact, Rogelio's goal surpassed Andrew's wildest expectations. His graffiti had inspired Andrew to help him become a graphic designer. Andrew had to admit, Rogelio had a natural talent and Andrew was a bit jealous. It had taken him years of sweat and toil and stubbornness to become a proficient artist. Andrew used to enjoy drawing cartoons and sketching people but now three-dimensional-art was his medium.

Working with steel made his past, those years in Vietnam recede to the dark recesses of his mind; and for a few hours, he actually felt joy. When he realized the first time that he was happy, he thought he must have been having a flashback because someone had slipped acid in his coffee. And then he realized that the feeling had sprung from the object in the center of his studio, the twisted steel he had cut and shaped into his own creation.

But at night sometimes...like tonight, he would wake from a deep sleep – sweating and scared – and sleep would elude him until morning. For the rest of the night, his thoughts would chase around inside his skull like two crazy squirrels chasing each other around the trunk of a tree, endlessly and without purpose.

Andrew sat up in bed and looked down at the sleeping form beside him. Debra slept on her back, her tangled blonde hair spread out in silky clumps across the pillow. And, so what, if he liked attractive women? Kit had no room to talk. His wife Rachel was hot. She may have brain cells pumping at supersonic speed, but Kit still picked Rachel because her measurements added up to a close enough proximity of 36-24-36 to make her nearly perfection incarnate. Kit refused to recognize his own imperfections. It was always someone else that had the defect, not him. Yep. Kit was wrong. Why didn't Kit mind his own damned business, anyway?

—

Daniel nursed his arm all through the night perplexed and angry at his body's betrayal. His wrist throbbed while a demon inside beat against his skin wanting to get out. Daniel heard his mother and Darrell enter the kitchen. Someone bumped into a chair and swore. His mother giggled. Daniel listened as his stepfather opened the refrigerator door, then he heard the snap and sneeze as Darrell flipped the top off a bottle of beer. Daniel heard his mother say, "Hey— what about me?"

And Darrell said, "Get your own fucking beer. I'm not your servant."

Daniel lay on his bed in the dark still wearing his day clothes. From his room he could hear them as if they were fighting at the foot of his bed. The walls were like paper. Once he'd heard his mother describe the walls that way after trying to get Darrell to shut up. Darrell had ignored her like he always did. It began like this sometimes, the yelling. His mother would feel hurt and say something mean and his stepfather would say something mean back. Daniel heard his mother shriek at Darrell. Daniel didn't understand the words. Then he heard flesh connect with flesh. That sound was also familiar.

He thought about his shop at the school. He pictured his workbench with all his tools put away in the shelves above his head: the diamond blade saw, the tumbler, the polisher, and his wet stone. He counted the rocks in his collection already cut and polished. The sudden quiet interrupted his counting. Five minutes passed. Daniel heard someone coming up the steps crying so soft he had to hold his breath to hear. The bathroom door across the hall opened and closed. Daniel heard his mother bolt the lock on the inside. He heard water running. Daniel thought about his rocks: the jasper piece that resembled mountains and a lake, the petrified wood that could have been a piece off a branch of an old, old, thousands of years old tree. Daniel fell asleep listening to Darrell begging his mother to open the bathroom door.

Chapter Two

Vera woke in the morning to the sound of a child squealing in outrage. Joshua opened his eyes and stared at the ceiling, "What the hell was that?" Sitting up and glanced at the wall adjacent to her bedroom where the strange child slept or had been sleeping, she mumbled, "It's a long story," as she kicked the bedsheet off her legs. When he said nothing, she added lamely, "I'll explain later."

"Where are you going?" he asked, his hand reaching for her. She slipped out of his grasp and headed for the bathroom.

"Shall I make breakfast?" he shouted. Vera heard the bed creak as he got out of bed followed by his bare feet padding across the hardwood floor to the hallway. Vera looked at herself in the mirror and wondered if she'd made a mistake with this man. Would he become possessive and try to change her? Would he become a pest? Hopefully not; she rather liked his mind. He was the first of many men she'd known that read more than Hustler or Sport's Illustrated. It was Sunday. Joshua had to be at the airport by noon. Vera wouldn't see him again until next Friday evening. She relaxed knowing Joshua traveled a great deal; therefore, he was unlikely to be a pest. He was perfect for her.

A male grunt and "What the hell!" alerted Vera to his discovery of the child. Vera ran out of the bathroom and out into the hall still holding her toothbrush. The child ran past Vera and absently slapped her on the thigh making little grunting noises. She couldn't be more than four years old from her size Vera decided, noticing the way the little girl entered the living room and touched as many objects as she could, not once, but three times or more, any object which seemed of interest to her, most of them unfortunately, breakable. Annoyed by the little girl's preference for the objects which were irreplaceable, Vera had to remind herself that the little girl was small, thin, fragile, and would soon be annoying someone else.

She noticed Joshua's confusion. "I found her swinging on that old swing set in the backyard. I'd meant to have that old thing removed. It's falling apart."

"Well, why didn't you call the police?"

"I plan to call. I just didn't want to bother them at two in the morning."

"You want me to call?"

"No!" Vera shouted. Embarrassed at her reaction she added, "I'll do it. I found her after all." She contemplated the little girl with growing mystification. The child continued to perform her touching ritual and Vera wondered if the touching was her way of claiming the objects around her or maybe just navigating through an unfamiliar environment.

Joshua said aloud what Vera had been thinking, "What's the matter with her?"

"She appears to be autistic," Vera said as she moved into the kitchen, walked to the red wall phone, and grabbed the receiver. As if her action (picking up the receiver) had been some sort of signal to the child, the little girl began to run through the house. The dining room and kitchen were one big room facing the backyard and there were two entry points to the kitchen/dining area one spilling out into the living room and the other leading to the bedrooms.

Unaccountably, the little girl chose the moment Vera dialed the police to run through the kitchen into the dining area, around the polished five-piece solid oak pedestal table with four matching chairs then disappear into the living room; after an anxious minute, the child reappeared and ran the gauntlet all over again. The little speedster made a point of running around the dining room table twice whenever she entered the kitchen and as she scampered past the sliding door, she would slap the surface leaving her prints all over the glass: sometimes fingers, sometimes palm exactly three feet off the floor – a continuous collage of horizontal prints on the glass. It was amazing how she managed to avoid clipping her head on the kitchen counter as she whizzed under its granite surface.

By the time Joshua showered and dressed, Vera had finished calling the police. The dispatcher also wanted to know why Vera hadn't contacted them the moment she found the little girl. Vera tried to explain her reasoning, but even to her ears, she sounded guilty of something. Predictable, Vera thought, talking to the police or encountering them in person made her feel guilty even when she had done nothing criminal. All the time she had been on the phone talking to the dispatcher, Vera followed the child's progress through the house watching anxiously as the three-foot imp raced through the rooms worried she would hurt herself or run out the front door. It was a good thing the phone cord was long enough for her to see what was going on in the living room and bedroom hall.

Once Vera set the receiver back in its cradle, the child chose to make her escape from the house altogether. Not only did she have more energy than a mouse on a wheel, she was a proficient escape artist. Vera had to lock the deadbolts on both the front and the back doors. Once the child managed to pull a chair up to the sliding glass door and pull the latch down. Whenever Vera touched her or tried to shepherd her away from the doors and windows, the child's grunts got louder and more desperate. Vera was fast losing her patience. It was a relief when she noticed a vehicle turn off the main road onto her drive. The sight of it was a disappointment she'd expected a police cruiser.

Vera opened the door and watched as the stranger climbed out of a battered green Jeep. He wore stone-washed jeans and a baggy cotton shirt. She couldn't tell from his appearance whether he was a cop. He didn't dress like one. He did look familiar though. Vera tried to remember where she had seen him before. She searched his face. He was a tall man with a narrow torso and long legs. He walked with a confident roll in his hips. His dark hair was straight and long. She hadn't seen a man with hair down to his shoulder blades in years; not since the '60s. He tied his hair back with a piece of leather.

From a distance, his appearance with his long hair, dark tan and blue jeans might have confused people into believing he was Native American. When he removed his sunglasses and she saw his blue eyes with lashes a woman would envy, suddenly, she felt scruffy and blamed Joshua for hogging the bathroom.

From his demeanor and appearance, Vera seriously doubted that this man could be a cop. No police force in its right mind would hire a recruit with hair longer than a woman's or allow him to dress as if he was on his way to *The Doors* concert and had the whole night to sit at a café and discuss psychedelics. Unless the county was so desperate, they could only afford to hire mavericks and misfits from the reject list of other agencies. Maybe he was one of those undercover cops like the ones who disguise themselves as drug addicts, dealers, or hippies?

As the stranger drew closer, he looked up at her with pleased recognition. Annoyed because she couldn't place him, she watched him mount the porch steps slowly. His expression changed to surprise. Vera out of habit tried to cover the white puckered scar along her cheekbone. She should have been used to people's reaction to her face by now. It had been nearly ten years ago. Yet if she were honest with herself, she would never get used to the way people looked at her with their eyes shifting away from her scar desperately searching for a safe place to land.

The man stood before her in his loose fitting faded 501 jeans with his lean body erect and his long fingers clasping a pad and pencil. His blue eyes lingered on her face too long for comfort. She had seen his eyes widen, seen the way he stumbled up the steps, his thoughts interfering with his forward motion. Yet by the time he had reached her, he had come to a decision. Wow, that had been quick. Perhaps his training as a police officer made the difference. He looked the part now, all business, all cop.

God knows how long they would have stood there on the porch mute and uncomfortable if they hadn't been interrupted.

"No, don't touch that, that's dangerous." Joshua said, his voice drifting out to them from the open window. Joshua was as clueless about children as Vera.

As the man passed her and entered the house he introduced himself, "I'm Andrew Treloar. Chief Steven Glenjones asked me to come by and check out the situation. You're Vera Lee, am I right? You reported an abandoned child, yes?"

"Yes," Vera said. "She's in here. I found her in the backyard swinging on the old swing set."

The man had to bend slightly so as not to hit his head on the door lintel as he walked into her house. His sharp blue eyes took in the sight of Joshua holding the child off the ground, his arms straight out in front of him. The tableau reminded Vera of images from her childhood mixed with images she had seen on the news – a male dangling a naked, angry, and frightened toddler in the air, as perplexed and unhappy as the child. How had she slipped off her clothes between the time Vera left the house and now? The girl swung her arms, her fists aiming for Joshua's face and more often than naught connecting with his arms and chest. The grunting becoming shriller and more disturbed the longer he held her.

"I've sent for Social Services to take charge of the kid," Andrew Treloar explained to Vera.

"Joshua, you can put her down now," Vera said. "She doesn't like to be touched."

"I figured that out for myself V," Joshua said and carefully set the child back on her feet. Once her feet made contact with the floor, she took off as if she were one of those windup toys that once on the ground proceeded to run into furniture and walls without feeling the pain. Vera managed to get to the sliding door before the little girl unlocked the dead bolt.

In desperation, Vera searched the kitchen cupboards for something to entertain the kid. She grabbed a box of cereal advertising healthy choices. The cereal included almonds and other assorted nuts as well as healthy grains. The sink was full of dirty dishes and the kitchen still smelled of salmon from dinner the night before. Vera managed to find a clean bowl and filled the bowl with her expensive breakfast cereal.

The child had been testing the durability of the cupboard door, the one under the kitchen sink, by opening and closing it repeatedly, until she heard the cereal hitting the bowl. Miraculously the grunting and the whacking of wood on wood stopped. Her eyes followed the progress of the cereal box. The contents were poured into a bowl and set on the kitchen table. Vera stepped back and waited.

The child stared at the food for several intense seconds and finally walked around the table and stood in front of the bowl. Vera realized she was looming over the little girl and stepped back to lean against the counter. The child grabbed Vera's hand and pulled. She was directing Vera's arm as if Vera's arm was a tool, something the kid could maneuver as she did the furniture. Vera dipped her fingers in the bowl and offered several pieces to the little girl. The child acted like a bird waiting for the worm. Vera popped the cereal in. The cop and Joshua stepped into the room and watched.

The cop cleared his throat and said, "Miss Lee, it might be a good idea to insist she feed herself."

Vera glanced over her shoulder knowing her face must have registered her surprise.

"What?"

"It's one of the traits of autism to maneuver others as if they were tools. Take her hand and place it in the bowl."

Vera did so. The child left her hand in the bowl. Vera assumed the little girl must be hungry; yet, she kept her hand in the bowl without retrieving the food.

"Around what time did you find her?" the cop asked seemingly unconcerned whether the child ate or not.

Vera wondered how Andrew Treloar knew she was single. She could have been Joshua's wife for all he knew. She wished she could remember him the way he remembered her.

"It was around midnight."

"Did you hear anything unusual – a car pulling up to your house or doors closing?"

"No, only the creaking of the rusty chains on the swing set."

As they had been exchanging information, Vera noticed the child curl her fingers around the cereal and slip several pieces in her mouth. Vera turned to face the men. Joshua's expression registered his annoyance and bewilderment. He obviously didn't know much about children which was reassuring. One of her worst fears was inadvertently getting involved with a married man, especially a married man with children. Andrew Treloar, on the other hand, appeared to have experience with children, especially autistic children.

"Would you show me where you found her Miss Lee," Andrew Treloar asked.

Vera unlocked the kitchen door and stepped onto the back porch. The porch roof sagged dangerously, especially at the far end where two 2x4s had been nailed together in order to carry the weight of the roof. The cedar floor boards had aged to a dull gray, the surfaces rough and splintered. It made her uncomfortable to have strangers seeing the old farmhouse the way it was now – going to seed – when in her imagination she envisioned a brand-new porch roof with a stained oak cedar floor and rails. Someday there would be fancy outdoor furniture, potted plants, and paving stones leading to a rock garden and herb garden.

"Be careful on the steps," Vera cautioned Treloar as she showed him the swing set. At one time, the swing set had been painted with red enamel; now, only tiny flecks of red paint remained in the corners and at the very bottom of the posts. There were two yellow plastic seats rubbed white in the center where children had swung themselves giddy.

Vera watched as Treloar inspected the property swinging around to get a good look in all directions from the meadow to the hill, from the porch to the barn, and finally to the sorry-ass fence and beyond the fence what she assumed was a cow path. The cow path followed the natural rock ridge along the hill up to the summit. It wasn't difficult to figure out what the man was trying to do. She had been doing the same thing only in her head because she'd had no time since discovering the little girl to really wonder how she had gotten into the backyard.

The cop redirected his attention to the swing set. Vera wondered how he saw the place, the old sagging wood fence along the northern side of the property, the insidious Trumpet Vine's thick bark as thick as her ankles growing up, between, and over the fence, the weight pulling the dog-eared boards toward the cow path. Vera hated to pull down the fence. The orange blossoms of the Trumpet

Vine added color and shape to the yard. In the northeast corner grew a willow nearly thirty feet tall.

On the east side of her property the fence had been removed. Beyond her backyard of yellowed grass, puncture vines, and dandelions stretched a meadow of wild flowers and cheatgrass. Beyond the meadow, about a mile away, she could see the Pass that led to the hilltop. Last night, she figured the kid's parents had taken a drive through the Owyhee Mountains along the back roads and lost themselves in the confusion of old and sometimes abandoned roads. Now with the sun warm on her head and shoulders, she remembered her dream. She had heard a chair being pushed along a rocky ledge.

Directly behind her house was the winding cow path. People had to go single file up the path to the top of the hill. At the start of Opal Road Access near her property, she'd slung a chain from her fence to a juniper bush and attached an old cedar board to the chain. She'd painted the words – Private Property No Trespassing. It did no good. She'd seen kids and even a few adults step over the chain and make their way to the top of the hill.

The cop searched the ground around the swing set carefully and Vera assuming she'd been dismissed returned to the house and to Joshua attempting to guard the sliding glass door to prevent the little girl from following them outside.

Within twenty minutes, Vera's home had been invaded by police officers searching her ten acres, Anderson Pass, Opal Road Access, and the top of Hunter's Hill for clues which might help them identify the child. There were no vehicles abandoned on the dirt road, no sign that anyone had come along the road recently and left a child to wander the Owyhee Mountains alone. It was as if the child had dropped out of the sky. Vera overheard Treloar discussing the situation with one of the other cops posted near her house.

The main highway less than a mile from Vera's farmhouse carried travelers from the small town of Marsing, Idaho through Mintlaw and on to Homedale which could take them in several different directions. Right out of Marsing, travelers could take U.S. 95 through the Owyhee Mountains to the Oregon border, and further south to Winnemucca, Nevada. There had been no car accidents or vehicles needing assistance on the Idaho side last night. Questions weaved in and out of her head as she watched the people search the grounds and the hilltop. Could someone have dumped the child in the mountains and left her to fend for herself? Or were her parents trapped in their vehicle somewhere beyond the hill, down some ravine or old mining shaft?

After an hour, Andrew Treloar returned to her house. He seemed to be the Mintlaw Police forces official spokesperson, "So far we haven't found anything to explain the child's appearance. It will take time to find an overturned or abandoned vehicle in these mountains. Altogether there's about 7,000 square miles in the Owyhee County alone. If her parents were sightseeing and lost their way or their vehicle overturned into a gully or along a creek bed, it could be weeks before we locate them. We'll check some of the tourist camps and scenic sites near here."

As he spoke, he knelt and studied the child thoughtfully. The little girl sat on the kitchen floor under the table. Some of Vera's books and magazines were strewn about the floor and the child flipped through the pages without interest. Every so often, she would pause at a page where a picture had been inserted. She would point at the picture and grunt. Vera wondered if her grunts were her only form of communication.

"She doesn't look as if she's walked far," Treloar said aloud. "You see the few bits of chaff from the cheatgrass stuck to her sock. If she'd been walking far, her legs would be scratched up and her tennis shoes and sock would show evidence that she'd traveled through the desert for a lot longer."

Vera looked closely at the kid's cotton print shorts and matching shirt with renewed interest, "She might have gotten the chaff bits from my yard, you know. I've been avoiding the backyard because of all the thorny weeds and cheatgrass. Look at her clothes. They look brand new. They've never been washed. See the creases, how stiff they are; the shoes though, their old and worn. See the hole in the toe."

Treloar twisted around to look up at Vera. He seemed proud of her as if she had said something particularly insightful, "That's clever of you to notice. Yes. Her clothes suggest someone had purchased them recently."

"She needs a haircut," Vera said.

"Yep," Treloar responded absently. "There are signs of neglect. It looks as if she hasn't had a bath in more than a week. Someone bought her new clothes, but didn't bother to cut her hair, bath her, or feed her properly."

Treloar stretched and stood up contemplating the child with a touch of anger and sadness in the set of his eyebrows and clenched jaw, "All the clues lead to someone prettying her up to be passed on. If she'd been an infant, the mother would have left her in a basket on someone's doorstep or. Well, I'll contact Chief Glenjones. He can check with the stations in Oregon and Nevada. Perhaps someone might have called in asking about her or her parents."

"What happened to her right sock?" Vera wondered aloud. Both men shrugged their shoulders and said nothing as if the question didn't seem that important. Had she dressed herself?

It wasn't until nearly eleven when the woman from Social Services arrived to collect Vera's orphan. Joshua had been pacing the porch for nearly twenty minutes. Treloar had offered to take him to the airport. Joshua declined. Vera wondered why. For the last hour, Joshua had been glancing suspiciously from Treloar to Vera. Then Vera remembered something Joshua had said in one of the meetings, something about a confrontation with the police and having been beaten up badly by some cops in Los Angeles, how his lawyer and the courts eventually managed to get the cops removed from the force.

Vera was surprised at her reaction when the woman from Social Services came into her house. It had nothing to do with the woman. She seemed very capable and kind. No Vera's reaction had to do with the child squirming in the woman's arms as she carried the little girl out to the blue nondescript car. Vera followed the woman outside and watched in astonishment as the social worker strapped the child in the back seat of the car in heavy restraints with strong clasps and thick leather belts.

"Is that really necessary?" Vera asked concerned for her former hell-raising guest.

The woman with cheeks flushed from the effort of restraining the squirming, grunting bundle backed her caboose out of the car and straightened to her full five feet eight inches. When the woman turned to face Vera, her expression revealed nothing. Either, she didn't seem upset by Vera's question or she was very good at hiding her feelings. You would have thought restraining children with prison style restraints was a daily occurrence. Her name was Archer as Vera recalled.

Mrs. Archer appeared competent. The woman stood by her open car door only long enough to answer, "Yes. It's for her own safety." Then she climbed into the driver's seat and started the engine. Vera backed away from the moving car and watched with arms crossed as the little girl was chauffeured to some temporary foster home.

As Vera turned to go back into the house, she noticed Andrew Treloar standing by the front door. He passed her as she climbed the porch steps saying, "Don't worry. They'll take good care of her until the police can locate her family."

"The police?" Vera asked. "So, you're not the police? I wondered. You don't dress like one."

Andrew paused to stand beside her as they watched Mrs. Archer's car turn and head toward the main road. "No. Steve asked me to come over since I live nearby."

Maybe she was angry with herself or angry with the whole rotten world; unfortunately, the man next to her received the brunt of her unhappiness. "You're not a policeman yet, you come into my home and ask me a bunch of personal questions as if you're a cop. I thought maybe you were a detective at the very least," she finished, as she reviewed what she had said and what had happened in the last few hours. She wanted to scream at him or hit him or call the local Chief of Police and make a formal complaint.

He didn't seem surprised by her reaction. He calmly walked away ignoring her tirade and climbed inside his Jeep. The situation had taken on the unreality of an avant-garde joke, Dada art, toilet as art, ordinary citizen acting like cop. "You had no right to pretend to be a cop and invade my home. Why didn't you make your position clear at the beginning?"

Andrew paused in the act of closing his car door and turned to face her. He slipped a strand of black hair behind his ear and shrugged, "I told you my name and that Chief Glenjones sent me out here. What's the big deal? I didn't arrest you."

"No, but you passed yourself off as a cop," Vera said holding her arms close to her chest in an attempt to hold in her temper.

"It's not my problem if you're perception of me was skewed. I never said I was a cop, remember. You just assumed I was."

"Hey!" she called out to him. He closed the car door and started the engine. "Will you let me know what you find out about the little girl? I mean when you find her parents."

He seemed pleased by her request. "Sure." Again something in the cadence of his voice sparked a sense of familiarity.

Since Andrew Treloar was the last to leave Vera thought she would be thankful at having her home nearly to herself once again; instead, she was getting madder by the second. The deputies and neighborhood volunteers from the fire department and town had long since moved beyond her property. She'd heard some of them talking about searching Poison Creek and Jump Creek Falls. Vera had never heard of those places. Their names conjured up images of danger and death. Was Poison Creek really poisonous? Did people jump from the falls to their deaths?

Her anger had more to do with the way the police thought they could wander in and out of her house with impunity, the way the volunteers peeked into her barn and searched her trash cans as if they would find the kid's parents inside them. She felt violated. She felt impotent. They carried themselves in such a way that infuriated her even more because they naturally assumed they were in charge and had every right to poke and pry and ask rude questions; yet, she as the homeowner who paid taxes and toiled endlessly to make her home attractive and comfortable could only look on helplessly.

Of course, a child was involved, and she understood the seriousness of the situation. Yet why treat her like a criminal? The juxtaposition of being allowed to shoot anyone who dared trespass on her property as stated by the Castle Doctrine while also being helpless to prevent the police from entering her home made her want to scream and pull her hair out.

While Vera had been talking to Treloar, Joshua had been listening. The first thing Joshua said when she entered the house was, "He's not even a cop and he walks through our house as if he has the right to be here asking questions? What the hell is this about anyway? Are the police so hard up nowadays that they have to ask nosy citizens to do their job for them?"

"Never mind Joshua, it's a little late to be pissed off now. I'll take you to the airport."

An hour and a half later, Vera deposited Joshua near the entrance to the airport feeling the familiar sense of relief and emerging excitement. Alone time, she thought, now I don't have to constantly worry about my scar or suck in my gut or watch what I say in case I make him mad. Before Joshua climbed out of her car, he pulled her toward him and kissed her hard enough to break the skin on her lower lip. Vera's lack of response annoyed him.

"What's the matter? Still worried about the lost kid; or, does your change in attitude have something to do with the man from Mayberry?"

"Stop it, Joshua. Jealousy doesn't suit you."

—

As far as Andrew knew, volunteers and police were still searching the Canyonlands for the child's missing parent or parents and as of seven in the evening the sun was slowly sinking behind the Owyhees. Soon the darkness would take over and the search would be called off for the day. Feeling particularly antsy Andrew thought of a way to help discover the child's identity and find her parents. Vera's accusation that he was a fraud hurt more than he imaged. He'd never really cared what other people thought of him. Plenty of drunks and snotty kids spray painting private property had called him ruder pejoratives. So that was why he was spending his precious evening hours at the local grocery store; instead of working on his recent commission.

Andrew decided to use the police stations resources and create a few posters in the hopes that someone might recognize the little girl and come forward. He was in the process of taping the posters on the inside windows of Peterson's Grocery store. The posters were still warm from the copier. Beatrice holding a box of canned peas in her arms paused behind Andrew.

"So that's the little girl you found, Andy?" Beatrice asked.

Andrew finished taping a corner of the poster and turned to face her. Andrew had known Beatrice since he had been a kid coming into her store to buy candy or some other silly thing he thought he really needed. Beatrice must be in her sixties now. Her short salt and pepper hair, more salt than pepper stood up in stiff spikes. She had also let herself fill out and discarded her high heeled boots for soft canvas shoes.

"Yep. Well, no, to be accurate, a citizen reported the child and we went to collect her. Does she look familiar to you Beatrice? You know most of the kids in town. What do you think? Do you remember her?"

As Beatrice peered at the poster with the child's face in the center, Andrew looked up in time to see Arthur at the checkout counter talking to Vera Lee. Vera's rigid posture and averted face made Andrew wonder what the hell Junior was saying to make her so uncomfortable. Jessie had to call out, "Vlasky, Vlasky, you're up," twice before Arthur spun around to face the cashier and realized Jessie had finished with the customer ahead of him in line.

Vera could have waited for Jesse to finish with Vlasky but chose to go down several stations removed and have Pamela check out her groceries. She had only a couple of items in her basket and dumped them on the counter waiting impatiently for Pamela to finish. By the time she'd paid for her purchases and picked up her bag, she was out the door long before Jessie had rung up Vlasky's last bottle of wine.

Andrew made sure Vera noticed him standing by the automatic doors. She peered up at him in passing forced to wait a second before the sensors acknowledged her presence and nodded curtly before rushing out of the grocery store. Beatrice who was still talking in his ear handed the box of peas to Andrew. Without protest, Andrew held the heavy box and watched Arthur pay for his groceries.

"Beatrice, if you don't know the little girl just say so. You don't have to wrack your memory clear back to the dinosaurs. I appreciate the sentiment though," Andrew said and dumped the box on the shelves with the others.

He managed to extricate himself from Beatrice's clutches and escape outside. He was in time to see Arthur standing by his Chevy Silverado with a four-inch lift loading his wine bottles and groceries in the vehicle. What a pretentious boob, Andrew thought. Daddy had found a way to get Junior out of the draft. He'd never served but the dumbass wanted to show how macho he was by buying himself the most expensive truck in the world. Andrew noticed how Arthur was trying to avoid eye contact probably trying to remember in his wine soaked befuddled brain if he had already promised to buy one of Andrew's pieces of art or maybe had forgotten to pay him for one he already had at home. When the guy's puffy red face relaxed into a smile, Andrew felt like laughing. The cheap bastard didn't know the difference between good and bad design anyway.

Andrew remained standing by the Silverado making the man even more nervous as Vlasky quickly put his cartons on the floor of the passenger seat. He could have climbed into his fancy truck and driven away without acknowledging Andrew at all. But Arthur didn't ignore him. He didn't ignore him because Arthur Vlasky was probably curious about recent events and thought he could get some juicy gossip out of him. Arthur stood by the open driver's side door and waited politely for Andrew to speak.

"That woman you were talking to in the store. You know her?"

"The woman," Arthur said looking confused for a moment. "Oh yeah, Vera. Sure, I used to know Vera. I hardly recognized her. Had to look twice. Holy shit, life has treated her rough, but Grandma said she was bad-news from the very beginning. Looks like some unsatisfied customer messed up her face good."

Andrew held on to his temper with an effort. He should have been immune to Arthur's needling ways, "How do you know Vera Lee?"

"Lee is it? Didn't know her new name. Her name used to be Vlasky. She used to be my step-mama."

"1973," Andrew said partly to himself.

Arthur frowned at him, "Grandma still believes that bitch caused the accident. And I'm of the same opinion."

Andrew would have dearly loved to wipe the stupid smirk off the dumbass's face. He took a step closer. Vlasky was so like his

41

arrogant old man. The alarm on Junior's face made Andrew want to smile. Now the dumbass understood the seriousness of the situation. He didn't give a damn if Vlasky was as rich as Midas. All the money in the world couldn't give this coward courage. Andrew was close enough to smell the alcohol on Vlasky's breath. He backed up and waved his hand in front of his face, "Holy crap. That's bad Vlasky. Maybe I should do my civic duty and make a citizen's arrest for public drunkenness?"

Vlasky looked uneasy about getting another DUI.

Andrew spoke in a voice he hoped remained professional and courteous, "It's my firm opinion that the past should remain in the past. Don't you agree, Arthur?"

"Sure. Yeah. Makes sense to me."

"Good. Quit whining about your old man and Vera. It won't do you any good you know. Most folks around here never really liked your Dad. Anyway," Andrew said taking another step back. "I heard you and your brother are planning a trip to Africa soon. Is that right?"

"Yes," Arthur said with a smile, all his good humor restored. "We're leaving next week. Pete wants to climb some damn mountain. I plan to bag a rhino."

"Well, have a good trip, Arthur. Don't you worry; we'll keep an eye on your granny and the ranch because that's what neighbors do for each other, right?"

"Sure. Of course. I appreciate that Andrew," Arthur said.

By the time Andrew reached his Jeep, Arthur was in his Silverado gunning his engine and racing out of the parking lot, his way of thumbing his nose at Andrew. Andrew could just imagine the little wheels in Arthur's brain spinning out of control. Arthur would probably complain to the Chief about him. It wouldn't be the first complaint Steve had received from the Vlasky family.

The beauty was that Andrew subcontracted out to the Mintlaw Police and sometimes the Owyhee County Sheriff's office when they were short of help; so, as an unofficial, poorly paid veteran of foreign wars, a sort of liaison between the agencies of law enforcement, the detective on the payroll, rent-a-cop, whatever; Andrew could tell Vlasky to stick-it-where-the-sun-don't-shine without worrying about a reprimand from Chief Glenjones.

—

Daniel stood under the shade of a locust tree near the dry creek and watched the people search the Anderson's field. They looked like ants crawling up and down the hillside and weaving in and out of the tall grasses and sagebrush. Daniel rocked from side to side and moaned. Go away, he thought, go away. They were trampling all over the burrows and winterfat. Some of them were crushing wild parsley beneath their boots. They were scaring away the whistle pigs and the jackrabbits. They were stepping on the ants and the spiders. What of the tailless frogs? Hide little frogs. Hide from them or they'll step on you.

They did not see him. They could not hear him. He listened for the sound of a car. He would rock his body side to side and hold his bad arm just so. He would watch the trespassers. They were trespassing. He knew about trespassing. He rocked and the thing inside his arm continued to beat wanting out. He remembered the school. Ms. Matthews needed him. Daniel started walking down the creek side in the safety of the lilacs moving quickly toward the road. When he got to the school, he spoke into the call box. The wrought iron gates opened for him. Daniel slipped inside and hurried down the driveway wanting to be near his shop. His shop was just around the corner and he had his own key.

Chapter Three

As Vera left Jarvis Hardware carrying a roll of hog wire under her arm and clutching a bag of nails, she wondered why Andrew had been in Peterson Grocery. The sight of Arthur's son so like his father in looks and temperament brought back old memories, memories she would rather forget. A lobotomy would be nice. No, too extreme. She didn't want to be a vegetable. Too bad there wasn't a surgery to remove unpleasant memories forever. If modern medicine ever discovered how to get rid of unpleasant memories, she would be the first to sign up.

As she turned onto her drive, she noticed some of her neighbors searching the hillside and the meadow near her house. She didn't mind if they searched the meadow but why were they peeking in her windows?

"Hey," she shouted. "What the hell are you doing?"

The teenagers jumped away from her window and scurried back to the meadow careful not to look in her direction. Should she be upset? It was close to four o'clock in the afternoon. The heat was intense, ninety-five degrees in the shade. Vera slowed to watch: middle-aged women, farmers and ranchers, grocery clerks, students, even off-duty police were studying the ground intensely. Some were using walking sticks, others poking under brush or whacking at tall grass with their sticks. She stopped her Corolla midway up the drive, turned off the engine and rolled down her windows.

It was too hot in the car. She climbed out.

Just standing by her car with the heat radiating off the ground and blinding her with white light made her long to run inside where the roof and the walls insulated her from the sun. And there they were all those people hunting for clues on the hillside and the field, the hot sun burning the backs of their necks, still searching long after the authorities had called a halt. She stood with this new image before her, her former perception of the world as a cold and frightening place receding into some dark place she stored for moments of melancholy. Those memories were still apart of her, still capable of torture; but the sight of people anxiously searching for the little girl's parents was a reminder that there were still good people in the world. They could have stayed home in their air-conditioned dwellings and watched the police and rescue teams search for clues. Instead they chose to come out and help.

Vera considered whether to join the search. She rejected the idea. It would mean involvement. It would mean having to open herself up to strangers, nodding and smiling, making conversation. No. Not a good idea. She'd had experience with friendly overtures that had turned ugly and sick. She attracted such people. Vera watched as her neighbors walked three feet apart and moved in unison as they combed the ground from Jump Creek Road to the top of the hill.

She remembered Joshua's joke about Mayberry and Andrew Treloar. His sarcastic comments were an ugly reminder of another tongue equally as viscous. Joshua acted as if he were jealous, as if Treloar's attention to her meant something significant. Vera seriously doubted Andrew had any interest in her other than as a potential suspect. If Joshua had only known Vera's personal aversion to the police or anyone associated with the law, he would not have been so jealous.

It was really hot today, she thought, without even the relief of a breeze in the air. Sweat beaded her forehead and the back of her neck, several drops slid down between her breasts. Vera's beige Toyota Corolla had air conditioning but that would be a waste of precious fuel. She had survived most of her life working for low wages dreaming of the day she would strike it rich and then when she turned thirty-five having to face reality that poverty was all she could expect from this lifetime.

It was rather ironic when she met the Armstrongs on the day she finally discarded her childhood dreams. They had made the difference, all the difference in the world. Vera, unused to kindness had been suspicious at first, wondering what they wanted from her. It took nearly two weeks before she could relax and accept them as the generous and funny people they were. Vera had never told the Armstrongs about Arthur or the accident or that she had been a resident of Idaho. Maybe they had known about her past life in Mintlaw and chose not to bring up those painful memories?

On October 31, 1973 outside her old bedroom window the leaves had been dressed in their autumn colors. The grass around the foot of the tree had been covered in yellow and orange leaves. From behind her, she heard heavy footsteps running into the room and Vera flinched bending her neck in anticipation of a blow. The blow came. The hand grabbed her head and shoved her face into the glass. Not hard enough to break the glass, that would have been wasteful, but hard enough to leave a bump on her forehead the next day.

A voice screamed in her ear, the words ringing and echoing in her head, "What did you do with my checkbook slut?"

An hour later he found his checkbook where he had left it the night before – in his car on the passenger side seat. Vera watched him drive away wondering if he was going back to the bar and hoping he would find someone to drive him home. It was Halloween night and Vera didn't want her neighbors to see her face and ask questions. She turned off the porch light and all the lamps in the house. She closed the curtains and dropped the blinds. She sat in the dark in the rocking chair by the phone and waited for her husband to come home preparing herself for another assault on her ears and body.

Standing by her Toyota ten years later, Vera did not feel the heat of a July afternoon. She was back in the past reliving Halloween night. He'd come home drunk and insisted they were going for a drive. She'd begged him to reconsider. Then she asked if she could drive. He smacked the side of her head and dragged her to the Firebird. The blow had made her nauseous. Part of her knew she had to get out of the car. If only her eyes would focus properly, she could find the door handle and open the car door.

Before she had a chance to escape, he started the car and peeled out of the garage. She found herself a prisoner in a speeding vehicle sitting in the passenger seat of Arthur's prize possession, his brand-new cherry red Firebird. Vera could smell whiskey on Arthur's breath clear across the space between them. Even his sweat smelled of whiskey. His hair reeked of tobacco smoke too. His hands on the steering wheel shook. Vera didn't remember saying anything wrong. She had just asked Arthur if he knew the girl, the one he had been talking to in the donut shop for nearly ten minutes the day before. The girl had been behind the counter. She had been blonde and pretty. Vera thought perhaps one of Arthur's sons had dated her.

Arthur responded to her question by smashing his fist into her face. She had thought he'd broken her nose. Vera recalled the pain and the shock, how she had clung to the door handle and pleaded with Arthur to slow down and let her out. She remembered how cold and calm he had been, how he'd pushed down on the accelerator and the car had leaped forward, their speed increasing until they were careening down the two-lane highway at over a hundred miles per hour. At that moment, she realized Arthur had gone from a sloppy drunk to a sober suicide. He would take her with him.

When Arthur heard the police siren and glanced in the rearview mirror and realized that the Owyhee County Highway Patrol was on his tail, Vera convinced that she would die at the age of twenty-four, began to pray silently to herself. But instead of trying to outrun the police Arthur took his foot off the accelerator. Unfortunately, he did so at a critical moment around a sharp curve and the Firebird sailed off the paved road and plunged down the ravine hitting a boulder at the bottom. Vera survived only because she wore her seat belt. Arthur died instantly the steering wheel embedded in his chest.

There had been an ambulance and a stretcher and staring up into a pair of blue eyes with smoky black lashes. The man had soaring black eyebrows too. He looked satanic. Now she knew his name – Andrew Treloar. No wonder he had stumbled at the sight of her this morning. He had remembered her from that tragic night.

At the time, Vera had been in too much pain to care how she looked or what she said. Later in the hospital, she agonized over what she might have let slip in her delirium. Now the memory clear as if she were in the Firebird once again played in her head: how the man had taken off his baseball hat and rubbed his short hair then leaned toward her and touched her shoulder. He'd asked for her name. She'd given her maiden name. Later she had to retract what she'd said and explain in a rambling discourse that made the other policeman impatient the reason why she had given her maiden name, even when she didn't understand why herself. Vera equated the name Vlasky with pain and unwarranted punishments.

Another memory came unbidden to the front of her thoughts, the conversation between Treloar and the deputy. Treloar had said, "I still can't figure out how she escaped with only a broken arm and a few scratches when the guy looks as if he'd been catapulted into the steering wheel like so much fodder. And she's sober, not a whiff of alcohol on her breath. The averages are that she would be the DOA and the drunk would have walked away from the accident."

The deputy said, "I clocked him at a hundred. The vehicle was all over the road. He was driving blind drunk. The lab will confirm that. It was weird though how the Firebird bucked as if he'd tried to stop, then shot forward and sailed through the air. I swear for a minute I thought I was watching Star Wars and instead of a space ship going into hyperspace, a tricked-out Firebird was attempting it. The damned thing soared into the air and up and up. I kid you not. Then as if the car realized the impossibility of what it was doing, all two tons of it dropped back to earth. Look at the depression here, no skids, nothing, not even a blade of grass disturbed until the vehicle crashed into the boulder below. This is one for NASA to figure out."

When the paramedics had lifted her gurney into the ambulance, Vera had seen Treloar's face one more time hovering above her like a dark angel. He touched her forehead and his last words to her were "You take care Miss. Everything's going to be all right." Vera remembered thinking – people use clichés after horrific accidents – people don't have the right words or know what to say after tragedies happen. No, she thought to herself, you've got it all wrong, what she wanted to say but was in too much pain to say was – everything had been bad, and everything wouldn't be all right ever again, even if he's dead, nothing will ever be right again.

Coming back to the present, Vera realized she had thought herself into a state of melancholy again. She climbed back onto the seat of her Toyota carefully, the seat already hot from the few moments she had spent standing by her car pretending to watch her neighbors search for clues. She wanted some balance in her life, something cheerful to think about. She hadn't always been like this, prepared for the worst, thinking the worst, settling between the lesser of two evils. She parked her car near the house under the catalpa tree and carried her grocery bags toward the porch thinking about those few seconds after Arthur accelerated and before she woke up on the gurney.

Arthur had been suicidal that night. She could have sworn he was bent on killing them both. She couldn't remember if he had tried to break. The memory slid back into the shadows. Something had happened something had happened just after Arthur accelerated. Someone had spoken. Not her. No. She'd been too terrified. It must have been Arthur. Maybe he'd screamed or shouted, "Oh my God." Perhaps he had tried to stop and that was why, so much speed combined with his attempts to slow down had carried them into the air. She realized disconcertedly that she'd been standing with her key poised to unlock the front door for too long. Once in the house, she switched on the television and put away her groceries and other supplies absently listening to the drone of the television, waiting with curiosity for the five o'clock news to start. Perhaps there would be something on the news about the abandoned child. Perhaps the police had located the child's parents. Vera hoped so.

48

As Vera sat in front of her television set and stared out the window waiting for the commercial to end and the news to begin, she remembered her first wish nearly a decade ago. She and Arthur had been married for two years. She had sat beside him on his couch, a couch much grander than her own and she had looked over at him as he watched the news. At that moment, the truth dawned upon her: she was sitting next to a stranger. She did not know him at all. They made love. They said, "I love you." They picked out furniture together and bought groceries together and exchanged gifts at Christmas and birthdays; and yet, he was a stranger. It was from that day forward, she began having daydreams about Arthur deciding to pack his bags and move to Alaska in search of gold. While in Alaska, she imagined him meeting an Eskimo woman and falling in love.

Her relief at the thought of him thousands of miles away, happy with his new life and she – she would be alone and safe. Every night for a month, she made it her special task to dream him a happy future. It didn't feel right. Somehow the dream wasn't working. Her instincts had been all wrong. It was time to stop worrying about his happiness and start concentrating on her survival. So, she changed the dream. Instead of a happy future with an Eskimo woman and gold in the bank; for two months, she conjured the same dream, her husband lying on a bed of cold steel in the morgue dead. And on Halloween night, her dream came true.

—

Last night during supper Maggie waited for Murray to complain to her parents about her behavior. Maggie could barely choke down the potato salad on her plate and the crisp chicken leg wondering when Murray would complain. Yet Murray said nothing. Maggie went to bed wondering if he would say something after she had left the room. It took her several hours to fall asleep. She tossed. She turned. She beat her head against the pillow. She counted to one hundred. She counted backwards. Then she created a fantasy in her head and wove in the people she knew. She dreamed about Jeremy, about meeting him in the desert.

In her fantasy, she was older, wiser, and oh so beautiful. Jeremy had been riding his horse through the mountains. He left his friends and led his horse toward where she stood. He offered to take her home. He pulled her up onto the back of his horse and they took off. Instead of taking her home, he took her further away. They wandered the desert just the three of them, Jeremy, his horse, and her. And she had her arms wrapped tight around his waist, the heat of their bodies keeping them warm.

Sometime in the middle of the night Maggie woke. The sound of a child crying woke her. She lay in her bed afraid to move. The sound stopped. It must have been a bird or a cat. Cats sounded like babies crying. Her limbs relaxed.

Maggie woke with a headache. A little man with a little hammer beat and beat against her forehead. Maggie dragged herself out of bed and grabbed her robe. She could hear her father and her mother talking in the kitchen below. She heard Murray's wheelchair roll toward the living room. He must have finished breakfast. The crying in the night had left a sour taste in Maggie's mouth. Her heart still beat so fast she thought it might pop right out of her chest. That little kid, that poor girl, Maggie thought. I feel so sorry for her. What a terrible life, what a terrible way to have to live, always being afraid and alone.

Maggie found her mother in the kitchen drinking a cup of coffee and reading the morning paper. It was the custom in Maggie's family for her mother to have a private discussion with Maggie if she had misbehaved, and if the behavior continued for her father to lecture her, and if that didn't work a suitable punishment. Her father did not believe in corporeal punishment. Unlike the boys, corporeal punishment wasn't necessary with Maggie. Just a disappointed or disgusted expression on her father's face could send Maggie into a fit of weeping. Evidently, Murray hadn't said anything about yesterday's rudeness.

Maggie poured herself a glass of milk and heard her mother cluck sadly. Maggie sat down at the table beside her.

"What's wrong Mom?"

"The woman up the road found an abandoned child. No one knows how the little girl came to be in this area. And the authorities still have no clue as to her identity. In fact, so far, no one has reported a missing child. Isn't that odd? And they say the child is autistic. I wonder if anyone called the Egg. What's the woman's name, the director of school for the blind and deaf?"

Maggie resented her mother using Maggie's nickname for the school. Maggie and some of her friends had been riding their bikes passed the new facility and the woman pulling weeds from around the snapdragons asked if any of them would like to work in the nursery or the kindergarten. Maggie had joked with Tish about how once the children graduated from the special school they would be known as Eagle Gateway Graduates and how the initials spelled Egg. Maggie remembered how Tish was so tickled by her joke; her high-pitched laughter seemed to ricochet off solid objects and peal through the air like a siren. She was sure every poor critter in the

Owyhees for miles around even some luckless farmer out in his field could hear Tish.

It hadn't been that funny. Unfortunately for Maggie the joke stuck, and her classmates started to call the kids Egg or Eggs, even the school was now known as Egg. Some people used the term as a condensed version of egghead, only in a contradicting way to imply the students at the Eagle Gateway were dumb. Maggie felt ashamed of herself. She'd been working so hard to curb her sarcasm and especially her need to get a laugh out of her friends and enemies.

She used to think, they were just stupid jokes, until her mother made her go to the Oxford English Dictionary and look up the word sarcasm. She read the excerpt from the book in disbelief: (mid 16-century French sarcasme, Greek sarkazein, later Greek to 'gnash the teeth, speak bitterly' ...Latin and Greek... sarkasmos, sarx, and sark ... "to tear flesh."). Today the word seemed so benign; yet, in the past people thought of those who practiced sarcasm as the act of "tear(ing) flesh." Yuck.

Now after Friday, having met the children in person, having been introduced to the staff and after talking to Ms. Matthews who seemed so nice, Maggie squirmed with guilt over being the instigator of that unflattering nickname especially when referring to the kids. Most of them were so cute and sweet, not that they had to be cute and sweet to be respected she reminded herself. She felt like such a monster whenever she heard the epithet and to hear her mother use the stupid label made her want to (gnash her teeth) she was so angry.

"Maggie," her mother said. "Are you listening to me?"

"Yes, sorry, I was thinking about something else. Sarah. Her name's Sarah Matthews," Maggie said and glanced at the paper and the picture of the child on the front page. Maggie had volunteered to help with the children on Tuesday through Thursday until school started in the fall. The children made her mother uncomfortable. Her mother, an elementary teacher used to work in the Twin Cities. Maggie remembered how her mother complained about certain students who were emotionally unprepared for school, not to mention the hyperactive and the potential future criminal types. In fairness her mother mostly objected to the time taken away from the rest of the class to cater to the particular needs of a few. She wanted those children to receive assistance a full-time tutor to go over the basics with them, someone who could work with them in the hall when they were upset or tired or confused.

Unlike her parents, Maggie remembered Grandma Liz often ridiculed those less fortunate and had an unhealthy aversion for anyone she considered abnormal or mentally challenged. Maggie's mother wasn't like Grandma Liz. Maggie's mother had been a Peace Corp volunteer. She'd worked in Africa for two years and passionately believed in equality for all in education. So why did she complain so much about Special Needs children in public schools?

At first, Maggie had to admit she had been uncomfortable around the children herself, especially the emotionally disturbed ones. Yet Ms. Matthews had assigned her the youngest group and even though Maggie had only been at the school for two hours, she had had such a good time with the little ones. They were adorable, and Maggie noted with astonishment and wonder how the most severely autistic were the handsomest of the group. It was as if to compensate for their estrangement from humanity, they had been blessed with beauty so that others would gravitate toward them and try to seduce them back into this world.

Of course, she had only a small sample to base her hypothesis on; yet, she resisted the logic of postponing her theory until she had more data. In her opinion, autistic children were beautiful humans choosing to wait for their moment to join the rest of humanity.

The newspaper photograph of the little girl showed her with wispy blonde hair imperfectly cut and eyes too big for her face. She looked so thin and pale. Maggie thought her skin color the oddest thing about her – whiter than paper, whiter than newly fallen snow, no, white as the creatures that swam in the deepest darkest caves. If the little girl had lived around here and played like a normal kid, she would be golden as a pecan or burned to the color of a beet.

Maggie's mother poured herself another cup of coffee and noticed Maggie staring fixedly at the picture of the child in the newspaper, "You recognize her?"

"No," Maggie said, "but she looks as if she's been kept indoors most of her life, doesn't she?"

"She is awfully pale. You'd think her parents would be frantic about her by now."

"Maybe they abandoned her. Ms. Matthew's says that autistic children are a strain on the family budget and exhausting to rear. If she comes from a single parent family the pressure is even worse."

Her mother pushed back her chair and moved toward the stove, "You want pancakes or an omelet for breakfast?"

"Where's Dad?"

"He volunteered to help search near Poison Creek. The police think perhaps the child's parents had an accident in the night and having gotten lost, they're wandering the Owyhee Mountains; and maybe even experiencing dehydration so severe they're walking in circles. The police think the child separated from her parents and wandered the area until she came across the swing set in that woman's yard."

"Why do you call her that woman, Mom? Her mailbox says Lee on it."

Rachel Treloar turned from the counter where she had been cracking eggs into a bowl and said in a hardy uncomfortable manner, "Miss Curious as a Cat. You read mailboxes, do you?"

"Her mailbox is right next to ours Mom. I couldn't help but notice. She's our nearest neighbor."

When her mother didn't say anything further, Maggie drank down the last gulp of her milk and put the dirty glass in the sink, "I'm thinking of going out and helping Dad search."

"You can wait a few minutes and have breakfast first."

—

Daniel sat in his chair in the shop and nursed his throbbing arm. He heard shoes tap, tap, tapping on the concrete moving fast toward the shop, then shoes crunching on the gravel, the sound keeping time with the throbbing in his arm. The door opened, and Daniel kept his head down afraid to look up. He saw her black high-heeled shoes with the pointy toes. He heard her say, "Pamela said I should talk to you Daniel. Why when she asked you to get the ladder, did you just walk away? Daniel, look at me, please when I'm talking to you."

Daniel obeyed her. Ms. Matthews was his friend. His treasure was safe with her.

"What's wrong? Why are you sitting in here?" her voice sharpened. "What's wrong with your arm? Let me see."

Daniel jumped up and backed away from her. His voice echoed off the shop walls, "Don't touch!"

Once Ms. Matthews explained what had happened to his arm and promised the doctors would fix it, he agreed to go with her. She had always been honest with him. Daniel believed Ms. Matthews more than anyone else. He sat in her car and stared out the window studying the contours of the mountains to his right. He kept his eye on them. When he looked at them, he forgot about his arm hurting. When Ms. Matthews left the highway and he could no longer see them, he looked down at his arm feeling the throbbing pain again. When they stopped at the hospital Daniel refused to get out of the car. He knew this place. Ms. Matthews had lied to him. Only bad things happened in this place.

"Daniel," Ms. Matthews said holding the car door open and waiting for him to get out. "You have to see a doctor. The pain will get worse, if you don't. Do you believe me?"

Daniel climbed out of the car and followed Ms. Matthews inside the hospital.

Chapter Four

A round seven o'clock on Monday morning when the heat was less intense, Vera went outside and walked to the barn in search of a shovel. After ten minutes of digging around the broken concrete that anchored one of the swing set poles in place, she realized she needed a sledge hammer. She'd decided upon waking that morning that the swing set needed to be removed, more so now than ever before. She would rather not attract anymore stray children or most particularly the curious police.

By nine o'clock with sweat trickling into her eyes, down her neck, and between her legs, and with horse flies buzzing around her head and the backs of her arms with all sorts of obnoxious insects landing on her flesh the most annoying being the tiny insects which seemed to delight in swarming near her face, Vera threw down her hammer in disgust and stepped back from her work. She'd managed to break apart three corners of the swing set and still had the fourth one to finish before she could pull out the cussed, damned to hell, stubborn pole.

As Vera wiped the sweat from her brow she turned toward the cool breeze from the east and noticed a tall skinny teenager walking down Anderson Pass. She was too far away for Vera to see her face. The girl noticed Vera noticing her and waved. Vera debated whether to wave back. She had worked diligently to keep her privacy intact and the occasional overtures of friendship from neighbors had been deftly rebuffed; Vera had found ingenious ways to decline overtures of friendship based on fictitious work or non-existent medical appointments, anything to avoid a coffee invitation from one of the farm wives.

With a groan, Vera recognized the teenager. She belonged to the Treloar farm across the street. She might be related to Andrew Treloar, the man masquerading as a cop. Perhaps she was his daughter. Not wanting to cause hurt feelings, Vera waved back and then sighed. The child took this response as an invitation to come over and chat.

"Hi," the girl began. "I'm Maggie Treloar. I thought I'd help search this area. My Dad's been looking over near Poison Creek, but I thought I'd check out the draw between the hills over there."

Maggie's slim brown arm lifted, and she pointed toward the hill above Vera's property, "Maybe she came from that direction. It's likely anyway because she found your swing set and the only way to see the swings is by being on the hillside."

When Vera said nothing but simply stared at the hillside surveying the walrus-sized rocks resting on top like sentinels guarding the gateway to the Owyhee Mountains, the girl continued in a soberer voice, "I mean, you can't see the swings from the street, so I figured she must have seen the swings from Hunter's Hill."

Vera turned to her, "In the dark?"

Maggie's red cheeks matched the red highlights in her brown hair, "Oh yeah, I didn't think of that."

Vera ashamed of her coldness offered an olive branch, "There was a full moon last night. I'd forgotten. From up above my yard what with the moon and all, the night would have been lit like a stage."

Maggie's eyes glinted with renewed excitement, "Sure. If she'd been standing up there, she would have seen the whole valley below and especially your yard." Maggie's eyes wandered over Vera's backyard as if rehearsing how the child might have seen the property; her attention caught by the broken concrete around the swing set and the shovel and the hammer and the way the swing set leaned far to the left. "You need some help here? My Dad could probably help you get the rest of the concrete removed."

Vera declined the offer maintaining a calm she did not feel, "Perhaps I don't have the muscle for the job, but it's my belief us-women are just as capable of doing what men do by applying a bit of brains and ingenuity to figure out how to get the muscle work done. Don't you agree?"

Maggie grinned, appreciating Vera's attempt to include her in us-women, "Sure. You've almost got it anyway."

Vera heard someone large wearing big boots on her gravel drive, "Excuse me Maggie. Someone's coming. Maybe the police have news."

Maggie followed Vera around the house to the front. Vera noticed the man, a very tall heavy-set man with a slouch wandering down her driveway and suppressed an urge to run into the house to avoid him. The man lifted his head from the contemplation of his shoes and noticed the women watching him. He looked at them without registering their presence. They were objects in his line of sight. They could just as easily have been trees or shrubs. His mouth hung open slightly and promptly shut.

He veered off her drive and across her weedy front to the open fields in the opposite direction of where he'd been going. Obviously, he had reacted to them; yet, his face expressed nothing of his thoughts. Vera noticed how he lowered his right shoulder and pulled in his neck as if by doing so he could hide from them. He wore a pair of baggy jeans torn in the knees and stained with paint. His t-shirt had spots of red paint smeared on the front and back. His square face pocked with old acne scars and black hair slick with oil provoked further comparisons with outsiders: the unfortunate homeless or hobo. He looked and acted the part. If he had been beautiful would she have reacted so negatively, she wondered?

"That's Daniel Harden," Maggie said over her shoulder. "He works at the Eagle Gateway School doing odd jobs for Sarah Matthews. Sarah runs the school. She's the director of the school and teaches sign language." Maggie pointed toward the east, "You see the school there on this side of the subdivision, just beyond the empty house with the cedar shingled roof. It's the place with the green lawn and playground."

"Yes, I've passed by many times," Vera said absently. "I remember when they first started construction last spring. At that time, the Andersons had brought me out to see their farm and I was deciding whether or not to buy it from them. I was under the impression the developers were expanding Prairie Star Estates."

"Prairie Star," Maggie said. "What a dumb name." She covered her mouth glancing at Vera with eyes wide. "Oops, that wasn't very nice."

"It could have been worse. It could have been Purple Mountains Majesty," Vera said with a shrug of her shoulders.

Once Daniel reached the Pass and disappeared over the ridge, Vera retraced her steps back to the yard and began gathering up her tools to put away. Maggie followed behind like an eager puppy enchanted with her new master. Vera had had way too much experience with children growing up from newborns to toddlers to teenagers and wasn't anxious to deal with any more. She would have preferred Maggie to be one of those bored teenagers allergic to adults. Instead, Maggie seemed to be enjoying herself. This must be her summer of strays, Vera thought, first the autistic child, now Maggie Treloar.

She tried to think of a way of encouraging Maggie to leave without hurting her feelings. Maggie helped her carry the shovel and the other tools into the barn chattering all the way, "You know the first time I saw Daniel on Hunter's Hill I thought he was from the college, a professor. And just yesterday, I saw Daniel yesterday up there. The first time, I was mad because that's where I like to dig for thundereggs. I've only found two really good ones so far. Most of what's up there has been picked through so thoroughly that you're lucky if can you find anything at all. Maybe Daniel saw the little girl and just doesn't realize what he's seen. Maybe I should let Uncle Andrew know. What do you think?"

"Who is Uncle Andrew?" Vera asked even though she suspected she knew.

"He's a sort of consultant for the local police around here. He's my Uncle Andrew. He's like Columbo in a way; he just looks more like Remington Steel. They're a year apart; I mean my Dad and my Uncle Andrew are a year apart not Columbo and Remington Steel. They act more like brothers than uncle and nephew. But sometimes my Dad lectures Andrew just like he was one of my brothers. My brothers Cody and Cameron are twins. They're freshman at the University of Minnesota right now."

Vera could still smell hay in the barn even though she'd gotten rid of the moldy stacks of hay the first week she'd moved in. Vera stood in the shade of the barn with the sun's light burning through the slates in the walls and the old shingles of the roof. It was so hot the sun's rays were practically cooking the ground where she stood. Vera soon realized if she planned to repair her house on her own, she would have to buy her own tools.

Whenever she had a little extra cash, she would go down to the D & B Supply store and buy herself a new tool. Her first purchases, of course, would be a hammer and an adjustable screwdriver with various size attachments for assorted styles of screws. Vera was proud of her wall, her pasteboard wall she'd nailed up along one side of the barn. She'd put up the storage shelves herself and now watched as Maggie Treloar carefully hung the shovel on a peg among all the other tools.

"Oops!" Maggie said as she tripped over the old push lawnmower near the barn door and instinctively grabbed Vera's arm to keep her balance. An image flashed through Vera's mind so sharp she thought she saw it before her very eyes. It was an image of Daniel looming over Maggie and the lost little girl she'd found on her swing set. Vera jerked as if she'd been stung and stepped away, so fast Maggie nearly fell face first at her feet. Vera glared at the offending lawnmower rusty with age to avoid Maggie's incredulous expression. Only once had Vera attempted to use the push lawnmower and after the ordeal and nearly having a heart attack maneuvering up a steep incline, she never used the thing again. Someday she thought I'll have enough money to purchase a brand new gleaming gas-powered lawnmower. Vera spoke her thoughts aloud in the uncomfortable silence.

"One of these days I'm going to buy myself a brand-new gas-powered lawnmower."

Maggie looked ill at ease. Vera didn't know how to explain what had just happened without convincing Maggie she was a total nut job for sure. Those images suddenly bursting upon her without warning had been a symptom of her childhood. She hadn't had one like it since puberty. Her mother called them signs from the spirits. Hog wash. Vera preferred to think of them as hallucinations generated by an overactive imagination. No wonder as a child she hallucinated so much and thought she heard voices.

It was all her mother's fault and maybe her entire clan of uncles, aunts, cousins, and traveling entertainers who had brainwashed her into believing their mumbo jumbo. And she shouldn't blame herself. She'd been at an impressionable age and they used her naivety to make her think she was somehow gifted with clairvoyance and other supernatural abilities. They had overheard her innocent remarks and fulfilled them thus perpetuating her childish belief that she had made them come true. She remembered once dreaming about a puppy. Two days later, presto, her mother brings home a puppy claiming the puppy had trotted up to her and asked to be adopted. Sure.

Vera glanced over at Maggie and realized Maggie feared her. Each time Vera moved, the teenager jumped back nervously as if she expected Vera to threaten her with bodily harm.

"I won't bite. I'm sorry if I scared you," she found herself saying then got angry for apologizing for an innocent accident. "Hasn't anyone bumped into you before? Well, don't look so shocked. It was an accident. Oh, for goodness sake – go home Maggie."

"And I suggest you stay away from Daniel," Vera called after her in a sharper voice than she'd intended as Maggie spun on her heels and hurried toward home.

Maggie paused to look at Vera over her shoulder.

"Why?" she asked with insolence Vera suspected was rare. "Is everybody supposed to be just like you? Anyone different from you must be sick or should be locked away, is that what you think?"

Vera put her hands on her hips, "Of course not. You know you've got it all wrong. I have nothing against Daniel. I don't know the man. It's just that you're awfully trusting. Most girls who've grown up in big cities that are your age are savvier. Hold on a minute. We've got off to a bad start. Let me explain. How about a soda? I have orange soda or root beer in the fridge?"

Maggie looked away from her, "I can't. Mom doesn't want me going into a stranger's house."

"You can sit on the front porch. I'll be right back."

Five minutes later when Vera walked out onto the front porch with a can of orange soda in her hand, she seriously doubted whether Maggie would still be on her property. Vera had to admit her behavior had been odd. Most wise children would have run on home figuring the lady was a loony. Yet she found Maggie sitting on the top step of the porch hugging her knees and surveying the view from the front of the house.

Vera handed Maggie the cold soda and sat down beside her. Maggie thanked Vera automatically. Politeness was the WASP way and Vera had become adept at imitating the people she lived among. Yet Vera had grown up in a different culture altogether where the people spoke a different language and survival was more imperative than Thank you or Sorry or May I. Her automatic resentment made Vera suddenly ashamed. This young woman was not to blame for Vera's unhappy childhood. Maggie seemed like a very sweet kid.

They sat in companionable silence enjoying the view.

Vera's house, Rock Wren House as she liked to think of it, sat in the middle of a stretch of fields on both sides. Beyond her ten acres on her right the graveled walkway skirted the field and led up to Hunter's Hill. While she'd been living in a trailer park in Vegas where a lot of snowbirds from other states spent their winters, the Anderson couple Carl and Annie used to invite her over to their motorhome for drinks and dinner. The couple would tell her horror stories about their attempts to keep dirt bikes and other vehicles off their ten acres. They told her they'd tried everything: fences, posting no trespassing signs, threatening to shoot a few of the hunters who thought they owned the entire Owyhee County. Eventually the Bureau of Land Management allowed them to create a barricade on the hilltop to prevent vehicles from taking the shortcut through the mountains.

The barricades worked on the vehicles but not the hikers and rock hounds. The Andersons finally gave up and created the Pass along the edge of their property. But their heart was no longer in the farming life. It had been a painful decision for them, after all, the farm had been in their family for generations; but times were changing, small farms were going the way of the dinosaur. It was time to sell the homestead. All they needed now was to find a buyer.

Fewer and fewer people were interested. The Andersons hated to sell their land to a developer but what could they do?

And that was when Vera knew she had had enough of traveling. It sounded so romantic to settle down and have a place she could call home. At the time, she hadn't thought the whole crazy plan through; she'd been so busy daydreaming about cute little lambs grazing in a pasture or Christmas trees growing on a snowy winter day that she hadn't realized how much work ten acres and a farmhouse would be for a single woman without family. Yet even now sitting on the porch taking a break from her chores, she didn't regret her decision. The air smelled sweet and the sun felt good. It would all work out. She would make it work.

Rock Wren House had been built snug against the hillside and was high enough up from the valley floor to see for miles. The graveled drive sloped and curved down to Jump Creek Road. Unfortunately, she couldn't see everything because the gigantic catalpa trees to the left of her porch blocked a view of her neighbor's property, well, a potato field wasn't all that spectacular; but there was no greenery obstructing the view directly below her and to her right. Along the ribbon of the two-lane road were more fields and farmhouses and beyond the farms the cluster of trees and buildings in the distance made up the town of Marsing, Idaho. The Andersons had warned her before she got too carried away about the farm that the nearest fire station was in Homedale; and if God forbid, there was a brush fire, she had only the well and a tank of emergency water behind the barn.

From her house, she couldn't see Marsing or Lizard Butte which was a shame. She remembered Lizard Butte from the time she was married to Arthur Vlasky, remembered on Easter how people would climb the butte for services. In her mind's eye, she could see the lizard's back with his legs hung over both sides of the hill and his snout sticking into the air; and like everything else in the world that humans did, her eyes finished the pattern imagining the lizard sunning himself on his warm rock with his eyes closed in contentment. Marsing and Lizard Butte seemed to be Maggie's focal point as well.

As Vera examined the porch steps critically, noticing the dry stiff husks which had once been pampered tulips and the thorny spindled twigs which had once been prized roses, her restlessness returned. There was so much work to be done. She felt so strange about owning a home. She was conflicted: excited and afraid. At least Arthur Vlasky couldn't take her home away from her. Now she no longer feared the angry knocking at the door and announcement of eviction or having to be a witness to her mother begging the police to let them stay for just a few days longer.

Since moving into the farmhouse, Rock Wren House, she reminded herself, Vera had been imaging what she would do with the place if she had enough time and money to landscape and improve it. Her list of things to do was a long one. The catalpa tree needed pruning, its low hanging branches brushed the roof of her Toyota. She could manage cutting the lower limbs, she supposed, but that would require tools which she didn't have at present. And some day, she wanted to plant a sentinel of arborvitae along both sides of the driveway to block the winds and keep down the dust. Also on the agenda were desert loving plants and interesting rocks. She would dearly love a fountain someday. Right now, what the house needed most urgently were new windows, a new roof, new doors, the house rewired and plumbing up to code, also the hardwood floors sanded and stained. There was so much to be done. The thought made her itch to begin.

She couldn't though.

She had a guest and it would be rude to jump up and start weeding or raking or pruning tree limbs while her guest sat on her porch and drank her soda.

Maggie took a long drink from the can then held the can as if it were a precious artifact between her hands. Vera laughed to herself, so what if the poor kid dropped the soda all over the dry splintered wood, all the sugary substance would do is attract the colony of ants living underneath.

"I'm a city kid Miss Vera," Maggie said remembering their earlier conversation. "I grew up in the Twin Cities. There are more people in the Minneapolis/St. Paul area than in the whole state of Idaho, you know."

Vera rested her elbows on her knees and stared down at the graveled drive, "When I was your age I was already working fulltime in the fields, picking strawberries or pecans or beans - wherever the road took my family - wherever we could find work." Vera paused wondering what had come over her. Why this sudden compulsion to overshare? The voice in her head reassured her. You can trust her. Vera mentally shrugged and her body began to relax.

"I had a spotty education. My husband didn't mind that I could only read at a sixth-grade level, but I did. I used to go to the community center and the volunteers taught me to read and write. My best friend became the public library. I went every week, sometimes twice a week, and picked up everything I could and books they suggested. Some of it was tough going. I had to keep a dictionary beside me and look up an unfamiliar word. I read stuff way over my head and conversely silly romance novels, funny mysteries, horror, and thrillers, just everything that looked good. I did that for years. Then my husband died," Vera paused and glanced at Maggie debating whether to tell her about Arthur. Vera decided to leave him dead and anonymous. "And ten years later I'm back in this neck of the woods after the Andersons sold me this house and the remaining property they hadn't sold to Stubben Real Estate. I wanted a home of my own, a home that stayed put, where the view might be different depending on the hour of the day but never changed too much."

Maggie appeared to be interested or Vera checked, polite attention had been drummed into her for so long the girl had lost the ability to appear any other way. Maybe she was secretly tuning out the speaker and thinking her own thoughts. Vera ignored her growing discomfort. She never used to talk as much as she was talking now, especially about herself. She sounded like a school teacher lecturing about the importance of getting a good education. Yet Vera had this inexplicable compulsion to tell her story, something she rarely did with strangers.

"Anyway, to get back to when I was a kid, well, wait a moment, let me ask you first if you've ever dreamed about an event before it happened and that day or a few days later the event happened exactly the way it had in your dream? Has that happened to you before?"

Maggie shook her head and frowned, "I know what you're talking about. I mean I've heard of precognition which some people call foretelling the future. My Dad says magic and fortune telling and all that ESP stuff is just wishful thinking because mankind can't control the weather or nature or natural disasters and definitely has no way of avoiding the ultimate end – death. So, Dad says people use magical thinking to make it seem as if there is life after death. He says people don't like to think that when they die there will be nothing, just nothingness."

"Is your father Agnostic?" Vera asked masking her annoyance with difficulty.

"Dad says the future is what we make of it and precognition implies that our lives are mapped out for us. He says the Great Plan is a hoax. He blames Christianity for selling people that stupid theory. Dad believes in free will. Uncle Andrew and Dad argue a lot about politics and religion. I think Uncle Andrew just likes to get Dad all stirred up."

"I see," Vera began and then couldn't figure out how to explain to Maggie why she had reacted the way she did in the barn when Maggie touched her. If Maggie had been raised in a home where the spiritual had no room, then Vera's gift or curse whichever way one looked at such phenomena would seem alien to the girl. Vera would just be confirming Maggie's preset convictions, then the young girl would conclude Vera was just another loony lady.

"Well, ah, I don't know what to say now," Vera said with a little laugh and threw up her hands. "You see I wanted to explain why I reacted so strangely when you tripped over the lawnmower and why I warned you to stay away from Daniel. I had this feeling, this feeling that you were in danger. I don't know maybe it was just my imagination. Sometimes people sense things that appear magical, yet they're simply instincts we all have which are based on observation and intuition."

"I don't understand."

"Take for instance earthquakes. You know studies have been done that suggest dogs can sense when an earthquake is going to happen long before the event. In fact, I remember Aunt Vista's shepherd how she came running toward us as we were eating lunch one day, acting so oddly, and hid under the picnic table. It was only a few minutes after she hid under the table when we felt the earthquake. I think she sensed the earthquake approach. Well, dogs do have a higher range of hearing and their noses can smell a hundred times better than us.

Don't quote me on the percentages. You know what I mean. If you believe in natural selection – those with the ability to sense danger are more likely to survive. I believe there are people who know when events are going to happen, and they prepare for them. They have a special gift and since they are survivors they pass on their special gift to their children, just as children inherit their parents coloring and build and maybe even intelligence."

Maggie appeared skeptical. Vera continued, "You see my mother was a keen observer. She used to warn me about things. I mean, not just ordinary things, obvious things like stay away from a hot stove or unplug the iron, but as if she knew the world and its secrets more so than ordinary people know. There was one time when she asked me to check on my Aunt Felance before going to school. I thought about ignoring her advice and taking the shortcut. She said *I see blood on the way to school. Go to Felance and ask her for a coin to keep you safe.*

Aunt Felance lived in the opposite direction. Something inside me wanted to believe. I did as she told me. And because I stopped at Aunt Felance's I ended up walking in a totally different direction. I learned later that some children were hurt on the way to school when the wall from an abandoned factory collapsed. Several of my classmates were hit by loose bricks. That's when I began to trust in my mother's warnings. Her premonitions made sense then. Now, I'm grown up and I'm not totally convinced. I think my mother had noticed the wall on previous occasions and didn't like the look of it, so she made up a story to get me to go the long way around. It's kind of a bummer though. It would be fantastic to have a mother with supernatural talents."

Vera also remembered her mother's last warning to her. She had been fifteen. Her mother familiar with Vera's daily complaints about their gypsy life and sensing Vera's decision to run away had sat her down for a woman to woman talk. Vera remembered thinking how silly her mother sounded sometimes. All Vera had wanted to do was get away from the poverty, humiliation, and fear. Most of all, she wanted to be accepted by regular kids her age.

"I can't keep you a child forever," Vera remembered her mother saying with the slow roll of the r punctuating her speech and the way she measured each word as if words had a magic of their own, especially if spoken aloud. "You will grow up someday and make your own decisions. But do something for me Vertina. That's what she used to call me—Vertina. I don't go by that name anymore. Vertina sounds too foreign. Anyway, she said, there will come a day when you marry. Before you decide to marry, ask the man to give you a token of his love.

If he gives you silver, then money is his love and not you. If he gives you flowers, it's the idea of love that enchants him and not you. If he gives you something he treasures, maybe a stone, a special stone he's found, something simple, something with value only to him, it's a sign he's a good man and he respects the earth and all its gifts. And then she said – promise to be careful Vertina. Watch for the signs."

Vera looked down at Maggie studying her face, "I know what I've told you must seem pretty crazy. But you see she did have some insightful things to say though. The more time passes when I think about her little daily adages the more I realize how on the mark she'd been —eighty percent of the time I'd say she was right. In retrospect, I wish now I'd paid more attention."

The young girl beside her made a noncommittal sound as if she were listening and simply encouraging Vera to talk. When the truth dawned on Vera she'd been speaking aloud embarrassment washed over her. What an idiot, she thought, was sunstroke to blame for her babbling? Feeling empty Vera lapsed into silence. Her mother had been a chatter box and sometimes she drove people crazy. Now that she was gone, gone forever, Vera missed her so much. Now that was a woman who could bend your ear all the way back and never let go.

Vera remembered the way her mother's short black hair curled about her neck and ears in the humid air; she remembered the smell of her, so musky, the musky scent still clinging to her cheap cotton dresses. Her mother's clothes, her speech, everything about her down to the smell of her made Vera squirm. Vera's teenage pity for her mother felt unnatural now. Her mother's death had given the woman dignity. And really Vera had the self-awareness and honesty to admit she'd been a stuck-up teenager thinking herself so much better than her mother and her family.

It had been unfair, really rather cruel to compare her mother with the other mothers who came to pick up their kids from the public schools in the neighborhood. Her mother and her extended family hadn't had the same advantages or opportunities as those soccer moms. Her family was automatically perceived to be a collection of thieves and con artists. Some people even believed the women in her family must be prostitutes the way the men ogled them, and the women gave them the stink-eye.

Vera's new-found pity, a revelation at the time, had been a painful experience. To pity the person, she used to adore seemed like a betrayal. Vera had never been ashamed of her mother before; now she was ashamed of the way they lived, the way her mother talked and dressed and spoke. Vera thrust the betrayal away. That earlier version of her had been naive and shallow, too absorbed in appearances instead of substance. Vera still struggled within herself, especially when she had to decide if someone was good or bad. She no longer trusted herself, not after her betrayal of her mother or the choice she made to separate herself from her family and culture, especially after a succession of no-good positively dangerous boyfriends.

Maggie shifted restlessly on the step and finally unable to contain herself any longer sprang to her feet. Vera hadn't realized how long the silence had stretched between them. Maggie said in a breathless voice, "I'd better be going Miss Vera. I promised Uncle Andrew I'd help search for the little girl's parents. They might be hurt. My parents told me I can't go up on Hunter's Hill by myself any more. They're afraid I'll fall in a gully or get eaten by a coyote. Funny, huh? Coyotes are more scared of us than we are of them."

Vera stood up, "You must think I'm crazy the way I've been rattling on."

Maggie skipped down the steps and glanced at her curiously, "No Ma'am. I don't think you're crazy. I liked your stories. It's just that you shouldn't worry about Daniel. He's just a kid in a man's body. That's what Ms. Matthews says. He'd never hurt anybody."

Vera watched Maggie walk purposely down the drive and run across Jump Creek Road to the Treloar Farm. As Vera picked up the empty can on the bottom step where Maggie had been sitting and entered her house, she remembered Arthur Vlasky had given her one of his precious coins from his coin collection as a gift. If only she had taken her mother's advice seriously; she might have avoided four years of misery. In retrospect, her mother had simply given Vera sensible advice woven with a bit of magic.

As Vera threw the empty cans in the garbage, she realized Maggie had never once flinched at the sight of Vera's face. It dawned on her also how she and Maggie had talked just like normal people. There had been no need to shield her scar or look away; there had no pity in the young woman's eyes, no evidence that she felt sorry for Vera. In fact, Maggie had treated her as if she were perfectly normal, just like any other person; well, maybe more like a respected teacher or counselor, someone worth listening to, worth admiring. Vera sat down in her rocking chair and found she was weeping, unable to stop the tears. She cried so hard, by the time she finished, her shoulders hurt, and her eyes were swollen nearly shut.

—

Andrew, while obeying the posted speed limit through the downtown area of Marsing (which in his opinion was about the same speed a snail might make crossing the road) happened to be at an elevation contusive for a panoramic view. He could see part of the town and the bridge crossing the Snake River. Like the other drivers in line behind his Jeep, he was waiting for a line of pedestrians to complete their journey across the busy road. They might as well have been ducks crossing the road for all the notice they took of the traffic.

This part of town was the most congested area, amazing since there were only about a thousand people in the whole town. But at this end of town people were either picnicking or fishing on the banks of the Snake River or drinking and eating at the bar or the restaurant. He should be content. Today's modern infrastructure was an improvement over Froman's Ferry of 1888. In the past, people and their wagons had to be ferried across the Snake River so, he shouldn't feel too put out by the tediousness of his wait.

At certain times of the day, depending on the weather, the season, or a particular celebration, this area of town could be congested with cars coming up from the shores of the Snake River or across the bridge connecting Canyon County with Owyhee County or from several different side streets, one being the Sandbar River House. Since it was May and the weather was warm and sunny, everyone had decided to be downtown or fishing under the Froman Bridge.

Most of the pedestrians in front of him were headed for the bar called the Pour House. They were in black leather jackets and chaps with their motorcycle helmets under their arms. Some had taken off their sunglasses and goggles. They looked pale, windblown, and extremely thirsty. He was getting kind of thirsty himself. He looked at the time on his wristwatch. He wasn't on a clock, not really. He was an independent contracted consultant for the Mintlaw Police and therefore he convinced himself, Chief Glenjones wouldn't begrudge him a beer or two.

The Pour House stood in an ideal location within walking distance of the bridge and the banks of the Snake River. The Pour House was a favorite stopping off point for tired travelers. Because he wasn't moving at the time, Andrew had a perfect view of the bridge, the traffic, and the pedestrians. Below him I55 sloped down the hillside and leveled off when it reached the edge of the Snake River where the bridge connected Marsing to Canyon County. Once off the bridge, I55 curved to the left along the Snake River and up a hill where drivers could see the remarkable rock formation called Lizard Butte.

Andrew looked down from his examination of Lizard Butte in time to see a cream-colored Datsun with Nevada license plates make an illegal U-turn near the Super 8 Market stalls. The Datsun had turned right off the vineyard road onto I55 then pulled off onto the shoulder of the road and made the U-turn heading back to Marsing. As Andrew drew closer to the bridge, he saw the Datsun waiting to merge with traffic. Andrew stuck the cherry globe on the roof of his car and followed the driver until he slowed down. The Datsun turned onto a side road and pulled onto a patch of dirt under a tree. Andrew called dispatch to have Erma check the license number.

"It's registered to a Mark Martin, 2001 Eucalyptus Drive, Las Vegas Nevada," Erma said, "It expires in January."

"Thanks Erma."

"George wants to see you at the diner at noon."

"I'm there, Erma."

Andrew climbed out of his Jeep and walked cautiously up to the driver's side door positioning his body out of the line of sight of a potential weapon.

"Your driver's license and registration please," Andrew said.

The driver wore his dishwater blonde hair in the mullet style which hung in greasy strands below the collar of his shirt. The wannabe-rocker looked at Andrew dressed in jeans and a white t-shirt with his long hair tied back in a ponytail and laughed.

"Are you kidding? What is this man? Are you making a citizen's arrest or something?" the driver asked as he leaned back in his seat and looked Andrew over with a smirk.

"What a bright lad you are. You guessed all by yourself that I'm not a cop. I'm impressed," Andrew said.

"Hey Man, you can't give me a ticket, so get lost."

"But this guy can give you a ticket, because he's a cop and has the important badge and gun. Man."

Andrew turned his head and watched as an Owyhee County patrol vehicle pulled up behind Andrew's Jeep. Vernon Clement climbed out of his patrol car. As he strolled toward Andrew, he slipped off his sunglasses and pulled a black leather citation holder out of his shirt pocket. The driver in the Datsun extracted his car registration from the glove compartment and handed Andrew the required documents. The name on the driver's license was Woodrow T. Kirk. Mark Martin's name was on the Datsun's registration. Andrew handed the documents to Deputy Clement confident Erma would have mentioned if the vehicle had been reported stolen.

"Mr. Kirk," Clement began.

"Yes, Officer," Kirk responded politely.

"Who is Mark Martin?"

From the driver's seat, Kirk twisted around so that he could look up at the deputy, "He loaned me his car for this trip. I'm visiting friends in Idaho."

"Well that's interesting. Hold on to your shorts Mr. Kirk. I'll be back directly," Deputy Clement stated in his fake drawl. Andrew stopped himself from laughing. Clement loved to play with the heads of the smug ones. He followed his friend to the sheriff's car and overheard him talking to dispatch.

"Erma, check out a Woodrow T. Kirk for me," Clement asked her. Kirk's driver's license had been issued in Portland, Oregon, Andrew noticed. Clement gave Erma the DL number off Woodrow Kirk's license and waited.

The radio squawked once more before they both heard Erma's voice, "Woodrow T. Kirk 1969 Lincoln Nebraska arrest: 1st citation illegal U-turn 2nd cultivation of illegal substance marijuana on Route 80 valued at $300,000, served one-year Nebraska State Prison, released December 1970. No other priors."

"Thanks Erma," Andrew and Clement said in unison. Andrew absently wondered if Woodrow had any connection with the missing child.

Deputy Clement wrote Kirk a ticket for an illegal U-turn then returned to his vehicle. Kirk had not denied making the illegal U-turn. He could have. When Clement drove out of sight, Kirk glanced at Andrew with impatience, "Are we finished?"

"Are you married Mr. Kirk?"

Kirk turned his head so that Andrew could see his long face and sharp nose. His skin had the pale look of someone who spends most of his time indoors. Andrew thought about Kirk's stats: age 39, height 6' 2", and weight 195 pounds. He looked as if he'd lost a lot of weight recently. His eyes were a light shade of blue and tended to avoid direct contact; otherwise, Kirk did not act as if he were guilty of anything as he offered up some surprising information considering he'd just been pulled over by a civilian, "I have a common-law wife. She lives here in Marsing."

"Any children Mr. Kirk?"

"No," Kirk said with a breathy laugh. "Why do you ask?"

Andrew handed Kirk one of his extra flyers, "Do you recognize her?"

Kirk looked at the picture of the four-year-old. The mullet cut was similar in outline to Kirk's but so different in composition and texture. The child's baby thin yellow hair glowed like spun silk and made her appear more vulnerable and endearing. Kirk's hair made Andrew think of drug dens. Although, he didn't act like a tweaked-out junkie or even a vacuous-eyed stoner. The only resemblance between the child and Kirk was their Nordic features: pale skin and icy blue eyes. After a careful examination of the picture, Kirk shook his head and said, "No, sir. I've never seen her before," with such an innocent air Andrew actually believed him. Kirk handed the flyer back to Andrew.

"U-turns seem to be your specialty. Drive responsibly Mr. Kirk."

Kirk dumped the ticket on the passenger seat and said, "Yes, sir. I will."

As Andrew turned to go back to his vehicle, Kirk called out to him, "Officer, ah, I mean sir, could you tell me how to find the Armstrong farm? I was told it's on the other side of the bridge, but I can't find it."

Andrew returned to the Datsun suddenly concerned, "Armstrong? I don't know any Armstrongs in this area. Who are you looking for exactly?"

"I'm looking for a friend of mine, well, actually my wife, my common-law wife, Vera Lee. Do you know her?"

"I suggest that you go to the nearest public telephone, call your wife, and get directions, Mr. Kirk."

Andrew wasn't about to give Woodrow T. Kirk directions to Vera Lee's house. If she had really been his wife, Kirk would have known where she lived and how to get in touch with her. He seemed like the type of guy a woman would avoid at all cost. Andrew returned to his Jeep and watched as Kirk snapped on his seat belt on (probably for his benefit) and started his vehicle. A wisp of blue-black smoke erupted from the tail pipe. The carburetor sounded dirty. There were a few dents around the trunk of the vehicle too.

Andrew waited until Kirk turned and headed back across the bridge. Andrew proceeded to follow the Datsun. The Datsun left Marsing and passed US 95 continuing down Jump Creek Road. The Jeep followed staying three cars behind. When the Datsun slowed to the speed limit through Mintlaw and eventually pulled into the parking lot of Lucy's Diner, Andrew who had been on his way to meet George Metcalf anyway pulled in behind Woodrow Kirk and parked his Jeep in a space near the door.

Kirk walked into the diner ahead of Andrew, glancing anxiously over his shoulder as if Andrew planned to stick a pistol in his back. Jumpy guy, Andrew thought. He wasn't amused. When he walked inside and found George waiting for him in a booth near the back, Andrew sat down at the empty bench across from his friend, "You see the guy with Rod Stewart wannabe who just came in? What's he doing now George?"

George looked up from his menu. He really didn't need to read the menu; he knew it by heart. His brown's eyes swept the room and stopped, "He's talking to Kimberly."

When Kimberly came over to their booth with her pad ready, Andrew waited until George had ordered his usual roast beef, mashed potatoes with gravy, and side of coal slaw, before asking Kimberly, "What did that guy want?"

Kimberly glanced at the man in question sitting at a booth sipping his cola, "He asked about some Armstrong farm. I think he must be confusing us with Homedale. I told him to go to Homedale IGA and ask someone there."

Andrew ordered lunch. George put down his menu, "What's up?"

"The guy made an illegal U-turn. I gave him a ticket. He's just out of prison."

"Uh huh," George said glanced at the man in question. "So, you gave him a ticket?"

"You know I didn't."

"Who then?"

"Clement."

"You got Clement to drive out of his way for a U-turn?"

"He just showed up. It's a gift. I got the gift. When I want a police officer, one shows up. Voilà, just like magic, here he is."

Kirk had noticed George in his Owyhee County Sheriff's uniform watching him. Kirk the wannabe rocker swallowed the last of his cola, stood up, dropped his money on the counter, and left the diner, careful to avoid looking at the two men. Andrew from his position facing the back of the diner could see through the glass as Kirk climbed into his Datsun and drove away. He followed the Datsun's progress as it headed out of town back toward US. 95.

Andrew got up, "I got to make a phone call."

Andrew used the public phone on the wall near the john. He dialed Vera's phone number. He let the ringing continue for another thirty seconds, finally gave up, and dropped the receiver back onto its cradle.

When he returned to the booth, George asked him with concern in his eyes, "What's bugging you Andy? We get drifters from Nevada in here all the time."

"This one says Vera Lee is his common-law wife."

"So?"

Kimberly brought their plates and Andrew picked up his fork, "I know trouble when I see it George."

"Well, let's not go looking for it just yet," George said and attacked his roast beef as if he hadn't eaten for days.

Forty-five minutes after noon, Andrew left the diner and returned to his vehicle. He headed down I55 and instead of turning left to go home, he continued down I55 until the highway changed to Jump Creek Road. As he passed the Eagle Gateway Boarding School, he noticed Sarah Matthew's sitting in the driver's seat of her white VW Rabbit. She was parked near the gate. Daniel wearing a cast on his arm climbed out of the passenger side of Sarah's vehicle and walked to the call box.

Sarah waved as Andrew drove past. Daniel looked around in bemusement and Andrew in his rearview mirror watched Daniel use his good arm and wave at his Jeep. A couple of yards from the school Andrew saw Maggie riding on the shoulder of the road on her ten-speed. He assumed she was headed for the Egg. Maggie's nickname for the school had caught on, at least in the Treloar family. Andrew saluted her as he whipped past by turning on the red cherry globe flashing on the top of his jeep. He left the siren off.

At the turn off to his father's farm, Andrew hesitated wondering if he should go visit his father instead. Maybe Vera would think he was stalking her? Maybe they really were common law? Then that would make her an adulterer because the guy he'd seen her with had obviously spent the night with her. Instead of going to his Dad's farm, he decided to risk another chewing out and drove slowly up to her house to give her time to notice his vehicle. When she didn't come out, he parked his vehicle near her Toyota. Kirk's Datsun was nowhere to be seen. He rang the doorbell and when that didn't get a response, he knocked on the door. Just as he turned to descend the porch steps and return to his vehicle, the door opened a crack and Vera peered out, her head swathed in a bath towel. Andrew returned to the door.

"I'm sorry to bother you Miss Lee. I just wanted to stop by and let you know that we still have no information about the abandoned child."

"Oh," Vera said and stopped.

Andrew debated whether to say anything about Woodrow Kirk. It was none of his business. He didn't want her to think he was nosy, "Well, that's all I have. No news yet."

"Thanks for stopping by, ah, Mr. Treloar. I appreciate the courtesy. I know you're busy."

"Yes, well, sorry to have interrupted," he finished lamely and left the porch. He heard the door shut behind him. He also heard her lock the deadbolt.

—

Maggie waved to Uncle Andrew and kept on pedaling. She had seen Ms. Matthews' car and recognized Daniel at the call box. By the time she reached the gates, the wrought iron portals were slowly opening, and Daniel had climbed back in Sarah's car. Maggie pedaled fast enough to keep up with Ms. Matthews. Daniel climbed out of Sarah's car and without a word headed for the shop behind the school. Maggie parked her bike near the steps and followed Sarah inside.

The three-story red brick boarding school stood in the center of the facility surrounded by blossoming pear and cherry trees and lawn on three sides. Inside the school, the main office was to the right near the central doors and down the hall to the left were the classrooms. At the back of the school were the cafeteria, bathrooms, and shower facilities. The boys and girls' dormitory rooms were east and west spread out like the wings of their namesake on either side of the building. From the air, the school resembled an eagle in flight. Maggie knew this because she'd seen the photograph in Ms. Matthew's office. Behind the school was a basketball court and beyond the court a baseball/soccer field. At the other end of the boarding school was the playground which included a pair of swing sets, two slides, a jungle gym, and several sand boxes.

Ms. Matthews, on her way to the cafeteria, paused when Maggie called to her in a breathless voice.

"This isn't your day to volunteer with the preschoolers is it Maggie?"

"Sarah asked me to come," Maggie told her. She noticed Sarah's preoccupied attitude. Usually Ms. Matthews concentrated all her attention on the speaker. Today, Ms. Matthews appeared a trifle angry. Maggie thought about Daniel's cast and wondered if Ms. Matthew's state of mind had something to do with Daniel's injury.

"I was wondering Ms. Matthews, if you still needed someone to work with the preschoolers in the afternoon?"

A classroom door opened across from them and the older students spilled out into the hall. At Egg there was no school bell to announce recesses or lunch break. Some of the students were deaf and the blind with their sensitive hearing didn't need any added annoyances. A few students were autistic, and others had to maneuver through the school in wheelchairs. Since the school housed some students year-round and most of the students spent their summers at Egg, a school bell seemed too institutional, too intrusive.

The hallway was large enough to accommodate wheelchairs; yet, some of the students just had to stop and say hello to Ms. Matthews and Maggie. The last to leave was Sam who stood beside Maggie and patted her on the shoulder every so often smiling his generous smile. Maggie greeted him warmly, but Ms. Matthews demanded the rules be obeyed. She pointed toward the cafeteria and said to Sam in a brisk voice, "It's time for lunch Sam. I'll see you in the cafeteria."

Sam moved off and walked alongside Mr. Tover patting him on the shoulder as they entered the cafeteria together.

Ms. Matthews glanced at Maggie frowning, "Afternoons? Yes, Pamela needs assistance in the afternoons. Why? Do you have someone in mind?"

"I think so."

"Well, has she ever worked with special needs children before?"

"Ah, no, I don't think so, but she seems really nice and so patient. I think she would be great."

"I'm sorry Maggie, but I must make an important phone call. Let's talk about this later, alright?"

"Sure," Maggie said and watched Ms. Matthews start toward the cafeteria, unexpectedly spinning around to throw Maggie a shrug and apologetic smile before heading toward her office. Maggie had never seen Ms. Matthews when she wasn't cool, calm, collected, and in charge.

—

Daniel tried to use his polisher to polish a piece of jasper, but the fingers on his left hand refused to hold the rock steady. In frustration he threw down the jasper and stood in his shop listening to the swamp cooler blow cold air into the room. The shop door opened, and sunlight followed Maggie inside as she entered the shed and shut the door behind her. Daniel lifted his head. Maggie wandered over to him and picked up the piece of jasper he had thrown down.

"This looks like a wolf singing to the moon," Maggie said. "Where did you find this one?"

Daniel nodded in agreement cheered by her interest in his rocks, "A wolf, yeah, it looks like a wolf. Stupid fingers."

Daniel stared down at his left hand where the cast ended just above the knuckles.

Daniel heard Maggie ask, "Do you need some help? I see you're polishing this one. I could hold it for you or do you have a brace? You could put it in a brace and use your good hand to polish it."

Daniel looked around the shop as if he could find a brace hidden somewhere in the room.

"If you don't have one, I can let you borrow mine," Maggie said. "I'll bring it tomorrow."

With his strong right arm, Daniel picked up a bucket full of thundereggs and set the bucket on top of his workbench. He started pulling out rocks and arranging them on the bench. He thought about each rock carefully. Some of them were the size of bowling balls others were as small as oranges. He believed the big one shaped like a head had something special inside. He would use his hammer and break it apart.

Daniel heard the shop door close. He took the rock he had selected and put it on the concrete floor at his feet. He lifted his hammer in his good right hand. With one stroke, he cracked the egg in two. He could only pick up one half at a time. He shoved the other thundereggs off to the right and arranged the two halves on the bench. He looked at each half, his eyes moving back and forth from one egg to the other.

They were beautiful: creamy opal in one half with a vein of red running down the middle and purple crystals in the other one with little crevices and holes and cavities like rivers and ponds. If he poured water into those crevices it would look just like the places he loved to go in the mountains. The only way to really see their beauty was to polish the cut parts until the rocks were as smooth as glass.

Chapter Five

M aggie left Daniel to sort through his collection and returned to the front of the school to retrieve her ten-speed. The heat from the sun burning on the exposed gravel rose up in waves and nearly blinded Maggie as she made her way around the side of the building. On the tree lined drive, as Maggie rode her bike toward the impressive gates, the gates opened admitting Daniel's mother Constance. She was driving a green Mustang convertible. Constance had the hood down and drove past Maggie without so-much as a glance. The sun's light reflecting off the windshield made Constance Harden's bleached blonde hair look a funny shade of green as if she'd paid someone to tint her hair the same color as her car.

Maggie used the smaller gate on the left-hand side of the entrance and pushed her bike through the opening. The small gate automatically locked behind her. Maggie wondered why Constance Harden had driven to the school, when she lived next door and could just as easily have walked the few feet to the gate. Maybe Daniel's mother never walked anywhere.

———

People's pity was despicable. She remembered the room, all the children waiting for their chance to dig through the leftover coats, mittens, boots, and used books. She remembered the greeter at the door to the cloak room with her sweet expression and her eyes swimming in pity for them all. Oh, yes. Vera despised pity more than any other human emotion. People pity because they haven't a clue what it's like to be poor and hungry and homeless. The ones who volunteer, more often than naught, have never dealt with poverty —not the ones that dole out the food at the shelters or the clothes in the cloak room. They don't even try to imagine what it's like to be poor, not really. She had to admit a few genuinely cared. It was about a difference in thinking – people who were the kind to care about the conditions of the poor hoped and worked toward eliminating poverty; whereas people who pitied the poor were just grateful they weren't poor or homeless or hungry.

Yes, there had been plenty of opportunities in her life to be the recipient of pity and the pity didn't end with her childhood. In the winter of 1973, Vera remembered sitting in the lawyer's spacious office with two sides of the wall covered in tinted windows. Over the lawyer's shoulder she could see the foothills that surrounded one side of the city of Boise. Arthur's lawyer Donald Whitcomb sat in his leather swivel chair holding some papers in front of him. Vera hadn't been sure if the papers were Arthur's will or something else he was working on. When he looked up from the papers she noticed the expression in his eyes. At that moment she hated him more than she had feared and hated Arthur.

"I'm sorry Mrs. Vlasky the will specifies very clearly that Arthur's estate and all his accumulated assets are to be divided between his sons."

"Did he leave me anything?" Vera asked unable to process the information wondering if there had been some stupid clerical error.

"No."

"What about the furniture, the cars, his coin and gun collection?"

"No, those bequests belong to the estate."

"What about my clothes and jewelry? Surely those are mine?"

"Of course, Mrs. Vlasky," he noticed something in her face and continued his voice dropping to a gentle murmur. "You know Mrs. Vlasky, it would be very expensive to contest Arthur's Will. Do you have the funds to sue the Vlasky family in court?"

The next morning Vera stood in front of the Boise bus terminal with the cash she had managed to collect from the pawn of her jewelry in her purse and her suitcase at her feet. Vera wondered how the clerks were dealing with her donations at the local Saver's Thrift Store as they pulled out the boxes of expensive dinner dresses, silk blouses, designer skirts, and assorted lingerie.

The thought of all those expensive gifts going to the poor gave Vera immense pleasure. In her present state of poverty owning such things would be useless. Where she was going, she would have to hunt for the cheapest, easiest job she could find. She may not be able to eat steak every night anymore, but a baloney sandwich will taste far better than the last four years of meals in Arthur Frank's dining room fending off blows and insults. Never again would his hand snatch food away from her mouth or his voice sneer at her about calories and fat little pigs eating themselves into an early grave.

With the sun shining down on her hatless head as if in joy with her decision, Vera stepped onto the bus and with her heavy suitcase banging against the seats and less joyfully her leg she made her way down the narrow isle looking for an empty seat preferably without another fellow traveler sitting next to her. She sat down in a seat near the back, dumped her coat on the empty seat, and thought about the day.

Today Arthur's children, his parents, his friends, and distant cousins, aunts, and uncles were at his gravesite, mourning the loss of Arthur Vlasky Senor. Vera mourned only the years she had lost. The knowledge Arthur was in his grave and not standing behind her ready to slap her on the head for some imagined wrong doing brought a smile to her lips. A rush of joy surged up from some place she had thought long since withered away. The feeling consumed her entire being so much so the Snake River, Lizard Butte, and all the orchards whipping past seemed so unbelievably beautiful so full of hope and love.

And as Vera closed the door on Andrew Treloar wishing he'd shown up when she was dressed and presentable a faint whisper of that long-ago joy tingled along her spine. She shoved the emotion down no longer trusting herself to know the difference between joy and lust. Or maybe she was really experiencing gratitude that an attractive man was paying attention to her after all these years.

—

Woody managed to park near an old creek bed and in the shade provided by a clump of runty dusty looking trees sat and contemplated the farm across the way. He used his binoculars to scan every inch of the place noticing with interest a dinky little foreign job one of those Toyotas parked under a huge tree. The tree's leaves were bigger than dinner plates. While he focused his attention on the Toyota, a long green pod the size of a short sword dropped from the tree and hit the Toyota's roof. The pod then bounced off the roof and landed on the ground nearby.

He moved the binoculars slowly to his left and examined the porch carefully. The hotel manager had told him that the woman he was looking for fit the description of a woman who had just moved into the Anderson's farmhouse. The place had been in the Anderson family since 1947. Everybody still referred to the place as Anderson farm. The name Lee meant nothing to the hotel manager.

He thought about what to say to Vera. He would say he missed her of course and that he was sorry. No. He would pretend ignorance. Woody counted the money still left in his billfold, two twenties. He needed some place to sleep, some place he could use as an address. People don't hire homeless strangers. No, better yet, he would persuade Vera to come back to Vegas with him. Aunt Vista had been a tough old corpse for sure. Telling him Vera had gone to Portland. Bullshit if she had. The old biddy had known all along where Vera was hiding out. From the beginning, Woody had suspected she'd been lying to him. Some people were just shitty liars.

The old bitch had never even invited him into her dumpy trailer. But he'd had a stroke of luck when later that day, a young man pulled up to her trailer and took her off somewhere. It was easy to jimmy the lock and slip inside. It took him an hour looking through the piles of mail and magazines before he found the postcard from Vera. She had written to her Aunt about some nice neighbors the Andersons. Kissing up to money, Woody thought, no surprise to him she would worm her way into their itty-bitty hearts.

He hadn't seen her in years, not since 1970. Two years in prison, four years living with fat ugly old women and then he found the Foss brothers. This past year had been the worst: living on the streets most of the time, sleeping in shelters if he got lucky, and doing the Foss brothers' dirty work. All he thought about these days was getting back with Vera. His friends told Woody she would make his life miserable. Screw them.

—

Andrew headed back to the police station in Mintlaw debating whether to call Vera and tell her that Woody Kirk was looking for her. He decided it was none of his business. Andrew heard the radio squawk then Erma's voice, "Andy. Chief wants to see you a.s.a.p."

Arthur Vlasky must have called the police station the moment he got home. Twenty minutes later, Andrew entered the station, greeted Erma with a nod, and knocked on the Chief's door. Steven Glenjones called out his name. Erma must have warned him. Andrew sat in the leather chair facing the Chief's desk. The Chief set his paperwork aside and studied Andrew for so long Andrew began to get mad.

"Vlasky claims you threatened him today. What's going on Andy?"

"I didn't threaten him. I gave him a piece of advice."

"And?"

Andrew settled himself more comfortably in his chair and considered how much to tell Steve, "I noticed Arthur Vlasky arguing with Vera Lee in the store. Whatever he said upset her. I had a talk with him, asked him if he knew her. He said he did. It seems Vera Lee is Arthur Vlasky's widow and Junior blames Ms. Lee for his father's death. I told him to forget the past and concentrate on the present."

"Is this about Vlasky's death back in '73?"

"Yes."

"The Vlaskys may be pains-in-the-asses, but they're voters and citizens of Owyhee County who we have sworn to protect and serve. Keep that in mind next time Andy."

Andrew stood up, "You've sworn to protect and serve them. I, thank God, haven't. I'm here as a favor to you and Metcalf. I'm retired, remember?"

Steve stopped him at the door, "No Andy, you're not retired. You're on the payroll as of today. It may not be much money compared to the artwork you sell but the people of Mintlaw and Homedale appreciate your service and the Mayor has already asked for more men. We'll be staffing temporary police officers for the next few years. Rural crime is up in the Owyhees as you know. You signed the contract agreeing to a temporary active duty position which reinstates your former rank and new responsibilities, so write up a report on the incident for our files. Please. And Andy, leave the report with Erma."

Andrew wondered whether volunteering to help the Mintlaw Police Department made sense anymore. The little he got from the department covered only basic household expenses and took precious time away from his projects which paid a hell of lot more money. He had three orders to fill as it was. And more aggravating, he resented having to write up a report about a situation which was personal and would reflect badly on him more than the idiot. Junior was a pathetic little cockroach.

Andy was sick and tired of the way the town kissed that family's ass. Everybody else had to pay speeding and parking tickets or obey fire hydrant rules yet, the Vlasky brothers were exempt from any citations. The single most egregious example of favoritism was the night Junior plowed into the side of Homeister's barn. It had been two days before New Year's Eve and the officer on the scene had neglected to give Vlasky the sobriety tests or to even question him about where he had been.

Junior claimed he'd hit an icy patch on the snow packed roads even though there were plenty of people in town who testified to his sloppy drunk-ass condition that night. Junior had been so drunk he'd tried to pee in the corner of the bar thinking he was in the john. He'd also had an argument with his sister about driving. At least there were still some decent folks in town because they pitched in to repair the gaping hole in Homeister's barn. All the cockroach did was contribute a few bucks and take off for Hawaii to let things cool down in Mintlaw.

—

Once back home, Maggie went straight up to her room to finish her homework. She thought about calling Vera to tell her about the job at the school; and then realized she didn't know Vera's phone number. She decided to wait until after supper. At the dinner table, Murray complained his iced tea had too many ice cubes. Maggie watched as her mother poured his glass of tea into a coffee cup and warmed it up in the microwave. Maggie wondered why her mother babied Murray. After supper, Maggie couldn't wait to get out of the house. She had to assure both her parents she had finished her homework. Nobody else her age had to write a paper about Idaho history during the summer. Most of her friends had long since forgotten what their teachers tried to teach them in the fifth grade about Idaho

Once Maggie had climbed on her bike, she thought about going over to Amy's house and then remembered that Amy had gone to Boise to visit her aunt and uncle. Instead Maggie crossed the road and walked her bike up the driveway to Vera's house. She would tell Vera about the job at the school in person. Vera seemed so self-sufficient it was hard for Maggie to imagine her needing anything or anybody.

Maggie leaned her bike against the porch rails and ran up the steps. She banged on the door and waited. No one answered. It was quiet inside. Maggie turned her head to confirm that the Toyota was still parked under the catalpa tree. She debated leaving a note under a rock and decided maybe Vera was in the backyard. She walked around the house; maybe Vera might be cleaning up the concrete and swing set. Maggie passed the barn and noticed the barn doors were shut and locked. The backyard looked just the way she'd left it earlier this morning. What was left of the swing set with the pole still stuck in the concrete might have been a helpless animal with its foot caught in a trap. Maggie returned to the front part of the house and climbed onto her bike.

A scream startled Maggie and she lost her grip on the handle bars and nearly fell off. She managed to find the brake pedal and skid to a stop. When she ran back to the house and banged on the door, calling out, "Vera! Are you alright?" no one answered. Maggie jumped on her bike and with arms and legs shaking hurried home.

—

Vera drew her curtains closed to shade the couch from the heat and lay down, her body aching all over. She hadn't worked so hard in years, not since she was a kid working the fields with her mother. She thought of all the tasks she had assigned herself left undone: the planting of bulbs, scraping the old paint off the shingle siding, pulling up the mildewed carpet in the utility room. Her body betrayed her, refusing to obey her thoughts. The work would have to wait.

She gave in to sleep and closed her eyes. In her dream, she saw the basement, the rectangle of a room with huge cinder blocks rising above her head to the beamed ceiling. The day's light coming through the open door above illuminated the stairs leading down to the basement. The railing of the stair was just an old two by four nailed to some blocks of wood. The railing had enough strength to hold a person's weight when that person needed to step down into the darkness in search of the light switch at the bottom. The fact that some idiot had put the light switch at the bottom of the stairs amused her foster family. Vera had never thought the position of the light switch particularly funny. She was the one they ordered to go down and fetch household items from the basement, mostly the laundry or a jar of pickles or preserves.

Sometimes the dry wood of the rail had splinters that speared themselves in her palm or the tip of her finger. She had learned to use the cinder block wall as a guide down to the light switch. The single light bulb in the center of the basement only illuminated the bottom of the stairs and about two feet around the bulb. Otherwise, the corners of the basement were in complete darkness.

In her dream, Vera could see the light bulb and the dangling string only because the door to the basement was open and the day's light penetrated down to her from the open door. She saw the way the light bulb illuminating the stairs made them seem to glow and how the dirt on the concrete floor seemed to dance as a gust of wind blew down from above. Vera saw herself standing in the center of the cellar, far from the light and the stairs. In the little window above the concrete wall overlooking the side of the house, something moved across the smudged glass something with long furry legs. She heard glass breaking and saw it standing at the top of the cellar stairs.

Vera sensed a gathering of shadows taking shape to her right, a stain among the gray cinder blocks which grew larger and larger until it was the size of a large animal. As in dreams, what had been outside and on the top of the stairs now shifted and she watched in growing fear and horror as the stain on the wall became a dark hole. A dog, a huge black dog with fangs sprang from the hole and landed on top of her. She saw his sharp white fangs and smelled his foul breath. Vera woke with her neck tingling as if the phantom dog had really got his jaw around her throat prepared to slash through her skin. Someone banged on Vera's door. Vera unable to control the quivering in her arms and legs listened to the fist strike the wood, once, twice, and a third time.

He had struck the wood so hard that the door shook. She had answered the door and he had pushed inside looking for Woody. Those other men, they had followed him inside, men with pits for eyes, men with guns in their pockets. He had shoved her into the bathroom. One of the other men turned on her cheap stereo, twisting the knob on the volume until the music sounded like it was inside her head. He told them to turn up the volume on purpose.

He had shut the bathroom door trapping her inside the tiny room with him. He had smiled down at her, his eyes cruising over her body with interest, his gaze lingering on her breasts. His hands roamed along her hip. She had become an animal frozen with terror, unable to think. Vera saw the fist and felt the pain like waves of hot electricity crashing inside her head. She screamed. Her scream echoed through the room bouncing off the living room walls.

Vera sat up and threw her legs over the side of the couch. With her elbows resting on her knees, she squeezed her head between her hands.

How long had she been dreaming? She remembered the cellar and the dog leaping at her throat. She remembered him. The time between leaving the couch and sitting in her rocking chair must have been only a minute or two; yet, she'd closed the curtains against the sun's bright light and now the day was over. She hugged her arms to keep warm, even though the house was airless and hot. Outside the kitchen window, dark clouds hung over the hills. Vera tapped her lamp and the light from the bulb illuminated the thing that lay in her lap. She didn't remember retrieving it from its hiding place. She didn't remember sitting down in her rocking chair either. She had lost more time moving from the couch to the chair. Maybe she was going crazy?

In her lap lay the only object Vera considered valuable; over the last twenty years, she kept the necklace well- hidden wherever she made her home. It had been a gift from her great grandmother. During the four years of her marriage to Arthur, she moved the necklace from one hiding place to another in his house afraid he would find it and use the necklace as leverage against her. As she examined the stone, the amber eye of the cat seemed to watch her. Her mother claimed the beads that looked like wood were really petrified wood from the Methuselah Tree, a very ancient tree full of history and magic. The Methuselah Tree had survived for over 5000 years on an arid mountainside. According to her mother, the tree was like Vera's people capable of surviving anything nature and man could devise. The tiger's eye symbolized rebirth; at least, that's what some people believed, supposedly representing the nine lives of a cat.

It wasn't until she was married to Vlasky and discovered (with a librarian's help) that her great grandmother couldn't possibly have tripped over the tiger eye stone on the moors of Scotland before immigrating to America in 1884. The stone had been discovered in South Africa in the 1800s; and by 1900 the stone once considered so precious had become semiprecious. Several new deposits had been discovered in other parts of Africa, as well as America, but there was no mention of Scotland and soon the market was flooded with them.

So, the family story had been her mother's creative imagination at work once again, one her mother had told so often she'd managed to convince herself. Vera wasn't surprised. Even though her great grandmother probably hadn't tripped over the tiger eye on the moors of Scotland; yet, she had designed and fashioned the necklace with her own hands. And when Vera was free of Vlasky and living in Oregon, she went to a jeweler and he told her the craftsmanship was the finest he had ever seen, and the wood was indeed unusual. He could see tiny insects in the life lines of the wood. He suggested she leave the necklace with him to examine more closely.

She refused.

The stone represented rebirth and courage to her. Vera suspected her great grandmother had been working on the necklace for many years, probably since the day she stepped onto American soil. She might have traded something she had at the time with another traveler for the tiger eye and created the necklace out of her own special pieces of silver, amber beads, and petrified wood. Her Nonnie had been known for her beautiful workmanship; so, it would not surprise Vera to find the necklace did indeed have some rare magical properties.

Knowing the necklace had been made for her by someone she dearly loved and respected meant more than empty family myths. Her mother had told the young Vera the necklace had been in the family for generations; her Nonnie never confirmed or denied her mother's story. As Vera recalled her great grandmother had simply draped the necklace around Vera's neck on her thirteenth birthday, kissed her cheek, and said a blessing in Gaelic. The family myth about the heirlooms, one for Vera and one for each of her other siblings were thought up by the chief storyteller of the family, their mother – Analetta Vera Lee Caumlo.

Vera moved about the room unwinding her stiff joints and tight muscles and with the necklace clasped in her hand walked to the wall clock. The time on its face alarmed her. How many hours had she been sitting in her rocking chair without being aware of herself or her surroundings? The necklace nearly slipped from her fingers; she grabbed it before it fell. She apologized to the memory of her great grandmother for hiding the necklace away all these years and held the stone to her heart. Kissing the tiger eye, she slipped the necklace over her head.

Unlike most necklaces which ended with a cabochon dangling from a bail, her great grandmother chose to design a necklace in the shape of the symbol for infinity. How she had constructed the intricate necklace was a constant marvel to Vera. There was no clasp or hook. It was one single piece made of seven intertwining silk threads that Nonnie had laboriously decorated with alternating beads of petrified wood and amber. There were four hundred and eighty-two beads minus the two spaces which were left alone so that the intertwined threads could pass through the tiny rings she had soldered to the back of a white gold rectangular plate. The plate held the bezel where the tiger eye was set. Years ago, Vera found when she looked through a magnifying glass, her great grandmother's initials SLC embossed on the back of the plate. SLC stood for Struana Lee Ferguson Caumlo. The name Struana meant stream.

Vera ran her fingers down the beads touching the petrified wood (wondering with a thrill if the wood really were from the Methuselah Tree); and as she examined the necklace with her fingertips, she was soothed by the tiny ridges and crevices coated in hard glaze, the repetitive motion of touching the beads relaxing and focusing her mind. Maybe the design had been intentional – to create a necklace which would give Vera confidence and focus her thoughts?

The clocks ticking reminded her of lost time. There was so much left to do. It was too late now. In another hour the sun would set, and it would be too dark to work outside. Vera remembered starting on the swing set around seven o'clock that morning; she and Maggie must have stopped to talk on the porch before noon. It was nearly six o'clock in the evening. What had she been doing for five hours? Where had she gone? To lose herself for so many hours frightened her.

The doorbell rang. As Vera moved toward the front door, she tucked the necklace in the coat pocket hanging on the coat rack on the wall. It was growing dark. Beside the door she'd placed a small table and on the table a lamp. The mirror hanging on the wall above the table showed her face so white and scared. She called through the door. The person on the other side spoke so low she could barely hear him. Someday she would replace the old thick wooden door with a new door that had a peep hole or window. She thought about Andrew Treloar. Maybe he had come to tell her about the little girl. Vera quickly unbolted the door.

She recognized the snakeskin cowboy boots first. Her eye traveled up the leg dressed in tight jeans to the torso dressed in a black t-shirt with a screaming Eagle on the chest and stopped at the narrow hairless chin. He said something to her. Vera slammed the door in his face and relocked the deadbolt. She ran to the back of the house and locked the sliding glass door and dropped the stick she'd measured and cut weeks ago in the bottom runner as an extra precaution. She had had nightmares like this before of madly running through the house locking doors and windows and all the while the intruder circled searching for a way inside.

—

Daniel returned home in his mother's car. The white around his mother's mouth meant nothing to him. He entered the house ahead of her and climbed the stairs to his bedroom. Darrell had the volume of the television up so high Daniel knew that he was watching *Terminator* again with Arnold as the bad guy. His mother had followed him upstairs. She opened his bedroom door without asking to come in. Mz. Matthews had told Daniel people should knock before they came into a room. His mother stood on the threshold holding the door.

"Well, Daniel, are you going to tell me how you fractured your wrist?"

Daniel repeated, "I fell down."

"Where? When?"

"Yesterday. I fell down yesterday."

"Sunday? You fell down Sunday?"

"No, Saturday. I fell down Saturday."

"Where?"

"On Anderson Pass," he said pointing with his good right hand toward the road in front of the old Anderson farmhouse.

"Why didn't you say anything before? All day Saturday you been hurting and all night last night and you say nothing to me? Why?" His mother didn't wait for him to respond, "You know what Miss Special Ed Smarty Pants said to me? She said if you get hurt again, she's going to sic the police on me, said maybe I didn't take care of you good enough. Maybe I should let you go live at that damned school. What do you think about that?"

Daniel thought about living at the school and being near his rocks, "Yeah," he said in an eager voice. "I want to go live at the school."

His bedroom door slammed shut. He heard his mother stomp down the stairs. Darrell had come out from the living room. Daniel couldn't hear what they said because the volume on the television was so high with a lot of explosions and gunfire. Daniel pulled out his suitcases from his closet and threw clothes inside, all his clothes, even the ones on the floor, on the chair, and under the bed, until there was no more room for any more clothes. He walked down the staircase one suitcase under his arm and the other in his good hand.

He heard Arnold on television say, "I'll be back."

A second later, he heard Darrell say, "Let him go for Christ's sakes. What's the big deal?"

Daniel carried his suitcases around the house and toward the locust trees. He looked out at the fields and up at Hunter's Hill toward his treasure spot. Something shiny caught his eye. He turned his head to the right and saw a car parked a few feet away under the trees and a man sitting inside the car. Daniel crouched down by the lilac bush that was almost as big as the locust trees. Daniel heard his mother calling to him. He made himself small and peered out to see what the man was doing. Daniel's mother called out again. Darrell told Daniel's mother to shut-up. Daniel crawled out from the lilac with both suitcases bumping against his legs.

He set the heavier one behind a tree growing near the garage and moved toward the dry creek like an Indian, quiet, quiet. He turned to see if the man in the car had noticed him. The man in the car had his head back on the head rest of the bucket seat. He looked like he was asleep.

Daniel walked along the bank of Poison Creek with his suitcase banging against his leg. When he came to the steep part, he used his suitcase to lever himself up. When he reached the top, he followed the cow path west toward the top of Hunter's Hill. At the edge of the hill overlooking the Anderson Farm and the meadow below, he sat down to rest on a slab of smooth rocks. From his vantage point, he could see everything below him. He was hot. The sun burned his eyes. He stood up and looked for some shade. Near the barricade of boulders just beyond Anderson Pass, he found a spot where a quaking aspen and some tall mahogany sage provided shade. He sat cross legged "cress cross applesauce," under the tree using his suitcase to prop up his sore arm. He closed his eyes.

When he woke, it was nearly dark. He pushed his suitcase out in front of him and crawled out from under the ledge. He stood on the edge of the cliff and looked down. He could see the house below and the light from a lamp illuminating the kitchen table near the window and he saw a human sitting in a rocking chair. The human was looking at something in her lap. She got up and Daniel couldn't see her anymore. Then a few minutes later, Daniel saw another human, a tall skinny one but not as tall as Daniel come around the house and stand on the porch.

The man pounded on the door and shouted, "Vera! Vera let me in. I just want to talk."

The woman opened the door and stepped out onto the porch. She pushed the man down the steps. The man tripped, righted himself, and stopped. The woman stood over him and said something funny, "Get!" she said as if she were talking to a dog. "Get! Go on!"

Daniel laughed and said to himself. "Get little doggy, you get."

Chapter Six

Once Maggie stood in her warm cozy kitchen with her mother sitting at the kitchen table reading and the smell of cookies backing in the oven, Maggie broke down and started to cry. Maggie blinded by tears felt an arm go around her shoulders and someone lead her toward a chair. Maggie struggled to control herself and heard her father's concerned voice call out and grow louder as he hurried into the kitchen.

"Just let her calm down Kit," her mother said.

Maggie used the dish towel her mother handed her to wipe the tears from her face. She controlled her voice and said, "I went to the school today and asked Ms. Matthews if she still needed an assistant for the preschoolers. She said she did, so I thought I'd go over to Vera's house and tell her about the job. But when I got there and knocked she didn't answer the door. Her car's there. I saw it. I went around to the back and she wasn't there. And when I was going to get my bike, I heard a scream from inside the house. I knocked and knocked but she didn't answer. I think she's hurt Mom. I think she's hurt and can't get to the door."

Her father said, "I'll go over and see if everything's all right."

Maggie sprang up, "Maybe we should call Uncle Andrew?"

Her mother frowned, "Let's wait until your father returns. Okay?"

Maggie heard Murray rolling himself toward the kitchen. He asked Maggie's mother what all the drama was about. Maggie stood by the door with her arms crossed and waited anxiously for her father to return. Maggie heard Murray say something about "morons." She couldn't stand to be in the room anymore. Jerking open the kitchen door, she ran outside and around the house. She saw her father reach Vera's porch. She saw him knock on the door. He waited for someone to come to the door with his head down as if he were listening.

Maggie stood under the willow tree and watched. When her father walked around the house and peered through a window, Maggie wanted to giggle. She'd never seen her father do that before. He disappeared around the back of the house. A few minutes later he returned and started down the drive way. Maggie walked toward him. They met in the middle of the road.

"She's not answering," her father said and led her toward the house. "I'm not sure what to do now. I mean if I broke a window and went in and found her sleeping peacefully in her bed, she could sue me for breaking and entering. And if something is really wrong, I would hate to think of her helpless and hurt. Come on."

They reentered the kitchen. Her father grabbed the phone. Rachel lifted the cookie sheet out of the oven and with her mitt awkwardly set the cookie sheet down to cool on the counter. Maggie leaned against the sink and listened to her father talk to the police dispatcher. Too many things had gone wrong this summer to let something like this pass unnoticed. Maggie's mother listened to the phone conversation without saying a word. Even Murray seemed subdued. Her father hung up the phone and turned to them.

"They say they'll send a car out to check on her. We just have to wait."

Maggie went outside ignoring her mother's attempt to stop her. Maggie sat on the front steps and watched for the patrol car. She thought about Vera, about her small frame and fragile bones, about the way Daniel had scared her, how she didn't seem comfortable around people. Then Maggie thought about her face and began to wonder how she'd gotten the white scar that ran from the corner of her eye down her cheek.

Maggie stood up when she saw Uncle Andrew's Jeep pull into the Treloar drive and park. Maggie's father had come out and she followed him toward the Jeep listening as her father explained to Uncle Andrew what had happened.

—

Andrew waited until Kit finished talking before leaving the Treloar Farm. He drove up toward Vera's house and parked behind her vehicle, then climbed out. Andrew glanced at Vera's car. As he climbed the steps to her front door, he noticed that all the lights were on in the house. He knocked on the door, but no one answered. He heard angry voices somewhere back of the house. He walked around the house and found Vera. He also found Woodrow Kirk.

Both had turned their heads to stare at him.

Andrew looked at Vera, "Are you alright?"

Vera had her arms crossed and held them close to her chest, "Yes, I am alright."

"Maggie heard you scream. She thought something might have happened to you."

K McVere

Vera looked puzzled for a moment then looked down at the ground.

Woody moved forward as if to touch her. Vera backed away.

Andrew looked at Woody, "Your wife doesn't seem to want you around, Mr. Kirk."

"Wife!" Vera shouted and lifted her head. "What have you been telling people Woody? That I'm your wife!"

"Well we are. We're common law. I checked."

"We are no such thing. You damned liar. Prove it. Show me the marriage license."

"It's not like that, Vera," Woody said trying to defend himself. "We're common law cause we lived together as man and wife."

"That's a lie."

Andrew thought it was time to intervene. He turned to Kirk and addressed him, "While you lived together did you refer to Vera as your wife? Was the rent under the name of Mr. and Mrs. Kirk? Or the utility bills? Did everyone know you as man and wife?"

Vera jumped in, "Never. It was my apartment and the rental agreement was in my name only. And I paid the bills. He just mooched off me."

Andrew noticed how nervous Kirk had become. There was something he was afraid Vera might say. Andrew waited in the hope she might say something that would give Andrew an excuse to arrest him.

Vera turned and walked toward the porch separating herself from them, "I think its time I got a restraining order," she said to no one in particular before walking into the house and slamming the door behind her.

Woodrow Kirk brushed passed Andrew. Andrew made sure Kirk left the property before he knocked on Vera's door. She opened the door and waited with her hand on her hip.

"Did he hurt you, Vera? If he did, we can take him in. Lock him up for the night."

"This we you're referring to – that would be the police, yeah? Well, since you're not a police officer, then I don't need to explain myself to you. And if I need the police, I'll call them. Good night, Mr. Treloar."

"As of a few days ago, Chief Glenjones reinstated me in the force with all the rights and responsibilities thereof. You haven't answered my question Ms. Lee. Did Kirk hurt you?" Andrew asked ignoring her remark. He would rather have been at home working on one of his commissions, than dealing with a domestic-

92

disturbance call. She could think what she liked about him. He would rather be a comical figure in her eyes than someone she feared.

"No. Mr. Treloar. As I said before, he did not hurt me."

"According to Maggie she heard you scream. Why did you scream, Ms. Lee?"

"A scream? You say she heard a scream? Yes, that was me. I fell off my step ladder. Woody had nothing to do with it," Vera said and without conscious thought placed her hands on his chest and shoved him backward. "I don't have to explain myself to you. You're not even a real cop. Go away. Now."

Any other cop would have arrested her immediately. He swallowed his pride and said, in as calm a voice as he could manage, "As I've already explained, I have been reinstated as a deputy of the Mintlaw Police Department." His statement sounded lame even to him since he was talking to her with the door closed between them. He knew she was still standing by the door.

"If you would rather talk to someone else, I can get another officer out here." He strained to hear her muffled reply.

"How convenient that you are now a cop again. No. I don't want anyone else coming to my house without an invitation. So, leave my property now."

Andrew returned to his vehicle. He saw Kirk walking away from the house onto the shoulder of the road. The catalpa trees hid him from view for a moment. At the end of the drive, Andrew paused to check for traffic and noticed Kirk's car parked on the blind side of the road. He had hidden it, so Vera couldn't see him coming. What a low life creep. Andrew watched Kirk drive away. He followed the Datsun as far as McBride Road. Once he was sure Woodrow Kirk was on his way back to Winnemucca, he turned around and headed home to Mintlaw.

———

Daniel waved at Andrew Treloar. Mr. Treloar did not see him up on the hilltop. Daniel picked up his suitcase and started walking toward the school. It was getting dark. Pretty soon the children would be in bed. Daniel made it passed his mother's house without getting caught. He arrived at the gate to the school and pushed the call box button. Ms. Matthews answered.

"It's me Ms. Matthews. I want to come and live with you."

The gates opened for him and he grinned. He walked down the drive, something inside tickling his stomach. Daniel remembered old man, old man Olsen. He remembered the first time he stood in Old Man Olsen's shop and watched him polish a piece of picture jasper. The ol' guy was planning to make a belt buckle out of that piece of white and green jasper. He had said something to Daniel.

What was it? No, he'd asked a question, he'd asked, "Why are you grinning?" Daniel remembered saying, "I don't know." Old Man Olsen said, "You're grinning because you're happy." Daniel remembered saying, "My stomach tickles," and Olsen said, "That's cause you found something you love to do, boy."

Chapter Seven

Yesterday, Ada Aleshire had been living a comfortable happy life in Winnemucca doing her thing and bothering nobody. Now she had become a case for the feds. She supposed kidnapping a child and transporting a dead body over state lines would be enough to get her a few years in Leavenworth, maybe life. She shrugged her shoulders philosophically – well her day job was equally as dangerous.

It was about eight o'clock in the evening as Ada drove along US 95 through the Owyhee Mountains. Occasionally, she glanced in her rearview mirror to see if the kid still slept. She'd given the kid a sleeping pill hoping she would sleep until she found just the right place to dump her. The pill was supposed to be good for eight hours. She sure as hell hoped so. Once the brat woke up, she suspected she would have her hands full keeping her in the car. The brat wasn't hers. She kept telling herself that. Carolina had had no right to dump the kid on her.

So, Carolina couldn't take life anymore and goes and kills herself in Ada's house – so what? Was the fact that life sucks Ada's problem? Why did she have to pay for some stranger's troubles? She hardly knew Carolina. They'd never been friends. They were distant cousins. Good thing none of Carolina's stupid mistakes had gone through the court or the welfare system. Good thing Carolina had just appeared out of the blue one day and asked if she could stay for a few weeks until she found a job.

Events had worked out in Ada's favor. Nobody knew she had the kid, not even her nosy neighbors. Carolina had shown up at midnight on her doorstep, just off the bus carrying a backpack and the kid. The smelly creature had been asleep. She and Carolina had argued for the better part of the night. By two in the morning, Ada gave in and let them sleep in her spare bedroom. It had been Ada's attention to throw Carolina Fletcher out at first light. Then Ada finds Carolina's body in her guest bedroom and the kid trying to slap her mother awake. The brat had annoyed her to crazy-town making those damn grunting noises non-stop.

Ada had to come up with a plan. Here was reality. The spaz had gone and died in her house. Ada wasn't sure what the hell had happened, maybe a heart attack, maybe an overdose. The police would investigate; they'd check Ada's background, ask a lot of questions; maybe even check out her income and discover Ada had more money in her bank account than she could justify. Her last employment had been around three years ago.

Back then, she discovered she could make much more money selling drugs if she cut out the middle man. A white woman who speaks fluent Spanish traveling to Mexico had a far easier time with border patrol than some tweaking male with long hair and tattoos. The kilo of cocaine formerly hidden away in her dryer in the basement was now close at hand. She couldn't risk a nosy neighbor calling the police and the police searching her house and finding the cocaine since her idiot cousin had killed herself in Ada's house – damn her, the stupid spaz.

Six hours ago, Ada desperate to come up with a plan had locked the kid and her dead cousin in the bedroom. Then turning up the stereo to mask the sound of the child's screaming, had put on a pair of blue jeans and a t-shirt; and as an extra precaution found her shower cap and put that on her head too. The last accessories to go on were a pair of rubber gloves from under the kitchen sink. After she disposed of the body and the kid, she would come home and clean the house thoroughly. With a combination of anxiety mixed with suppressed fury, Ada riffled through her junk drawer for masking tape and searched the garage for rope. She thought about how it would look with the kid in the backseat of her car tied up with rope and masking tape over her mouth. No, that would be a bad idea, a really shitty stupid idea.

A brilliant solution came to her out of the blue. Ada mashed a sleeping pill into crumbs and mixed the crumbs in with the peanut butter. She offered the kid the special sandwich, but instead of eating the sandwich like a good girl, the brat spits the wad onto Ada's newly cleaned champagne carpet.

The deliberate ruination of her carpet was the last straw. While holding her nose, Ada rammed a sleeping pill down the kid's throat forcing her to swallow. It took the pill thirty minutes to work. When she was confident what's-her-name was asleep, Ada carried the kid down the stairs. The kid hardly weighed anything, might as well be carrying a sack of groceries. Ada carried her limp body out to the garage and dumped her in the back behind the driver's seat of her van, a cargo van which cost her a mere five hundred bucks and had formerly belonged to a fellow pothead who's carpet cleaning business had gone bust. Once she had the kid securely wrapped up in a blanket inside an empty box, she threw a sheet over her not in the mood to watch her drooling in her sleep. No sense in someone seeing the little monster and crying child abuse.

The rest of Ada's time she spent madly cleaning out the carpet cleaning junk in the back of the bed of the van to make room for Carolina's body. The van had been Ada's prop in case any of her nosy neighbors wondered why she stayed home more often than she worked. Carolina would be a much more difficult problem to solve. Carolina was practically a stick, so she wouldn't be too hard to lift into the van. But they were about the same height five feet six inches tall and that might make things more awkward. She needed a gurney or something with wheels.

Again, the brilliant idea came to her out of the urgency of the moment. Ada lifted Carolina's body onto her black leather executive chair. The chair was equipped with wheels, so all Ada had to do was wheel her out to the garage, untie her from the chair and lift her into the back of the van. Not knowing what she would need once she found a place to dump Carolina, Ada threw the chair into the van just in case. Before climbing out, she realized she might need some other things and went in search of masking tape. Once she was satisfied with her plan, Ada locked the van and returned to her kitchen. Sweat was pouring down her forehead into her eyes, the salty stuff burnt. When she looked in the mirror, she looked like a tomato, round and red and slightly green in places. She had to take a break.

After a cup of coffee and a cigarette, Ada grabbed her purse and keys and climbed into the driver's seat. The seatbelt was a bitch to secure, so she chose not to mess with it. Before she opened the garage door, she noticed in the rearview mirror that she was still wearing the shower cap. Shit! Why the hell was she wearing a shower cap, it was her frigging damned house! She'd been watching too much television. Crime shows had screwed her up for sure. She should have put the shower cap on the kid or Carolina's head. Yes, she thought, I'll have to vacuum the entire house, scrub down the bathroom and the spare bedroom – clean the van too. What had she done to deserve such a fate?

A conversation she'd had with one of her customers gave her another brilliant idea.

She laughed and beat the steering wheel with enthusiasm.

It would be the perfect revenge.

As Ada passed the Oregon border, she pulled off U.S. 95 onto several different dirt roads wanting one which looked less traveled, oh yes, nice that, a road less traveled, for sure. It took four attempts to find the perfect backroad and just in time because she was running out of backroads. This last one was particularly rough and as she searched for a good spot to dump the evidence, she thought about her cousin's side of the family. Would someone miss her? Did they know she'd shown up on Ada's doorstep begging for shelter? Her parents had died in a car accident five years ago. Her father had been one of those guys who drove under the speed limit and in L.A. that had been a big mistake. Carolina had been an only child and she'd never married. She'd been a real smarty pants, a college graduate, but a loner. Somehow, homely Carolina, with zits and an overbite and her pencil curves managed to get herself pregnant at one of Ada's pot parties.

As far as Ada knew, the kid had never been in a public school and had never, at any time, been in one of those institutions for the mentally retarded. Ada also knew that Carolina made a good living as some kind of nerd at a techie place. Carolina hated people. Carolina had been a social failure – one of those weirdos terrified of people.

Yeah, Ada's stepmother used to say Carolina's kid had turned out just like her, another idiot from a branch of idiots, not only a retard, but an illegitimate retard. Ada's stepmother although claiming to be a good Christian (while never being seen in a church that Ada knew of) had definite opinions about certain groups – the Jews were all good with math yet would steal you blind; the blacks were mostly dumb and would try to steal the clothes off your back; whereas the mentally retarded do not belong in society and should be locked away and never seen. Also, her stepmother believed that anyone not a Baptist was destined for hell everlasting.

Unfortunately, Ada had had only a few good years with her father. When she turned eighteen, her father was arrested after being caught robbing a convenience store and once he was in jail, her stepmother threw her out, so Ada was a free agent and never looked back. She still carried within her a bone-deep conviction that her father and her stepmother were right about some things.

Her present troubles were proof that idiots like her cousin should never have been born.

The van rocked and bumped and slid down the washboard dirt road and Ada holding onto the steering wheel for dear life thought about her van uncomfortably conscious of the damn logo in large white letters emblazoned across the left side the logo *Dust Bunnies*, an old phone number which was out of service now, and an image of a huge vacuum chasing a rabbit. She gritted her teeth determined to stick to her plan.

Someone might remember the van. It was conspicuous anywhere but that was the beauty of it. Who would think something so innocuous would be carrying a couple of bodies inside? But she had no other plans and it was too late to change this one anyway. The shocks would never be the same either. At a certain point near a rise in the road that wandered up and up and required four-wheel drive, Ada stopped and surveyed the area. What a dump! She saw broken glass from beer bottles thrown along the side of the dirt road and other garbage left by hunters and drunken adolescents, even some used toilet paper among the bushes. It was still too bright out to dispose of the bodies. She would have to wait until dark.

The kid stirred in the backseat. Ada thought about Carolina whining over losing her job and how the daycare had refused to take the kid back because the retard had climbed into an infant's crib and tried to hurt some baby. Ada couldn't imagine, not for one minute having to care fulltime for the little monster. No way would she be stuck with her. Ada's plan would be to get rid of the mother and the kid, go home, clean up any evidence of them from her house, and close out her bank account. If she moved to another state and changed her name maybe she could get rid of her other annoyances as well? She'd always wanted to travel to Europe, not South America for sure, not where the wetbacks lived, but in a civilized country, maybe where her ancestors had come from in Germany. Her father had told her about her grandpa and how he'd been some kind of scout when Hitler was in power; how, her grandpa had been fifteen when he'd fought to keep Germany pure; and when the war was lost how he had come to America.

—

Woody Kirk sat on Ada Aleshire's concrete steps with Aleshire's porch light flickering above him and waited. He crushed his cigarette butt out on the step below him with his boot heel noticing the five other ones near the new one. Ada would be pissed. He picked up the stubs and tossed them behind her ornamental bush, then lit another cigarette and took a sip of his beer. The beer was as warm as the temperature outside. Here on the step with the porch light above his head illuminating only the door and the welcome mat while his body remained in shadow, Woody thought about what he would say to Ada. She didn't like it when he came over to her place. She didn't want her nosy neighbors knowing her business. Woody figured this was too important to miss. She made him nervous, her and her ball busting attitude. But there was worse.

Woody wished now he'd never answered the phone this morning. He'd been ringing her house all day. At ten o'clock, he figured he'd come over and see if she was home. The van hadn't been in the garage. She must be out doing her business. He'd left because the lady next door was peeking out her window and might just call the cops thinking he was casing the place. He left and waited and returned at midnight. He'd been waiting three hours now. He glanced at his watch. It was three fifteen everybody on her street had long since gone to bed. And an hour ago, he'd climbed over her fence, tried her door and some dog in the other yard began to bark.

A vehicle swept around the corner and headed toward him. He threw the half-finished cigarette in the street watching as the vehicle drew closer. He recognized her van by the whine of the loose belt. The van pulled into her driveway and he could see the Dust Bunny logo on the side. She hadn't seen him yet. The garage door opened. Woody walked toward the garage and watched her park her van. He slipped inside before the garage door cut him off. Ada climbed out of the van and stopped when she saw him. She stared at him, not with surprise, not even with a squeal like some women might do, just stared, and dangled her keys between her strong fingers and watched him.

"What the hell do you want?" she asked.

"Two bags."

"And you're going to pay how this time?

He pulled the roll of cash out of his pants pocket. She took the money and counted it as she walked through the side door. Woody followed her inside.

"You're going to have to wait. I've had a long drive and I stink."

While Ada showered, Woody made his phone call. It took Ada twenty minutes. Woody listened to the sounds from the bathroom, the fan sucking the hot air up into the ceiling vent, the blow dryer whining. Then all was quiet and in the quiet Woody heard the Camaro pull up outside her house followed by the protest of heavy car doors opening and the crash as they were slammed shut. Before the men had reached Ada's stoop, Woody had the front door open and greeted them on the steps. He led them inside.

As Ada walked down the hall and entered the room, she was in time to see two men making themselves comfortable on her couch, "Who the hell are you?" she asked and glared at Woody.

"Ada, this is Mark and Sim Foss, friends of mine."

Sim stood up, padded his coat pocket, and said, "Sit down cow. We want to talk." Woody watched Ada obediently and without comment sit on her couch and look up at Sim Foss expectantly. She didn't seem like such a ball buster now.

—

It took an hour of patient listening and groveling before Sim Foss shut his flapping mouth and the smirk on Woody's face disappeared. Ada knew all about the proper behavior when confronted with douchebags like these guys. Woody was a kiss ass, a complete Igor to Sim's Frankenstein. And Sim's brother Mark? Well, Mark had a few screws loose too. Only Mark wasn't as vicious as his older brother. She could probably deal with Mark. Thank God, she'd managed to dump Carolina and the kid before Woody showed up. Her problem now was getting rid of these stinkers.

She'd had plenty of time to figure out that Sim wanted something for nothing. While he yapped on and on, she thought about what she could afford to lose and decided that giving the brothers her cocaine was well worth her life. He'd convinced her nearly twenty minutes into his rant. She didn't want to let on though and she was patient. She didn't want to appear too eager or he'd think she had more to hide.

"You see how working my neighborhood has been a mistake, don't you?" Sim finished leaning in, so his stinky breath stirred the hair on her forehead.

"I didn't know. Nobody told me this was your, ah, neighborhood," Ada said all of the sudden having an overwhelming urge to laugh out loud. The whole stupid scene reminded her of West Side Story. Where had Sim come from anyway? He sounded like a wannabe mob boss, "Okay, what do you want from me?"

He slapped her so hard she toppled onto her side. She lay there thinking that he might be a spaghetti sucker, but she couldn't let her feelings of contempt show on her face and rather than jump up and make a run for it she would wait patiently for him to finish hitting her. She was a bit surprised when he stepped back and watched her with a smile, "Tell Woody where you keep your stash and maybe I won't kill you."

Ada carefully pushed herself up to a sitting position and looked straight into Woody's eyes. Even though she was careful to keep her thoughts to herself Woody flinched, "I gave my stuff to the gyp."

"She's lying," Woody said moving as if to he wanted to punch her himself.

"Where do you think I've been all damned night, Woody? I've been on the road driving to Idaho and back. You think I did that for the fun of it?"

K McVere

Sim looked at his brother than at Woody and gestured between Ada and Woody, "Are we talking about Vera? She knows where Vera lives?"

This was Ada's opportunity to give back, "Woody knows where she is. He told me he'd found her. She's living on some big farm in Mintlaw, Idaho. It's some dinky farming town between Marsing and Homedale. Some old couple felt sorry for her and gave her their run-down farmhouse. The house looks like it has got leprosy but oh well, now she can pretend she's a regular person and not the scum of the earth she really is. I bet the Vlasky family love the fact that their daddy's widow is living so close to them. You remember Arthur Vlasky don't you Woody? Vera's ex-husband, the one she married after dumping you?"

"I was in prison. She didn't dump me. He was an old man with money. He had maybe a few good years left in him."

"I heard different," Ada began. "I heard Arthur Vlasky made her feel safe and she just knew he would protect her from a crook like you. Yeah. He protected her by driving them both into a mountain, killing himself, and marking up that 'face' you have the hots for."

Sim stepped between them, pointed his finger at Woody and said, "You lied to me," then turned and glared at Ada and said to her. "You're going to take us to her house and we're gonna get my cocaine."

He glanced over his shoulder at his brother, "You follow in the Lincoln."

Mark protested, "Why don't we take your Camaro? It's faster."

"You're taking my Camaro home and bring your Lincoln here. I'll keep an eye on them until you get back. When we're ready we'll all go to Idaho and visit our old friend."

Ada corrected Sim in her head: *The proper term is "bringing not bring" dumb shit, Ada thought; it's called parallelism, ass wipe. Not taking and bring, ass wipe, dumb shit, shit, shit. Taking and bringing. Okay?* She so wanted to smash in his face. No, better yet, she would squeeze his nuts until he screamed for mercy. Resigned to doing nothing for now, she leaned back and stared at the front door. A few hours ago, dumping Carolina and Kat practically on Vera's doorstep had seemed fucking hilarious.

Now what? She forced herself not to look at the garage door where she knew her van waited for her. Sim might buy the idea she was scared shitless. Yet, Woody wouldn't, not if he noticed her interest in the garage. Um hum. Woody wouldn't. She swallowed the hysterical giggle bubbling up in her throat. Woody wouldn't, would he? Woody may seem like an idgit most of the time, but he had an uncanny knack for sniffing out the truth.

Woody looked so dismayed by the turn of events that Ada wanted to laugh in his face. Unfortunately, now all her plans were awry. She loved that word. It was so fancy. Yes. And knowing fancy words reminded her. She was damned smart. All her teachers knew she was smart and told her so and said if she only did this or that she'd go places. What a bunch of losers.

After Mark left, Sim ordered Woody to sit next to Ada on the couch and he sat in the chair facing the front door with a gun resting in his lap. He might even know how to use it. No sense in testing him.

—

By the time Mark returned to Winnemucca and stepped inside Ada Aleshire's house with the Lincoln Continental parked in her driveway, Woody was sitting down to breakfast which Ada Aleshire had been forced to prepare for the three of them. The looks Ada shot his way when Sim wasn't looking made Woody choke on his scrambled eggs. He remembered what Vera used to say about Ada, how Ada never forgot an insult or an injury, never, and she had a Machiavellian way of paying back anyone stupid enough to cross her. Vera had to explain Machiavellian to him. When he read some more about Machiavellians, he enjoyed pontificating on the subject with his customers, especially going over the details of the awesome cruelty of that fucked up family.

Sim Foss interrupted Woody's thoughts and demanded the keys to the van from Ada. He then ordered his brother to drive the Lincoln and carried the van keys out to the garage.

Ada protested, "I have to lock up the house."

"You've got a garage door opener, don't you?" Sim asked and climbed into the passenger seat of the van unlocking the driver's side door for Ada. "Get in. You're driving. Woody you'll be in the back of the van."

Woody wanted to protest but held his tongue. The look on Sim's face scared him. He waited until Sim unlocked the back of the van then he climbed inside. He swore under his breath realizing he had to sit on the dirty floor among all the cleaning equipment. He noticed the large commercial freezer set up against one side of the van bolted to the floor and heavy duty black electrical cords snaking along the inside of the van which must provide power to the freezer. The cords ran the full length of the cargo van from the driver's seat where Ada sat to the double doors in the rear.

He had to shout over the others to be heard, "Hey, why do you have a freezer in here? Isn't this van supposed to be for your rug cleaning business?"

"Shut up Woody," Ada said as she climbed into the driver's seat and waited for Foss to hand over her keys.

"Answer his question," Foss demanded holding the keys in his hand.

Ada turned her head to give Woody the stink eye and said, "This van used to be owned by a caterer. You know what that is dumbass?"

Woody didn't dignify her question with an answer.

Ada turned to face the back and glanced at the freezer, "The guy I bought the van from kept the freezer for his own personal use on long trips, so I decided to do the same."

"Look in the freezer Woody. See what she's hiding," Sim ordered.

The idea that they wouldn't have to go all the way to Idaho spurred Woody into motion. He opened the freezer lid eagerly, "Turn on the overhead. I can't see anything in here."

Ada turned on the overhead light and Woody grunted in disappointment. He slammed the lid and returned to the floor, "It's empty."

Woody heard Sim say, "Let's go."

Four hours later and several stops for gas, bathroom breaks, and munchies they finally arrived in Idaho at the intersection of US 95 and I55. It was late in the afternoon and Woody would have dearly loved a nice dinner and a couple of cold beers. Of course, now that they were in Idaho, Idaho's idea of a rest stop was a patch of dirt next to an open field of weeds and highway litter. Sim was in the front seat beside Ada and Woody was still sitting on the floor of the van like a kid. Woody heard the three of them talking, Ada, Sim, and Mark. Mark had pulled up next to the van in the Lincoln and rolled down his window ignoring Ada in the driver's seat and addressing all his remarks to his brother Sim next to her.

"So where is this farmhouse?" Mark asked lighting his cigarette and blowing the smoke out the window and into Ada's face.

Woody snickered.

Ada turned her head and gave Woody a look that promised retribution then focused her attention on Sim. She told him, "Vera's house is in Mintlaw like I told you before. It's between Marsing and Homedale. The shortest way is this two-lane highway. We head west for a couple of miles. There'll be a farm right across the road from her house and the owner's son is a cop. So, it might be better if we go the backway in. We'll have to turn around go back up U.S. 95 and turn right onto Poison Creek Road. It's a dirt road and bumpy. Your brother might want to get in with us unless the Lincoln has better shocks than mine?"

Woody could hear the slam of a heavy car door and the crunch of boots on gravel as Mark exited his car and walked around the van to the cargo doors. The brief sight of the intersection showed him fields on either side of the highway. When a car carrier stopped at the intersection to wait for his chance to turn, Woody noticed the new cars on the carrier he assumed were going to some dealership in town. He was jealous, jealous of those guys who could afford those beauties. He would love to be driving one of those fine-looking rides right now. While Mark climbed in the back of the van with a six pack of beer in one hand and his sunglasses in the other, Woody was forced to lean sideways to get a better view of the new cars.

Once Mark shut the door, Woody could no longer see all the cars. Woody changed his mind, the car carrier was probably on its way to Oregon because none of the farmers around here could appreciate or afford any of them. Woody knew which one he would choose if he had the money, the bright red 1985 Chevrolet Corvette convertible. Mark glared at Woody as if to say what the hell are you staring at? Obviously, Mark had no appreciation for luxury, beauty, and speed.

When Ada started the van up, Mark settled down facing Woody and proceeded to light himself a cigarette. "Hey, no smoking in my van," she called over her shoulder.

"Screw you. I'll do what I like," Mark told her, taking a deep drag on the cancer stick.

Ada stopped the van so suddenly Mark and Woody nearly fell over onto the floor, "There are combustibles back there, Mr. Foss, stuff I use for my carpet cleaning business, ammonia and other shit. Do you want to blow us up?"

From the front, Woody heard Sim order his brother to put out his cigarette.

It was a damned good thing he did because once they were on Poison Creek Road and Sim had to climb out several times to open the barbed wire gates to let the van through, they were jostled and jolted along the rutted shit-eating road and a lit cigarette would have ended up on the floor of the van anyway. That didn't stop Mark from trying to take a sip of his beer. Most of the beer ended up on his chin, his jeans, and the van.

While they made their miserable way over the rocks that seemed to be everywhere, Woody tried to peek out the window to see where they were going while keeping an eye on the back of Sim's head. The crazy bastard was looking unhappier by the second. Try being in the back, dickhead. An hour later, at long last, after making their way up a hairpin dirt road just on the edge of a long drop, they finally came to a plateau. Once on top of the hill, they had to continue down a stretch of old road full of weeds and musky smelling bushes where it appeared no one human had been in a long time. Woody was grateful when they cleared a rocky bend, bounced over a cattle guard, and stopped.

Ada turned off the engine.

Woody was relieved to be out of the stuffy hot vehicle. He took a deep breath of the cool mountain air and looked around. It looked as if they were up high but there were rock cliffs on both sides of the rutted road. It looked like it hadn't been used in a long time. There was grass and weeds growing in the middle of the road and the van really couldn't go any further. At the other end where the road seemed to drop into an abyss, he could see a barricade of boulders. Maybe there was a sheer drop beyond the road? Between the cattle guard they had crossed and the gully a few feet from where he was standing was a clump of thorny bushes. Half in and half out of the gully below him grew several old willows. They were gigantic. Their leaves shaded them and the van.

He watched as Ada and Sim stood in front of the van and argued. Finally, Sim must have agreed to whatever Ada said because he climbed back into the van leaving the door open. Mark had gone off to stand behind the willow tree and piss. Woody went over to stand near Sim's door.

"So, is she going to Vera's house now?" Woody asked nodding his head in Ada's direction as he watched her walk purposely toward the end of the road where the barricade of rocks warned drivers not to go any further. She slipped between two boulders and disappeared from view. When Sim didn't answer him, Woody looked up. Sim was staring at him with a speculative look as if wondering if he could trust him.

Mark showed up and lit a cigarette. He was in the act of taking a deep satisfying drag off the cigarette his expression blissful.

"Mark, you watch the van and make sure the bitch doesn't come back and try to take off. Woody and I are going to see what she's doing."

They walked side by side toward the barricade. By the time they got to the line of rocks, they could see the valley below. About a mile away, they could see the road and cars moving fast along its two lanes of blacktop. To their right they could see some sort of fancy red brick building encircled in fancy iron fencing with manicured lawns. The high-pitched caterwauling of children carried to them from across the field. The fancy school and the playground looked odd with the miles of farmland and tiny farmhouses. In fact, the school looked as if it belonged in some snooty big city.

Beyond the school, he could see a new subdivision and construction going on with several two-story houses already built. Expensive vehicles were parked in the driveways. Then he turned to look to his left and that's when he spotted a well beaten path along the edge of the hill winding its way toward an old farmhouse. He saw signs that someone had been making improvements on the property. There was a fresh coat of paint on the house and a new roof and the beginnings of a garden in the back. With a jolt he realized that that was where Vera lived. She might be down there right now. He searched for her and for Ada. Evidently, Sim was looking for Ada as well and from his expression getting madder by the minute.

They both saw Ada at the same time. Instead of being anywhere near the farmhouse, she was on the highway with her thumb out. She looked up and saw them on the hill and began frantically waving her arms. A farm truck carrying a big plastic canister of liquid in the truck bed stopped and she spoke to the driver. After a few minutes of earnest discussion, the driver opened the passenger door and she climbed inside.

"Oh, you lying-filthy-bitch," Sim growled. Woody wanted to scream her name and shake her until her neck cracked. But it was too late. The truck took off down the road. Sim was trying to fish something out of his pocket. Woody hoped it wasn't a gun or knife.

"Did you see the license plate number?" he said pulling a small notebook out of the back pocket of his jeans.

"No. I can't see anything from here."

A deep booming voice shouted at them, "What are you doing here? This place is private. We have permission to be here. You don't. Go away."

Woody looked at the man. He carried a white bucket and wore dirty overalls and hiking boots. He was more than seven feet tall, a gigantic man with huge muscles. His legs looked like the muscled limbs of a wrestler and his biceps rippled with every movement. He looked as if he could easily crush their heads between his hands. The group behind him frightened Woody more. Sim noticed them too. There were about seven ordinary people of different ages and professions with the giant and they also carried buckets. An older woman walked up to the angry man, "Now Daniel, this is public land. These people have every right to be here too. Let's keep moving and leave them alone to appreciate the scenery. Sorry folks. Have a lovely day."

Woody was in a shit load of trouble.

It didn't take a rocket scientist to know he was now Sim's hostage. Ada had gotten away. He was the one who told Sim about Ada's drug business. Sim would hold him responsible for losing the cocaine. Maybe Vera had the cocaine. Woody didn't think so though. He was sure Ada knew where it was and it sure as hell wasn't anywhere near Vera, the woman Ada hated the most. At that moment, Woody was trying to convince the Foss brothers of this fact, "I thought Ada's story was fishy. Ada wouldn't trust Vera to take care of her stuff. She must have left the cocaine at home. She's probably on her way back there now."

The speculative look Sim gave him made his stomach sink. And then his brother Mark came to Woody's rescue, "It can't hurt to check. Let's go back to her place and see."

Sim glared at his brother, "Then what was she doing out all night in the van? Was she just joy-riding in the middle of the night? Cleaning carpets? Sleeping with some shit uglier than her? So, what was she doing for ten hours, smartass? You called me several times yesterday whining about how long she'd been gone. If she wasn't in Idaho hiding the cocaine on Vera's property what was she doing?"

"I don't know."

"Well, we're going to wait until dark and go down to the farmhouse and find out, you understanding me?"

"Yeah, sure."

Mark leaned toward his brother, "Let's get out of here. That lady is staring at us. You want her to remember the van and our faces?"

They waited for Sim to come to a decision and realize staying put wasn't an option. Sim climbed into the van. Ada had left the keys in the ignition. Mark wrapped his arm around Woody's shoulder for the benefit of the rock hounds who were busy searching the ground and tapping rocks. Mark pretended to hug Woody and with a strong grip on him dragged him toward the back of the carpet cleaning van, "Climb in good buddy."

Chapter Eight

Maggie said nothing about Vera Lee at dinner on Tuesday evening. Andrew explained the scream she had heard was because Vera had fallen from a ladder. He finished by praising Maggie's neighborly concern. Maggie had her doubts about Vera's version though. That scream hadn't been the scream of surprise. No. She'd been screaming bloody murder. At dinner, her parents talked about the missing child exclusively as if there wasn't any other news and Murray consumed his food as if it were his last meal. Maggie facing the kitchen window was the first person to see her Uncle Andrew approach the house. Everybody in town came to the backdoor. Only lost motorists, salesmen and Jehovah's Witnesses knocked on the front door. Her Dad jumped up before she could and swung the door open, "Your timing is impeccable Andy; we were just sitting down to supper. Come on in."

Tonight, Andrew wore his nicest clothes: pressed stone washed blue jeans, a tailored polo shirt, and a pair of comfortable canvas shoes. He smelled of aftershave and cologne. As her brother Cody would often joke, Andy had on his professional trawler duds. Maggie's father had to explain what trawling meant in Cody's lexicon. Trawling was Cody's euphemism for men fishing but not for fish. In this case, trawling meant fishing for women in nightclubs. Ou-la-la.

Andrew grabbed a plate, a fork, and a knife with customary efficiency and sat himself down next to Maggie.

"Hey Mouse, you feeling better now?" he asked.

"OK," Maggie said. "I guess."

"Just ok?"

"Well, yeah I guess so. It was scary thinking that Vera might be hurt, and I couldn't help her. It was funny when Dad peeked in her window though," Maggie said as she glanced at her father and smiled. "Dad had to stand on tiptoe. He looked like a burglar."

Maggie paused wondering how her mother would react to her other news, "When I stopped by Vera's house, we talked about the little girl and other things. She gave me a soda then we saw Daniel Harden. Daniel made her nervous. I tried to explain that he's harmless. I don't think she believed me. She told me to stay away from him. I guess she's never been around people like Daniel before. And that's why I was so scared when I heard her scream. I thought maybe she'd seen Daniel again."

Uncle Andrew appeared interested in what Maggie had to say, "Ms. Lee may be naïve about autistic children and the disabled, but she doesn't strike me as prejudiced one way or another. She handled Baby Jane Doe just fine."

"Baby Jane Doe," Maggie's mother said quizzically. "That's what you're calling her?"

Andrew grinned up at Maggie's mother standing by the stove, "Yes, Rachel, until we locate her next of kin, that's what Metcalf and the others are calling her—Baby Jane Doe."

Murray ignored their conversation and asked for the bread and butter. Maggie's father without a word handed him the butter dish and a plate of sliced bread. Her father and Murray had been arguing again Maggie guessed probably about the farm.

Maggie sat up straighter in her chair, "Oh, oh, now I remember what I wanted to tell you Uncle Andrew! Listen!"

He jumped back in his chair with his hands raised in surrender and an astonished look on his face imitating the excitement in her voice, "Great Scot! Yes, do tell!"

Maggie slapped him on the shoulder, "Stop teasing me. This is serious."

He put on his serious face, "Please, proceed to enlighten me."

Maggie's father chuckled, "If that's supposed to be an imitation of me, I'm insulted."

Would everybody please listen," Maggie pleaded, familiar with the way her family jumped from one topic to another and that she rarely if ever managed to hold onto the conversation without someone jumping in and interrupting her.

Andrew gave her his full attention. Maggie continued, "You know when I saw Daniel at Vera's house; he was cutting across her property to get up to the hills beyond. He goes there often, you know. I've seen him looking for rocks and things in some of the old pilings. You know the one's I'm talking about Dad, what I used to call Rock Castle City."

Kit Treloar looked up from his plate, "Do you remember what I said about digging in the hills?"

"I don't take a shovel Dad," Maggie said quickly defending herself from another lecture. "I just look on the ground and pick up cool rocks. Honest."

Her uncle sipped his iced tea and appeared to consider her idea seriously as if she were one of his contemporaries at the police station, then he shifted in his seat slightly to give her his full attention, "It might be difficult to get any information out of Daniel. Have you considered that?"

"He loves to talk about rocks, Uncle Andrew," Maggie said.

"I know he does and little else."

"He might have seen the girl and maybe someone who was with her. He might let something slip. He's done it before. He got Joann in trouble when he told Ms. Mathews that she took naps during the afternoon like the little kids. It wasn't deliberate or anything. I mean, he wasn't trying to get Joann into trouble, just telling Ms. Mathews what he'd seen."

Andrew laughed so loud he made Murray jump in his seat. "Sorry Dad," patting the arm of his father's wheelchair. "Maggie's tickling me."

Maggie's parents responded differently. She couldn't tell whether the teacher's naps bothered her father or amused him. Her mother's frown reminded Maggie of her disapproval of the unskilled and downright lazy people schools sometimes hired to oversee children.

"It's not like that Mom. Joann is a good teacher. She works long hours and sometimes the kids just wear her out. Really, the kids love her."

Uncle Andrew bit into his chicken and after swallowing interrupted Rachel's tirade about the class of person such institutions attracted by saying, "I may need your help on this one Maggie since you know Daniel better than I do. He might feel more comfortable talking to me if you're along. What do you think?"

Maggie jumped at the chance to ride with her uncle and said quickly before her parents had second thoughts, "Sure, I'd be glad to help out."

"I'll swing by tomorrow and pick you up around eight or so, How's that?"

"Well the school doesn't open until nine thirty," Maggie told him.

"Then I'll come by for breakfast and we'll go together. Is that a plan?"

Maggie agreed and studiously avoided her mother's eye knowing full well that her mother disapproved of her working at the school. Her father beamed at her. Unfortunately for Maggie having two teachers as parents meant that she had to excel in all her course work and if she failed in one area, they were prone to give her extra assignments at home until her grades improved. None of Maggie's friends had to deal with so much extra homework. Sometimes Maggie wished she had regular parents, parents who hardly remembered there was such a thing as homework. Then Maggie remembered Vera telling her how she had had only a fourth-grade education and taught herself to read. Maybe Maggie didn't have it so bad after all.

—

The heat had collected in the house during the day and even with the windows open and the fans moving air about, the heat preferred to remain inside. It was so hot that the paint dried on the brush before she could get it on the wall. Vera threw her paintbrush. The brush hit the unpainted wall, leaving an imprint of blue droplets like tears radiating toward the window. Vera stood in the center of the room, her bare feet standing on old newspapers with paint drying on her body. The skin beneath the paint tightened. She glanced down at her bare legs. A blotch of paint had dried on her right knee. She bent her knee and the paint cracked. Vera picked up her brush from the floor, wrapped the brush in a sandwich bag, tightened the bag around the handle with a rubber-band, and stuck the brush in the refrigerator. She hammered the lid back on the paint can, switched off the light in the bedroom, and in the bathroom tried to wash the paint off her cheek, her hands, her elbow, her knee, and the bottoms of her feet.

Without much conscious thought, Vera changed into a clean pair of shorts and cotton blouse, grabbed her purse, and drove into the tiny town of Mintlaw, population 806, make that 807, she thought, her mind on ice cream and an iced coffee at the local drive-in. It wasn't until she was almost at O'Reilly's Ice Cream Shack; she remembered little Mintlaw didn't have iced coffee. This wasn't Seattle after all.

Vera pulled up to the drive-in window ten minutes before closing. The clerk took her order with a smile which still managed to amaze Vera. Most fast food establishments these days employed the young and the impatient. Yet in this small town, she supposed the employees knew everyone and anticipated seeing them again, so the savvy ones refrained from annoying their customers. As Vera waited for her order, a familiar Jeep pulled up next to her car. She glanced at the man in the vehicle and recognized Andrew Treloar at the wheel. He leaned toward her with his arm resting on his car door.

"Evening Ms. Lee."

Vera acknowledged him then turned back to accept the clerk's change.

"Would you mind pulling over to that parking area," Treloar said pointing to his right. "I've thought of a few more questions to ask you. It won't take but a minute."

The sweet kid handed her a brown box. Something stopped her from complaining about her order. She thought the clerk had mixed up the orders. When she glanced inside and discovered the clerk had prepared a sixteen-ounce glass of coffee mixed with ice cubes, a small carton of chocolate milk, and an extra-large portion of banana split which included a long handled red spoon, Vera gave the young woman a generous tip, "You're a life saver. Thank you."

"Anytime Ma'am," the young woman said with a grin. "I remember you from last time. You asked for an Iced Mocha that time too."

With reluctance Vera parked her car in the spot Treloar suggested and when he climbed out of his vehicle, Vera followed suit, thankful that he hadn't climbed into her car to have a chat. Vera had never met Treloar before Friday night; yet, gossip had a way of circulating quickly through Mintlaw even landing in the vicinity of new neighbors. Vera had heard enough about Treloar's reputation as a ladies' man from conversations she had heard between clerks and customers in the one grocery store in town Peterson's Grocers and at the one and only restaurant Lucy's Diner. Before Vera had ever met him, she remembered Beatrice talking to a customer about the Treloar black book and how his book had more pages than Boise's Phone Directory.

Treloar held a notebook and a pen in his hands and flipped to a blank page then began the cross examination, "You said that it was about midnight when you heard someone on the swing set. May I ask why you didn't call the police as soon as you discovered the child?"

Vera leaned against the passenger door of her vehicle and crossed her arms then uncrossed her arms knowing that her body language might betray her, "I've gone over this with you before," she began and then sighed. "I don't know why I didn't call them right away to be honest. I was tired and half asleep. I guess I thought the police station might be closed until morning. Actually, I wasn't sure who to call. Where is the police station anyway? The phone doesn't list a Mintlaw Police Department."

"I see," Treloar said. "Well, perhaps you have an old phone book. Mintlaw citizens are taken care of by both the Homedale and Mintlaw Police. We even have the Owyhee County Sheriff's Department keeping an eye on us. Contrary to popular myth, citizens in this county receive the same service citizens in Boise enjoy. Next time, just give Homedale Police a call and they'll switch you over to our dispatch office, ok?"

"I will," Vera said, using the excuse of leaning inside her vehicle to retrieve her drink in order to hide her annoyance. The undercurrent of amused speculation in his eyes made her nervous. She was probably older than him, yet he treated her as if she were a child. Vera sipped her drink and stared at his hands. His fingers were long and supple. He kept his nails trimmed and clean. In fact, her senses were receiving more details as she tried to relax, how his cologne smelled wonderful reminding her of something outdoorsy maybe wild grasses. He looked dressed for a date in his fancy polo shirt, pressed jeans, and preppy shoes.

"Now then, you say that you heard nothing but the creaking of the swing set. Are you sure you didn't hear a car driving past your house or any other sound you couldn't identify with the normal night sounds around here?"

Vera tried to remember if she'd heard any other sound. She wanted the child's parents to be found just as much as Treloar. He waited for her response. She should have known the man wasn't a police officer. Vera had encountered the breed before. Most police she had met in her life were humorless and prone to consider a person guilty based on looks, class, and attitude. The policemen she'd encountered in her life seemed to think Roma were subhuman and treated them accordingly. Her mother remarked once that homeless and undocumented immigrants received better treatment than Roma.

Vera remembered only two incidents that proved her mother right. One had been when they had camped on private property and two patrol cars showed up with the cops ordering them to vacate the premises. While still in her pajamas, she and her family were forced to pull down tents and throw all their belongings in their vehicles. Her mother drove a station wagon and her Aunt Vista drove an old bus. They were forced to leave the meadow in the middle of the night. Those few who owned trailers or campers simply collected their lawn chairs and tables and drove away.

But her mother had to struggle with the tent and roll up their sleeping bags before departing. None of the policemen offered to help her. Vera's youngest half-brother Gordo had been two at the time and clung to Vera's mother making her task even more cumbersome. Vera remembered sitting in the grass staring at the guns in their holsters too frightened to move. Eventually, Vera had to carry Gordo across the meadow and deposit him among the bedrolls where her younger siblings were curled up in the back of the station wagon. Vera remembered the police standing on the roadside near their patrol vehicles with arms crossed and eyes watchful. Vera would never forget them.

The other time had been when she was riding in the back of her Cousin Tony's old Chevy pickup with some of his friends. The police had stopped them at a diner near Eureka, California. Vera noticed how they were prepared for trouble with holsters unsnapped. They came at the truck from either side like wolves circling prey. Vera had grown accustomed to mistrustful looks even homeless people looked at them as if they might cheat them or steal from them. When she reached her teens, Vera had to endure cat calls and insulting come-ons from strange males.

Yet that day, she had experienced a new reality, the wary coldness of policemen who were convinced Tony and she and her other relatives were gang members. Some overzealous citizen on the road had radioed the police to tell them a gang of kids had been driving drunk. The police had assumed Tony's vehicle had been stolen. Once Tony had shown the cop his proper papers and remained calm and polite proving he wasn't intoxicated by taking the nose test and the walking forwards and backwards test, the police left. Their mistrust stayed behind in the memories of Vera and Tony and the others. Vera's future encounters with the police left her feeling dirty as if a standard had been set and she did not measure up.

Yet times were different now. She was a homeowner. She owned property. She had a few bucks in the bank. Nobody knew she was Roma here. Most people treated her as if she were ordinary. Not even Joshua Adams and the other members of AA knew the truth about her and she trusted them more than she had ever trusted anyone. This man though, this wannabe cop didn't appear easily convinced of anything. He pretended to be easy going and friendly. It was a clever way to get people feeling comfortable and when people trusted you they talked. Vera wasn't going to play his game. She sensed steel under the smile.

Vera accepted her dreams as legitimate expressions of reality. Treloar didn't appear to be the kind of man who would accept a dream as evidence. Vera felt an overwhelming compulsion to tell him about her dream though. She was amazed at how patient he stood there waiting for her response. Enough time must have passed for most people to start feeling uncomfortable. She'd been arguing with herself for a while now. She looked up from the ground where she'd been daydreaming and noticed Treloar had moved. He had opened his car door and settled himself on the bucket seat with his notebook and pen resting on his left leg. Vera straightened and moved closer to his vehicle.

"You're probably going to think I'm crazy or something, but just before I woke, I'm not sure what time it was, it could have been a few minutes before or even an hour before I heard the creak of the swing set, I dreamed about my Aunt Vista slamming her car door over and over again. Then I saw my Uncle Frank pushing his chair, you know those fancy chairs, leather chairs with the little wheels on the legs, yes those, he was pushing his chair across the rocks. Sounds crazy huh?"

Treloar made a few notes, threw his notebook and pen on the passenger seat and climbed out of the car, "No, it doesn't sound crazy to me. You told me the other night that your bedroom window was open. That's how you could hear the creaking of the swing set. Perhaps earlier you heard what sounded like a car door slamming and inserted the sound into your dream. The chair doesn't make sense though. I'll have to think about that one."

Treloar looked up at her and smiled. His finger pointed at her throat, "You've got something on your neck."

Vera rubbed at the spot, "I've been painting."

In the semi-dark where they stood with the florescent lights of the drive-in casting the parking lot in shades of amber, Vera could see the whiteness of his teeth between his lips. He had nice lips. Vera looked down at his shoes.

He moved closer.

Vera took a few steps back, "How's the little girl? Have you located her parents?" There was something about Treloar, the way he stood with his shoulders erect and arms relaxed at his sides which made Vera's pulse race. His striking blue eyes and long lashes weren't bad either, all together a perfect package. Yet he was an odd-ball, she reminded herself. He might even be delusional.

Watch yourself Vera—you've been taken in before.

Treloar ran a hand through his dark hair and let down his guard enough to reveal his frustration, "No news as of yet. Social Services found a temporary home for her in Boise. We don't have the necessary facilities to keep her in Mintlaw. In a few days, they'll take the case away from us and the feds will probably step in to solve this one. The local police can handle child abuse cases but kidnapping over state lines, that's different. I'd really like to find the degenerate that would dump a kid off in the desert in the middle of the night."

Treloar continued to surprise Vera. Under the assumption the interview was over, Vera started moving toward her car.

"You probably don't remember me," Treloar said.

Vera froze. "No," Vera lied. "I'm sure we've never met."

"We did. It was back in 1973. You were in a car accident and pretty banged up, that's probably why you don't remember me. Your husband was driving a Firebird as I recall. I wanted to say something the other day, but I figured it was the wrong time, wrong place."

"I'll never forget it. I'm sorry though, I don't remember you," Vera said in a breathless voice anxious to leave. "That was ten years ago, goodness what a phenomenal memory you have."

Treloar followed her. Vera hadn't expected him to do that. She opened her car door and slipped inside. Treloar placed his hands on her car door and leaned in. There was something else she detected in his expression, a sorrow she couldn't comprehend.

"Just out of curiosity what made you move back to this part of the country?"

Vera started her car, "My ice cream is melting. I should get home now."

"Don't be afraid, Ms. Lee."

"I'm not afraid."

Treloar straightened and tucked his hands in his pants pockets, "Sure thing, thanks for the information. If we learn anything further, we'll let you know."

Once safely in her house with her melted banana split sitting in the sink, she dropped fresh ice cubes into her coffee and poured the chocolate milk into the glass now a warm watery sort of Mocha. She sat in the dark kitchen contemplating the view outside her bay window. She could see the shadowy outline of the swing set leaning like a drunk. The swing set had become a symbol of trouble. It had attracted an odd little girl and brought the police into her home.

So, what if Andrew had brought up old memories and seemed uncomfortably curious about her, his gorgeousness compensated for his other defects. The fact that he was not only handsome, but smart made him even more dangerous. And now a further foreboding washed over her, the FBI might soon involve itself in the case. There would be more intrusions into her privacy, more questions and background checks. She couldn't run away; she was trapped in the home she once believed would make her respectable in the eyes of the world.

This time, she'd done nothing wrong. Ten years ago, she'd wished a man dead and the wish had been fulfilled. In her family to ill-wish someone had consequences. Vera had gone beyond ill-wishing back then. She'd used a talisman and a curse. Vera pulled the necklace out of her coat pocket and held the thing away from her body as if it might contaminate her. Ten years ago, she'd spent thirty days dreaming about her husband dying. And when Arthur Vlasky had dragged her out of the house on that Halloween night, drunk and crazy, she had been wearing the necklace; she could feel its smoothness next to her skin. She'd prayed to the night, to her Nonnie, to any ancestor listening so that her misery would end. She had been hoping they both would die. But fate had allowed her to live. Perhaps meeting Treloar tonight hadn't been such a coincidence. Perhaps she had called him to her.

The moonlight allowed Vera enough illumination to bury the necklace. She'd chosen a spot near the barn, so that if necessary she could retrieve the round cake tin without too much trouble. Vera held the cake tin next to her chest. She'd wrapped the necklace in a soft cloth and put it inside. Now she wondered if she was a fool. Away from the comforting light of her kitchen, standing here beside the barn, she could imagine her Nonnie frowning down at her in perplexed contemplation and hear her say, "What's the matter with you child? Do you really think you have power over life and death? If you're so powerful, how come your still alone and unhappy and poor?"

On the gold painted lid Santa Clause rode through a winter's snowy night. The motif seemed an inappropriate container for what lay inside. The necklace had once been a gift from someone she dearly loved and missed. The necklace had giving the young Vera a sense of security and belonging. Ten years ago, she had perverted the gift's true purpose. She had directed all her humiliation and hate at the tiger eye allowing the necklace to become the recipient of ugly evil thoughts. It was tainted now.

She'd wished him dead, wished him dead every morning when she woke, every evening when she got ready for bed, for thirty days straight. Vera dropped the cake tin into the hole and covered the hole with dirt. If she'd had a wood stove, she would have thrown the necklace into the fire. When the sun rose above the hill, Vera finally felt tired enough to sleep. The sound of an ambulance and several police sirens woke her around three o'clock the following afternoon.

——

Andrew watched Vera Lee drive away. The scent of her remained behind. He tried to place it, vanilla, no, cinnamon, yes definitely cinnamon. It was nearly ten thirty before he arrived at Prairie Star Estates. Andrew stood before the woman's house without knocking. She must have heard him climb the steps to her door. The door opened, and Andrew could smell the floral scent of a plug-in deodorizer. The smell clashed with her heavy jasmine perfume. He entered the hall breathing in a mixture of scents: Pine Sol, Windex, lemon furniture polish; all sorts of cleansers and deodorizers assaulted his nostrils, scents to cover up smells and scents to remind people of cleanliness.

The room was immaculate, not a pillow out of place, not a wine glass out of order. The appliances gleamed. As his shoes brushed against the carpet another floral scent rose up from the floor and clogged his nose making him sneeze. She had a bottle uncorked. She poured him a drink. Andrew drank it down in two gulps, set the wine glass on the polished coffee table, and over the country western wailing said, "I can't stay long."

She looked disappointed and sat down next to him on the couch, "Why? Is there another emergency?"

"You've been following the news?"

"Oh, you mean the kid they found," she said. "Yeah, I heard."

"Well we're going to be working around the clock trying to solve this one. I just don't have time to go off and leave Steven to take care of things. And the weekend in McCall, I'll have to cancel, sorry."

He stood up his eyes burning from all the scented products in the air noticing how the vaulted ceiling fan spinning round and round blew cold air mixed with dust modes down upon them. In desperation he said, "I've got to go. Sorry. I'm meeting Steven at the office."

She followed him to the door, her mouth slightly open in dismay, still holding her wine glass. Andrew noticed for the first time that she wore a black lace nightie.

—

Daniel lay down on the cot in the shop and listened to the silence. The cot was a little small, but he liked it anyway. He had a comfortable pillow and some army blankets. His rocks were on the workbench ready for him. Mz. Matthews had given him a locker and some drawers made of clear plastic from the D & B to store his clothes in. She even promised to find him a radio and television set. Daniel had turned off the swamp cooler, so he could hear the sounds outside, the night noises of traffic in the distance, a cricket singing to his mate, a dog or maybe a coyote barking at the moon.

—

Vera sat in her kitchen in the dark and listened to the music. It was The Woods of Old Limerick on her turntable. The music filled the room and reminded her of other moments of longing and joy.

K McVere

Vera hadn't danced since the age of twelve. She danced in the room, arms extended, remembering the little girl who danced as her mother played the pipes. Her bare feet rubbed against the wood floor marking the house as her own.

Chapter Nine

T reloar arrived at his father's farm a little before eight o'clock, sober with his gut twisted in knots after two nights spent in his apartment alone wondering what had gotten into him lately. He'd arrived Monday night at Metcalf's house prepared for good food and good company. Metcalf had invited a few other patrolmen and a couple of his wife's single friends. After an hour of watching the two women use their maneuvers on him: wriggling of hips, flinging of hair, pouting of lips Treloar began to feel cornered and left early. And last night, after leaving Prairie Star Estates, he'd unplugged his phone and sat in front of the television watching a movie. When the movie ended, he couldn't recall what it had been about or why he'd wasted his time.

This morning, even though he had had plenty of rest, he felt tired and irritable. He could have kicked himself when he drove past Vera's house and all the hairs on his arms stood at attention with extra blood coursing through a vein he used to have power over. His response to Vera reminded him of his adolescent insanities.

She was completely wrong for him.

He'd never been attracted to her type of female, liberal feminists with their loose peasant dresses and wall to wall bookcases.

She probably spoke a dozen languages and read Sartre for fun.

While interviewing her about Baby Jane Doe he'd noticed her collection of books: Camus, Marquez, Joyce, Woolf, and Vonnegut. In college, he'd met women like her – smart, opinionated, and independent. He knew if he were around them too long, he would end up forced to defend his choices in life which would lead to quarrels.

So, he avoided them.

And avoiding such women had made life so much more peaceful, so much healthier.

She would make his life miserable in the long run.

Yet, she had courage.

And she was kind.

He suspected she even had a sense of humor.

Why had she come back here, especially right on the doorstep of her late husband's home? The Vlaskys are arrogant ass-wipes, the kind of gluttonous tightwads that never tip anyone and drink themselves into a mental stupor. It was no surprise to Andrew that the elder Vlasky's Firebird ended up wrapped around a boulder. His first sight of Vera Vlasky had been a shock. He heard through the grapevine Vlasky had found himself a young wife. Somehow, he'd never expected to see the likes of her with the likes of him. He'd been expecting some silly vacuous female who'd managed to seduce the old geezer into marriage.

Andrew turned into the driveway leading to the Treloar farm and just by his proximity to Vera's home no longer felt tired or dispirited. Someone had once said maturity brought dullness to the senses. They were wrong. Andrew's senses were at a peak that made him jumpy. Jumpy was not good. Jumpy got you into trouble. He made himself picture Vera nagging him to join the Communist Party. He couldn't sustain the picture. She didn't strike him as an anarchist.

Last night at the drive-in she barely spoke above a whisper and when she mentioned her dream, he was astonished how touched he was by her honesty and willingness to help solve his case. The way she had handled Baby Jane had been rather cute, her attitude one of perplexed affection. She seemed to instinctively understand the child's sensitivity to touch and respect her need to explore. Her boyfriend Joshua was a real tool. He'd reacted to the kid as if she was an alien from another planet, not even bothering to hide is annoyance and impatience. What did Vera see in him? He was obviously using her. If Andrew wanted to he could easily conduct a background check on the guy and find out all sorts of nasty secrets. But he wouldn't. It was none of his business.

Before Andrew entered his father's house, he thought about going over to Vera's place and finding some other reason to talk to her. A memory surfaced unbidden, Andrew remembered the coyote he'd had in his sights once. The coyote was poised on the hillside above him looking down into the chaparral with intense interest. She stood motionless for nor more than half a minute. It was weird and wonderful. She must have felt someone watching her and turned in his direction. She didn't move. When she took off with that natural loping gait down the other side of the hill, Andrew remembered he wasn't supposed to be in awe of coyotes, remembered Native Americans believed the coyote was a trickster. Yet he'd been thrilled to see her, so wild and untamed, so dismissive of him. It was as if the coyote knew he wouldn't pull the trigger, as if she knew Andrew wouldn't dare harm her.

The kitchen door opened before Andrew had a chance to grab the doorknob. Maggie's eager face looked up at him. She was dressed and ready to go. As Andrew entered the kitchen, he smelled fried bacon and hot coffee. At the breakfast table, Kit stood by the table sipping his coffee and discussing crops with Murray. Maggie chattered at Andrew. Rachel was silent throughout the meal, completely unlike herself. He knew Rachel believed everyone deserved a sound education; yet, he thought she might be worried for Maggie. Daniel wasn't a small child to be coaxed into good behavior with a cookie or a promise; he was a huge scary looking young man who could potentially hurt Maggie if he were frightened or upset with her questions.

Once outside in his Jeep with Maggie sitting up front beside him, Andrew cautioned Maggie about their interview, "Just let him do the talking, ok."

Maggie crossed her arms and stared at the highway, "No problem."

Andrew drove past the Eagle Gateway school grounds and turned onto a dirt road in order to back up and have his car facing the way he had come. Andrew wanted his vehicle off the main road under the shade near Constance Harden's property. He would rather not have nosy Mintlaw residents wondering why he was at the school.

Earlier that morning, Metcalf had bumped into him at Lucy's Diner getting a coffee to go. Rachel's coffee tasted like burned scrambled eggs, "I hear you've been doing a bit of private interviewing, Andy?"

"Speak plainly George. I've got to be on my way."

"Well a little bird told me you were interviewing the Lee woman at O'Reilly's Ice Cream Shack at closing. A bit unconventional don't ya think? Find out anything interesting?"

"No. Not really."

"The Chief says we'll be working in tandem with the Feds, but you're supposed to pass on any info you get to him."

"I know that George," and gave him a warning look. Andrew continued, "You got something else on your mind?"

George threw up his hands, "Sorry, just curious."

"You mean your wife is curious. Don't worry. The Chief will know whatever I know."

While Steven Glenjones, now Chief Steven Glenjones had been spending his youth in a college dorm back east, Andrew had been dodging bullets in Vietnam. While Steve had been surviving the police academy, Andrew had been spending time in Mexico, Alaska, Canada, and other parts of the world he no longer wanted to remember, doing idiotic stuff he most definitely wanted to forget. Sensibility returned to him when he sat in his father's parlor and looked across the room at his mother sitting in her rocking chair knitting a christening dress for another grandchild. He decided there and then to come home to Mintlaw for good.

His father had wanted him to help at the farm. Andrew chose to spend his college years learning Art History and practicing three-dimensional art. He had disappointed his father once again by avoiding any responsibility to the farm. Before Murray's stroke they had come to an agreement. Murray wouldn't nag him and Andrew wouldn't discuss his current project. At the moment, Andrew thought about the piece left unfinished in his studio; he would have much rather been at home working on the piece than babysitting his great-niece Maggie. Such compulsions came over him without warning. This was not the time though. Steve, without saying so in so many words, had given Andrew the go ahead to do some snooping on his own. Maybe Daniel had seen something. Andrew had his doubts Daniel knew anything about the abandoned child; Daniel seemed too obsessed by his rock collection to care about anything else.

The Chief had told him, "You've got a knack for uncovering dirt, Andrew. Even as a kid, I remember how you could sniff out the most innocuous information. You can get people to confess like no one else I know. Yep. You've got a talent for this gig. You could have gone to the academy and become a detective, a really good detective. I'll never understand why you choose to spend your time soldering scraps of metal together. Seems like a strange occupation for a grown man."

Andrew stood beside his car and stared at the poplars without really seeing them. The poplars had been planted by Michael Harden, Daniel's father. Michael had met Constance in some small town in Oregon and brought her back to Idaho. They'd been married in a hurry by the Justice of the Peace and rumor was Michael had been forced to marry Constance because she was pregnant. Michael had had no intention really of joining up; yet, for some inexplicable reason a week after Andrew's older brother Stewart was shot by some unknown assailant, Michael joined the marines. Murray was convinced Michael had had something to do with Stewart's death. At the time, Andrew thought his father's grief was making him see enemies where there weren't any. Now he wondered if his father might have sensed something.

"Uncle Andrew, are you alright?" a voice asked him.

Andrew looked down and focused his eyes on Maggie's face. Maggie reminded him of Stewart.

"I knew Daniel's father," Andrew found himself saying. "His father died in Vietnam. I was thinking about Michael Harden. Michael was so proud of his son. Then he learned that Daniel was disabled. Michael would never acknowledge the fact. He kept saying Daniel would grow out of it. After Tommy was born, I kind of understood a little of what Michael had been feeling – disbelief and guilt."

"Dad told me about Tommy," Maggie said not quite sure if she dared talk about him.

"Yes," Andrew said, clearing his throat of an obstruction. "Okay, let's go talk to Daniel, shall we?" He searched his back pocket. "Wait I forgot my notebook. Go ahead and let them know we're here Maggie."

Andrew returned to his Jeep and retrieved his notebook and pen.

Maggie wandered over to the gate. Attached to the gate was a black call box. She pressed the button. Andrew heard a voice bark from the speaker, "Yes. What now?"

Maggie leaned forward with her lips practically kissing the box, "It's Maggie, Mr. Peterson. Ms. Matthews knows I'm coming today. Can you open the gate please?"

Andrew flipped to a blank page and scribbled a reminder:

Michael Harden rejoins Marines November? 1974; dies February 1975 Vietnam.

Stewart Treloar dies October 31, 1974; Poison Creek Road.

Arthur Vlasky Sr dies October 31, 1973; Firebird, US 95.

Dec 2, 1973 Vera Vlasky/Lee disappears, returns to Mintlaw Mar/Apr 1985.

On a previous page he'd written down his conversation with Vera:

Baby Jane Doe May 1st, 1985 Midnight? 2 am?
Swing Set.
Brand new shorts & blouse.
Old worn tennis shoes.
Missing sock.
Needs bath & haircut.

Social Services report: child drugged, between 3-4 yrs old, no signs of sexual abuse.

No profile in database.

Found 3 miles from US 95 & 50 yards from Poison Creek Road.

Vera's dream:

1) Aunt Vista & car doors.

2) Uncle Frank & sound of someone pushing a chair across rocks.

Woodrow Kirk. Common-law husband? Las Vegas plates, prison Nebraska 1970.

Andrew had added a question mark beside Vera's name remembering her confusion after the accident, how she insisted her name was Lee, not Vlasky. Andrew added another question mark beside Woodrow Kirk's relationship with Vera. What did he want with Vera? How did Woody find out about her return to Mintlaw? Was Vera her real name? He'd done a full background check on her using several databases – the DMV and credit reports, as well as, local and federal criminal record checks and couldn't find her name in any of the databases before 1979. There should have been a marriage record for her in the early 1970s. He found nothing. Had Vlasky claimed he and Vera were married as a cruel joke?

On Halloween of 1973, Vera had been evacuated by helicopter to St. Alphonsus Hospital in Boise; her condition critical. He wasn't sure how long she'd been admitted. She disappeared right after she was released from the hospital. If he knew which city and state she had been born in, he could have contacted the county clerk's office and obtained her legal name and parentage. The fact that her credit report began in 1979 and her social security card had been issued six months prior to her establishing credit made him uneasy.

It had become routine lately for parents to apply for social security numbers for their children to claim them as dependents on their federal tax returns. Only employers hiring domestic help part-time need not require social security numbers when they file their returns and need not supply an equal amount of FICA for those types of workers. In the past, a worker would go to the social security office to apply for a card providing their birth certificate as evidence of their U.S. citizenship. Vera Lee had obtained a social security number in Vegas only a few years ago. How could she have gone all these years without one? Was she even a citizen of the U.S.? If she had been a part-time domestic, he supposed she could have gotten away with not having to file taxes. Or if she had been a farm laborer, she may have been paid with cash?

Her surname Lee sounded suspect to him too. Something Rachel had said at the Treloar Farm during dinner came to mind. In response to his remark about Vera's last name, Rachel had said something about the name coming from Lea or Leigh. She suggested the surname might be English Roma.

"I know this might sound kind of silly but from the look of her I would say there is some Roma heritage – you know, her thick black hair and skin tone and the almond shape of her eyes," she looked mildly embarrassed and rushed on. "Lee is a perfectly good English name. When I was in college, my roommate was fascinated with the history of Roma migration into England during the 13th and 14th centuries. The new immigrants borrowed the surname of wealthy landowners as a way of protecting themselves from persecution. The prejudices and scarcity of work during the 19th century forced many Roma to migrate to America. Maybe you could ask her if she has another surname. Roma families usually have a public name and a private name."

Everyone at the dinner table that night seemed to assume Rachel must be right based solely on her impromptu lecture about the history of the Roma in the United Kingdom. Well, Andrew preferred hard evidence not simply intellectual conjecture. Although the fact that Vera had obtained her social security number so late in life made him wonder if perhaps Vera might have come to the U.S. illegally or she might be using a false identity. The fact Woodrow Kirk assumed they were common-law made him wonder what kind of company she had kept in the past.

He looked at his notes again, noticing with alarm how both Stewart and Vlasky had died on October 31st. If he was a superstitious man, he might have leaped to the conclusion their deaths had something to do with black magic. What nonsense, Andrew thought. There was a logical explanation for their deaths. His brother had been shot by a criminal while pulling a driver over or by some dumb hunter shooting game at night in the Owyhees.

Studying his notes had taken at least five minutes, yet Maggie was still standing by the black box. She turned to Andrew and shouted, "Mr. Peterson says there's something wrong with the gate, maybe an electrical problem."

Maggie waited patiently for the groundskeeper to walk down the drive and let them in. By the time Andrew stood beside Maggie, he spotted the groundskeeper jogging toward them. He was a short man between thirty-five and fifty years of age with a receding hairline and pale complexion. His paleness surprised Andrew. He would have expected someone who worked all day out of doors to have a bronzed tan and leathery skin. This man looked as if he spent most of his time in the basement.

"Hi, Mr. Peterson, sorry I interrupted your class. Where's Jeremy?" Maggie asked with an attempt at casualness. Andrew wasn't fooled. Evidently, Maggie had a crush on this Jeremy character. Andrew would have to check him out.

By the time Mr. Peterson unlocked the gate droplets of sweat were rolling down his temples. The man's expression reminded Andrew of Murray – pissed off at the world in general.

"I have no idea where Jeremy has gotten to, nor does there seem to be anyone else capable of coming down here to open the gates," Mr. Peterson said in a voice tight with suppressed fury.

As Andrew assisted Mr. Peterson in securing the gate behind them, he heard two vehicles approaching. Andrew turned in time to see a golf cart driven by a teenager bump across the clipped lawn toward them. From the direction of the school, a white VW Rabbit convertible appeared with a woman at the wheel.

The cavalry had shown up at last.

The golf cart and the VW Rabbit stopped in front of the gate. Andrew recognized Sarah Matthews, the director of the Eagle Gateway Boarding School. Andrew assumed the blonde, six-foot-two god-like creature driving the golf cart must be Jeremy. Miss Matthews took it upon herself to perform the introductions, "You've met our speech therapist Mr. Peterson, and this is Jeremy Stubben our groundskeeper. You must be Andrew Treloar. I spoke with Chief Steven Glenjones. He said you are a former police officer and now a private consultant and have jurisdiction here in Mintlaw. A pleasure to meet you sir. Welcome to Eagle Gateway Academy."

She turned to face Jeremy, "Have you seen Daniel around?"

Jeremy shook his head in the negative then shrugged, "No Ma'am, haven't seen him since he let me in this morning."

When Miss Matthews offered to take Maggie and Andrew up to the school, belatedly she noticed Peterson's ruddy complexion and offered him a ride as well. Mr. Peterson promptly climbed into the front seat. Andrew heard Jeremy asking Maggie if she'd like a lift in the golf cart, Andrew interrupted Maggie before she could accept, "Why don't you go with Miss Matthews Maggie and I'll hitch a ride with Jeremy."

From the crestfallen expression on her face, Andrew guessed he was no longer Maggie's favorite uncle. On the way to the two-story red brick structure in the center of the complex, Andrew pumped Jeremy for information.

"You wouldn't happen to be related to Richard Stubben?" Andrew asked Jeremy.

"He's my Dad."

"Isn't working here a conflict of interest?" Andrew asked.

"Why?"

Andrew dismayed at the total lack of interest Jeremy showed for anything beyond his small world sighed and said, "Well, your father tried to buy up this land from Mrs. Harden, I mean Mrs. Schmidt, and she sold the land to the investors of this boarding school instead."

A light in the murky depths of Jeremy turned on, "Oh yeah, you mean cause of Prairie Star and all. Nah. My Dad's just happy I found a summer job."

"How do you like working here?" Andrew asked confident he had found a topic that would bring some enthusiasm into the boy's voice.

"It's okay," he shrugged.

Maybe Jeremy wasn't comfortable talking to cops. Not bothering to hide his relief, Jeremy let Andrew off by the door to the school. Mr. Peterson and Miss Matthews had disappeared inside. Jeremy waved to Maggie as he drove off nearly hitting the back of the school bus. Andrew quashed the urge to lecture the kid about safe driving and hoped for the sake of the public Jeremy hadn't obtained his full driver's privileges just yet. In Idaho, children as young as fourteen were permitted to drive but only during daylight hours. He wasn't sure if Jeremy had his full license. Mentally he stored the question away to jot down in his notebook. Check DMV records for Jeremy Stubben's info.

"I found Daniel," Maggie shouted out to him. "He's in the shop out back fixing the lawnmower. Come on I'll show you."

Andrew found Daniel under a blue tarp which he had tied to two trees near the school's large metal shed. Daniel was sitting on the ground cleaning the lawnmower's filter. Maggie made the introductions, "Daniel this is my Uncle Andrew."

Daniel kept rubbing away the oil and dirt from the filter.

Maggie didn't seem discouraged by his reticence evidently – this was typical of Daniel, "Did you find any good rocks this weekend?"

Daniel looked up. The child-like beam of pleasure on the young man's face was unexpected. Andrew associated the expression with young children then remembered his son Tommy's delight for the most innocuous objects.

"Yeah, Maggie, I did. Want to see um?"

Daniel struggled to his feet and Andrew instinctively stepped back feeling slightly uncomfortable as if he were encountering one of the creatures from that movie about acid-for-blood aliens. It was rare for someone to be even taller than Andrew. He supposed he'd gotten so used to being the tallest in a crowd that when someone even taller loomed over him he felt uneasy. Not only was Daniel tall, his shoulders were massive, his arms incredibly long, and his thighs like a wrestler's thighs. Andrew stared at Daniel's hiking boots (which looked new) and guessed them to be a size fourteen. Maggie, walking behind Daniel looked like a shrimp in comparison. She didn't seem to mind Daniel's size or his imposing presence. They seemed to be on very familiar terms which he supposed had to do with her work at the boarding school.

Daniel took them inside the shop where the swamp cooler blasted wet cold air into the room. He moved purposely toward a work bench where a collection of rocks had been thrown onto the surface and another pile of rocks sat in an old plastic container that had formerly held five gallons of green paint. Daniel tenderly picked up half of a gigantic thunderegg and showed his treasure to Maggie. Maggie made appropriate sounds of interest. Andrew wandered around the shop examining the equipment. Privately, Andrew wondered why anyone would store tools and electrical equipment in such an environment, might as well store your drill and jigsaw and hammer in the bathroom.

"Where did you find this one?" Maggie asked, and Andrew thought to himself: *my miniature detective at work.*

"I found it up on the hill near that old farm the lady lives in, the lady with the long black hair."

"You mean on top of Hunter's Hill?" Andrew asked.

"Darrell calls it Stoner Hill," Daniel said enunciating every syllable.

"I saw you Friday. You were coming down from the hill. Later you went back up. Did you see anybody else up there?" Maggie asked.

"I found this Saturday by some sagebrush."

"Daniel, are you sure you didn't see anybody else up there on Friday?" Maggie asked again.

"I had to wait," he said and held up a smoky quartz crystal the size of a baseball, "to go back and get this one. I spotted it by that place where the cattle don't cross."

130

Andrew moved a little closer, "You mean the cattle guard? Can I see it?" Daniel grudgingly offered his prize to Andrew keeping a watchful eye on the rock to be sure Andrew didn't try to abscond with it.

"Why did you have to go back for it if you saw the crystal Saturday?"

Daniel lifted his face to the ceiling and screwed up his eyes in thought, "The human told me to go away."

"Who told you to go away? Was it a man or a woman?" Andrew asked.

Daniel's confusion prompted Maggie to explain, "You know Daniel, a boy or a girl. Was the human a boy like you or a girl like me?"

"No. I don't know. The human said - Get lost you moron."

Andrew moved closer, "What do you mean by no, Daniel? No, the person wasn't a girl like Maggie."

"No. The human wasn't a girl like Maggie. I don't know what the human was. I never got a good look," Daniel went back to examining his thunderegg. "It was rude, very rude. Mz. Matthews says rude humans haven't been properly educated and we must educate them."

Maggie touched the rock and asked, "Was the human like Ms. Matthews or your mother, a big girl?"

Daniel bobbed his head in agreement and grinned at Maggie, "Big girl."

"What did she look like? What about her car what did it look like?" Andrew asked.

"The human said Get lost you moron and I was afraid it would take my rocks," Daniel said, suddenly reminded Andrew still held his rock. Annoyance flickered for a moment in the scrunching of sun bleached eyebrows and narrowing of brown eyes as Daniel snatched the rock from Andrew's hands and held it close to his chest. "Mz. Matthews says that word is a bad word and only mean people use that word."

"Can you show me where you found the rock Daniel?" Andrew asked.

It took the combined efforts of Ms. Matthews and Maggie to get Daniel out of the shed and up to the hilltop. Andrew stood near Daniel by the cattle guard and watched as Ms. Matthews urged Daniel to remember what had happened on Saturday. Daniel pointed to where he had seen the human in the vehicle. Andrew walked toward the area Daniel had indicated and searched the ground for tire tracks. Andrew found several. He cautioned the others not to walk in that area. Andrew stood up and searched the land noticing some broken brush where a vehicle might have driven over them. He followed the tracks to a clump of crushed hopsage where they ended at the edge of the gully.

Willows and different varieties of brush supplied by snow and rain grew down in the gully. There were a few large boulders at the bottom; the rocks had cracked off the top of the cliff side and tumbled down to the bottom. Andrew crawled down the side of the gully slipping and sliding in the loose sandy soil. At the bottom, he had to climb over a pile of rocks to get to the brush beyond. He pushed aside the thorny limbs of a wild blackberry to get a better view of the ground. Andrew stood in the deep depression and looked around. Beyond the blackberry bush, he could see how the gully had carved a channel nearly a mile long meandering parallel to the rutted road, the gully narrowing beyond the willow. The largest willow grew a few feet away; some of its roots exposed, their humps reminding him of elbows and arms. A creepy image he would rather not dwell on today.

Andrew crawled under the blackberry bush and once on other side, he was able to stand up and move around. He searched the sloping sides and the bottom of the gully. The willow cast this part of the gully in shadow. He stood in the only spot of sunlight near the blackberry feeling the sun's heat soak into his scalp and warm his shoulder blades. Stepping over rocks and brush, Andrew made his way to the trunk of the willow. He had to pull aside the hanging limbs to see what was underneath. He saw the bones and his heart jumped imaging them to be human. With relief he realized the bones were too old. They were from a cow, a cow that might have fallen into the gully or been brought down by some wolves and finished off here.

Andrew circled around the willow and looked up toward the ridge. He could see no evidence a child had been here. He returned to the rock mound. When he looked up, he could see the wind moving the blackberry branches and blowing dust motes in the air; yet, here at the bottom, the air was hot and oppressive. Andrew brushed aside the sweat trickling down his forehead resisting the urge to climb out. He'd seen the tracks and the crushed hopsage. Something had been dumped down here. Along the ridge, he noticed a dimple in the loose soil between wedges of lava rock. The indentation was too uniform and regular to be animal prints. Then he thought of Vera's dream about hearing the wheels of a chair rolling on rocks. The dimple in the sandy soil between the lava rocks could be the impression left by one of the wheels. Andrew's eye followed an imaginary path from the impression to the bottom of the gully.

He stumbled over small broken rocks to stand where he thought his imaginary object would have landed. Andrew searched the slope in front of him and took a good look at a thorny bush level with his waist. He knew the name. His father had told him the name. He remembered his father telling him the plant was poisonous. It was on the tip of his tongue, yes, there it was, horsebrush. He knelt near the horsebrush and swept the thorny white limbs carefully aside using only his arm protected by the sleeve of his denim shirt. It was one of his best shirts too. When his eyes focused on what lay beneath the horsebrush, he put aside his petty concerns.

Andrew found her lying face down. She had landed on part of the horsebrush, her fall having broken some of its limbs, but the momentum of her fall stopped by a buried boulder's edge. She lay cradled in a bed of decomposing yellow flowers from the brush. Andrew ducked his head using his arms to protect his eyes to get a better view.

She lay on her side her upper body covered in a pajama top, something resembling a long cotton t-shirt, formerly white, now covered in dirt and the gray powder of fallen pebbles. The ends of the pajama shirt were pulled up to her waist exposing her underwear. The sight of her with the decomposing flowers for a pillow, the sandy soil a mattress for her torso, and the white thorns of the horsebrush as a blanket for her bare legs overwhelmed him with sadness. He preferred to think of her asleep at home in her bed, not like this, not exposed to the harshness of the Owyhees.

Then he heard Miss Matthews calling his name from above, her voice alarmed.

"Mr. Treloar! Where are you?" she asked. He heard her step carefully over lava rocks and looked up in time to see her peering down at him. With his arm holding back the prickly limbs of the spiny horsebrush, Miss Matthews had a perfect view of the woman's body resting beside his bent knee. He heard her draw in air then break into a coughing fit. Andrew looked down at the sleeping woman and around the area searching for further evidence, wanting desperately to find the filth that had dumped her body in this gully as if she had been nothing but garbage.

Chapter Ten

Vera went out on her back porch to watch as an ambulance, now with its siren silenced attempted to climb Hunter's Hill and failed when its tires began to spin in the sandy soil midway up. Two patrol cars chose to park at the bottom of the hill near the Pass. Vera looked to her right and noticed a white VW Rabbit parked on the shoulder of I55. Vera moved into the spare bedroom to get a better view and noticed Andrew Treloar and the other officers of the Mintlaw Police Department, as well as, a volunteer rescue team made up of citizens of Marsing, Mintlaw, and Homedale townships who were searching the field and the hillside.

The ambulance having decided not to attempt to reach the top backed down the hill and parked near the patrol vehicles and the coroner's van. The top of Hunter's Hill was brightly lit with emergency lights and the occasional smaller beam of light from individual's searching the area. Vera noticed the paramedics wheeling a gurney out of the bed of the ambulance and her pulse began to race. Either someone had been hurt or the police had found a body. Vera couldn't stand the suspense any longer. She left the house, being careful to lock the front door, and climbed to the top of the hill by way of her fields.

The winding path behind her house would have been the most direct route but the way was too steep in the dark. By the time she reached the top, a policeman posted near the barricade of boulders ordered her to stop and told her she could go no further. Vera noticed at the other end of the rutted road, a woman about her age shepherding Daniel away from the cattle guard. He was searching the ground and making their progress as slow as a toddler's amble.

The woman held Daniel's arm and led him to the barricade of rocks and the yellow security tape. As she passed Vera, their eyes met in acknowledgement of each other's presence. The woman paused. She appeared pale and tired, "You must be Vera Lee. I'm Sarah Matthews. I run the Eagle Gateway Academy."

Vera acknowledged her but could hardly swallow much less speak. Ms. Matthews seemed to understand and led Daniel back to the car. The police were cordoning off the area. Treloar was crouched near the edge of a gully and staring at something below. Vera could see the slender limbs heavy with leaves from the locust and willow trees growing on the sides of the gully and there were a few bushes and a straggly tree growing at the very bottom. There must be a creek bed running somewhere nearby or perhaps during the rainy season water collected in its deep basin. She heard him tell another policeman to find a rope. When he stretched and stood up he noticed Vera for the first time. Vera watched him walk towards her. She tried to read the expression on his face.

"Miss Lee."

"Mr. Treloar."

They stood staring at each other in a weird sort of silence for a moment which gradually made her uncomfortable. Vera's feet remained stubbornly rooted in the same spot.

"Some reporters have been banging on my door since early this morning," Vera said to explain her presence on the hilltop. "They're driving me crazy with questions."

"I'll take care of it, ma'am," Treloar said. He looked annoyed. At first, she thought he might be annoyed with her then eventually figured out the television news crews and curious were also contributing to his annoyance.

"I'm in the way. I'll go back to the house," she finally heard herself say but couldn't move.

Treloar took her arm and led her in the direction of the barricade of rocks which now was embraced by yellow crime scene security tape. There was just a small opening big enough for a gurney to pass through and she could see the emergency personnel struggling to lift the gurney over one of the boulders. As Andrew led her back to the barricade, she heard him say, "We found a body, the body of a woman. She might be the little girl's mother. Stay in the house and when this is finished I'll stop by. Will you be alright? Do you need assistance?"

His icy tone galvanized her into action. She slipped her arm out of his hold and picked up speed saying over her shoulder, "Yes. I mean no. I'm alright. I'm sorry. I just needed to know what's going on. Thank you for the update. I'll talk to you later."

She had hoped to see the woman's face to know for sure.

—

Maggie watched the activity across the road as the coroner's van drove up the steep incline toward the top of the hill. At the bottom, several television news vans were parked on the side of the road with crew filming the activity. The police were keeping the reporters and news crews off the field and the top of the hill. Earlier,

Maggie had seen several patrol cars and an ambulance arrive. There were police milling about the hillside and they and Andrew seemed to be searching for evidence. Men in suits were up there also. She could see the yellow crime-scene tape fluttering in the breeze as the police and the FBI and the detectives from Boise searched the area for clues. Word had spread quickly. Uncle Andrew had asked Maggie not to say anything to anyone about what she knew. Maggie had kept her word.

Unfortunately, the curious and the rubberneckers were being typical ghouls especially Daniel's stepfather Darrell Schmidt. Ms. Matthews had to get parental permission before Daniel could leave the facility and show them where he had seen the litterer as he called the human who may or may not have dumped the body. Schmidt had given his permission for Daniel to leave the school and show them where he had heard the disturbance on the night the child had been discovered. So, Schmidt knew beforehand why the police were up on the hill.

Maggie and her father had been near the road when Schmidt approached them. Maggie plucked at her father's sleeve to get his attention. Schmidt wandered over as if he were some sort of tourist, busily sucking on his cigarette filter and glancing at the activity all around him. He stopped by her father's pickup. Maggie's father ignored the man and adjusted a metal intake tube with a slightly crooked head to allow the water to flow more swiftly down the row of mint.

Each row had an intake tube at the head which captured the water flowing through the ditch and down the rows of mint. Kit had seventy-two intake tubes, one for each row of mint. He kept his eye on the icy cold water flowing down his grandfather's ditch. His grandfather had bought the land in the late1940s and created his own furrow near the shoulder of the road surfacing the furrow with concrete for a faster runoff. It was still in damned good shape for its age.

The Owyhee Project had been approved back in the mid1920s and finished by 1939 which allowed the creation of the Owyhee Dam in Oregon and the reservoir and numerous conduits for water to flow to farmers in eastern Oregon and southwestern Idaho. The Owyhee Reservoir stored runoff and water from the Snake River for the farmers in Malheur and Owyhee County who were allotted their share from the three divisions: Mitchell Butte, Dead Ox Flat, and Succor Creek Divisions. The water supplies 105,000 acres of land with an additional 13,000 acres of supplemental land.

Kit remembered his grandfather talking about how the Owyhee Project had been a test for a future Hoover Dam. Its success had paved the way for the Hoover Dam. And here he was standing in Mintlaw, Idaho which had once been a desert and now bloomed with corn, wheat, potatoes, and mint; anything, you name it; whatever the mind could conceive of could grow here.

Mr. Schmidt hailed Kit and pointed toward the activity up on the hillside.

"They found a body up on the hill," he said to her father. Maggie stood in her thigh boots by the ditch and watched Schmidt get closer then abruptly stop when he noticed her father's expression. He threw his cigarette butt on the ground and turned to face the hill, "Your nosy uncle took Daniel up there this morning. I guess he found what he was looking for, huh? What a lot of drama over some homeless nobody, big deal."

Her father glanced at Schmidt and back to his crops. Schmidt behaved as if Daniel had done something wrong. Maggie had met Daniel's step-father once before and on closer observation she still was of the opinion he was a braggart and a bully. His nervous movements made her itch to smack him. Wow, what was the matter with her lately? Even when he stood in one spot, Schmidt's arms jerked about brushing off flies or his fingers played with the sweaty dirty cap on his head or he rubbed the stubble on his chin; and at one point, he touched his pack of cigarettes in his shirt pocket as if he thought somebody might steal them. Her father said Schmidt and Daniel's mother spent a lot of time in the taverns. Maggie watched Schmidt acting like an insane puppet and replayed the dinner conversation from months ago in her head. Andrew had been there.

"I feel sorry for anyone that spends most of his time especially on a beautiful summer day inside a dark bar," her father had said.

"Schmidt's an oxymoron – an ugly, unappealing gigolo with a talent for living off lonely women," Andrew said.

"andy alwa us upid," Murray said.

"Ghee Dad thanks," Andrew said.

"No ou. andy!" Murray said and wiped the spit off his chin.

"He said Candy always was stupid," her father translated.

"I remember Michael Harden. He was a heavy drinker, so it's not surprising Candy would find another Michael nine hundred miles away from home. She's destined to attract the worst type of men," Andrew explained. "Remember Dad how Candy's father drunk himself to death and her grandfather died in a bar brawl up in Idaho City."

"Well I feel sorry for her. She's known no other life. It isn't her fault. The system is at fault for not having given her a chance to move beyond the dysfunction of her family," Maggie's mother said.

"Ood ill alwa ell," Murray said.

"What'd he say?" Andrew asked.

"Blood will always tell," her father said.

The subject of Darrell Schmidt and Constance Harden ended at that point. Only Maggie heard her mother say under her breath, "Medieval."

Maggie had met Schmidt once at the Egg. Her first impression had been of a skinny guy with cold brown eyes and lips set in a perpetual sneer. Maggie had never heard so many foul words come out of someone's mouth at one time. He smoked constantly and snapped his gum between his lips like a cow chewing cud. He had been talking to Sarah Matthews and told her about his strip club in Boise and how he'd met Candy in Sacramento where she'd been a stripper. Maggie couldn't believe someone would just come right out and tell a stranger such stuff. He even seemed rather proud of his strip club and his stripper wife. He told Ms. Matthews his wife had retired from stripping. Ghee whiz, Maggie should hope so Daniel's mother was old, nearly thirty or maybe forty.

While Darrell Schmidt bragged about his money and his sexy wife, Maggie wondered about Daniel and what kind of a life he'd been living with parents like Darrell Schmidt and Constance Harden. It amazed her that Daniel had managed to reach the age of twenty-seven without hurting himself or someone else, especially since it appeared he spent most of his days and nights unsupervised. Well, Maggie thought, at least now, Daniel has Sarah Matthews to watch over him.

Since Daniel had started living at the school, his attitude had changed dramatically. He seemed happier and more relaxed. He even joked about things now. He talked to Maggie more and smiled more often. Maggie admired the way Sarah Matthews persuaded Constance to give Daniel more opportunities for independence. Instead of confronting Constance with criticism about Darrell Schmidt as a role model, Ms. Matthews found excuses to keep Daniel at the facility on the weekends and during the day. Sarah made the argument that the Eggs and the school couldn't do without him.

Daniel's parents could have cared less but for one thing – she'd heard from people in town since Daniel was over eighteen now and seemed to be managing his independence, the social security disability checks were going to stop coming to the Harden house and be delivered to Ms. Matthews as his proxy guardian. Maybe the Schmidts were hoping to keep the money flowing? Maggie noticed the way Darrell looked at Daniel as if just by being alive Daniel irritated him. And his mother, Candy Schmidt teetering on her high heeled shoes in the hallway while students went to their next classes looked out of place in her tight dress and feathery earrings.

Maggie noticed the quizzical look she gave her husband and felt a tug of sympathy. Constance reminded Maggie of a frightened kid. When Constance tugged on his sleeve for a second time, Schmidt pulled away and scowled, "Do you god-damned mind, Candy? Can't you see I'm talking to the teacher?" Maggie noticed the odd way the woman reacted to Schmidt's rudeness. She'd expected just such a reaction and didn't appear to be embarrassed her husband used profanity in public. Maggie pitied her but worried more for Daniel's health and safety.

While her father ignored Schmidt, Schmidt tried to talk to Maggie. Maggie moved away pretending to examine an intake tube with concern. After a time, Schmidt walked away from them and returned to his vehicle. Maggie looked beyond Schmidt's tall skinny body and noticed Vera Lee climb Anderson Pass and stop to talk to Uncle Andrew, "That should do it, Maggie," her father said in his quiet voice. Maggie compared her father's voice to the scratchy phlegm-clogged voice of Darrell Schmidt. She appreciated her father even more for being the kind of man he was – smart, kind, and generous. She was so lucky to have such parents.

It was late afternoon now and nothing exciting had occurred in the last two hours since Maggie had been sitting on the window seat watching the road. The sound of the wheelchair bumping across the uneven boards of the hall alerted Maggie to Murray's presence. Maggie turned in time to see Murray maneuver his wheelchair around the corner and enter the living room. Maggie dropped her unread book and waited for Murray to roll himself toward her and the big bay window.

His sharp eyes observed the activity across the road and with a lopsided smile he said, "ose suits ave no'ing on my boy," and Maggie translated his words into, "Those suits have nothing on my boy." Murray's pride in Andrew had merit. Maggie agreed. In her opinion, Andrew could do no wrong. Maggie said nothing though because Murray habitually contradicted her or tried to make her feel small and unimportant.

Here she was babysitting Murray again while her mother shopped for groceries in town; yet, there was so much excitement going on just across the road. Maggie had been thinking of a way to get closer to the action. Dad was in the fields keeping an eye on the irrigation. Mom was in town and wouldn't be back for probably another hour. As her eye traveled around the room trying to come up with an excuse to be outside, she noticed the set of walkie-talkies on the coffee table. Dad had bought them, so he could communicate with Murray while out in the field. Dad had left them behind because it was Maggie's turn to babysit and she wasn't scheduled to work at the school today. Even though Murray would probably lecture her about curiosity killing the cat, Maggie gave the idea a chance to blossom.

"Hey, Murray. What do you think about me going over to Vera's house and finding out what's going on up on the hill? I'll take one of the walkie-talkies with me and tell you what I find out."

Murray had been staring out the window and watching the coroner's van creep down the hillside heading for Jump Creek Road. When she spoke, his blue eyes focused on her intently, "Wha'd ya ather ay out noop'in?"

"Not to get in the way of a police investigation. I know. But I'm not going up the hill. I saw Vera go up there earlier and come back down. Maybe she knows something more."

"Um."

Murray twisted around in his seat to reach for the walkie-talkies. Maggie didn't try to help. It only made Murray angrier if he thought people pitied him. He dropped them in his lap, then with a shaking hand and fingers curled into a claw dug one of the handheld devices out of his lap and offered her the other walkie-talkie in a shaky palm. Maggie caught the thing before it fell to the floor, "Ou no ow ta oose?"

"Sure Murray, I press this button and your box rings and then I talk to you. When I'm finished I say over and out and you press your walkie-talkie's button then it's your turn to talk to me."

With an impatient wave of his right hand he motioned her to go. Maggie jumped up from the window seat and left the house. She paused on the front lawn and turned back toward the bay window where she could see Murray sitting in his wheelchair. She pressed the call button and waited patiently for Murray to press the talk button. She could barely hear his slurred, "What?"

Maggie talked into the box, "Just making sure they work Grandpa. I'll check again after I cross the road."

Once across the road and standing on the sloping gravel drive of Vera's property, Maggie called Murray again and sensed from the tone of his voice that he was tickled with their new game. She thought he said, "I hear you fine" and responded with "Good. I'll check back with you on Vera's porch, Grandpa." Her father had said the walkie-talkies could transmit at least as far as five miles. Murray knew this to be true. Maybe this way of communicating with her great-grandfather allowed him to keep in touch with the world and still remain a dignified loner. She called him once more from Vera's porch then knocked on Vera's door.

Vera must have been watching Maggie because before Maggie had finished signing off the door opened.

She appeared as edgy as Maggie felt, "Hi, Ms. Lee; it's just me."

"Who are you talking to Maggie?"

"My great-grandfather Murray. Mom's in town shopping and Dad's in the field. I thought maybe since Dad and Murray use the walkie-talkies, Murray and I could use them," Maggie said noticing with surprise that Vera had a lit cigarette between the fingers of her right hand, "Did Uncle Andrew tell you we went to the school to talk to Daniel?"

"No," Vera said trying to hide the evidence of her burning cigarette behind the door. "So, the man we saw yesterday, he saw something up there?"

"Yes, he said he saw a lady and the lady told him to go away. She wasn't nice. Uncle Andrew and Ms. Matthews took Daniel up there and Daniel must have shown them where he'd seen the lady. I noticed the ambulance and the other patrol cars. There's even some FBI I think," Maggie said knowing full well she was fishing for information and wished she had the courage to just come out and ask Vera what she knew.

Vera sensed her curiosity, "I'm not sure if I should say anything until your uncle comes down. He said he'd let me know more later on today."

Maggie wondered if Vera's reluctance to speak to her had anything to do with her age. If Maggie's mother had shown up on Vera's doorstep maybe Vera would have been chattier. Vera's expression changed, she looked annoyed. Vera was staring at something beyond Maggie's shoulder. She swore under her breath then said, "Excuse me a minute Maggie," and disappeared inside the house without closing the door. In a few seconds she was back slamming the door firmly closed behind her. Maggie turned and watched as Darrell Schmidt made his way up the drive toward them.

"Who's that?" Vera asked unhappily.

"Darrell Schmidt. He's Daniel's stepfather."

Darrell must have figured a way to get rid of his wife. Why was here?

He walked toward them the long greasy black hair sweaty at the ends. The beads of perspiration on his forehead didn't help. Why didn't he just wait until Daniel went back to the school and collect all the dirt from him? He'd replaced his dirty t-shirt with a powder blue sleeveless shirt which contrary to his intentions accentuated his scrawny arms while his blue jeans which bagged in the rear made his butt look like a child's. All told it was a sad pathetic sight.

As he got closer, Vera noticed more details. The holes in his tennis shoes made her strangely sad. For a split second she pitied him. Then she glanced at his face. Pimpled with unshaven black hairs and old acne scars his face made her even more nervous. There was something exceedingly seedy about him. Bathing wasn't a big issue with him, number one. He had the corpse like paler and emaciation of a junkie, number two. Number three was the unnatural shine in his eyes which reminded Vera of someone she'd known in the past and had learned to despise. She recognized the signs of avarice and dependency in this loser too. Here was a drug dealer with an addiction to his own supply.

"Morning Ma'am," he said with a lopsided smile he erroneously believed to be seductive. "I see you've noticed all the excitement up there on the hill," Maggie was relieved that Schmidt's eye roamed elsewhere.

"Yes, I've noticed," Vera said conveying from her tone her lack of interest in getting to know him better. His greedy eyes fingered her body from legs to breasts to hair. His attitude that a woman should appreciate a man appreciating her "attributes" annoyed Vera even more. Not once had he looked her in the eye for more than a second. When his eyes finally focused on her face, he stepped back as if she'd thrown something at him and the lustful attitude died.

"You've seen action, yeah? You one of those martial art chicks?" he asked bobbing and weaving pretending to box.

"From the sickly green color of your skin and your emaciated body, I'd say your action is usually inside four walls, maybe with a needle and a spoon, huh?"

Maggie watched with admiration as Vera put Schmidt in his place. She appeared to be so unruffled by creepy Schmidt. And she seemed to know just the right words to make him nervous.

In his drugged brain there must have been a moment of remembered manners. "Hey, that's not fair. I'm your neighbor. She knows who I am," he countered as he waved his arm in the general direction of the Eagle Gateway Academy, then in Maggie's general direction. "I own the farm next to the school."

Maggie broke in.

"Mr. Schmidt is Daniel's stepfather," she told Vera helpfully and moved toward the end of the porch to watch the activity on the hill. Maggie preferred lots of space between her and creepy Schmidt.

Vera decided it was time to end the conversation, "Well, Mr. Schmidt if you came over here to find out what's going on, you're out of luck. I know as much as you do and maybe less. I'd suggest you go back to the road and ask the police what's going on."

When Schmidt did not move or appear to notice her gathering discomfort, Vera decided she would have to resort to bluntness to get rid of him, "I noticed on your way up here you walked through my garden. I'd appreciate it if you kept to the gravel on your way back, Mr. Schmidt. Do we understand each other?"

Schmidt weaved back and forth on his feet and Vera feared he would collapse. The sun burning down on his head and the alcohol in his body were probably broiling what little brain cells he had left. The amount of grease in his hair wasn't helping matters either. The oil shone like blue globs in the blinding light. Vera wondered at the insanity of a man coming out into the light of day with police everywhere after injecting himself with a speedball. It looked as if he'd even brought himself a thermos of Jack Daniels. The combination of alcohol, drugs, and noon day sun were either going to stop his heart or put him in a coma.

Schmidt waved a floppy arm in her general direction, "Sure, sure. No problem," he managed to say. "This frigging heat is frying me alive. You got something to drink in there?"

"No Mr. Schmidt. I don't have any alcohol in my house," Vera said between clenched teeth wondering again why when she wanted to be alone, she seemed to attract even more attention and even more unwanted visitors. Of course, the discovery of the body on Hunter's Hill was a huge sensation in this small rural community. While she tried to figure out a way to rid herself of Schmidt, she noticed with outrage several reporters snapping pictures of her house and the three of them standing near the house.

Great, Vera thought, just great. Now she would get no peace at all until the body had a name and the murderer was found. If she stayed outside much longer, the reporters would think she wanted to talk to them.

Vera heard Schmidt mumble, "Too bad;" then remembered he'd asked for something to drink. Vera stood with her arms crossed in front of her chest and watched him with a freezing look until her disgust with him finally penetrated his thick skull.

"I'm going," he said. "I'm going." Vera watched with relief as he weaved his way down the drive toward his car. She should have been impressed with the car. It looked expensive. But Vera had never been impressed by flash, especially not little shiny red foreign cars driven by drug dealers or pimps or any person stupid enough to get behind the wheel while intoxicated. Schmidt and her dead husband Arthur might have been twins in their shared stupidity. One of the news crew managed to waylay Schmidt and ask him some questions, a cameraman showed up to record Schmidt's words. God knows what he might say in his condition. Vera familiar with the degree of puritanism running rampant in this part of the world and mirroring itself on the local news channels doubted Schmidt would ever be on television tonight or any night.

As Vera contemplated her neighbor's inebriation and wondered how he had the nerve to climb into his car while police were roaming the area, Maggie spoke up, "Hey, looks like my uncle is on his way down to see you Ms. Lee."

"Maggie," Vera called to her. Maggie turned toward her. "If we're going to be friends, I suggest we call each other by our first names."

Maggie appeared pleased, "Sure-thing Vera. I'd better let Grandpa know what's up." She pressed the button on the walkie-talkie and spoke into the device, "Grandpa, hey Grandpa, you got your ears on? Uncle Andrew's coming down now. How're you doing?"

Vera could barely understand the man's muddled rambling discourse.

Maggie and Vera didn't have to wait long before Andrew appeared around the side of the house and when he noticed Maggie on the porch his smile turned into a frown, "Maggie, what'd I say about bothering Ms. Lee?"

Maggie looked crestfallen. Vera stepped in, "She was keeping me company."

"Go on home, Maggie," Treloar ordered.

"Murray's alright," Maggie said holding out the walkie-talkie. "I've been talking to him on this."

"Maggie, you've been asked to keep an eye on Murray. Standing here gawking at a crime scene isn't your parents' idea of caregiving," Treloar told her sternly. His tone set Maggie hurrying off the porch and sprinting down the driveway.

Vera watched Maggie marsh away her skinny arms pumping and sensed from the rigidity of adolescent's shoulders the girl was struggling with embarrassment and tears at being publicly chastised. As soon as the words were out of his mouth Treloar seemed to regret his outburst. She assumed his anger had something to do with the body discovered on Hunter's Hill. He turned to face her. She watched his eyes.

"I came down to tell you the FBI agents are interested in this case. Someone will be down shortly to ask you a few questions."

Vera puzzled by Treloar's sudden reserve pressed her arms to her chest and looked away, "Do you know who she is? Is she the child's mother?"

"We should know more in a day or two," Treloar said and continued, "but I'd appreciate it if you just stayed inside until we're finished."

"Of course," Vera murmured and turned to enter her house. "Tell them I'll be at home when they're ready to talk to me."

"Wait a sec, Ms. Lee," He called after her. She turned. He looked into her eyes then quickly away as if he wasn't sure how his question would be received. "I noticed Schmidt talking to you. What did he want?"

Vera thought about her parting comment the other day and wondered what had possessed her to speak so rudely to Treloar. She heard in her head what she'd said to him and compounded her stupidity from the day before by saying, "I don't need protection from the likes of him. I'm a big girl. I can take care of myself."

It irked her that her words brought a smile to his lips. She supposed she wasn't fooling anyone with her tough-girl attitude, least of all Andrew. Later that afternoon, the FBI showed up at her door. They were irritatingly predictable. They talked to her as if she were a criminal and repeatedly asked her questions she had already answered. Vera omitted mentioning her dream about Aunt Vista and Uncle Frank haunting the hilltop. The FBI would never understand and might even discount the rest of her story as the product of an unsound mind.

—

The only moment that turned Maggie's humiliation into triumph came strangely enough from Murray. Murray acted as if he and Maggie were co-conspirators and when Uncle Andrew entered the kitchen and warned Maggie to stay away from the hilltop until further notice, Murray defended her right to know what was going on. Murray and Maggie were reduced to speculating, since Maggie's attempts to wriggle information out of Andrew came to nothing. Maggie had to wait until the five o'clock news to find out what the police knew. They had found the body of an unidentified woman in the gully on Hunter's Hill. A witness to the potential crime, a woman was a "person of interest" to local authorities and if anyone could identify her from the artist's sketch, they were to contact the number on the screen.

The drawing of the woman resembled hundreds of women with wide cheekbones, stubby nose, and a square chin. Maybe the police artist had had trouble understanding Daniel. Since Daniel only paid attention to objects not people, Maggie suspected the drawing was nothing like the real "person of interest."

—

Vera switched off her television set and settled herself in her rocking chair to think about the events of the day. Maybe her decision to move back to Idaho had been a mistake. The ring of the telephone made her jump. Vera waited until the tape played and recognized the voice on the other end before picking up the receiver. Vera had been getting calls from the local news stations and the newspaper and didn't want to talk to anyone, but when she recognized Joshua's voice she suspected he had probably heard about the body from cable news. Joshua speaking from his hotel room in Pocatello sounded annoyed with her, "What's going on in your neck of the woods V? I've been watching the news. You hear about the body they found near your house?"

"Yes, I heard Joshua."

"Do they know who she is? Is she that kid's mother?" Joshua asked. Vera heard papers crackling and bed springs creaking and could tell Joshua was prepared for a long chat. The idea of chatting long distance annoyed Vera's frugal soul.

Vera managed to convince Joshua all was well. By the end of their expensive chat Vera had agreed to pick him up at the airport on Friday evening. Unfortunately, she couldn't think of a good reason to brush him off. She would have preferred to be alone. Mintlaw and her property had become big news locally. Having busybodies sniffing around her property and nosing their way into her private life made her agitated wanting to pack her bags and flee.

By a supreme effort of will she pushed aside the voice telling her to run and pretended to be unconcerned by the calamity she knew was coming her way. Joshua's mistrust, jealousy, and neediness were becoming a major turn off. She suspected there was more to him than he was letting on. He was hiding something from her. She might have cared a week ago what he thought or if he were going to spend the weekend but not anymore. Danger was on its way and she needed to find safety or some sort of protection. Joshua was a contradiction of personalities for sure: demanding commitment yet spending most of his working hours on the road in strange hotels all over the country. And he continued to ignore her insistence on boundaries. She would have to make herself clear this weekend.

A part of her felt guilty – was she suddenly ready to move on because there was someone else she found more attractive, someone more her type? Her sponsor would be disappointed. She remembered Judith's warning. First you have to learn to live with yourself before you're ready to share your life with another.

Vera woke up with a startled oath realizing she had fallen asleep while sitting on her rocking chair in the dark kitchen. Knowing her house so well, she walked through the dark rooms avoiding obstacles with practiced ease. She fumbled her way to the lamp on the countertop managing not to bang her toe or hit her knee on the furniture and switched on the light. The soft yellow glow illuminated her kitchen and the dining room making the atmosphere appear cozy and safe, hopefully casting the evil spirits to the dark corners.

She wasn't ready for bed yet. Her nerves were on fire. Things had been going so well lately and that was a bad sign. She knew from experience that when life was good inevitably something bad was on its way. She walked through the house not bothering to turn on the lights imagining some nosy news reporter wondering why she was up in the middle of the night. She paused for a moment in each room and listened to the familiar sounds of the house, the protests of an old lady shrinking into herself arthritic and tired. The familiar sounds were oddly comforting. No demons here.

When she ended up back in the kitchen, she poured herself a glass of water and sat at her table staring up at the path that led to Hunter's Hill. The willow hid part of the hillside from her view, its morose branches pressing down upon her poor old fence. Vera thought about the little girl swinging on her swing set in the middle of the night with the moon shining down upon her. She hadn't been afraid to be in the dark alone at night. She had a single madness of purpose – to swing up into the air higher and higher. Unbidden surfaced the question of what had been up there on Hunter's Hill while the little girl swung her legs up and up and up into the sky. And Vera was afraid.

Camus had been right –life is absurd.

From her vantage point, Vera could see the kitchen and the living room. She hadn't drawn the curtains yet; so, when she saw car lights heading up her driveway, Vera left her chair and moved toward the front of the house to peer out the window. The car stopped by her Toyota. Vera drew the curtains peering between the slit and watched as a man climbed out of the vehicle. She recognized Treloar's Jeep but choose to wait until Treloar knocked on her door before moving. The clock on the mantle told her it was ten thirty. He wore jeans and a plain cotton shirt which emphasized his broad shoulders and lean hips. When she opened the door, he smiled down at her his eyes appreciative and apologetic. Vera preferred this Treloar to the earlier version.

"May I come in Ms. Lee?" he asked. "Sorry to be here so late."

Vera showed him into the kitchen switching on the light as she entered, "Would you like something to drink – coffee, tea, or a soda?"

They sat at the kitchen table as the coffee perked. Treloar sat with his back leaning against her kitchen chair and his elbows resting on the table. He looked tired with lines she had never noticed before along his forehead and around his mouth. His voice, a rich tenor reverberated inside her head, down her neck, and into her stomach.

"There was no identification on the woman's body, nothing that could give us a clue. All we know is that we've found a woman with blonde hair and blue eyes approximately one hundred and twenty-five pounds, five feet eight inches tall dressed only in her underwear and the top half of some cheap pajamas." Treloar informed her then paused and when she looked toward him he continued, "I shouldn't be telling you this." He stopped and turned his head toward the window.

Vera watched him, admiring his profile, the perfection of black soaring eyebrow, black eyelashes, high cheekbones, and most of all she admired his nose. His nose was just right, not too skinny, or too broad – yes – a noble nose. Maybe he had Spanish or Native American ancestors? And then the thought came to her in a deprecating voice unbidden – or he's just an American racist who if he knew her true ancestry might decide she was a mongrel and unfit to be seen with him.

A minute or two passed and in the silence Vera poured him a cup of coffee and set the cup in front of him. As if he had come to a decision, Treloar started talking again, "It looks as if someone dragged her out of bed in the middle of the night and drove to that

spot to dump her in the gully. Daniel said the woman driving the
vehicle told him to get lost; that the litterer (his name for her)
caught in the act threw rocks at him and screamed at him. He said
she was heavy set. He mistook her for a man at first. He said he
couldn't see her eyes because it was dark, and he couldn't see her
hair because she wore a hat. She might have been bald for all we
know. The vehicle she drove didn't interest him. He wouldn't even
have remembered her, if she hadn't been so snarky with him.

That's what we have so far. After the coroner's investigation
we'll know more about how she died and when. Yet we still won't
know her name. No one's reported a woman missing that fits her
description. The lab will do a DNA test to determine whether the
child and the woman are related. DNA testing is fairly new and may
not be conclusive enough. It seems obvious to me they're related in
some way, but we have to be sure."

Vera sat across from him and sipped her coffee, "What's
going to happen to the child?"

Treloar's expression softened, "She'll be in the foster-care
system until her relatives claim her. Otherwise, she'll stay in the
system until someone adopts her. Her chances of being adopted are
minimal though. The Egg (that stands for Eagle Gateway School or
their Graduates by the way, an acronym dreamed up by Maggie) has
offered to care for her temporarily."

They sat across from each other in silence. It was a
comfortable silence. Vera didn't feel the need to keep the
conversation going as she did with other people. Treloar leaned back
and stretched his aching muscles, rubbed his face, then took a sip of
his coffee and finally said with a self-deprecating smile, "Maggie is
sulking right now. I'm no longer her favorite uncle."

"Teenagers are prickly creatures," Vera offered and shrugged
philosophically. "Of course, I'm only speaking from personal
experience."

His grin charmed her. A thought unbidden popped into her
head – *he has always been loved, loved by his family, his friends,
and even his women*. Vera swept aside a momentary self-pity and
found strangely happiness coursing through her body. He deserved
to be loved. He was a good man. She was sure of it. Evil could never
penetrate such confidence. For a moment, she thought she saw a
flicker of self-doubt in his eyes. It must have been an illusion.

"I was wondering," he began staring down at his cup, his
long fingers wrapped around the porcelain, "if you might be
interested in dinner and a movie some night."

Vera's surprise must have shown on her face. Treloar interjected an escape, "Of course not. Sorry. I'd forgotten about your boyfriend."

Vera thought about telling him the truth. Instead she got up from her chair and poured him a fresh cup of coffee. The silence had become uncomfortable. She supposed it was her turn to reveal something, "I've known Joshua about three months now. We're still getting to know each other." At that moment she floundered and just stopped talking, unable to think of anything sensible to say which might explain her relationship with Joshua.

"I suppose you've heard the gossip about me?" Treloar asked his expression open and honest.

Vera could only nod her head in agreement. She thought about Treloar and his women. She thought about the last twelve years and how she had managed to avoid most entanglements. Her scar had helped some. But there had been a few who persisted and because liquor made all things palatable she could barely remember most of them. The few she did remember were memorable because they had turned out to be the worst shits ever.

"I've got my baggage as well," she said meeting honesty with honesty. "I've chosen my relationships carefully since, well, since Arthur."

She paused knowing she'd forgotten someone, belatedly remembering that Treloar knew about Kirk, "Well, that's not quite true."

Treloar acknowledged her moment of confusion with a grin.

She finished her thought in a breathless hurried way, "Since Woody and Arthur I mean. Woody was before Arthur. I was lucky with him. He ended up in prison and I found a new life. I didn't know how lucky I was until he showed up the other day. I'd never thought of him as a stalker before. Now I do. I know what I've become. Some people might think I'm selfish. Our society sets great store by marriage and family."

"And you prefer the single life?" Andrew asked.

Vera decided to believe he really wanted to know. Not being able to figure him out made her uncomfortable. He wasn't a real cop just a temporary one. Yet he ran around with cops and helped them investigate cases. She wondered what he did for a living. He dressed as if he had money, yet his car was at least fifteen years old. He often visited his father and his nephew. He seemed to know all the locals. He had no obvious job. She thought about ways some people might make money at home. He didn't look like a computer nerd. Up on the hill when he was doing his job, he'd been distant and reserved.

150

Her trust in people had gotten her into trouble before. No one was ever as they appeared. If he was into drugs or something else illicit surely the cops would know? She decided she didn't care.

"I used to think marriage was the only way to find peace. Now I know some marriages can be the worst kind of prison," she said in an emphatic matter, so he understood her completely; pretending she didn't care if her words pushed him away.

"I've seen enough domestic disputes to agree with you," Andrew replied, "although I've also observed marriages which have worked. Kit and his wife Rachel are a perfect example. They love and respect each other."

"Then why haven't you married?" Vera asked despite her reservations about getting too personal with him.

Andrew shrugged, "I haven't found the right woman, I guess. No, wait, that's not entirely true. To be honest, I've made it my business to avoid the kind of woman looking for a husband. I've chosen the other kind of woman. You know what I mean."

Vera stirred the cream in her coffee slowly, "Even during the first few years of my marriage, I hated the whole situation. I longed for privacy. I longed to be able to take off somewhere on a whim and not have to worry about checking in with hubby to get his permission. You know I became aware that I was living in a prison on the day my husband put a padlock on the garage door and refused to let me drive to the library without him. Can you believe it? He was so jealous and possessive even the library seemed a threat to him."

It was unexpected when Andrew grabbed her hand and squeezed her fingers. He didn't seem like a touchy feely sort of person. Vera let him hold her hand wondering why she was having trouble breathing. She was the first to pull away. Her hand still tingled where he had touched her. Her body had betrayed her again. In a voice she hardly recognized, she said, "It's getting late. Thank you for being so honest. If I learn anything that might help identify the woman, I'll call you."

Unused to being rebuffed, Treloar stood up his jaw stiff his body radiating embarrassment. Vera regretted the way she'd spoken to him the moment she opened her mouth. He hadn't deserved her rebuff. Treloar didn't give her time to apologize. He pushed in his chair and started toward the front of the house, his boots ringing across the hardwood floor. His reaction seemed so out of proportion to what had taken place. He was already out the door and stomping down the porch steps by the time she got herself together and followed him outside. He was already climbing into his Jeep and prepared to drive away.

Vera called to him.

He climbed into his vehicle and turned on the engine. She thought he hadn't heard her and called his name again. He turned to watch as she approached. He was just a shadow of a man sitting behind the wheel of his car. In the dark, she couldn't read him.

Standing with her arms hugging her chest, she blurted out the words without thinking how he might interpret them, "Don't leave angry," she began.

"I'm not angry, Vera," he said in a voice she hardly recognized as his own. "I'm just embarrassed. I suppose I had it coming."

"No. You didn't deserve that. You've been so kind. Please, don't leave angry."

Andrew switched off the engine and climbed out of the vehicle. The porch light illuminated his face for the first time. He looked puzzled, "I told you Vera, I'm not angry with you. What's wrong? Are you alright?"

"I'm fine," she said annoyed at exposing herself to his scrutiny. "I just, I don't know my own mind right now. Can we remain friends? Or would that be too humiliating for you?"

His chuckle eased the tension between them, "This is new to me. My God! A woman wants to be friends with me. I'm not sure if my ego can handle it."

They stood in the dark with the light from the hall illuminating the porch. A passing cloud dimmed the light of a three-quarter moon, a light that barely penetrated the dark. The crickets were going crazy warning the listener of another scorching day tomorrow. A car moving down Jump Creek Road zoomed past thinking he was safe from the cops on a rural road. Vera thought perhaps she should reconsider his unspoken invitation. She might not have another chance once her world blew up in her face and the truth came out.

Treloar threw up his hands, "No, Vera. I don't think I'm prepared to be just a friend. I'm sorry."

"I'm sorry too."

"Goodnight."

Vera remembered how possessive Woody had been and after Woody, how Arthur had been a carbon copy albeit much older. She remembered how Woody jealously watched her and monitored her every move. In the end, she fled from him and his possessiveness as if she'd been the criminal. She still regretted leaving behind some of her possessions especially her books. Her pathetic paperbacks had hardly been valuable. Vera wondered if like the men in her past, she was doomed to find only possessive males bent on keeping her caged up. Andrew didn't appear to be possessive. Yet her track record suggested she had a knack for finding just the wrong man for herself. There had to be a man out there who wasn't a shithole. Maybe Andrew was the right man?

Vera returned to the porch and watched him drive away. Sometimes, Vera wondered what her life would have been like if she had found a good man and settled down and had a bunch of kids. Other women were married with children and still managed to be independent. Children were such odd creatures though, so dependent on adults. Vera could barely take care of herself much less a child. And to have a child just to placate a man's fear of abandonment was seriously flawed.

—

Andrew drove home without remembering how he got back to his house. He had three messages on his machine: one from George and one from Steven. The other message he deleted. He had no memory of the woman and no interest in renewing their relationship. From the third floor of his house on the banks of the Snake River, he thought he could see Vera's roof. That was impossible. It could have been the Harden house for all he knew. Andrew sat back in his chair and stared up at the ceiling. Rejection was new to him. He could have sworn Vera was interested. He'd been around long enough to recognize the covert sizing up, the way if a woman's eyes lingered over a man's mouth or his hands or the back of his neck, she was interested.

Feeling sorry for himself wouldn't help him. Unbidden the image of the dead woman surfaced. He didn't brush the memory away. He had seen something which still bothered him. There had been something odd about the scratches on her legs. He saw where the spikey thorns of the horsebrush tore the skin but there was no blood. You had to be alive to bleed, didn't you? At least he thought so. He hadn't wanted to touch her in case he contaminated any important evidence. The coroner had established time of death. And then he realized what was bothering him. She must have been preserved in some way inside a cold room or a freezer. Of course, the nights in the Owyhees were cold, even in the spring, and she had been down in the gully. If she'd been kept in a cold place time of death might be wrong.

—

Daniel stood by the fence facing the hill. He watched the ambulance drive down the graveled the Pass and pause by the main road. The ambulance driver did not turn on the lights or the siren. Daniel wanted to see the flashing lights then he'd know the humans were gone and no longer contaminating his special place. He turned to follow the progress of the ambulance as it drove slowly down the road and out of sight. Daniel had done everything Andrew Treloar and Mz. Matthews wanted. He had shown them where the angry human had thrown rocks at him.

He told them about seeing the human get back into the car and wait, how he had hidden himself and watched until the light faded to purple, and he could not see the van anymore. He told them about hearing car doors opening and closing. He did not know if they believed him about the bobble head in the chair and the wheels rolling across rocks. He told them, most everything, except where he had been hiding. They didn't need to know about the cave either. If they knew about the cave, they might come back and disturb his collection.

Daniel sighed in relief to see the ambulance disappear and the angry human leave his favorite place. The angry human was gone now – forever and ever gone. And Darrell and his mother were over there, and he was over here. He could see the lights on in his mother's house and see Darrell sitting in his lazy-boy chair watching television. Daniel saw his mother hand Darrell a beer and sit down in her chair. Darrell had laughed at Daniel when Daniel said his mother should have a lazy-girl chair to sit in.

Darrell was a jerk.

Thinking about Darrell made him angry. He had better things to do. He turned to look at his home. The outside was cool tonight, so he'd left the shed doors open and turned off the swamp cooler. He could see his cot and his table beside the cot and the lamp on the cot and his pictures hanging on the walls and he could hear his little TV going and recognized the opening credits of his favorite television show. He hurried inside his home and sat down in the chair Mz. Matthews had brought him. He heard the opening credits of, The A-Team and with a thrill of anticipation followed the team as they took care of the bad guys. The episode was called *A Nice Place to Visit*.

Chapter Eleven

T oward the end of August, Vera had finally managed to break apart the rest of the concrete around the last of the poles holding the swing set in place. She dumped the poles along the side of the barn and threw the old swings in the garbage. With some extra money from her new job at the Egg, Vera had bought herself a few plants from a nursery in the city. The white cedar tree she chose was about a year old, the trunk about the size of her wrist. Her most pressing need was to make her backyard a sanctuary rather than a zoo; some day, she hoped the cedar tree would give her some privacy. When she learned the old cow-path was a public access path for hikers and hunters to get from Opal Road up to Hunter's Hill, she decided she had to find a way to keep nosy people from staring down into her backyard or looking into her windows as they traversed up the path to Hunter's Hill.

She discovered the truth about Opal Road Access by pure accident, ironically not from the Andersons who probably didn't want to spook her or from the county clerk she paid her taxes to because the county clerk probably could care less; but instead she learned the truth from Kit Treloar during a discussion about the ten acres she hoped he would lease from her. They had been standing in the shade near her house looking out at the field and Kit had been helping her understand the survey map the county clerk had given her. In her opinion the map looked like a bunch of squiggles and straight lines and nothing like her property.

While she stood beside him and tried to pretend she understood what he was talking about, he glanced down at the map and then pointed straight ahead of him and said, "You see there where Anderson Pass runs near the irrigation ditch by the school? That's where your property begins. The Andersons donated part of their field to the town for public use." He turned slightly to his left and pointed in the general direction of Jump Creek Road, "and you see the shoulder of the road, well, about three feet from there that's where your property begins. The shoulder of the road is considered public use in case someone breaks down or the road crews need to widen the road."

He pointed with his thumb over his shoulder behind them, "And of course, back behind us is all your property for about eighteen feet beyond your barn." Then he paused to look at the rising slope of Hunter's Hill. He was probably thinking about the body. It wasn't something anyone could forget for long especially since no one knew her name or if the child might belong to her.

He turned to face her and looked over her head and pointed toward the narrow cow path beyond her old fence and she spun around to follow where he was looking and heard him say. "And I'm sure you already know beyond your fence is Opal Road Access. It's considered public domain."

"Hold on there," she said spinning around to face him. Her expression made him smile and he quickly tried to take it back. He looked so much like Andrew she was confused for a moment. Only for a moment because the news that just anyone had the right to trespass on her property and peek into her windows made her boiling mad, "This is the first I've heard that Opal Road Access is public domain. You mean just anyone can come up from the road, anywhere on my property and climb that old nasty cow path?"

"Oh no, let's step back a bit," he said in a soothing voice. "People can't trespass on your fields, even though they've been doing that a lot lately or walk up your drive and into your backyard. They only have permission to use the Access from Opal Road."

She looked around shading her eyes from the burning sun, "Where is Opal Road?"

He pointed at her catalpa trees, "On the other side of your trees there's a dead-end road. Your neighbor Homeister, that's Hugo Homeister, he owns the farm on the other side of you and uses Opal road to access his crops. Opal ends at the cow path among a cluster of locust trees. Years ago, Homeister and Murray cleared the area for a turnaround when people realized Opal Road didn't take them into the backroads of the Owyhees. They've also posted signs by Jump Creek, but kids keep shooting holes into them. So, they got the BLM to pay for the construction of a post surrounded in stone with a metal placard drilled into it which explains to tourists and locals their rights and responsibilities on the road. You can drive over there and read the sign if you're curious."

"I will one day but for now could you just give me the short hand version?"

Kit looked down at her and smiled. He had a disarming way about him. Like Maggie, he was a people person, "Well, let's see. Basically, BLM permits people to drive up to the turnaround, park their vehicle for the day, and climb the Access to the top of Hunter's

Hill and beyond. It warns that litterers will be fined up to a thousand dollars and the property below the Access is private. The Andersons used to have No Trespassing Signs along their fence. I see the fence isn't doing so well. If you'd like a pair of extra hands, my family can help you cut away the lower branches of the willow and build a new fence, maybe a taller one. Oh yeah and I forgot to mention, the BLM sign also warns the public if they trespass on private property, the owners have the legal right to use deadly force."

"I don't own a gun but," Vera volunteered, "I could probably weld a cast iron pan and do some damage."

His laughter was infectious. It hadn't taken them long to hatch out an agreement about the leasing of her ten acres and Vera was pleased imagining the extra money she would earn without having to lift a finger. Her good mood lasted until Kit had gone back to the Treloar Farm and she had spun around thinking he had driven back with a question or more information only to see a stranger's SUV coming up her drive and a woman looking confused asked her the way to the body discovered somewhere in Mintlaw.

Hunter's Hill had become a nuisance bringing unwanted attention to herself and her property. Once the news got out, more people would drive up to her house and ask for directions to the place where the body was found. She was forced to block off her driveway from the road with orange cones until the handyman she'd hired finished her country style utility gate. She would have preferred one of the fancy gates the salesman wanted her to purchase but the price made her gasp. The local man out of Nampa had given her a better deal. He was also a brick layer and he built her two stone façade pillars on either side of the black lacquered utility gate for far less than she would have had to pay someone in the city. She was pleased to discover the gate wasn't all that heavy for her to open or close.

The last few months had been terrifying. She expected trouble to arrive any day and it didn't. But she knew it was on its way. The best way to keep herself from worrying was to distract herself with work. She started digging her hole for the cedar tree four feet from the teetering fence midway between the start of Opal Road Access and her willow tree. Maybe when she could come up with more money, she might buy a series of arborvitae as a year-round camouflage against nosy trekkers.

Maggie had become a regular visitor and one day had asked Vera why she used her hose to water her garden when she had a perfectly good irrigation ditch supplying water from the Owyhee

Reservoir. Vera had been pleasantly surprised to discover that she had access to water just like the farmers. Maggie demonstrated how the ditch worked, showed her the water box, showed her how to steer the water into her ditch and flood her back and front yard. Vera's ditch ran the full length of her property. The ditch began at the culvert on the east side of her property and ran south veering parallel to the house and finally spilling into another ditch on the west side. No one had told her she had the right to flood irrigate her property using the water from the ditch. Vera had always assumed the farmers owned the water. Maggie set her straight.

A few days later, Kit casually walked across the road, interrupting Vera's weeding to offer his help setting up her irrigation ditch. Since May when Andrew told her he wasn't the "just friends" type, she had seen nothing of him. Andrew and Kit looked so much alike in their dark coloring and high cheekbones that Vera felt a momentary twinge when she saw him walking up her drive mistaking him for Andrew for a moment. Vera suspected Kit's friendly attitude had something to do with Andrew's former interest in her. She didn't care. She was happy to get as much help as possible and accepted Kit's offer with genuine gratitude. He told her the ditch hadn't been used in years and she would need to contact the ditch rider and find out how she could access her water rights. Kit explained that she had already being paying the fee along with her property taxes.

For the most part the Treloar family left her alone. Maggie, believing she was Vera's special friend cheerfully stopped by whenever she wasn't babysitting or volunteering at the Egg. Maggie borrowed books from Vera and pitched in to help Vera paint the house. The painting was done in spurts, whenever the day was cool enough to apply paint to the thirsty cedar boards. Vera accepted Maggie's overtures of friendship without suspecting Maggie had an ulterior motive.

—

Maggie knew without a doubt her uncle had the hots for Vera. He never said anything to anyone about his feelings, but Maggie knew. All the signs were there. No one in the family talked about Andrew's strange behavior lately. Instead of going out on his nights off with some new girl he'd met, he stuck close to home or came over to the farm to play cards with her father or watch television. He rarely went out and seemed depressed, even when he ate Sunday supper with them. Maggie's father had jokingly asked Andrew if he was thinking about joining a monastery. Andrew's silence worried Maggie. At first, she assumed he was concerned about the body found and determined to find the person or persons who had dumped her in the gully.

It all became clear to her right before Memorial Day on Friday night. He'd arrived on their doorstep just in time for supper and after supper stuck around to watch a movie with them. Murray had gone to bed early and her mother was reading in her parent's room. Maggie noticed that unlike her Dad, her Uncle Andrew ignored the movie and sat staring out the window, a strange thing to do since the curtains were closed.

At one point when Maggie's father stopped the movie to pop some popcorn, Maggie heard the familiar sound of Vera's Toyota coming down the road. Her uncle jumped up and pulled back the curtain and she and her uncle watched as Vera stopped the Toyota and a man climbed out to open the utility gate. When her uncle closed the curtain nearly tearing it off the pole and left the room without a word, Maggie knew he was upset. A few minutes later when he didn't return, and her father came back with a bowl of popcorn and said, "It's just you and me kid for movie night. Andrew had to take off; he said he forgot something at home," she knew that he was not only upset but jealous.

—

Vera ignorant of this event so many months ago, dug around her hole until she was satisfied the size was just right for her new tree. The bark of a dog and Maggie's voice interrupted Vera's concentration on her task. Vera turned in time to see Maggie and an unfamiliar canine come around the corner.

"I didn't know you had a dog, Maggie," Vera said and dropped her shovel deciding this was a good time to take a break anyway. It was hot and muggy, and the sweat was dripping down into her eyes. She rubbed the sweat away with the corner of her shirt.

"He's not my dog. He's Jeremy's dog. Jeremy calls him Lazy."

Vera watched the collie chase off the birds near the sprinkler then come up to investigate Vera's hole and sniff all the interesting smells on Vera's tennis shoes. The collie returned to the hole and decided he would help her dig, "No!" Vera shouted. He was not only a lazy animal but a badly trained one. Maggie dragged the dog away from the hole and held onto his collar.

"Sorry Vera."

Vera stooped down to look at the mess. Her perfect hole had been widened. A piece of material protruded from the side. Vera pulled out a playing card and examined it. On one side was a cartoon and on the other a title that she read aloud, "The Balancing Soda Bottles." It looked like something a child would have collected, something from the 1950s or 1960s. Maggie let the dog loose and stood beside her to look at the card.

"Wow, that's neat. Some kid must have forgotten it and over the years it just got covered up with leaves and dirt."

Vera headed toward the house with her prize held between her thumb and finger, "I'll just wash it off. Come on in. Would you like a glass of lemonade?"

"Sure," Maggie said, then remembered the dog and called to him. Jeremy had asked her to watch Lazy while he floated down Indian Creek with his friends. Maggie had been disappointed he hadn't invited her along. When the dog didn't answer to his name, Maggie stomped toward the barn, vowing never again to babysit anything human or animal. She was sick of being stuck at home.

She heard the dog digging behind the barn and called to him sharply. Vera came out of the house holding two glasses of lemonade and saw Maggie disappear around the corner of the barn closest to Opal Road and the beginning of the Access. Maggie's scream startled Vera; she dropped one of the glasses. The glass bounced off the top step of the porch and shattered on the cracked concrete sidewalk. Vera set the other glass on the top step and ran toward the barn.

As Vera came around the corner, she saw Maggie struggling to get possession of something the dog had in his mouth, "Give it to me. Give it to me now, you stupid dog."

Vera ran to help and pulled on his collar until he was nearly choking. As the dog gasped for air he let go of the object he held between his teeth. Maggie lifted the backpack in the air. Vera let go of the dog and stared at it. It was a child's light green backpack with Ninja Turtles prominently displayed on the canvas.

"It looked like a jacket. I thought, maybe." Maggie never finished what she'd been about to say but Vera could have finished the thought for her.

"Do you recognize it? Is it one of yours?" Maggie asked.

Vera brushed the dirt and leaves off the pack and answered with a resounding, "No," then unzipped the bag and peered inside.

"You shouldn't do that. It might be evidence."

"I'll call the police," Vera answered, obviously unhappy about having her home invaded once again.

"We could call Uncle Andrew," Maggie suggested.

Vera carried the bag between her fingers into the house. Maggie listened unabashed as Vera telephoned the Mintlaw Police

Department leaving the pack on the porch chair. She didn't want the police entering her home again. She and Maggie waited on the front porch for the police to arrive.

—

Lazy scratched on the barn door to be let out. Maggie ignored him. About ten minutes later when the white four-wheel drive patrol vehicle with the gold star swept up Vera's drive, Maggie was in an excellent position to see the expression on Vera's face when Vera recognized the passenger sitting next to the police officer. Maggie shivered inside, not fully understanding the implications, but convinced that she had been right all along. Officer Metcalf walked up to Vera and introduced himself. Andrew stood by the vehicle with the side door open and retrieved a pair of rubber gloves out of a case. Fifteen minutes later, Andrew had stuffed the backpack in a large plastic evidence bag, the Ninja Turtles starring at them through the plastic. Andrew put the bag on the back seat of the patrol vehicle and turned to face Vera and Maggie.

"Who found it?" Deputy Metcalf asked.

Maggie showed her uncle and the deputy where Lazy had found the pack. Andrew took the lead and climbed half way up the hill among the locust and underbrush growing near the barn until he came to the spot where the dog had found the bag. A limb growing from the bottom of one of the trees had been broken and a piece of the strap from the backpack lay on the ground beside the limb.

Andrew peered through the leaves of the trees up toward the hillside. Maggie supposed he was picturing how the pack ended up on Vera's property. Someone must have thrown the bag into the cluster of trees and brush where the branch broke. The bag must have caught on the branch and hung there for quite some time, nearly three months now. Maggie wondered how the police and volunteers could have missed the bag dangling from a branch.

It was like he'd been reading her mind when her uncle said, "I thought the search crew had been all over this area and combed through the underbrush thoroughly. Unless the pack hasn't been here all that long and the person who dumped the kid and the woman is still around."

—

Vera watched as another patrol car pulled up to her house and parked near Officer Metcalf's vehicle. Without speaking she stepped out onto the porch and directed the deputy toward the barn. Vera thought about the child's backpack and the police and knew they would want a sample of her fingerprints now.

—

After Andrew found the bag, Maggie returned to the house to tell Vera she would take Lazy home. Vera acknowledged Maggie's presence with an absent nod. Maggie could tell that Vera's thoughts were miles away. Maggie left the house mindful of, once again, disrupting Vera's life. She imagined her uncle and Vera together, perhaps on their wedding day. Her uncle is surrounded by his family and friends. Vera has no one. Well maybe she does have someone, the stocky man who visits her on the weekends. Maggie pictured the man again sitting in Vera's car – all brown, his hair and eyes a similar shade of brown and his tanned skin with the tiny black moustache growing under his jutting nose.

He wore suits on Fridays, baggy shorts on Saturdays, and 501 blue jeans on Sundays. He must keep some of his clothes at Vera's house because his habit was to bring only a small black bag with him when he visited her. Maggie knew he liked to eat at fancy restaurants when he came to spend the night. They were always leaving the house around supper time and from what Maggie could gather they didn't eat at Lucy's Diner in Mintlaw.

Once, Maggie had seen them in Beatrice's store looking at steaks in the meat section. Their cart had been loaded with fancy crab salads, rolls, and lobster. Vera had been preoccupied and reserved with Maggie that day. Her attitude had made Maggie uncomfortable. At the time, she wondered if maybe Vera was ashamed of her boyfriend. She'd introduced him to her and Joshua had shaken Maggie's hand. A brief handshake and a big smile that's all Maggie remembered about Joshua. He'd seemed overly jovial, the smile on his lips real, but his eyes blank. He reminded her of a determined pushy salesman on the brink of a tantrum.

He can't be at Vera's wedding, stupid. He'd be an old boyfriend and he didn't look the mature type willing to let the better man get the girl.

Maggie entered her house convinced Vera belonged with someone else, someone with more class, someone who wants to be with her all the time, not just the weekends, a person who would protect her and take care of her and buy her pretty clothes. Joshua didn't buy her pretty clothes. Maggie had been observant enough to notice that Vera habitually wore an old pair of jeans and matching tennis shoes and when she did dress up for work at the school, Vera wore clothes that had been out of fashion for at least ten years.

And even worse, Joshua didn't offer to help Vera with expenses or chores around the house. Maggie remembered the day she had entered Vera's house without knocking and seen Vera searching through drawers and her purse for change. Vera had made a joke about it, said that it was the middle of the month and her bills had to be paid first. Vera must be hard up for money if she had to count all her nickels and dimes to come up with enough for a carton of milk. Why wasn't Don Juan offering to help out? Didn't he eat her food and drink her milk? What a creep.

—

Unaware of Maggie's negative impressions of Joshua, Vera had been debating whether to call Joshua and let him know about the discovery of the backpack. Last time, he had resented having to learn about the body found on the hill from a news broadcast instead of from her. He had sounded hurt on the telephone as if she had tried to exclude him from the important parts of her life. Vera supposed he must be off work by now. Vera called his home number and let it ring ten times and when she heard his voice telling the caller to leave a message, she hung up.

She wandered around the kitchen touching the counter, the top of the bar stool, and other objects as she moved. Her behavior reminded her of the little girl's, the girl she had found swinging on her swing set in the middle of the night, the girl someone had dumped in the Owyhees, a child Vera now knew to be Carolina Fletcher's daughter.

Instead of Andrew bringing her the news, George Metcalf had stopped by to inform her the artist's sketch of the face of the woman discovered in the gully which had been televised on the local news and in newspapers all over the Pacific Northwest had generated many dead ends until the day before when a coworker had seen the resemblance and could positively provide proof the body belonged to Carolina Fletcher formerly of Seattle, Washington who had lost her job in April and hadn't been seen since.

Deputy Metcalf had volunteered the information, information she probably didn't need to know, as some sort of gesture to prove to her he considered her one of Andrew's friends and therefore by degree Metcalf's friend. He told her Carolina Fletcher had been an orphan, her parents having died in a car accident; Carolina evidently had had few friends at work or in her private life. The other information he gave she already knew. That Carolina was the mother of the three-year-old autistic child who had been swinging on her former swing set three months ago.

The entire time the deputy was talking to her, Vera could barely swallow just waiting for the moment when he would grab her arm and demand to know why she hadn't identified the woman months ago. She could have told him the truth. She could have said she hadn't seen Carolina Fletcher in years, not since they were teens, and only after a couple of weeks did the truth dawn upon her who the drawing reminded her of and then she knew she couldn't say anything for fear she'd end up in the same condition. The pieces of the puzzle had come together, and she was terrified. From that point on, she was determined to keep the truth to herself. As long as she kept silent, maybe, the danger would pass her by. If they believed she would keep her mouth shut, maybe, they would leave her alone.

When Deputy Metcalf left, and she realized he wasn't going to arrest her or interrogate her, she went to the refrigerator and stood with the door open searching for a beer and getting mad as she realized there was nothing to drink. Then it dawned upon her she hadn't had an alcoholic drink since October 31st, 1983. Her sobriety date brought her back to reality. An overwhelming desire for a smoke quashed the need for a drink. She went outside in her backyard to have a quiet smoke walking to the overturned clay pot in the corner where she kept her pack of cigarettes and her lighter.

After finishing two cigarettes, Vera went back into the house and remembered Joshua had told her he would be in Spokane. She called directory assistance and got the number of the best hotels in Spokane. Eventually, she located a hotel where the clerk recognized Joshua's name.

"Shiloh Inn, may I help you?" the woman said.

"Yes. Is Joshua Adams registered with you?"

"Do you know his room number?" the clerk asked.

"No, I'm sorry, I don't."

Vera heard the woman talking to someone else. Another woman got on the line.

"May I help you Ma'am?" the other clerk asked.

"Is there a Joshua Adams registered at your hotel?" Vera asked again. "I was just wondering if you could leave a message for me. I don't know his room number."

"I've already left two messages for him this morning, Mrs. Adams. He still isn't in his room. I'm sorry. I'm sure when he gets to his room he'll contact us for his messages and call you straight away."

Without being aware of it, Vera thanked the woman automatically and hung up the phone. It was nearly nine o'clock in the evening. Monday evenings seemed to be Vera's day for unmasking chimeras. Vera knew Joshua would call at his usual time. Instead of being mad, Vera was elated. Here was her perfect opportunity. Although, she did wonder how she could have been so naive. Her friends at AA had told her about thirteen stepping, people who just went to meetings to find mates or sexual partners and weren't really interested in sobriety.

Vera played back what she knew about Joshua. He had told her he worked for Simplot and traveled all over the northwest overseeing the various Simplot plants located in Montana, Washington, Oregon, and Idaho. He'd taken her to his apartment in Caldwell once. The bareness of the rooms had struck her as typical bachelor pad decor. She remembered sitting on the uncomfortable couch and noticing with a deprecating smile the card table and four lawn chairs in the kitchen.

In retrospect, she realized the apartment had been a hideaway, a temporary home where he could bring women without his wife finding out. No wonder the discovery of the child had upset him; he'd probably been terrified he would be found out. Vera wondered if Andrew knew Joshua was a married man. She got mad only when she realized with a lurch of her stomach how if Andrew knew he must think she was some sort of desperate woman willing to accept crumbs from a married man rather than be alone.

—

Andrew and Chief Glenjones talked about what they'd found in the backpack. Before they contacted the FBI, they took pictures of each item and recorded the items in a ledger. It had been Andrew's idea. Steve had agreed. The billfold had included identification. Now they knew the identity of the dead woman – Carolina Fletcher. They also found two credit cards, a MasterCard and Visa, about twenty dollars in change, and a prescription for anti-depressants. Tucked among miscellaneous notes and receipts, Andrew found a telephone number. He traced the number and came up with an Ada Aleshire living in Winnemucca, Nevada.

As usual the FBI refused to talk to Andrew. Steve might trust Andrew's judgement but not the FBI. Andrew wanted answers. He drove to Winnemucca to the address of the Aleshire woman. He didn't care if he was interfering with the FBI. If they wouldn't talk to him, he would find his own clues.

Andrew stood on the sidewalk and looked up at the two-story white stucco house. There were signs the FBI had already been at the house, the yellow crime scene tape was a dead giveaway. He peeked through the garage window. It was empty. Either, the FBI had confiscated the vehicle, or the woman had done a runner. Andrew noticed a woman next door watering her roses. He walked up to her and gave her his best smile.

"Hello Ma'am. I'm Andrew Treloar. How are you today?"

The woman was near her fifties and paused to look him over with interest, "If you're from the FBI, I've already told the other man what I know. Nothing. I didn't even know there was a woman living in that house for nearly a month until Doreen across the street told me. She kept to herself. She might have been a vampire for all I know."

"Why do you say that?"

"Because I never saw her leave or enter her house until after dark. That's why."

"Do you know what she drove?"

"Your other guy, he asked me the same question. Don't you people keep in touch?"

"I'm not with the FBI, Ma'am. I'm helping the Mintlaw Police Department."

"Oh," she said turning off her hose. "Sorry about that. Thought you looked different somehow. I know you're not wearing the suit, that's what makes you look different."

"Yes, Ma'am, what did you tell the FBI about the woman's vehicle?"

"I'd like to see some identification if you don't mind."

Andrew pulled out his wallet from the back pocket of his jeans and showed her his old badge. He had yet to receive a new one. Most people never even look at the inscription. Satisfied with his badge, she continued, "She drove a van, a red van, carpet cleaning van, I guess. She must have shampooed carpets in the middle of the night. That's all I got to say."

"Did she have any visitors?"

"No. According to Doreen, she's been living in that house for nearly a year. Maybe her visitors crawl over the back fence and ring her back door or she doesn't have any friends. Well, wait. That's not true. I did see somebody come to her door once."

"Was it a woman, a woman with a child?"

"No. A man, a tall skinny guy with greasy hair wearing ugly boots."

"Ugly how?"

"They were the ugliest color I've ever seen on a grown man, a dirty yellowy green. Weird color for a pair of cowboy boots, don't ya think?"

Andrew pictured Woodrow Kirk. There couldn't be many men wearing snakeskin cowboy boots. Maybe the Mintlaw volunteers and police had been thorough in their search and the backpack in the trees near the barn had been left there by Woodrow Kirk on the day he'd been pestering Vera? Perhaps Kirk wanted to implicate Vera in Carolina Fletcher's death? Or maybe Ada Aleshire and Woodrow Kirk were involved in something else and Carolina had been a witness and a problem they needed to get rid of?

Andrew left Winnemucca and drove back to Idaho. Once at the station he contacted Agent Butlin the FBI man in charge of the case. Butlin listened to what Andrew had to say: all polite that conversation, although information passed only one way – from Andrew's mouth into Butlin's ear. He thanked Andrew politely and hung up. Andrew sat back in his chair and wondered if the FBI would follow through with his information. Probably not. Andrew had questions, questions about where Kirk had gone, whether Vera still had something going with Kirk, and how Kirk knew Ada Aleshire. Andrew knew, even before he climbed in his vehicle, he wanted to question Vera about Kirk. This time his personal interest wasn't a priority. He had a legitimate reason to learn more about Vera's relationship with Kirk. Sure, he thought in self-disgust, if this is police business why are you so nervous?

It was Monday, nearly three months since the Fletcher child had been found. Andrew had a name now for the kid now – Katherine Fletcher, her mother called her Kat. Her mother preferred to be called Carolina by her coworkers and neighbors. Carolina had worked for a software company. *Father Unknown* had been typed on Kat's birth certificate. Andrew suspected Carolina had had an affair with someone at work. He discovered she'd been fired shortly after giving birth to Kat. Subsequent work in other areas had resulted in lay-offs or dismissals. For a single parent raising an autistic child could be financial and emotional bankruptcy.

—

By five o'clock Vera had located all of Joshua's possessions, his casual clothes, his shoes, his toothbrush, and shaving cream. She dumped them in a black husky trash bag and set the bag on the back porch. Vera sat in the dark and waited for Joshua's call. Right on the dot, just as the big hand reached the six, the phone rang. Vera answered on the third ring.

"Hi honey," Joshua said.

"I'll make this brief Joshua because I know you've probably already spoken to your wife today and must be exhausted keeping all your lies straight. So here it goes. If I ever see you anywhere near my house again, I'll call the cops. I'm leaving your clothes and things at your apartment in Caldwell, so don't think you can come here to collect them and try to pig your way back into my bed. And by the way, the next time I see you at one of my AA meetings I'm going to warn the women that you're married and on the prowl," Vera said, then with barely enough breath left in her lungs dropped the phone in its cradle, cutting him off as he said, "Vera, wait, let me." Her legs began to shake in reaction to her fury. It had to be a curse. No one could be so unlucky. Her mother must have cursed her before dying.

Vera drove passed the bar in town, conscious of the lights inside, the dull rhythm of the jute-box playing, the motorcycles and cars sliding in and out of spaces, the constant opening of the door with people exiting and entering. Vera drove to Karcher Mall in Nampa. It was still too close. She drove to Boise and found a store. As she stood in front of the checkout counter with a bottle of scotch and two plastic bottles of seven-up in her cart, she woke up.

Pretending to have forgotten something, Vera left the line and pushed her cart back toward where she had picked up the whiskey. She'd never liked whiskey anyway; Grasshoppers and White Russians had been her preferred drink of choice but only when she could afford them. Most of her high had come from drinking cheap beer and doing free lines of coke. Low maintenance drunk, low maintenance lover that summed up her life.

Vera found the number written on a slip of paper at the bottom of her purse, the paper gray from coins which had left metal deposits on its surface. The number was still legible though. Vera recognized the voice that answered on the third ring.

"Judith? It's Vera Lee. Do you remember me?"

"Where are you Vera? I'll fetch you," Judith said and Vera heard her sifting through drawers as if she might be searching for paper and pencil.

"No, Judith, that's not necessary. I'm sober. I just want to talk."

"Sure. Come on over," Judith said and gave Vera directions to her house.

Thirty minutes later, Vera was standing in front of Judith's house near Municipal Park. As Vera climbed the stone steps to the door, the door opened as if Judith had been watching for her. The light from the hall spilled out into the night. Judith hugged her before Vera had a chance to step inside. Vera thought she could handle almost anything, but that hug undid all her fine resolutions.

—

Around six o'clock Tuesday evening, Andrew pulled up to Vera's house conscious that Joshua Adams had spent the weekend there. As he climbed out of his patrol car, he imagined Joshua sleeping in Vera's bed, showering, shaving, eating meals with her, learning more about her than Andrew would ever know. Friday evening, Andrew had seen Vera driving through town with Joshua sitting beside her in the Toyota. Andrew knew where they were going. He could picture the two of them entering the church and sitting among others like them, drinking coffee, exchanging histories and war stories. Last month, Andrew had followed Vera to the airport and watched as Joshua lifted Vera up into his arms and kissed her roughly, while passengers veered around the couple.

I'm not stalking her, Andrew had convinced himself. I'm just keeping an eye on her. A year ago, his actions would have been unthinkable. Women were easy to find. When he wasn't around his particular woman of the month, he rarely thought about her. The man that he had been a few months ago would not have recognized the new Andrew. Other guys, weirdoes and suspicious pimps stalked women. Other guys lurked in doorways and hid themselves behind bushes or watched women through binoculars.

Vera wore a sleeveless tank top speckled with paint and a pair of gray sweat pants tied with a white string. The string had come loose and swayed back and forth as Vera held the door open for him and led him toward the kitchen. Andrew glimpsed exposed skin as Vera's pants began to slip. He saw a smooth hip the color of pecans then hit his head on the door lintel as he entered the hallway. By the time they reached the kitchen, Vera had the string tied and her top pulled down.

At the table, Andrew chose to sit opposite her, so that he could watch her face. Vera gathered up some papers she'd left on the table. Andrew recognized insurance papers. He'd also noticed the address of a local plastic surgeon in Boise on the return envelope. Andrew looked up at her. Vera offered him a glass of lemonade.

"No thank you Vera. This is an official call," he said, knowing the futility of posing as just another cop but determined to pretend. "I'm here because I've been to Winnemucca. Remember the backpack you found."

"You mean the one Lazy found."

Andrew chuckled, "Yeah, the backpack Lazy found. Well inside there was a telephone number. The telephone number belongs to an Ada Aleshire. Aleshire's stepmother told us Ada hasn't been heard from since May. Her stepmother is insisting we contact the FBI's missing person's unit and have the FBI find her. The FBI won't tell me diddly-squat. I think they don't care because Ada Aleshire dropped out of sight voluntarily. I think you know something. It's no coincidence Woodrow came to see you, is it? Ada and Woody know each other. Tell me what's going on, Vera?"

Vera's body stiffened. She sat in her chair with her hand around her sweating glass and stared at him as if he had changed into a rabid dog before her eyes. Andrew waited for her to respond. He tried to ignore the sudden dullness in her eyes, the resigned slump of her shoulders. Somehow, he had disappointed her. He couldn't go back. He couldn't unsay the words.

Vera spoke as if speaking had become a chore, "Get out of my house. Get out now."

Andrew hadn't expected outrage, "So there is something you're not telling us. Does it have to do with Kirk?"

Vera jumped up. Her ears had tuned out the sound of the chair hitting the floor. She did not flinch or look away from him, "You assume a great deal. Now I'll tell you again, get out of my house. You have a lot of damned nerve. You're not even a real cop. You're some sicko prancing around as if you have some special authority. You're nobody. Just a thrill seeker looking for dirt on people you don't even know. Your friends Steve Glenjones and George Metcalf should be questioning you. You're the real danger around here asking questions, poking around, following people when you don't have the authority to do so. You should be locked up to protect the rest of us. Get out. Now."

Andrew got up and walked around the table, "I'm not here to hurt you. I need answers. You tried to help us once before. What's different now?"

From his perspective, all Andrew could see was the top of Vera's head. He heard her say. "I'm going to call the real police if you don't leave now. Woody is no longer a part of my life. He hasn't been for ten years. He's gone, remember. I saw you follow him out of town, Dick Tracey. Get out."

Andrew leaned forward, so that he could see her face. He could smell her shampoo, an almond and raspberry scent. The rest of her smelled of sunshine and cinnamon. Her hair, the black curls resting on olive skin hid her eyes from his view. He leaned closer. He saw her breasts rise and fall as her breathing quickened. He saw her nipples grow large.

"Don't," she said.

Andrew stepped back realizing too late he had exceeded his authority; he had tried to intimidate her. He stood in the kitchen with a blade of sunlight warm on the back of his hand, unwilling to move. When he lifted his hand to tuck one of her curls behind her ear, his hand felt cold. She stepped away from him and collided with the overturned chair. Andrew caught her before she fell.

Andrew with his hand wrapped around her left arm and other hand touching the small of her back held his breath for a moment, unable to focus on the room, unwilling to move away. Her bare arm and backbone were warm and smooth beneath his hands. When he slipped his hand under her sweats and his fingers made contact with her skin, Vera leaned back and moaned. Andrew bent his head and kissed her forehead, the bump of her nose, the white scar along her cheek, and then her lips. He tasted coffee and chocolate and salt.

When he let go, Vera walked away from him. The space between them hurt so bad he had to bend over to keep his focus on something other than her. He saw the chair and picked it up, all the while listening to her footsteps walking purposely toward the front door. He waited for her to call his name, tell him to leave, sick at the thought of having to leave. He heard her shut the door and lock the deadbolt. She stood in the hall and looked across the space between them. Andrew walked toward her. She led him down the hall. He followed her into the room and shut the door behind him.

—

Daniel stood on the edge of Hunter's Hill and looked down on Miss Vera's house. He saw Andrew Treloar walk toward Miss Vera's porch. His teachers had told him the police protected people; but Daniel knew Andrew Treloar wasn't a real police officer. He was just a guy. He didn't even have a real job. That's what his stepfather said. His stepfather said the man was a wannabe Colombo. Daniel didn't understand what he meant by Colombo. Long ago, Daniel's real father had told him the police were nosey. Darrell called them oinkers. Mr. Treloar wanted to be an oinker. Why would he want to be that? Maybe he should go down and make sure Miss Vera was safe, maybe tell Andrew Treloar to leave Miss Vera alone?

Daniel sat on the rocky ledge and watched the house. It was quiet as if the people inside were asleep. He waited and watched. He saw a bird of prey circle the sky above him. It looked like an eagle. He had gone with the other children to the Bird Sanctuary and Swan Falls Dam. He had stood by the stone wall and looked down into the canyon where the Snake River flowed looking just like a long winding green snake. He had seen the birds perched on the cable wires strung across the river canyon. Mz. Matthews told them about the diverse kinds of predatory birds around the Snake River Canyon. She said they hunted jackrabbits and rodents and were good for the environment. They had better vision than humans.

Daniel looked down at Miss Vera's house. He saw Andrew Treloar and Miss Vera walk toward the Jeep and climb in together. They had been inside the house for hours. Mr. Treloar's hair looked wet. Daniel watched them drive away. He jumped up; the truth dawning upon him now that he understood. The truth made him mad.

—

Vera followed Andrew into his house. From the outside, the house appeared to be abandoned. The wood siding hadn't seen a coat of paint in years. The yard had been cut, but there were no plants or landscaping to show off the place. The property was close to the banks of the Snake River. One side of the house faced the river with floor to ceiling glass in different sized old window frames. When Vera stepped inside and followed Andrew down the dark hall, she came to a threshold filled with light. She entered the huge room separated only by untreated beams and looked around in awe. One side of the room was in shadow, the other side near the windows was bathed in the afternoon's light. High above near the ceiling, the individual windows had been tinted. Only the windows near the floor and just above her head allowed sunlight inside the room.

There was even a sky light at the other end of the room, the room that might have been Andrew's living quarters. She saw a couch and a television, and a stereo placed in the far corner above the sky light. But where Andrew stood, she had an uninterrupted view of the Snake River flowing by. She stepped out of the shadow into the light of the room gradually getting closer to Andrew who stood near a gigantic piece of metal sculpture in the center of the tiled floor. There were scraps of metal in one corner. On a long metal table were tools, pry bars, hammers, saws, and soldering equipment. He had cans of spray paint and sealers lining the shelf above the table.

Andrew ran his hand down the piece which reminded her of a soaring wing. The wing had been painted with silver enamel. Andrew turned toward her. Vera responded by lifting her arms in the air, "Wow. This is fantastic. This is what you do in your spare time. You're an artist."

"Yes, I'm an artist," he said reminding her of their earlier conversation and her comment that he wasn't a real cop. "I've even sold some of my pieces. Come on I'll show you the rest of the house."

Vera followed him up a spiral staircase made of wrought iron to a loft where she noticed the view of the Snake River first then the king size bed with its rustic beams which nearly reached the roof. She liked his taste in furnishings; the expensive gray silk coverlet covering the mattress matched the gray framed pictures on the wall and blended well with the burnt wood look of the walls. Andrew pulled her toward him and began to unzip her jeans. His hands moved behind her and slid beneath her shirt to unsnap her bra. She tried to breathe.

"Does this house belong to you?" she managed to ask.

He kissed her neck, "It belonged to my older brother Stewart."

He slipped off her shirt.

Her bra fell to the floor.

He continued answering her question, "After Stewart died, my father bought the property," then he kissed her left breast and straightened to look into her eyes. "And I bought the house from my father."

Chapter Twelve

S eptember had been as hot as July, then, one night the weather changed and by the first day of October the weather cooled into the low forties. Most of last night had been overcast. This morning, storm clouds raced across the Owyhee Mountains promising snow on the peaks. But on the valley floor, the weather remained crisp and cool.

Vera had been back to work at the Egg since September when the public schools reopened, and Egg received day students from the surrounding area. Her scheduled days were Tuesday through Thursday afternoons from one until six o'clock. The preschoolers were her responsibility. On this her fifth Wednesday afternoon, fresh from a night's sleep she hadn't had since she had been a child, Vera entered the Egg breathing in with pleasure the smells of chalk, paint, children, and baking bread.

Joann Bitterroot taught the preschoolers and Vera assisted her. Vera greeted Joann with a nod and a smile. Joann, a tall woman with salt and pepper hair cut neat and tidy just above her earlobes sat at her desk in the corner. Today, Joann wore a suit jacket over her blue silk blouse, a wool pin-striped gray skirt, and sensible black shoes. She had pinned an inlaid gold brooch with a ruby rose on the lapel of her jacket. She looked pressed and prepared as always.

The older woman looked up from her paperwork as Vera entered. Joann made a point this morning to drop her pen and greet Vera, "Aren't we full of sunshine today," Joann said with a grin which revealed a smear of pink lipstick on her upper front teeth.

Vera wondered if her face betrayed her alarm at Joann's uncharacteristic friendliness. Then Vera remembered this was a small town and Joann usually drove past Vera's house on her way to the school. Perhaps, Joann had seen Andrew's Jeep parked beside Vera's Toyota this morning? Joann paused by the mirror hanging near her classroom door and noticed for the first time the lipstick on her teeth. She scrubbed the offending color off her teeth with her usual determination. The maneuver with Ms. Bitterroot's typical no-nonsense manner made Vera chuckle to herself. Vera relaxed figuring Joann had no time for gossip or chit-chat or anything as time wasting as conversation.

She reminded herself of all Joann's good qualities, her masterful organizational skills, and her command over the unruly children. Joann's unusual height and mastery of any chaotic moment reminded Vera of General Patton. And no matter what the situation, Joann's inner yogi always remained serene even when confronted with a blind child kicking and screaming and banging his head on the floor or Misty quiet in a corner ripping out pages from one of Joann's favorite children's books.

Joann left her chair to walk toward the reading circle table and while selecting a book to read to the preschoolers announced, "By the way Vera, we're expecting a new student this morning. Her name is Katherine Fletcher. She's the little girl they found near here. You remember? The one discovered by your house?"

Before Joann spoke, Vera had been about to mention the smear of lipstick on Joann's teeth. Ms. Bitterroot's attention to detail had relieved Vera of one potentially embarrassing social conundrum: pointing out a flaw to a female – and replaced it with another. How should Vera respond? Why would the authorities hand the child over to the Egg? She debated on whether to mention her part in Katherine Fletcher's discovery. Then she lost her courage and decided to keep quiet. Maggie might say something though and Joann would wonder why Vera hadn't told her about her connection with Kat.

It was difficult to keep up with Ms. Bitterroot as she maneuvered her way through the room leaving the bookshelves and darting toward the art table. Ms. Bitterroot's broad back was bent over the table as she proceeded to pour macaroni dyed in primary colors into individual plastic bowls. Absently, Vera questioned the logic of blind children working on art projects. Yet Joann insisted these activities provided a creative outlet for the blind and stimulated their highly developed tactile abilities. Weren't their tactile-abilities stimulated all the time?

Before Vera could mention her part in the discovery of Katherine Fletcher, the door opened, and the children began filing inside. Vera watched Misty head for the bookshelf like a robin darting for a tree branch. The little girl had long black curly hair and eyes as large as compasses. Her sense of direction was equally uncanny. Even though blind from birth, she knew the room better than Vera. Jimmy followed her inside. He was pale and thin with light brown hair so fine that you could see his pink scalp. Katherine Fletcher was the last to enter the room with Maggie in tow. The child performed her ritual of slapping objects and people as she circumnavigated the room. Maggie followed close behind Katherine, as if an invisible umbilical cord stretched between them only allowing Katherine a foot or two of separation.

Joann gathered her flock around her; six children in all and had them sit on the reading matt. Katherine's skinny bottom covered in brown corduroy jumper touched the surface of the matt for three seconds before she sprang up and started circling the room again. Maggie attempted to pen Katherine down, "Come on now, Kat, time for Reading Circle."

Maggie's nickname for Katherine was perfect. Like a cat, she roamed and sniffed and searched spaces. Like a cat, she insisted on her freedom and independence. There were no other autistic children in the preschool. Misty and Brian were blind. Jimmy and Denika were deaf while Josephine was partially blind/deaf and rarely if ever spoke. Josephine had been born in the Ukraine and had lived all her young life in an orphanage. When she was three, she had been adopted by an older American couple. Unlike American children, Josephine stayed where she was put, rarely exhibited emotion, and entertained herself by rocking her upper body forward and backward as if she were bowing to some invisible audience.

For the time being, Joann allowed Kat to roam the room and Maggie to follow her and keep her occupied. It was Vera's job to assist Joann. During reading time, Vera had nothing to do but sit in one of the small chairs in the room and watch the interpreter Mr. Burtman sign for the deaf children as Joann read. The reading took a lot longer than usual because Joann liked to give the deaf children an extra moment or two to examine the pictures on the book's page.

With a certain dramatic flair all her own, she would point at something in the picture that she thought the children might find interesting. Vera would then hand out embossed copies of the picture pages for the blind students to explore with their curious fingers. Throughout the day, Vera thought of herself as a giant jumping bean: a jumping bean which could sit, hop, sit, jump, dash, sit, crawl, hop, and sometimes skip. She was grateful the picture book Joann chose today was a short one.

By four thirty, Vera knew her ordeal was nearly over. It was Vera's job to lead the children into the alcove off the school cafeteria and get them seated at the dinner table. Unlike the cafeteria style folding tables, the students who boarded at the school during the school year used the family table, a polished oval oak table covered in a delicate linen tablecloth with matching oak chairs. The table included an attractive homey center piece, china plates (which terrified Vera especially since Kat had joined the diners), heavy crystal glasses, and silverware wrapped in matching linen napkins. The sharp knives were a real worry.

The Egg table, as the kids and staff called it, was reserved for teachers during the day and the boarded students in the evening. Dinner for the preschoolers meant urging picky eaters to choose something, anything from the food platters. Vera went to each student with the heavy platter waiting patiently for each child to choose a meat and a side dish; in the beginning she felt rather outraged by her feudal position until she arrived one evening to find Ms. Matthew's serving the students with a similar platter. It was Maggie's job to offer the children the gravy bowl and the butter dish and assist them if necessary so that their clothes weren't covered in dollops of sauce or fat.

Among Vera's other duties was to clean up spills, wipe sticky hands and faces, and intercept a child's attempts to wiggle down from a chair and escape outside. Her reward was a free dinner three evenings a week. The kitchen staff at the Egg was nothing like the staff at a typical public school; this kitchen staff happened to be students from the culinary schools in Boise who planned and prepared weekly meals and were paid a little extra for their time and trouble.

Every term there would be a new batch of future chefs and sous-chefs; and no one was foolish enough to miss a meal at the Egg because Ms. Matthew's not only checked the culinary students' backgrounds but vetted the students by requiring them to prepare a meal for the Egg staff and students. At the end of the test, the Egg students and staff voted for their favorites. It was always a treat to savor a delicious meal that might have come from a four-star restaurant. And since many of the parents who sent their children to the Egg happened to be rich and well connected, it was a real triumph for these future chefs be chosen by the Egg.

From the very beginning, Vera had been impressed with the blind students' grace and agility with utensils. And Vera had to remind herself every so often that even sighted people left a table with milk moustaches and tomato sauce on their chins. The first, second, and third grade students sat at the Egg table with the preschoolers. Vera enjoyed this part of the day as she watched the deaf students' fingers fly and heard the high-pitched giggles of the blind students. Instead of having to stand in line during the lunch break, these students were served at the table as they would if they were in a home surrounded by family. Instead of hearing the familiar cafeteria cacophony of children giggling, shouting out to friends, shoes shuffling, canes tapping on linoleum or the kitchen staff asking for the one hundredth time, "Carrots or corn, white or chocolate milk, empty your trays in the blue bin please," These full-time in-house students were encouraged to eat slowly, demonstrate proper table manners, and learn the art of polite conversation.

Among the minority attending the school were a few quadriplegic children and children with Down's syndrome. There were also a few teenagers who were developmentally behind their peers whose parents paid for their children to attend the Egg. Some of the students were day students, others were boarded full time during the school year, and still others were temporarily sheltered until the authorities could find foster homes for them. The criteria Ms. Matthews insisted on for these temporary students were that they be special needs or handicapped in some way. The criteria had something to do with government funding.

Josephine and Jimmy had already left for the day. Denika, Brian, Misty, and Kat were arranged around the table facing each other with Maggie and Vera at each end keeping a watchful eye on the children closest to them. Maggie did her best to prevent Kat from choking on the food she sucked down her throat. Vera watched the four children and Maggie with astonishment. None of them spoke. Brian and Misty both blind could hear perfectly; yet, they continued to eat and drink in silence. Denika, the only deaf child at the table looked up from her plate once but spend most of her time absorbed in the food.

Kat locked inside her own world protected her plate with one arm and ate with the other. The sight disturbed Vera enormously. The child's behavior reminded Vera of pictures she had seen of prisoners defending their food. Vera tried not to think about what her life must have been like as a child living most of her day in daycare and her evenings with a depressed mother who slept all the time and had no family or friends. If she imagined all the sad and cruel truths of this child's life she would just work herself into a fit of misery and rage, perhaps infecting all the children. She mentally shook the ugly feelings away.

"So how was your day Misty?" Vera asked a little too loudly tapping Denika's small shoulder to get her attention and attempting to use her newly acquired sign as she spoke. Lucky for her, Denika was an expert lip reader. Maggie with an uncanny sense of timing interpreted Denika's rapid signing for Vera's benefit and the blind children.

For the first time Kat looked up from her plate and watched the curious symphony as if she were at a tennis tournament, her fine blonde hair whipping her cheeks as she turned to stare at Vera conversing with each student in turn as Maggie interpreted the conversation for Denika's benefit with her beautiful hands creating language in the air.

At one point, Kat who was sitting next to Maggie slapped her arm to get her attention and Maggie shook her head gently and simultaneously signed and said Kat's name, her fingers shaping the letter K and running the K down her hair to signify Kat's long blonde locks followed by the admonishment, "Kat, please be patient. You will get a chance to speak soon."

When Kat nodded her head in acknowledgement, a thrill of delight ran down Vera's spine. It was an astonishing sight to see the two of them so easy with each other. Maggie was brilliant with the little girl, so good with all the children really. Then Vera remembered that both Maggie's parents were teachers and concluded Maggie had inherited their talent as educators.

Once the children had finished dinner each child was assigned a job to do. Denika went around the table accepting the plates and handing them to the blind students Brian and Misty who were waiting on either side of the trolley. The blind students scrapped the food off the plates and into the waste bin. It was Kat's job to empty the glasses into the liquid bin on the trolley with Maggie's help. Kat's idea of helping was to toss the glasses into the liquid bin. Maggie's job was to fish the glass out and hand it back to Kat with a little liquid still in the bottom and encourage Kat to try again. Vera's assignment was to collect the utensils and the Wedgewood serving platter.

By quarter to six, Vera was handing out canes to the blind children. Kat followed Vera and the other children to the double doors in the back of the building. Vera held one side of the doors open as the children filed out. Denika raced down the grassy green slope to the playground equipment below. Maggie and Kat exited the building with as much speed. Kat's response to being outdoors reminded her of a devilish imp suddenly set free from purgatory.

Vera was grateful for Maggie's assistance since she doubted she could match Kat's speed.

Brian passed by Vera, his cane nearly as tall as himself. The end tip of his cane smacked the open door then landed on Vera's shoe. Brian giggled. Vera stared into Brian's gray eyes and for a moment thought he was looking straight at her. It must have been a trick of the light.

Misty threw down her cane near Vera's feet and lifted her arms, "Up, up," she said.

"No, Misty, you're too big to carry. Come on, take my hand."

Vera picked up Misty's cane and while holding her hand led her outside. There were no steps in the school, no need to worry about a child tripping. Brian used his cane like a divining rod waving it about in front of him. Vera stopped beside Brian, "What do you want to do first?"

"Swings," Brian said. "Let me fly."

Vera looked down at the top of Misty's head, "And what about you Misty? What do you want to do?" Misty sat down on the grass nearly pulling Vera's arm out of its socket.

Vera pulled her up on her feet again, "No not today. Let's go to the swings. Follow my voice, Brian."

As a concession to Misty, Vera allowed the little girl to sit on the grass near the swing set then helped Brian into his seat. When Brian asked for a push, Vera gave him a gentle push to start. Once he was settled in the seat and she had given him a few pushes, Vera returned to sit beside Misty and watch as Brian pumped his chubby legs with his face screwed up in fierce concentration. Misty's busy fingers played with the buttons on Vera's blouse and the end strands of Vera's hair. The first time Misty had done this Vera had been uneasy.

No one had told Vera what to expect from a blind child. Vera had had to adjust to a new set of social boundaries as inquisitive fingers touched her face to "see" her. That first day, the blind children had explored her face and hair with their fingers and discussed among themselves their individual interpretations of the way she smelled and the texture of her skin and hair. Their comments had been surprising and made her uncomfortable. They all agreed she smelled like cinnamon cookies.

Misty began to play with Vera's fingers. Her touch made Vera's scalp tingle. Touching was so intimate. Vera thought about Andrew and yesterday and last night. She padded Misty's hand gently and stood up, "Come on. Let me push you on the swing."

—

After showering at Vera's place, Andrew slipped on his clothes from the night before and with reluctance left Vera standing in the kitchen drinking her morning coffee. The sight of her wearing only a bra and underwear with her bare feet propped on the barstool he had recently vacated remained with him the rest of the day. Before he turned onto the main road with the intention of driving to his house to work in the shop, he saw Kit in the front yard raking leaves. Andrew considered driving on without stopping then groaned knowing full well he would never hear the end of it if he did. Andrew drove across the highway separating the properties and pulled to a stop near Kit.

Kit threw down his rake and walked toward Andrew.

"Morning Uncle Andrew," Kit said at his most cocky. "Had a pleasant night, did you?"

Andrew rested his left arm on the door of his patrol car and looked up into Kit's grinning face. Kit sobered, the knowing grin replaced by a whistle, "So that's how it is, huh? Maggie was right then, you got a bad case of commitmentitis."

"Hold on," Andrew said. "Give us a chance will you."

"A chance for what? To get to know her better? Andy, you've been mooning around Grandpa's farm for weeks but in the last few days I see your Jeep more than I see you," Kit pantomimed waving to an imaginary Jeep going south then waved at the same vehicle going north, and finally waved at Vera's house.

"Yeah, yeah, very funny. Do me a favor kiddo and don't say anything to Rachel until Vera's ready to meet the family properly."

Kit shook his head his expression reminding Andrew of a mournful hound dog, "Too late, old man. She told me the news. Remember most ordinary citizens get up at six in the morning and start work by seven. We don't see much of you lately. Why don't you come inside and have some of Rachel's quiche? It's really good."

When he entered his father's house, he found Murray in the living room listening to the farm report and exercising his right hand with a medicine ball. His father lifted his hand and waved, his eyes were sparkling. It pleased Andrew to see his father smiling, well, he still had trouble with one side of his face but there was a definite aura of hope in the way he looked and moved. It must have something to do with Rachel's cooking.

In the kitchen, he found Rachel pouring a fresh cup of coffee in her cup, after glancing over her shoulder at the men, she grabbed another cup from the cupboard near her and poured Andrew some coffee. The sound of thundering elephants coming down the stairs alerted him to the other member of the Treloar household. When Maggie saw him, her grin got wider, "Hey Uncle Andrew, how are you doing?"

"I'm good Mouse," then he threw up his hands and said. "And no, you can't ask."

Everyone laughed having anticipated Maggie's next question. Because they were so happy to see Andrew, his family respected his wishes and brought up only neutral topics during breakfast. When Andrew learned Maggie's bike had a flat, he offered to drive her to the Egg on his way to the station. As Andrew got up from the table and Maggie ran up to her room to grab her purse (when did she start carrying a purse?) the black rotary phone resting on the telephone nook rang.

He had been present when Murray and Rachel had their showdown about the telephone nook. Murray had won. It had been his mother Mattie's pride and joy, that old telephone nook built into the wall. It had been handcrafted – old school kind of crafting with an arch above and a fancy border beneath the ledge. Rachel tried to get him to replace the rotary phone with a touch-tone phone and Murray nearly turned purple all over, so she dropped the whole idea of revamping the telephone nook.

The only concession Murray would allow was that Kit could scrape off the old green paint and put on several coats of semi-gloss white paint. In Andrew's opinion, the telephone nook was perfect for the period of the house; while Rachel's renovations looked inappropriate, the way his Jeep would look odd with pink carpeting and doilies on the headrests.

Rachel was at the sink washing dishes and Kit was drying them. Kit draped the dish towel over his shoulder and grabbed for the phone. Andrew scraped the leftovers off the plates and handed them to Rachel; there were very few leftovers since Rachel was practically a Julia Child. As he handed the last plate to Rachel, he heard Kit say, "Yeah, he's here. Just a sec," and turned to Andrew. "It's George for you. How does he know you're here anyway?"

"Thanks Kit," Andrew said and took the phone from him. Andrew could have told him George kept tabs on everyone in Mintlaw but decided he would be better off keeping the truth to himself. If he'd revealed George's unpaid but enthusiastic surveillance team made up of Mintlaw Quilters Club, VFW members, and nosey neighbors, Kit would have started on his favorite topic throwing in Orwell's book *1984* as proof George's behavior was a precursor to the enslavement of modern civilization. "Hey George, I promised Maggie I'd take her to the Egg today. If you need an extra hand, it'll have to be later this afternoon."

He hated to lie to George, but he knew since Carolina Fletcher had been found on federal land and transported across state lines, those facts meant the case belonged to the FBI and he had no jurisdiction. He also knew if the Chief were aware of his plans to drive to Winnemucca and interview Woody Kirk, there would be hell to pay.

"No, Andy. We're good today. We may need you tomorrow. Dusty's wife is due any minute and the pool says it'll be tomorrow. Hey, you've got a call, Andrew. The Feds are on the other line, I'm going to hang up now and you can talk to Agent Butlin. Agent Butlin, he's all yours."

"Andrew Treloar?"

"Yes, it's me. How can I help you, Agent Butlin?"

"Thought you should know since you were instrumental in discovering Carolina Fletcher's body, we've uncovered new information. Your coroner in Idaho was wrong, sir. Carolina Fletcher did not die of an overdose. I repeat. She did not die of an overdose. Who hired your coroner anyway? Disney? Is he even a pathologist? Never mind. I don't have time to lecture you on hiring people unsuited to their jobs. Our pathologist discovered Carolina Fletcher didn't die from a drug overdose. She died from eating poisoned mushrooms.

We decided we would do our own forensic examination. We found the poisonous mushroom Destroying Angel in her stomach along with evidence of sumac leaves, all mixed in with spaghetti sauce and noodles. Our forensic expert and pathologist agree she ate some kind of exotic meal before dying. In her backpack, we found a clear plastic bag full of dried plants and the poisonous mushroom. We believe her death was suicide. We're basing it on three pieces of key evidence: her recent visit to a lawyer, the autopsy, and the bequests in her will.

We've informed your Chief that the case is closed. At least as far as murder is concerned. The illegal disposal of human remains we're leaving up to the Owyhee County Sheriff's Department and Fish and Game. As for the kidnapping of a minor over state lines, we have since discovered Carolina Fletcher's will gives custody to her cousin Ada Aleshire for the guardianship of Kat Fletcher; therefore, there is no impropriety for a legal guardian to take her ward over state lines. We cannot confirm whether the person Mr. Harden saw was Miss Aleshire and must conclude she may have met with an accident herself. If Carolina Fletcher had known the dangerous company Ada Aleshire kept, she might have had second thoughts about leaving her daughter with her cousin. But as it stands, we have closed the file on murder and kidnapping."

Into the sudden silence, Andrew spoke quickly knowing he probably wouldn't get the chance to talk to the agent again, "In Idaho our coroners are allowed discretion when deciding whether to call in a doctor to determine cause of death. Yes, perhaps our coroner was too quick to judge. He saw signs of drug abuse and decided it was an overdose. And that's a shame. But we can't throw the entire case out. Your coroner may be thorough but even if Ada

Aleshire was Kat's legal guardian, I'm pretty sure Aleshire is guilty of attempted manslaughter. At the least.

Think about it. She left a four-year-old child in the mountains and our witness testified that he saw the woman prepare to throw Kat into the gully which would have seriously injured her.

Aleshire is a dangerous person, Agent Butlin, and we need to find her," Andrew concluded. His annoyance increased as the silence punctuated an already legendary assumption that the FBI were made up of arrogant agents who refused to listen to local law enforcement.

While attempting to convince the FBI agent to keep the case open, in the back of his mind, Andrew was cussing out Mintlaw's coroner and his lazy, no-good, mediocre mind. He had obviously been too stupid or too lazy to bother to request a medical professional examine the body. But that was no excuse for the agent to close the case so quickly. Either the man was more interested in checking off another win for himself or there was something else going on.

"I have informed your Chief, Mr. Treloar," Agent Butlin began in a voice which conveyed his astonishment that an ordinary citizen would have the nerve to question his decisions, "that we have closed the file on Carolina Fletcher and Kat Fletcher. We are still pursuing leads to the whereabouts of Ada Aleshire but no longer need Idaho's assistance. And I will repeat what I told your superior, sir. Do not attempt to look for or interview Ada Aleshire on your own. She is still a person of interest for us but on a different matter. Do we have an understanding, Mr. Treloar?"

"I understand, but—

"We appreciate your help Mr. Treloar. Have a nice day, sir."

Agent Butlin hung up and Andrew looked at the receiver in disbelief. What a tool, he thought. The case might be closed for the FBI but not for him. He still had a lot of questions unanswered and if he just happened to bump into Ada Aleshire, he was going to, by damned, have a few words with her. He was genuinely happy the Feds would no longer be involved in the Fletcher case. Now he wouldn't have to sneak around behind the Chief's back.

—

A small body collided into Vera's back and the impact made Misty lose her hold on Vera and fall face first into the grass. Misty began to cry. Vera turned in time for Kat to slap her. The slap aimed at the back of Vera's head ended up connecting with Vera's cheek. Vera's cheek stung. Instinct prompted Vera to grab Kat's tiny wrist preventing another slap. Maggie ran up and tried to pull Kat away.

"No," Vera shouted. Maggie stopped in her tracks her face registering alarm. Vera held onto Kat's shoulders and tried to speak in a calm voice imitating Joann's tone. "Maggie, would you help Misty please? See if she's hurt. I'll take charge of Kat."

Maggie lifted Misty into her arms and rubbed her back and soothed her with nonsense words. Vera pulled Kat into her arms and held her firmly preventing the little girl from slapping her again. Kat bit her on the cheek instead. Even though her cheek burned where Kat's teeth had penetrated the skin, Vera hung on. They were locked together, she and Kat like conjoined twins. Kat leaned her head back and squeezed her eyes shut. She began to scream with all the power of her considerable lungs.

Vera's ears were ringing long after the screaming stopped. She refused to be intimidated. She held on. Something inside her wanted desperately to break through the barrier between them. She shouldn't care so much about this strange child. But she did. If only Kat would communicate with words and stop biting and slapping people. There was so much Vera needed to know. If Kat had been a different kind of child, everyone would know by now what had taken place the night Carolina Fletcher died. Even at four years old, child psychologists could have potentially found ways to learn something about what had gone on that night. Don't experts use drawings to help children through their trauma? And what about substituting dolls for the people?

Vera began to gently rock Kat. She thought about her own childhood and started singing her Nonnie's lullaby softly in Kat's ear. Surprised Kat began to relax her tense muscles. From far away, Vera heard the night duty nurse call her name. Without warning, Kat became soft and spongy in her arms. Vera loosened her hold. Kat stopped screaming and slipped through her arms. She leaped to her feet and began running toward the swing set. As Vera watched Kat grab hold of the seat and attempt to climb on by herself, Vera saw the night duty nurse's comfortable canvas shoes.

"Your cheek looks inflamed," Miss Paterson said, "If you've been injured, we have the necessary forms in the office for Workman's Compensation."

Vera looked up at the woman for the first time, "Give me a moment here Miss Paterson, please," as she searched for Maggie and found Maggie moving toward Kat with Misty in her arms and Brian following closely behind "Maggie, would you take Misty and Brian inside now please? Kat and I will be along soon."

"I'll fetch Ms. Matthews," Miss Paterson said her tone sour.

Kat and Vera stood alone in the playground. Inside the school, Vera could hear the fulltime residents making their way toward the private rooms on the second floor. The sound of cars driving up to the school and doors opening and closing mingled with the sounds of children calling to parents and friends. From the highway, Vera heard a semi-truck brake and start up again as it drove slowly through the town of Mintlaw toward Marsing and on to parts unknown.

Vera sat on the grass facing Kat. Kat had her eyes squeezed shut and her hands were clenched white fists. The little girl began to pound her fists into the grass and grunt. The grunts became sounds which might have been attempts to communicate but made no sense.

"I know you understand me Kat," Vera said and touched her cheek where Kat had bitten her relieved to discover there was no blood. "I'll give you all the space you want. But when you hit me or anyone else, I'll do it again, I'll hold you and hold you and make you very unhappy."

"Sounds like a plan to me," a voice said behind Vera. Vera turned and looked up into Ms. Matthews' face. "Before you go home, I want Miss Paterson to look at your cheek Vera."

—

Andrew arrived on Vera's porch before midnight. He'd called ahead. When Vera opened the door, the light from the hall lamp illuminated the bandage on Vera's cheek. He kissed her before stepping inside. When he dropped her back on her feet, he said, "I see you've had a tough day too."

Vera, instead of explaining the circumstances behind her wound led him toward the bedroom.

Andrew stopped her before they entered, "I want us to live together. I've been thinking about it all day. My clothes won't take up much room. What do you think?"

Vera held his hand. Her eyes refused to meet his.

"Well? What do you think? Am I going too fast?"

Vera looked up at him, "No. Yes. I don't know. Let's give it a few weeks and then decide. Ok?"

—

Maggie stood outside breathing in the crisp air of Halloween night and listened absently to the loud music and even louder voices inside Amy's house. Maggie's costume itched just along her shoulder blades. She tried to scratch the itch without being observed then decided to come outside and find herself something to rub up against. She had to carry her long trailing gown with both hands.

She and her mother had made the copy from Godey's Fashion Plate last winter in Minnesota which her mother had managed to get from a friend who took a picture of the fashion plate and a picture of the life size reproduction on a mannequin displayed at the Smithsonian. According to the fashion plate it was made from a dark Green Empress cloth and included a black straw Tudor hat with white plum, white gloves, and black gauntlets. She wore buttoned up boots and carried a lady's riding whip. It was ridiculously warm and heavy. It had been her idea and she wished now she'd never said anything to her mother about wanting to be a historical figure from one of her favorite books.

And come to think of it why would Jo wear anything this fancy? As she looked desperately around, she noticed the trees. The locust tree near the road seemed promising. Maggie rubbed her back against the trunk of the locust and ignored the thought of all the nasty insects living in the tree that might drop down on her head.

Someone laughed wickedly. Maggie turned. The laughter had come from one of the cars parked along the side of the road. There were a few couples necking. Maggie thought maybe someone she knew had seen her using the tree trunk as a backscratcher. A voice from the nearest vehicle hailed her. She recognized him and peered closely at the blue Trooper with a bent front fender and noticed a dark silhouette sitting inside.

"It's me. Jeremy," the voice called out.

Maggie wandered toward the Trooper and peeked inside. If Jeremy had seen her rubbing her back against the tree like an animal, he didn't act as if he thought she'd done anything silly or stupid.

"Come on in and talk to me," he said invitingly opening the passenger side door, "Ah, little lady?"

Maggie debated whether or not to climb inside, "I'm Jo March from *Little Women*. Don't worry everybody's been asking me." Her mother would have a fit if she knew Maggie was getting into a boy's car.

As she leaned forward to look inside she asked, "You haven't been drinking or anything?"

Jeremy lifted his can of orange soda for her to see, "Only pop."

"Okay.," she said and opened the door realizing with real disappointment her skirt was too long and bulky to fit in the bucket seat of the Trooper. "Hold on a minute," she told him untying the ribbons that held the skirt and jacket together. She refused to wear the chemise, stockings, and garter, as well as the corset, even though her mother had pleaded with her to be as authentic as possible. As if some fairy godmother had worked her magic to make Maggie's night a success, all Maggie had to do at that critical moment was drop the skirt and petticoat, step over them, lean down and pick them up off the ground. She rolled the skirt and petticoat into a ball and held them to her chest like a warm comforter.

Jeremy laughed when he saw what she was wearing underneath the skirt. Instead of black stockings and a garter, she wore a pair of gymnastic stirrup leggings. She climbed into the passenger seat of the Trooper and smiled up at his beautiful face thrilled to be sitting beside him.

—

Daniel sat on his perch on the hillside near the ledge above Vera's house and watched as Andrew Treloar unloaded boxes from a moving van. He remembered the first time he had met him when Daniel was just a kid before he started growing so fast his knees and elbows ached every day. Andrew had knelt, so Daniel could see his face. He'd shaken Daniel's hand and said, "Call me Andrew. I knew your father Michael Harden. We went to the same school. You probably don't remember this, but I met you when you were just a baby. You sure are growing, Daniel."

His mother had said Andrew was Andrew Treloar and that she had known him when she was newly married to Daniel's father and Daniel should call him The Pig or The Fuzz because he had been a cop then and was still a cop now. And Daniel had asked other people what they called Andrew Treloar. He found out he had been a soldier like his father and his friends had given him a nickname. They called him Scrapman and when he asked what Scrapman meant Deputy Metcalf laughed and said because Andrew created works of art with bits of discarded metal and other materials and because he had always been a scrappy guy getting into fights so, they gave him the nickname. Daniel decided to call him Andrew or Mr. Treloar because people got confused when he called him Scrapman.

When Daniel saw Andrew Treloar take the boxes inside Vera's house, he began to feel real uncomfortable and a little concerned. Was Miss Vera moving out of the Anderson farmhouse and Andrew moving in? Daniel knew Miss Vera. He liked to watch her with the little children. He liked the way she laughed and hugged them. He liked the way she smelled and the way she talked to him. She was more than a human. She was different from Mz. Matthews. Daniel began to worry about what was going on down there. The first time he'd seen Miss Vera he'd felt things happening in his private parts; and each time he saw her, he got just as excited, but he had learned to hide the fact from the other kids when Mz. Matthews talked to him privately and warned him that if he got too excited, she would have to ask him to leave the school for good.

He didn't want to leave the school and go back to his mother's house. He loved the school. He was somebody here at the school. He was taller than anyone else and could climb ladders and work on the roof and the windows and clean out the gutters. He was needed, and no one had needed him like this before. Sometimes he couldn't help himself like September 25th the day Miss Vera helped him put the volleyball net up. She had bent over to pull out the black netting from the box and things began to happen down near his zipper.

He wanted to touch her. He put his hand on her breast. She jumped back and said in a cold voice, "Don't. Don't ever do that again Daniel. I don't like it. It's not polite to touch people without permission." On September 27th, Daniel had bumped into Miss Vera in the supply closet and his hand had brushed against her hip. He remembered how she rushed out of the closet without looking at him. He remembered how at night when he thought about her he woke up in his bed with his underpants all gooey.

Daniel watched Andrew's nephew Kit, the one everybody called Professor Farmer help his uncle unload boxes. Daniel tried to make sense of it all. Then he saw Andrew and Miss Vera alone by the moving van and how Andrew Treloar pulled her to his chest and kissed her. Daniel's throat tightened so he could barely breathe. He scrambled up from his perch and ran toward the place he felt the safest. He shoved the sagebrush away and crawled into the hole of the cave and made his way to his treasure. Only when he was near it was he able to stand up. Still mad at what he had seen, he punched the wall of the cave and cried out when the pain shot through his hand and all the way up his arm.

"Shut them out," he told the cave. "Shut all the bad thoughts out." He used to think Andrew Treloar was Scrapman. Now he hated him. He hated him so much; all he wanted was for the oinker pig to be dead, dead, and gone. When he looked around his cave with the tears making the walls weave and shimmer, he thought he saw something in the corner. There were a few holes in the ceiling of the cave over there and at certain times of the day, bright light made that spot glow. It was usually dark when he came to check on his treasure. He saw it and froze suddenly scared. What was it doing here? Where had it come from?

When he remembered what Maggie had told him during harvest time, when those kids had been working beside them at the orchard and started throwing the hard-green apples at him, laughing, and thinking they were so cool, and the way some of those hard-green apples had hit him in the legs and stomach and really hurt, she had said, "Why are you so scared of those creeps? They should be scared of you. You're bigger and stronger than them. Go on. Stand up to um and see if they don't run away." And she'd been right; and when the farmer had wanted to fire Daniel, she had taken his side and explained what really happened. It had ended well because his friend Maggie had been on his side and the farmer believed her. He got to finish the day and received an extra two dollars for his hard work.

So, stand up then, he thought, *you're bigger and stronger than anybody*. He made himself get moving and crawled toward the corner of the cave to see what lay on the ground.

—

Jeremy started the Trooper. Maggie didn't protest. He drove south toward the highway. Maggie rolled down the window and let the wind blow through her hair. The wind snapped Jeremy's vampire cape into a frenzy. Jeremy drove faster, the snapping seemed to come from everywhere inside the car. Maggie thought about the two of them, the Vampire and the Victorian Lady flying through the night along the unlit highway with only the Owyhee Mountains to see them. Maggie forgot about her father. Maggie forgot about Amy and Amy's party. She felt more alive than she had ever felt in her whole life.

Chapter Thirteen

J ump Creek National Park was their destination this fine Sunday afternoon, Vera learned as Andrew drove. He'd been astonished to discover she had yet to visit the park. It was a sunny Sunday afternoon, most of the snow had melted and the dirt roads were dry. While at breakfast he mentioned several other landmarks, Leslie Gulch, and Succor Creek National Park, which made her a little nervous. Somehow, she'd given him the impression she was the outdoorsy type. She seriously wondered if she had the necessary grit to endure the great outdoors with its bumpy roads, dust, bugs, and dangerous critters.

Vera suspected her driver had figured out she wasn't the outdoorsy woman of his dreams because Andrew drove all the way to their destination like a little old lady. When he turned off the highway onto Poison Creek Road, she made herself relax. He'd chosen Kit's blue Ford pickup rather than his Jeep. He'd told her before they left the house, he intended to look for scraps of metal to use as material for his art projects, also to collect any garbage litterers might have tossed out their windows or left behind at campsites.

"People dump all sorts of junk around here," he started to say.

"That's shameful," Vera interrupted.

"Sure," he said with a lifted brow. "But sometimes when they do, I find a piece of a scrap that's perfect like rusty tailpipes or bumpers. I found an old canteen once after a heavy rain. I'm pretty sure it must be at least forty years old."

Vera sat beside him with her window rolled down, her arm resting on the door, and the sun warming her skin. They drove by farms and roads named Hogg and Gem. Just when she thought they were going to keep on driving south on the smooth blacktop of US 95, Andrew slowed the truck to a crawl, switched on his turn signal, and proceeded down a dirt road stopping long enough to open a gate made of barbed wire. Once on the dirt road, Vera had to hold onto the handle on the truck roof near the window to stay in her seat. The truck swayed and bucked over the dips and humps forcing them to move at a snail's pace along the winding dirt road where thick brush and weeds grew beside the road and an occasional big rock squealed in protest as it rubbed up against their undercarriage.

Several times, Vera had to use both hands: one on the roof strap and the other on the door handle to keep herself from crashing into the windshield or hitting her head on the ceiling or falling onto the floor in a heap. As they ascended the steep rise and leveled off, Vera thought they were safe at last until Andrew was forced to slam on the brakes as a teenager on a Honda ATV tore across the dirt road in front of them. The boy showed off by driving with only the right-side wheels touching the ground. Small rocks and dirt collected in a blanket of brown projectiles. Vera rolled up her window as pebbles hit the glass, the heat inside the cab made it difficult to breathe.

The boy passed them again and stopped on the other side of the road next to an old rusty pickup and a blue sedan full of teenagers. Two older men stood by and stared with hostile expressions as the Trooper maneuvered past them. One man had thick salt and pepper hair and a round face like a pumpkin's head. His eyes were black, his expression unreadable. The other man with his rounded shoulders and beer belly had an identical hostile look. Unlike most of the people they had met on this god-forsaken road who upon passing each other would wave or nod or smile, these men acted as if Andrew and Vera were trespassing on their private property. Even though they hadn't seen any signs posted indicating private land, Vera wondered if they were indeed trespassing and worried they might be shot as a consequence.

"Is this private property?" Vera asked.

"No, this road is on BLM land. I wanted to show you a view from the top of Jump Creek Canyon and then come back down to show you the park. You're probably wondering why the McGown and Spencer men look so ornery. I think it's because Kit's license plate is pissing them off. They think we're from Minnesota. In the last few years, we've had loads of people moving here from California. Property taxes are outrageously high in California and people are buying land and houses here because it's so damned cheap. Many people born and raised in Idaho resent these intruders and are worried about their lives changing for the worse. You know more cars on the road, more crime, that sort of thing."

"I see," Vera said. "I thought for a minute their hostility had something to do with me."

"Well, sure. They probably think you're one of those uppity Yuppies who stole the Armstrong farm right out from under those poor folk's noses."

Glancing at Andrew's smug face, Vera countered, "Or maybe they know you're an official cop again and they hate anyone who's a cop."

Andrew drove the truck to a barbed wire gate, got out, opened the gate, and got back in the truck. He stopped again to hook the gate back to the post. Vera surveyed the curving dirt road with unease, noticing the deep wash on her side. As Andrew drove close to the edge, Vera clutched the door handle and stared straight ahead afraid to look below. She'd always hated heights. The truck kept moving higher and higher up the hill. Soon it reached level ground and Vera unclenched her fingers from the armrest. She had no time to relax because her ordeal wasn't over yet; in a matter of minutes, the truck took an even worse road, barely a road at all and started climbing straight up toward the sky.

Vera shut her eyes. She heard Andrew chuckle. She didn't care what he thought of her cowardice. All she wanted to do was get the hell out and walk the rest of the way behind him. But she couldn't find the words. Instead she clung to the door, feeling trapped and terrified certain at any moment, they would plunge sideways down the hill and be nothing more than marbles pinging from side to side and up and down in a glass jar.

When the truck stopped, Vera opened her eyes and saw the view. Below her she could see how the land sloped steeply downward and gradually leveled off to end at a rocky ledge. She sensed open space beyond the ledge, open space where the crack in the earth could carry one into nothingness. Vera made herself get out of the truck and follow Andrew down the slope to stand on the ledge. Andrew helped her navigate the steep incline showing her how to walk sideways. Once on level ground, he let her go and walked toward the edge and stood with his hands on his hips enjoying the view.

Vera got down on her hands and knees and crawled toward the edge. She didn't care what he thought of her strange behavior. What if she looked childish? Heights had always frightened her. Then she peered down into the canyon. She heard the ruffling of wings and warning cries below and saw a few big birds fly out from their holes in the rock face. Birds of prey, Carl had told her. They were predatory birds who took care of the rodents and rabbits. She saw trees and shrubs and grass growing on the canyon floor. She could not hear the water because her ears were roaring with fear. Andrew did not laugh at her as she inched her way back to solid ground and finally stood up. He walked toward her and took her hand and rubbed the knuckles tenderly with his thumb.

"You'll get used to it," he said.

Vera didn't think she would ever get used to crawling up a mountain side and parking on a bit of land only as wide as her porch, then walking like a man with a stubby leg down to a ledge just to see a creek running through a canyon, a canyon so narrow, she would have to be hanging from the middle of a rope between the two-sheer cliff faces to see everything.

The park, Vera discovered, was soon reached by way of a gravel road leading beyond an old farm. The road dropped and wound down to a cavernous bottom where one could see the canyon up close. Unfortunately, the canyon could not be seen from one end to the other because of the thicket of shrubs, trees, rocks, and vegetation growing along the water's edge. This canyon must have been created by a tremendous force of nature. It was an incredible sight.

Down in the canyon, Vera noticed a bathroom and a bit of landscaping. She also noticed a well-trodden path something pygmies or goats might use. Vera did not think of herself as a goat or a mountain climber and her rediscovery that heights terrified her made her examine why she chose to live in this part of the world. Although she belatedly remembered being equally terrified standing at the top of the Eiffel Tower and as a child when unbeknownst to her in the elevator, she discovered after the doors opened she was in a box in the sky.

Later her mother apologized assuming Vera was like every other Lee—perfectly comfortable in the clouds. When those elevator doors had opened, and she'd seen a glimpse of sky from the skydeck of the Sears Tower in Chicago and people from behind her were pushing her to move forward, she'd dropped to her knees and crawled out and clung to the wall with her eyes closed. She would rather have been safely on the ground.

Andrew had been studying the canyon below him with an intensity which made Vera nervous wondering irrationally if he was thinking about flinging himself over and into the creek below. Vera couldn't stand the silence any longer and asked him what he was thinking. He looked down at her sitting on the ground near his feet. He looked at his watch, then back to her.

"I'm trying to imagine Kat walking in the dark between here and your house."

"You think maybe her family lost her at Jump Creek Falls? That maybe she walked all the way from here to the hilltop above my house?"

"Maybe, I don't know. Why would they have been on Hunter's Hill in the first place? It's known only to locals and a few park rangers. It makes more sense that Carolina and Kat Fletcher were some place well known. They might have seen the posted signs and drove here to see the falls. Or they stopped at the park to use the bathroom and somehow they got separated."

Vera interrupted his musings to say, "You'd be surprised how often strangers to an area while on their way to a town or a city end up getting lost. It could be some stupid cosmic accident."

"No," Andrew responded firmly. "It wasn't an accident. It was premediated. Carolina Fletcher was murdered, and Kat Fletcher had been drugged. There's nothing innocent or accidental about those conditions. Your statement and Daniel's statement don't match up. Daniel went home at ten o'clock Friday evening. According to him everything was over, the litterer drove away. You say you heard the wheels of a chair at midnight and got out of bed. Which time should we believe?"

"I don't know. You're making my head spin. Or maybe it's this place. Perhaps Kat heard the creaking of the swing set and followed the sound to my backyard," Vera suggested.

"Did she find your swing set by flying down from the hill into your yard? We found no footprints small enough to be a child's, no evidence she had been there, and no blankets Daniel swore he saw."

"She was carried then."

"That's what I think happened. The perp frightens Daniel away. The perp pretends to leave. The perp returns and finds the blankets with Kat still sleeping inside. This individual carries Kat down the Access to your backyard and Kat wakes. The perp panics and puts Kat on your swing set to calm her down. Now how would a stranger know Kat would be soothed by a swing set?"

"Why do you keep using the word perp? Didn't you say you thought this person might be Carolina Fletcher's cousin?"

"Because I want to keep my mind open to other possibilities. Once you think you know what happened, you end up going down a dead end. I don't want to create evidence to fit my theory. And yes, I did suspect Ada Aleshire. But we can't find Ada Aleshire or her van and that worries me. We have to consider all the possibilities."

"You think Woody's involved?"

"I do."

Vera returned to the truck and climbed inside. A few minutes later, Andrew followed her to the truck and started the engine. He glanced at her face. She lifted her head to look beyond him at the view and saw with a thrill a bird of prey soaring in the sky above Jump Creek Falls. As they began to descend the winding dirt road and the bird disappeared from view, Vera found her voice.

"How? In what way?" Vera asked him.

"What are you talking about?" Andrew asked swinging the truck around a sharp curve.

"Woody, how is he involved in all this and in what way?"

"He knew Ada Aleshire. He had been seen at her house shortly before she disappeared. She may have needed his help in disposing of the body. Perhaps he was the one who carried Kat to your swing set. Daniel insisted there was no one, but the angry litterer."

"You said Kat had been drugged. She was probably asleep."

"Yes, she had been drugged, but according to the doctor drugged only long enough to sleep six hours at the most. Let's suppose Ada Aleshire was the mastermind behind all of this mess. Winnemucca is two hundred and twenty miles from Mintlaw. That's roughly about a three hour and thirty-minute drive if the driver was going sixty-five all the way. Supposedly she'd been seen at nine-thirty by Daniel. She would have had to leave Winnemucca around six o'clock. Knowing how energetic Kat can be, I'm assuming she drugged Kat in order to have time to prepare. She would have given Kat the drug long before she left Winnemucca; maybe two or three o'clock in the afternoon. We know Kat was awake and swinging on your swings at around midnight."

"What's your point?"

"Someone must have carried Kat down the hill and set her on your swing set. A few weeks ago, Woody showed up at your door having tracked you down, so he could harass you and claim you as his wife. Why would he do that? Woody's a former drug dealer. He ended up in prison. You knew him. I think your rejection of him may have made him think he could punish you by dropping his mess in your backyard.

He gave Carolina Fletcher her last meal which killed her. He drugged Kat to put her to sleep. He convinced Ada Aleshire to help him dispose of her cousin's body and the child. Then after the body was dumped and the child safe, he realized Ada Aleshire knew too much and killed her too. She's probably buried somewhere between here and Winnemucca and Woody thinks he's safe."

"If Woody were the mastermind behind all this, why would Ada Aleshire throw rocks at Daniel to scare him off? I would think she would ask for help or tell him to run get the police if she thought her life was in danger?"

The truck reached the plateau and as they drove past the gate, Andrew said, "But we found only Daniel's footprints and the tire tracks of a Chevy Cargo Van. If Ada Aleshire had been throwing rocks at Daniel, why isn't there any evidence she'd been in the vicinity?"

"She could have wiped her tracks away with whatever was at hand, a branch off some sagebrush or long grasses maybe, anything would do. Although, now that I think about it sounds like you're trying to say Daniel is lying. If that's the case, then your careful time frame goes up in smoke and your back to square one."

"I'm trying to figure all the angles," he continued speaking more to himself than to her. "I've known Daniel most of his life. He's not a liar. I just want to be fair and not get caught up in my own prejudices. Another puzzle is the backpack? The same person who carried Kat down to the swing set must have also thrown the backpack into the trees near your barn. The person must have the most powerful throwing arm in the world to pitch the pack that far. It was stuffed full of coloring books and clothes and toys.

A woman might be strong enough to pick it up and throw it, but she would have to be an Olympian shot putter. So, it seems to me (even though I don't know much about Ada Aleshire) that it makes more sense a man was involved: the weight of the body and the chair, where the backpack landed, and getting the van in and out of Hunter's Hill all are much easier to believe when you factor in a man's upper body strength."

He shifted in his seat to look at her in an effort to bring his point home, "Woody could have done it all by himself. Ada Aleshire would have needed help."

Vera stared out the window at the narrow tracks of the road leading back to civilization. She kept her mouth shut. She was done trying to help him. She was afraid if she looked at him he would be able to read her mind. Fear paralyzed her. She wanted to pick up her thermos of cold water and take a long deep drink, but her arms refused to move.

She thought about Woody instead. Was he capable of disposing of a body? Why would he bother? What profit would there be for him to sneak around and try to lead the police in her direction? She may have injured his pride, but Woody wasn't seriously interested in getting back with her. He'd always been wrapped up in himself, manipulating people to serve his needs. Deep down inside Vera knew Woody wasn't involved in this mess. He was like a cat – he had a talent for avoiding unpleasantness. Yes, he was a moocher and a womanizer and a pathetic addict but not an abductor of children. At the first sign of trouble, he would have figured a way to disappear and be long gone. She was sure he was probably in another state by now looking for a new meal ticket to charm.

She began to relax and with a pretense of nonchalance picked up her water and took a long drink. Andrew kept watching her. She made herself turn to face him. A pair of keen blue eyes studied her face with an intensity she didn't like. She saw him frown then shake his head and turn back to the road.

They drove along in silence until the truck reconnected with Poison Creek Road then Andrew said, "We did find a dead rattle snake where the van had been parked."

Vera turned from her contemplation of the alfalfa fields to his profile, "You think maybe Carolina Fletcher died of snake bite?"

"Carolina Fletcher didn't die from snake venom. The Feds think it was suicide. Their coroner found poisoned mushrooms Destroying Angel in her stomach. The FBI thinks she ate a fancy meal before dying and all evidence leads to suicide due to her previous bouts with depression. She'd signed a will giving guardianship to her cousin. Ada Aleshire is Kat Fletcher's legal guardian.

I'm going to do something about that. Kat is still in the care of Social Services and I'm going to make damned sure Kat is protected from the likes of that bitch. The Feds have closed the case. They think her cousin Ada Aleshire got scared and dumped the body in the gully. Now according to their thinking, it's nothing more than the unlawful disposal of human remains on federal land and Idaho law enforcement need not worry themselves over the Fletchers or Ada Aleshire."

"I don't understand. What about child endangerment?"

"I've told you too much already," he said.

A minute or two passed then he shrugged and with a smile said, "So what, I'm just a temporary cop assigned to Mintlaw Station during a personnel shortage and I'm a nosey neighbor. I doubt if you're going to spread this bit of news all around town. You don't strike me as a gossip."

"I'm not apologizing," Vera replied. "You did seem rather odd. And I didn't know the circumstances, I didn't know that they deputized you right afterward."

"Yep, George thinks I'm a nosey son-of-a-bitch too. He told me once that I should go back to school and become a detective or maybe start my own private agency. That I'm good at finding missing people."

"Why don't you if that's what your good at?"

"To tell you the truth, I've seen too much ugliness in the world and just want to pay attention to its beauty. So that's why after the war, I decided to go back to college and concentrate on art."

Vera pulled out her sunglasses from her bag and slipped them on, "Too bad. You're good at finding missing people and even better you're an altruistic snoop. I'd say you were trying to balance the ugliness in the world with your own sense of beauty. I think that's a good thing."

"I suppose. Anyway, whenever they have a tricky case or something they think I might be able to figure out, they come by and deputize me and give me the details, promising me a big paycheck. Most of the time, I'm not interested. This time, I really want to know what the hell is going on. Something stinks. There is more to this than the feds are letting on."

Too late, Vera made a sound and crossed her arms tight to her chest.

"Damned," Andrew said. "I've upset you. I'm sorry. You've been so kind helping Kat and listening to me rambling on. The ugly details of this case are none of your business. You ready to go? Maybe stop by Three Fingers?"

Vera glanced at him and forced herself to smile, "I have no clue what you're talking about but OK."

"It's a bar and grill. The grill part specializes in (pardon the pun) finger foods. What's odd about the whole thing is that the bar is in Mintlaw, but the famous rock formation called Three Finger Rock is in Malheur County Oregon. From the look on your face, you don't get it. Ah, well, why don't I show you what I mean, I'll show you the landmark first. We'll have to go out US 95 and head to the Oregon border. About a mile or so from the border there's a graveled road we can take, and you can see it in all its glory from a distance. It's better that way. When I was a kid, I tried to climb all three fingers. I managed not to break anything – myself or the fingers. But once I navigated the Three Fingers I checked it off my bucket list."

The ride back on the bumpy twisting road took an hour and that hour seemed like an eternity. She didn't want to think about what he'd told her. She was afraid of betraying herself. God, she hated them, every last one of those dipsticks. She'd managed to escape their perverted world so many years ago only to fall into a trap of her own making with a different brand of scumbag – her ex-husband and his family. Once she sobered up and found a sponsor, she realized she'd been doing the classic drunk's dance. It was all about seeking the comfort of the familiar. In AA people joke about arriving at a party and among hundreds of partygoers the drunks are going to find each other and wallow in their mutual addictions. And at the same token, do psychopaths and narcissists inevitably meet their future victims? Woody had found her. Who would be next?

Once she survived the insanity of Poison Creek Road, she gritted her teeth for another washboard teeth rattling experience just to get a look at Three Finger Rock. She was pleasantly surprised to find herself on a smooth blacktopped highway then a well maintained graveled road which wound through an incredible canyon of fantastic hills and rocky ledges. When she saw the unique rock formation, she nodded her head in the affirmative several times and said, "Okay. I guess it does look like the earth rose up out of the ground to give us the finger. So, what?"

Andrew looked at her and grinned, "I agree. But the people around here think it's funny for another reason. Mickey named his pub and grill after the Three Fingers Rock formation, not because he's a great fan of the landmark but because he's figuratively giving the finger to Oregon. He hates Oregon. I have no idea why. Personally, I love Oregon. It's a beautiful state."

Andrew and Vera pulled into the parking lot of Mintlaw's Three Finger Rock House which in fact was a physical manifestation of another pun – the exterior of the pub and grill was covered in local rock with thin seams of cement between. When Andrew held her arm, preventing her from entering the bar then looked down at his wristwatch as he counted the seconds, Vera played along. At first, she was perplexed. Gradually, she grew curiously intrigued for she became aware of other people congregating in front of the building as if in anticipation of seeing something fun.

Without warning she heard familiar music blaring from the outdoor speakers. It was Sousa's *Stars and Stripes Forever*; and while the music played, Andrew pulled her backward toward the street. She stood beside him among several other tourists and townspeople watching in astonishment as a trap door cleverly disguised on the roof opened and crashed backward exposing a hole, the size of a large suitcase. Mingling with the sound of Sousa's stirring music was the sound of someone vigorously turning a crank. Only a few seconds passed before she saw the apparition appear above the roof top and slowly rise to salute the town.

"How does he get away with that in this conservative part of the world?" Vera asked in astonishment staring at the plaster cast of a gigantic middle finger and its matching pink nail directed roughly west. She assumed the finger was pointing at Oregon.

An old man in a huge dirty cowboy hat wearing saggy blue jeans looked over his shoulder at them and said, "It's the first, you know, the first amendment right of ours— free speech."

"What Ty is trying —saying in his own way," another man said as an unofficial translator for the old cowboy. "Is that Mickey went to court so as he could call his bar Three Fingers. Then he had to go to court again, so he could use the plaster cast. Back in 1980 we got to watch the middle finger twice a day: openings and closings. Now, cuz of complaints from old ladies, Mickey only raises the finger once a month." The man ended his lecture by giggling. Then the giggling turned into a fit of snorting

Once inside, Vera sat on the stool and realized how long it had been since she had been inside a bar. Andrew started to order her a beer and she touched his arm to stop him, "I'll have a coke or an iced tea."

Andrew ordered her a coke and himself a nonalcoholic beer. Vera munched on peanuts and looked around. The bar was crowded. There were men and women in the uniform of Harley enthusiasts. Some of them looked good in black leather pants and jackets; others looked kind of sad, elderly, and overweight. They had removed their goggles. Yes, she thought whimsically to herself, they were a bunch of raccoons enjoying the contents of this trash can. The analogy made her smile.

Her smile encouraged one of the raccoons to stand up and move toward her. She scowled and turned back to face the bar. As she stared at her face in the large mirror hung behind the bar, through the glass, she saw a woman get up from a table in the far corner, a medium sized stout redhead her face obscured by a pair of large sunglasses. The redhead was moving toward the door. It was the way she walked that reminded Vera of someone. The jukebox bellowed out a country music song with twanging guitars and a baritone voice lamenting about lost love. The patrons contributed to the noise by talking over the music.

Before Vera could get a good look at the redhead, a group of people entered the bar and she disappeared outside. A trivial uneasiness disturbed her tiredness. Now she was fully awake and wondering, wondering if she had seen Ada Aleshire. She thought about running outside and confronting her. But then what would she do? Make a scene? Call the cops? And what about Andrew; what would he think if he knew the truth?

Vera hated being inside these places. She hated sitting on barstools in the dark. She hated the smell of stale beer and the blue haze of smoke all around her suffocating her with its stench. What the hell was the matter with these morons? It was a beautiful sunny day. The mountains were a few miles from the bar. Why were they cooped up in this place? She'd spent the best years of her young life sitting outside these kinds of places waiting for her mother and her mother's newest boyfriend to come out. And when she got old enough to go inside and look around, she discovered how dingy, dirty, and dumb people were when they were drunk.

In her young alcohol-free superiority, she thought the people drinking inside the dark gloomy bar were certifiably nuts.

When she did discover how much she liked the taste of liquor and the way it made her feel, instead of wasting her hard-earned money on expensive drinks in a bar, she bought her liquor cheap and drank her bottles in the privacy of her home. Now that was certifiably nuts in another way. If you drink alone, where no one can see you, then you can't be a drunk, she rationalized. At least for a while she was able to justify her solitary drinking till the day she was trapped in an elevator in Vegas for two hours and couldn't get to her rotten little apartment for her breakfast of cigarettes, gin, and poached eggs on toast. She thanked her lucky stars she'd been in that elevator alone.

Vera could barely hear Andrew over the music. When a large man smacked Andrew on the back and said, "Well hello stranger," Andrew introduced him as George, a friend. Vera remembered George Metcalf arriving at her house when Lazy discovered the backpack. He looked as if he had just stepped out of a poster for Go Army with his buzz haircut, his strong jaw and tall muscular body. George's handshake left her fingers numb. She watched him watching her. His examination reminded her of other cops she had known, the eyes taking in all the details: the face especially, also registering the height, the weight, the coloring, and distinctive features like tattoos or scars; all for storage in long term memory for future identification.

Vera climbed off the stool and moved towards the lady's room. When she returned George had left. Vera climbed back on the stool and finished her soft drink. Andrew finished his drink, stood next to her, and without a word took out his truck keys from his pocket. She got the message loud and clear. He led her to the truck his hand on her back gently guiding her down the street. Once home, Vera began to relax. She entered the house and Andrew followed. The drive had taken fifteen minutes but the silence between them had made the time seem to go on for eternity. Andrew had moved in a week ago. Vera had spent most of the time rearranging her bedroom closet and drawers to accommodate his clothes. Thankfully he had left his furniture at his house on the river. At first, she'd been afraid his intention had been to burn all his bridges.

A strange sense of hollowness made her wonder why she had agreed to this arrangement. Their relationship consisted of tumbling around in her bed at odd hours of the day and night and Andrew getting up and getting dressed and leaving her at home, so he could work in his shop or help his buddies at the Mintlaw Police Station. Now that he was living with her, she sometimes wondered if he was secretly gloating at his victory and one day she would wake up and he would be gone for good. While he was at his studio, sometimes she would be at the Egg helping with the children wondering if he was regretting his decision; but most of the time, she was in the yard weeding or watering or finding some new fix-up project to keep her mind off her stinking-thinking.

The drive to Jump Creek Falls had been their first outing. Would he now expect her to cook his meals and wash his clothes? She had no knowledge of what a couple's successful relationship looked like and no prior experience to draw upon, only her disastrous marriage to Vlasky and before him, her Uncle Frank and Aunt Vista's marriage. They squabbled all the time; and on occasion threw things at each other. Nonnie and Cawley's great love came secondhand through her mother's stories. Vera suspected her mother had been trying to recapture such a love in her own life by insisting the men she met had to be faithful to her no matter how badly she behaved. The only two realities in Vera's life had been Nonnie and knowing the family would soon be on the road again. Had she thought finding a permanent home would give her an advantage over her mother? It hadn't worked out so well with Vlasky.

Did Andrew expect her to wash his dirty clothes? She stared down at the hamper full of his clothes and decided the next time she was in town, she'd buy a hamper for herself. Maybe he would get the message.

Vera thought about his body lying next to hers, the way she would wake to find his arm hugging her close and his long leg draped over her hip. His smell was imprinted on her brain now, the scent of him still on the pillow. At first his confidence and intelligence frightened her; now, as she was getting to know him better, she noticed his moments of gentleness and kindness. He could be stubborn too which wasn't so bad. Everything about him had taken possession of her mind and her senses and she could no longer remember Joshua's face or his smell. This new male, exciting, interesting, and sometimes puzzling had transformed what had once been her desires into a desire to please him.

In the past, she had to put up with a man forgetting to put down the toilet seat or leaving crumbs on the countertop. Unlike other males, Andrew seemed to have been born with an insatiable need to put everything in order. And he was much better at organization than her. Just as encouraging was the fact that he took less time to shower and shave than Joshua. And Andrew liked to keep his toothpaste tube and toothbrush in a fancy holder in the medicine cabinet. The only habit he had which bothered her was his insistence on flossing every time he ate and fussing over the condition of the bathroom and kitchen. They had to be clean and tidy. Otherwise, she didn't know much about his past or his experiences in Vietnam.

Well, she was equally reticent about her past. And if he found out about her past what would he think? He already despised Woody. If he knew she was Roma, would he leave or worse would he pity her? Not ready to open a discussion about her first encounter with Andrew's close friend George Metcalf or their visit to Mintlaw's famous watering hole, Vera wandered into the kitchen and started preparing something to eat for dinner.

Andrew came out of the bedroom with the hamper in his arms, "Time for laundry duty," he said with a grin and opened the folding doors that separated the washing machine and dryer from the kitchen. While she chopped onions and mushrooms, Andrew separated the whites from the colored clothes and started the machine. Wow, she thought, can he be for real?

—

Daniel sat on the ledge above Miss Vera's house. He had been watching the house since the day Treloar moved in. He rubbed a bit of picture jasper between his fingers. He'd found the piece of stone in an abandoned test hole. There were other rocks around the sides of the hole, but nothing that interested him today. Someone had dug the hole a long time ago. He knew this because there was already cheatgrass and winterfat growing where the dirt had been deposited.

He didn't know what to do about Miss Vera. She liked him. She smiled at him and showed him that she liked him. But she never got close enough for him to touch. Daniel knew about mating and reproduction. The kids at school told him all about males and females and how they had sex and produced babies. But that wasn't always true. His mother and Darrell slept together, and he could sometimes hear them doing something fun, but his mother did not end up having a baby afterward. Mating must be fun the way his mother and Darrell behaved. Daniel thought about mating with Vera.

—

Jeremy turned the Trooper onto a dirt road leading to the left just before the Oregon line and swung the vehicle around to face the highway. He shut off the engine and turned off the lights. Maggie stared out the windshield at the shadow of the mountain on the other side of the highway. There were no lights anywhere for miles not even a nearby farmhouse with maybe the glow from a window or porch light.

It was so dark she could barely see Jeremy's face. She began to get nervous, began to wonder if Jeremy had assumed something she wasn't prepared to do. And then she started to think about her father and wondered if he expected a phone call from her by now. He knew she was sleeping over at Amy's houses and had still insisted she call him when the party ended. What if he had tried to call Amy's house and Amy told him she had gone off with Jeremy?

She wasn't sure of the time. She knew where she was. She had seen the *Welcome to Oregon* sign before Jeremy turned onto this road. She had been in this general area with her parents and uncle before. It just looked desolate and ominous in the dark. Many times, her family had driven their ATVs up and down the backroads of Oregon. But now, in the dark, with only passing vehicles' headlights and a black sky filled with white stars and a cloud passing over the moon, she couldn't even see her hand in front of her face.

When she heard rustling outside the Trooper and peered out Jeremy's passenger window, she searched the shadows trying to pick out the cause of the sounds she was hearing; all she could make out were a few shapes resembling sagebrush and rocks with a larger hump beyond. She tried to remember if there was a mound on this old road. The entrance to this off-road had a turnaround made by numerous vehicles over the years packing down the soil and killing the vegetation.

Maggie tried to imagine what sort of animal was out there moving around in the night. It could be anything: a coyote, a jackrabbit, even grouse. No, not grouse, birds clucked and flapped their wings. Perhaps it was a badger? They hunted at night, didn't they? Badgers looked cute, but they were mean. She hoped it wasn't a badger. Maybe it was a snake? No, snakes sleep during the fall and winter; she was sure her uncle had told her they sleep in burrows and only come out to warm themselves on rocks in the afternoon.

"Did you hear that Jeremy? That noise," Maggie asked him. "What do you think it is?"

Jeremy inched closer to her wrapping his arm around her shoulders and with his face near her face said, "It's probably a jackrabbit." Then he kissed her.

Maggie tasted salt from his potato chips and smelled beer on his breath.

She pushed him away, "I thought you said you hadn't had anything to drink."

Jeremy settled back in his seat, "I had a couple of beers earlier, before I got to Amy's house. That was two hours ago. Don't sweat it, Maggie. I'm not drunk."

The rustling got louder. Maggie rolled up her window and looked out. About two feet away from the Trooper, she saw several furred shapes prowling around the mound. The dark cloud slipped passed the moon and with the moon's light bathing the area in white, Maggie saw a van with its back doors open wide and what might have been a wolf or a coyote jumping out of the back end with a bone between its jaws. Maggie screamed.

Chapter Fourteen

Andrew Treloar arrived at the turn off near the Oregon border and noticed George's patrol car parked off the dirt road with his lights flashing and his headlights illuminating the van. Andrew parked his vehicle beside George's patrol car and left his headlights on. He walked over to Jeremy's Trooper first. Maggie sat in the passenger seat with her head down and her hands clasped in her lap. Andrew opened Jeremy's car door and said, "Jeremy would you step out of the vehicle for a moment, I'd like to talk to Maggie."

Jeremy nearly catapulted himself out of his Trooper bumping into Andrew in his eagerness to remove himself from what he imaged to be a furious male relative, "Sure thing, Mr. Treloar," he said and stood well away from the Trooper as if he thought Andrew might be tempted to punch him.

Andrew climbed into the driver's seat and looked across the space between himself and his niece, "Why didn't you call me Maggie?"

Maggie lifted her head, "I told Jeremy to go straight to the police station. And when we got there, Uncle George, I mean Deputy Metcalf said to show him where we found the van. I didn't have time to call you. I asked somebody to let my Dad know where I was. Does Dad know?"

"Yes, when the station called, I called your father. He's not pleased that you left Amy's party without contacting him first. Anyway, you don't need me to tell you how your father's taking this. Do me a favor and get in my car. I'll take you home directly."

"Jeremy can take me home."

"I promised your father that I would bring you home. Go on. Get in the car. Do it now."

Maggie climbed out of Jeremey's Trooper and climbed into the front passenger seat of Andrew's Jeep. Andrew called out to George, "Hey George, you need to question Jeremy?"

George turned, and his flashlight hit Andrew in the eyes, "Oops, sorry, Andrew, No, the kids can go home now."

Andrew signaled to Jeremy. Jeremy approached him with a wary look, "Go on home Jeremy. If we have any further questions, we'll contact you."

"I'm real sorry about Maggie seeing this. Would you tell her father I'm real sorry?"

"You can tell him yourself. Now go on, it's late."

Andrew watched until Jeremy reversed his Trooper and took off down the highway back in the direction of Mintlaw. Andrew walked toward the van and stood beside George. George's gloved hand stopped Andrew from proceeding any further, "Let's just wait for the investigators to get here from Homedale. I don't want another ass chewing for messing up the scene of a crime."

"Anyone inside do you think?" Andrew asked wondering if perhaps Ada Aleshire's body or whatever was left of it might be inside the vehicle.

"Can't tell from here? We'll know more when the sun comes up. Hey, you don't have to stick around. You can take Maggie home and get some breakfast. By the time you get back here, I'll be ready for bed."

Andrew glanced back at his Jeep, then at the van. He was reluctant to leave. This was the evidence he had been waiting for, the vehicle which he assumed belonged to Ada Aleshire and had been driven up to Hunter's Hill, the same vehicle she had used to transport Carolina Fletcher's dead body and Kat wrapped in blankets. Andrew had more than enough curiosity to want to stick around and see what forensics might find in the vehicle, "No, I'll stick around a bit longer. Maggie can wait. It'll do her good," he paused before looking back at the van. "I've got my camera in the car. I want to take some pictures while I'm here."

There was a strip of gold along the edge of the mountain peaks. Andrew fished in the Jeep for his camera case and paused to look at the back of Maggie's head, "I want to take some pictures of the scene. The sun should be up in about twenty minutes. I'll ask George to radio in for dispatch to give your Dad a call that I'll be bringing you home. Ok?" When there was no sound from the front of the Jeep, Andrew slammed the back of the door and walked to the passenger side carrying his camera case.

"Maggie," he said looking in on her. Her head was lowered, and she had her hands covering her face. "Well, you just take all the time you need to get yourself together. Just stay in the Jeep please."

Andrew returned to where George stood by the back of the van his flashlight skipping across rocks and sagebrush and wild grasses, "Looks like some rock hounds have been here lately."

Andrew glanced over his shoulder and waited for the sunrise. When he could see well enough to get out his camera; he made sure he had plenty of film. Another ten minutes passed, and he began to take pictures of the area around the van, the inside of the van (at least what he could see from where he was standing) and the tire tracks from the blacktopped highway to either side of the road for about half a mile. The invisible line George had drawn prevented him from taking pictures of the other side.

The headlights of a vehicle coming fast down US 95 heralded the arrival of the coroner and behind him Andrew noticed another vehicle. Andrew soon discovered the Chief had left his warm bed to follow the coroner out to this lonely spot right on the Oregon border. Steve was probably feeling more pressure than Andrew to solve this one. Even though this area was the jurisdiction of the Homedale Police, everyone in local law enforcement seemed to be on the scene ready to assist.

"Can I borrow your flashlight George?" Andrew asked. Andrew used the flashlight to check his watch. It was 5 a.m.; in approximately thirty minutes there would be enough light to see inside the van and hopefully he would be allowed to take some pictures. Andrew heard another patrol car's siren in the distance. Reinforcements were arriving.

Andrew helped the Homedale Police and Mintlaw's other deputy Charles Davis Dougherty set up the lights around the parameter and with George's assistance everyone set stakes in the ground and encircled the van with yellow caution tape. Maggie had not moved from her spot in Andrew's Jeep. At one point, Andrew thought she might have fallen asleep. A few minutes later, when her head popped up, he realized she'd just been looking for something on the floor of his car.

—

Vera awakened by Andrew watched him enter the house and grope for the light switch. She had positioned herself on the couch with a blanket over her legs and an unobstructed view outside her window. Every so often when she heard a car on the road, she would pull back the curtains to peek outside. It was 6:30 a.m. Vera greeted him at the door. He lifted her up into his arms and hugged her so tight she could barely breathe. He let her go and said, "Nice."

Vera followed him into the kitchen. "Well?" she asked.

"Curious, that's what I'm thinking, curious indeed."

"What did you find?"

"I left before the real work started. I'm going back after I shower and change."

"You said something about an abandoned vehicle. What happened? Is anyone hurt?"

"Maggie and Jeremy found a van near the Oregon border. It looks as if we've found Ada Aleshire's carpet cleaning van. But I'm not sure what else is inside. I'll know more later on today."

"What's so curious?"

Andrew sat down at the kitchen table with a bowl of cereal. He paused before plunging his spoon into the bowl, "It's been five months since Daniel saw the van and the woman. And the location of the van so close to the highway doesn't make sense. There is definitely something underhanded about this whole affair.

Two months ago, everyone was looking up and down this entire area from Leslie Gulch to the Owyhee Reservoir, from Marsing to Homedale, even searching the entire route to Winnemucca and they found nothing fitting the description of that van. Yet, now, at this very moment, the Chevy van shows up. The vehicle isn't that hard to spot. It has a giant vacuum chasing a giant white bunny on one side with the logo Dust Bunnies detailed in fancy script on both sides. How could anyone not notice that?

In fact, weeks ago, I passed that stretch of road on my way to Aleshire's house and back again and I didn't see it there. Now all of sudden, the van is sitting in plain view with its cargo doors open and ... well, I can't say any more about it. I'm thinking the van was hidden away in someone's garage or maybe a storage yard, no, more likely a junk yard, a place nobody would think to look and then it was driven to the Oregon border recently and parked on that road. Somebody is playing games with us and I want to find out what the hell is going on."

—

Maggie stood in the kitchen and listened to her father with a face as white as salt, "Have you heard nothing I've said in the past? Do you really expect me to believe that I gave you permission to get into a boy's car and drive to Oregon? What is going on with you lately Maggie? You're grounded, grounded for two months. No parties. No movies out. Your only outside excursions will be to school and home again. Are you listening to me?"

Nodding her head unable to see for the tears blurring her vision, she had known exactly what would happen if she got into Jeremy's car. She had known and got in anyway. Two months! Then she thought about Egg. She found enough voice to ask, "Will I still be able to volunteer at Egg?"

"The Eggs can do without you for the time being. You're grounded Maggie. Now go to your room."

Maggie glanced at her mother sitting at the table in her bathrobe. She looked crisp and prepared, her hair combed and pulled back into a tight ponytail. It was the expression on her face that shocked Maggie. She looked so pale and haggard. Her mother hadn't said one word since Maggie had entered the house. Maggie left the room and just as she reached the stairs she heard her mother say, "Don't be so hard on her Kit. We've had nothing but success and hard work from Maggie all her life. Everyone deserves a mistake or two. Let her help out with the children after her regular classes."

"Jeremy works at the school you know," her father said.

"Only during the summer, let her work at Egg for the summer. Daniel will be in charge of the grounds in the fall. Jeremy hasn't been pulling his weight lately."

"How do you know that?"

"I've met Sarah Matthews for lunch a few times. I admire her and think she will be an excellent influence on Maggie."

"God Rachel, I am so angry and disappointed. I've been thinking all sorts of dire thoughts. How can you be so calm?"

"I've been just as worried as you Kit. I handle stress differently that's all."

Maggie turned to climb the stairs and noticed Grandpa Treloar watching her from the parlor room which was now his bedroom. He waved to her. She waved back and climbed the stairs grateful that at least one person in the house didn't hate her.

—

A dream woke Daniel. He'd been running, running across the desert in the dark with the moon as a guide. The moon was a trickster. The moon kept the bad creatures hidden from him. The moon showed him the sagebrush and the boulders; yet, it made the burrows and snakes invisible. He stumbled several times, never quite reaching the road. The snakes hissed at him. As he ran past the homes of the whistle pigs, a few popped out of their holes with their front claws tearing at his pants and their sharp teeth sinking into his right ankle. He sat up on his cot and threw back his army blanket. Burrs and thistle thorns coated the bottom of his sheet near the foot of the cot. He couldn't remember how the burrs and thistle thorns had come to be in his bed.

He thought of magic and Halloween. He thought of jokes the kids had played on him in the past. He saw Robbie's face again: Robbie peering down at him, Robbie with his missing front tooth, his red gums and long tongue; Robbie coughing up a big wad of snot and Daniel just lying there on the ground waiting for the spit to land on his head. He shook himself awake. Robbie couldn't hurt him anymore. He was bigger than Robbie now. He found his socks stuffed down among the sheets at the foot of his bed. His socks were covered in burrs and thorns. He must have pulled them off in the night and shoved them away from him with his feet.

Daniel hopped across the room as his bare feet met the cold concrete. He jumped into his pants and sat on the cot to put on a clean pair of socks. He liked to put on one sock and one shoe, then the other sock and the other shoe. He especially liked the part where his mother wasn't here to tell him to put his socks and shoes on the way normal people do or to tell him to go back upstairs to put on socks that matched. Always the matching, match this puzzle with that puzzle, match this card with that card. Find the same color. Find the same face. Find the same, same, same. He liked brown and green and black. He liked pictures on his shirts. He liked shapes that reminded him of rocks. He didn't like square pockets and white buttons. And he definitely didn't like short sleeves.

Mz. Mathews promised to give him some money to buy new clothes. He thought about going to the store with Mz. Mathews and finding himself a shirt with a picture of mountains on it. He wanted shirts without buttons, shirts with long sleeves. He wanted army pants to remind him of his father. He wanted to find himself a good hat, a hat like those people in that land called Australia wear. He got excited thinking about how he would look in his new clothes and how Miss Vera's eyes would shine when she saw him.

—

As Vera drove toward the school down the tree lined driveway, her eyes were filled with all the colors of autumn: yellow, orange, red, and brown leaves whirling through the air, some floating to the ground, some still stubborn clinging to the tree branches; the way the grass had greened up with the onset of cooler weather, the way the mountain peaks had taken on a shade of violet against the darker sky. Even the air smelled fresher, almost newborn. Not all the flies had died, but compared to August, October's flies were a minor annoyance, an occasional unwelcome visitor at the door.

Andrew had left the house before Vera had finished showering. Vera's assumptions about Andrew's chauvinism had been erroneous. She should have realized Andrew, a bachelor for most of his adult life, would have had plenty of time to domesticate himself. His habits were rather peculiar though. He only washed clothes if he ran out of underwear and socks first. He had enough underwear and socks to last him a month. He sent his uniforms to the dry cleaners and rarely wore blue jeans to the Mintlaw Station anymore.

If he did wear blue jeans, they were more likely designer jeans. In comparison, her clothes appeared shabby and sloppy. Once she had enough extra money, she would go to downtown Boise and buy herself some clothes worth wearing, something tailored and soft against her skin, something well-stitched and durable, something in bright colors with beautiful patterns.

Vera waved as Sarah Matthews with Daniel in the passenger seat passed her on the road. Daniel waved back enthusiastically. Vera was relieved to know that Daniel would be away from the school this afternoon. She knew she shouldn't be afraid of him; yet lately, Daniel had become more intensely interested in her and sought her out most often when she was alone. Vera didn't know who to turn to to ask how she should respond to Daniel. The situation was delicate, not a topic she could readily bring up with Joann and she most certainly didn't want to prejudice Ms. Matthews.

When Vera entered Joann's classroom, Joann sighed and said, "I just received a phone call from Maggie's father. Evidently, Maggie won't be volunteering after school for quite some time. It is a shame. Now Vera this might seem like a setback, but we must be flexible. You understand?"

Vera nodded absently, wondering if the "flexible" part was Joann's own mantra to herself. She passed the teacher as Joann sat at her desk. Vera hung her jacket and purse in the closet feeling like an intruder breaking into someone's private sanctuary. Joann had asked Vera not to leave her purse or her jacket on the countertop because she needed the countertop which extended the length of the room for school projects and papers. Yet there were days when the closet was locked, and Vera had nowhere to put her personal belongings.

For a few weeks, she kept her coat and purse in her car. But when she had to go out with the children, she was forced to run to the front of the school and grab her coat. On the third day that she left the classroom to fetch her coat, Joann had insisted she bring her coat inside. Yet the woman kept giving her mixed messages, some days leaving the closet door unlocked, other days locked.

After glancing around the school room, Vera began gathering up toys and books and putting them away before the children came in and tripped over them. She didn't let her thoughts show on her face. What the hell was that all about—be flexible? Why was Joann lecturing her about flexibility? All her life Vera had to be flexible. If she hadn't been flexible, she would have been dead by now. Mentally shaking off other people's stupid remarks, Vera turned her attention back to the task at hand. The deaf children had yet to acknowledge the blind children's need for orderliness. Vera straightened the room and bundled up the children's artwork cluttering the tables and floor.

She thought about confiding to Joann the real reason why Maggie would not be volunteering in the classroom any longer. Once the room was tidy, Vera decided to keep quiet. It was up to Maggie to tell Joann. Joann didn't need to know. Joann might have understood having teenagers of her own; but, if Maggie returned, she would be disappointed to learn Vera had gossiped about her to the staff. It was a revelation to discover how a fifteen-year old's good opinion had become extremely important to Vera.

The more she met people half way, the more she valued their good opinion of her. Now that Vera lived with someone, she found herself trying to second guess Andrew's thoughts over something she had said or did that day. Why was she being so obsequious lately? She had been the same way with Vlasky. The slightest criticism would be shuffled and reshuffled in her head and would make her writhe in self-contempt. Was it because they were gadjo? Had she always been afraid of them? No. There had been a time when she used to challenge criticisms, when she was self-confident and independent, and stupidly brave. She was the Muddy Puddle when she was under attack and a fierce Cath Palug fighting the mighty King Arthur when standing up for the underdog. A few bloody noses and bruises hadn't frightened her back then.

And then her Nonnie died and the gadjo took her away from her family.

She brushed aside the memory, really, more of a feeling now. A distraction brought her back to the present.

Misty entered the room in her usual way, flinging the door open and letting the door crash against the wall. Her chubby figure had been squeezed into a pair of corduroy pants and a lacey blouse. Her curly hair had been pulled back into a ponytail and that ponytail whipped from side to side as she navigated the room with her new-found skill with the stick. She smacked the chairs, the bookshelves, the toy shelves, Joann's desk, ending up collapsed in a heap on the floor near the toys running her fingers along the shelves for her favorite speak-book. The others had filed in behind her.

Vera stood in the corner of the room near the closet and watched the children find their places. Misty lifted her head, then jumped up and started toward Vera. When Kat noticed Misty moving in Vera's direction, Kat made a point of reaching Vera first and grabbed hold of one of Vera's legs. Kat's usual greeting —a smack on the leg or on the backside became a tap on the knee today. Misty sensed Kat's nearness and stopped in her tracks listening intently. Kat was exhibiting jealousy.

Vera pried Kat's fingers off her leg. She led the girls toward the reading circle mat, her hands trapping their small fingers, gently but firmly steering their small selves toward a space they did not want to go. Vera disliked being the instrument of entrapment. She disliked energies contained and suppressed and aligned to fit someone else's objective. Her work at Egg reminded her increasingly of prison wards and she the guard on duty shuffling the prisoners from one room to another or from one area of the room to another.

Joann enjoyed her work, she enjoyed containment and suppression of energies; she enjoyed molding and shaping these children into regular people. Vera had her doubts that these children would ever be regular anything and suspected ordinary folks weren't regular either. Everyone had some spark of craziness inside themselves which needed to be fulfilled. She wished the world would let them find out what made them happy. We all can't be little soldiers marching in the same direction.

She should be resigned to the idea that these children, so full of energy and anger and eagerness to explore the world would someday run out of delight and discovery. They would become the hollow chambers of one of Daniel's thundereggs, all too aware of their limitations. It made her mad just thinking their futures would be so bleak. Her morose thoughts were getting her nowhere today. She decided to turn off the stinking thinking and pretend to be one of the little soldiers.

Once outside in the cool autumn air with the wind blowing down from the mountains and the clouds obscuring the sun from moment to moment, Vera watched the children run to the box and dig their fingers in the sand and roll and scream and catch each other's flying coats. The patterns on the green lawn shifted from light to shadow to a haze that bleached the earth the color of dandelion wine. Misty and Brian blind to the light and shadow and haze perpetuated by the clouds could still feel the sun on their faces and when the clouds obscured the sun could feel that too.

They could also "see" the world with their other senses, their noses, their ears, hands, and bodies, bumping into the other children and the swing set and the pole of the basketball hoop.

It was fun watching all the children abandon themselves to play. Vera held Misty and Brian's sticks under her armpit and had her hands in her pockets to keep them warm. Denika sat on one of the swings and pumped her legs until she and the swing had become a pendulum fighting gravity. From the corner of her eye, Vera noticed Kat running away from the playground area across the green lawn, her pink jacket lined with warm goose down open and flapping behind her as she ran.

Every so often Kat would pause and look back to see if anyone followed. Vera let her run knowing the fenced yard would contain her, knowing once Miss Paterson arrived to relieve Vera, Vera would have to go in search of Kat and play the game out to its bitter end. Vera was in charge of all the children and couldn't leave the rest of them to chase down one. Kat's habit was to stay within sight of an adult, gradually separating herself by some invisible measurement of distance, about three or four feet, a distance only she understood, and she maintained that distance for as long as possible.

Today, Vera lacked the impetuous to stalk or trap anyone and winced at the idea of having to carry Kat kicking and grunting all the way back to the school. If she had her way, Vera would set Kat loose, let her run free and wear herself out, poor kid. Vera had no more energy or enthusiasm for games. Maggie would have played the game. Maggie would have coaxed Kat to her and rewarded her with treats, just as if Kat had been a puppy. Vera compared the school's strategy of rewards and punishments with puppy training techniques. She found the whole miserable bag of tricks distasteful.

Joann had tried to explain the reasoning behind the children's training and Vera had tried to accept the situation. Yet, she wished there were some other way of educating children like Kat. Vera had this overwhelming urge to pick Kat up and take her home. She disliked the idea of these children sleeping in cots alongside other children without the comfort of home to remind them of their humanness and connection to something deeper and more durable. Yet familial warmth and protection was also a myth. Her experience with her own family reaffirmed her opinion people could be shits twenty-four hours a day.

Vera thought about the van out in the Owyhee Mountains, a van which at one time had belonged to Ada Aleshire. Someone had driven the van from Winnemucca, Nevada to these mountains and dumped Carolina Fletcher in a gully and left a child to wander the desert alone. Vera compared Arthur Vlasky with Ada Aleshire. Something ugly drove them to do the things they did. Something inside them had become misshapen. Was their selfish cruelty hereditary? Vera didn't know. Maybe. Who gave a damned? It was academic anyway. Reality was much more complicated. All she wanted was to be left alone. But there would be no solitude for her.

First to arrive in Mintlaw and her home had been Kat followed by Woody; soon they would all come.

A voice calling her name interrupted Vera thoughts. Vera turned around and watched as Miss Paterson walked toward her across the lawn. Vera waited for the woman to approach. Denika noticed Misty and Brian heading toward the school and stopped pumping her legs in the air. Denika took her time slowing the swing down. Vera waited for Miss Paterson and for Denika. It seemed as if Vera had nothing to do but wait.

Andrew was probably asking probing clever questions in his job and gathering all sorts of fascinating details about the van and Ada Aleshire and Woody Kirk. He had a really important job. He was valued. And how about her, Vera Lee wondered, what was she doing that was valued? She was—once again—waiting for others to finish playing or working or making important decisions. She was a statue in the lawn waiting for someone to see her.

No, she wasn't as grand as a statue, she was more like a lawn fixture. You knew where it was when you needed it but otherwise didn't pay it any mind—sort of a glorified garden hose. When Vera felt someone standing near her, she realized she had gone off again on a tangent of self-pity. Mentally she shook herself awake. Stop moping, woman. Be grateful you're alive. Be grateful the vengeful goddess hasn't knocked on your door and insisted you help her in her evil deeds.

Miss Paterson stood beside Vera. Vera opened her mouth to acknowledge Miss Paterson and stopped herself. Miss Paterson kept her face averted her body vibrating with some suppressed emotion. Vera sighed. Now who was the child in this playground? She decided to address Miss Paterson in a voice louder than normal for the children's sake, so that they could locate the two adults, "Good afternoon Miss Paterson. Now that you're here, I'll look for Kat."

Once the children were within snatching distance, Miss Paterson grabbed hold of Misty and Brian's hands and trotted back to the school. Denika followed behind the three glancing back at Vera twice before entering the school. They were all good people, every one of the staff members were all dedicated kind souls, Vera told herself. They were only doing their job.

Vera decided not to run after Kat. Instead she walked toward the swing and sat down. She wrapped her fingers around the chains.

The chains were cold. A gust of wind blew sand into her eyes. She blinked away the tiny irritants and her eyes watered. Through a haze of tears, Vera heard the swing next to her creak. Vera wiped her eyes and dried her wet fingers on her pants leg then looked over at Kat pumping her legs to get herself going really high. Vera watched her swing higher and higher reminded of the night she found Kat in her backyard swinging under the moon.

A half an hour passed before Kat lost interest in the swings. October dusk turned to night. The older children were inside probably in the recreation room playing games or watching television or sitting on their cots reading or listening to music with their headphones separating them from the other children, their only real privacy. Vera could barely see Kat in the dark. Her instinct was to snatch Kat's hand before she leaped off the swing and chose to prolong the game of cat and mouse. Vera stopped herself. Kat jumped off the swing, fell to her knees, grunted, jumped up, and started running toward the trees. It took a great deal of willpower to walk purposely toward the school doors, wondering if she was doing the right thing, wondering if she would end up spending the entire night outside searching for Kat.

Vera stood inside the school in the small lobby between the outside door and the door leading to the hall. She leaned against the cold brick wall and stared at the opposite wall with her heart pumping double time. It seemed as if she had spent way too much time waiting. Maybe she should go out and drag Kat inside? The outside door swung open and Kat stood holding the door open with her eyes large staring at something above Vera's head. A gust of wind blew through the vestibule and lifted a strand of Vera's hair. Vera shivered and waited.

Kat stood for a moment contemplated the vestibule. Kat made her decision and entered the vestibule cautiously, touching the door with the palms of her hands, pushing off the door with her body as if the door had pushed her into the hallway. Then Kat slapped Vera's leg in passing and began trotting down the hall in a serpentine fashion as if moving through an invisible maze. Vera had become used to herself as an object, sometimes seen and used, sometimes not seen, not heard.

While the drama had been playing out between her and Kat, she had not noticed someone else in the hall. Sarah Matthews stood outside her office door dressed in casual jeans and a simple pink blouse. Vera thought she looked good in pink. The sight of Sarah Matthews wearing anything casual seemed out of place. By this time of night, Vera was usually home preparing her dinner, so perhaps

Ms. Matthew's attire wasn't so out of the ordinary. Both watched as Kat wandered toward the recreation room. Both heard her litany of grunts and saw Kat tap the wall with her knuckles as she moved down the hall. Just before Kat disappeared into the recreation room, Kat switch from grunts to another sound, a sound that had a different rhythm and pitch.

Sarah glanced in Vera's direction, her scrubbed face free of makeup, the skin glistening under the florescent lights. Vera noticed Sarah's blue eyes widen. What was so surprising to Ms. Matthews? Or maybe it wasn't something surprising but something shocking. Was she shocked? Why? Perhaps Sarah was upset with Vera for keeping Kat out so late or maybe Vera had overstepped her duties by staying longer than Sarah could afford to pay. Vera considered reassuring Ms. Matthews about overtime.

"Did you hear that?" Miss Matthews asked Vera.

"I heard something. It might have been a word. I wasn't close enough to hear," Vera admitted.

"I thought I heard her say – go creak, creak, creak."

Vera shrugged, unable to think of anything to say. She felt so tired and dispirited she could barely make herself walk down the hall. Ms. Matthews lifted her hand to stop Vera from leaving. In the time it took to stop and turn to face the woman, Vera had made up her mind. She wanted to speak before Sarah spoke.

Sarah spoke first, "Vera, I want you to know how much I appreciate your services here. You are doing such a wonderful job with the children. They often talk about you."

Vera changed her mind. She would quit later, no, soon. Tomorrow, she would start looking for a new job. Yes, and she would give two weeks' notice. It was only fair. Kat speaking for the first time had delighted Sarah. And of course, since we're all cause and effect creatures, Sarah assumed Vera had done something miraculous. So what miracle had Vera done? She had done nothing. She'd kept her distance and kept her mouth shut. Big deal. Sarah Matthews erroneously believed Vera had taken something out of Mary Poppins' bag of tricks and magicked the child. That was absolutely insane. Vera felt like a worm. She thought about setting the director straight, changed her mind, and allowed the guilt to wash over her. A few seconds passed for civilities sake before Vera bolted from the school with a brief wave and her head down.

▬

Daniel stood by Miss Vera's car in his new clothes. He waited for a long time until he saw her slip outside and run down the steps. When she stopped half way to her car and stood without speaking by the lamp post, Daniel walked toward her. Under the light Miss Vera's eyes were shadowy reminding him of a Halloween mask. "I got new clothes," he told her. She said nothing. He tried to touch her arm and she backed away from him. "I like you Miss Vera," he said in the sudden quiet. The wind picked up her hair and she looked witchy.

Daniel stepped back, her silence made him uncomfortable. He thought about how much he wanted her to notice his new clothes and stepped real close and hit her in the arm. She muttered something under her breath. He missed the words for the roaring in his ears. He caught something else under his skin, something that burned and hurt. He did not know how he had fallen. He heard Miss Vera's Toyota start up and the sound the beige ball of metal made as it spun around. Bits of gravel hit him in the head. It was Robbie spitting on him again, spitting on his head and laughing. Daniel's chest hurt, and his head pounded. The tears remained inside.

—

Andrew returned to the abandoned van. The coroner had arrived. Andrew walked up to the back of the van and peered inside. Big mistake he realized. He made himself stand his ground even though his stomach wanted to puke up his dinner. George turned to face him with an evidence bag dangling from his hands and noticed Andrew for the first time, "We think it might have been a cougar got him." As George moved toward the back of the van in the process of climbing out with his hands full of bags, Andrew noticed the snakeskin boots.

"Oh shit. Oh shit. Holy hell and damnation; I recognize those boots."

"What? You recognize these boots?"

"Yes. You remember the jerk that claimed he was Vera's common law husband? He wore boots just like these."

George jumped down from the van and faced Andrew, "Would his name be Woodrow Kirk?"

"Yes. Yes, it would. And when I spoke to Ada Aleshire's neighbor, she said she'd seen some scruffy looking guy sitting on Ada's stoop wearing snakeskin boots. I bet this van belongs to Ada. I bet the two of them were in cahoots."

"Um hum. Good to know. Let's let the Doc finish his work before we jump to conclusions and take these back to the station. You can tell the Chief all about your little visit to Winnemucca," George said looking peeved.

Andrew ignored George's disproval and thought about Woodrow Kirk and the van, "No self-respecting cougar would eat something that was a rotting old corpse. The van's been missing for nearly two months. Where's it been and how could Woody be freshly dead?" he asked aloud not really expecting an answer from George.

"There's a large commercial freezer in the back of the van," George offered as an apology for his attitude earlier. "Maybe somebody stored his body in the freezer."

"That would require the engine running constantly or maybe the freezer hooked up to an electrical source. It couldn't have been left in a junk yard. Someone would have noticed. Maybe the van was stored in somebody's garage or in a rented storage unit with a source of electricity?" Andrew said.

"Maybe," George said walking past him with the evidence bag. "But right now, I just want to finish this grisly job and go home and take a nice hot shower."

Chapter Fifteen

V era had forgotten to leave the porch light on for him again. Andrew groped in the dark and entered the house by touch alone. He'd had to use his key light to find the lock. He left the groceries outside and searched for the hall light switch. The bulb flickered and went out. Andrew entered the dark kitchen and noticed the halo of orange light in the corner of the dining room where Vera's rocking chair stood.

After depositing the groceries on the counter, he wandered down the dark hall toward Vera's bedroom using his hands to guide him. He assumed she was asleep and was surprised when he peeked into her room and found the lamp on and the bed as he had left it this morning. The room was empty. He searched the rest of the house. He had parked next to her Corolla. She had to be here. He checked all the windows and the back door. There was no evidence of forced entry. He stepped out on the back porch and surveyed the dark. What he imagined to be trees and the fence and the barn in his mind's eye might have been something else altogether. A darker shape near the barn separated from the shadows and moved toward him. With a sense of relief Andrew watched as Vera walked up to him. She held something to her chest.

Once inside the kitchen with the lights on, Andrew noticed that Vera's hands were covered in mud with mud stuck under her fingernails as if she had been digging into the hard ground with her bare hands. One of her fingernails was bleeding. He saw smears of blood on the bottom of the cake tin she held so tight to her chest. Andrew watched as Vera prowled around the kitchen like a cat sniffing strange smells. He stood in the warmth of the light and shivered as if a cold blast of winter had swept past him. Andrew called out to her.

Vera ignored him. She switched off the light by the rocking chair and sat down. She began to rock back and forth. Her eyes were in shadow. His eye traced the path of mud she had made as she walked from the kitchen door to the counter to the table and finally ending up at the rocking chair. He noticed she was wearing only a sleeveless tank top and gray sweat pants. There was a hole in the knee of her sweat pants. He wanted to touch her, but instinct told him to remain where he stood. It was a primitive sense of strangeness, of something unfamiliar, even alien.

Andrew made himself relax. He began to pull the groceries he had bought out of the bags and put them away. The clock told him that in six hours it would be daylight outside. He would wait as long as he could before he made a move. He wanted to give her time to come back to him. Was this sleepwalking? He'd read about sleepwalkers. As far as he could recall, it was best not to touch them or scare them. He had planned to make himself something to eat before going to bed. Now he could not imagine eating. Once the groceries were put away and the bags folded neatly and tucked inside the bottom drawer near the sink, Andrew switched off the kitchen light and made his way to the table in the dark. He sat down in the chair that faced the room, so that he had an uninterrupted view of Vera. He sat in the dark and waited.

The silence was broken by a voice, a voice he did not recognize murmuring words he did not understand. The sound was coming from Vera, coming from her throat, but unrecognizable as human. It reminded him of the wind sweeping through a corn field and how the dry stalks of corn rubbed against each other. Andrew smelled mud and wet leaves and the perfume of Vera's hair. Then the voice changed. He relaxed. It was Vera again. She clutched the cake tin closer to her chest. He heard her clearly now, when the words registered on his tired brain, he felt sick inside.

"I'll take this curse, throw it in the river."
"Yes."
"Tomorrow."
"I'll take this curse, throw it far away."
"No one will find it."
"No one."
"Take out the trash."
"No."
"Eat your beans."
"No."
"I'll kill you."
"Someday I'll kill you."

The sunlight coming through the open kitchen window warmed his shoulder and woke Andrew. He lifted his head from the hard surface of the table and rubbed his eyes. When he could not find Vera, he went in search of her and found her in the bedroom asleep under the sheets and blankets. He saw the cake tin under her pillow. Andrew slipped off his uniform and slid between the sheets naked. He pulled her body to him and held her tight. He could care less if he held a mad woman in his arms still dressed in clothes smeared with mud, with a dried-leaf stuck in her tangled curls and her body smelling like a grave. She murmured something in her sleep and Andrew was relieved it was her voice speaking, not the nightmare voice of yesterday.

All the forensic evidence collected by the experts from the van, all the prints discovered at the scene, the questions and mysteries of the van's existence receded in the face of this new problem. He lifted his head and looked at Vera's profile. His eye traced the shape of her nose, the white puckered scar along her cheek, the full lips, and the narrow chin. She had a habit of trying to hide her nose. He could read her. She thought she looked monstrous. Her nose was fine, better than most. Even with her imperfections, she still made his blood race as if he were seventeen again.

—

Maggie climbed out of her father's pickup and merged with her classmates into the school hall. Amy was waiting for Maggie by her locker. Maggie pulled her textbooks out and walked with Amy to their first class. Maggie had become a celebrity in Amy's eyes and Maggie thought her sudden adoration was stupid. Maggie wasn't a rebel, far from it. She'd always been the good girl, the boring girl, the one teachers counted on to raise her hand and answer the question no one else knew or didn't want to answer in case they might be mistaken for a smarty pants.

Now her father mistrusted her, and her mother looked bereaved as if someone had just died. Even her Uncle Andrew avoided her. Realistically, Maggie had to admit the discovery of the van occupied most of his attention these days. And Vera, of course, had become extremely important to him. He rarely dropped by any more and when he did he seemed impatient to be gone. Her parents thought Andrew's attachment to Vera kind of cute. Maggie thought their romance was so romantic. Vera was intriguing: a woman alone, a woman with scars inside and out, a woman with an unknown past. Yet Maggie couldn't help feeling a twinge of jealousy because she and her uncle used to do things together and had always been so close before.

After math class, Maggie saw Jeremy walking down the hall with his friend Joe and realized how just the sight of him made the pulse race in her throat and her legs shake so that she had trouble navigating, so much so, she kept bumping into people like some stupid drunk. After their humiliation during Amy's Halloween Party, these days Jeremy avoided her too and refused to look her in the eye. It made Maggie sick to her stomach. She knew she'd lost something important and she blamed her uncle and father for the loss. Sometimes, when her mind weaved what-ifs, she almost hated her father.

He had threatened to drop her off and pick her up from school every day for as long as she was grounded; but by Thursday of that week, her mother had said something to her father and her father had told her she could ride her ten-speed to school instead. Her mother worked part-time in Boise, so she was long gone before Maggie had to leave for school. Grandpa Treloar was the only person left in the house by the time Maggie stepped out the door. Grandpa Treloar made a point of waving to her from the living room window each morning. Maggie knew the old man was proud of her, not for running off with a boy in his car on a school night maybe, but because they shared a secret.

As she stepped outside a familiar Trooper was parked near the Pass and she saw Jeremy walking up and down the graveled path searching for something or someone in the irrigation ditch and the cluster of locust trees. She considered calling out to him but changed her mind. Then he saw her and ran down the rest of the way. Her heart started pumping so fast she thought she was going to keel over wondering if he had changed his mind and didn't think she was such a dope after all. He dashed across the road and stopped in front of her breathing hard and looking worried. He had to bend down to catch his breath and when he could speak straightened to his full six feet two inches and said, "Have you seen Lazy? I've been looking all over for him. I'd forgotten that you watched him that one day when he discovered the kid's backpack."

She shook her head wishing she could give him some good news, "No, I'm so sorry. I haven't seen Lazy since that day. Maybe I can help you find him."

He backed away from her with his palm up as if he were warding her off with a spell, "No. That's fine. He's probably chasing a rabbit. I've looked up on the hill," as he pointed to Hunter's Hill, "and I didn't see him. I'll check at home, maybe he got tired and went home. But thanks anyway. Ah. Yeah. So, I got to go." She watched him head back to his Trooper and drive away, all her fears confirmed. He no longer wanted to have anything to do with her.

Riding away from her grandfather's farmhouse, Maggie glanced across the street and up the slight rise to Vera's house. She saw the beige Toyota parked under the catalpa tree and Andrew's

Jeep parked on the other side. Maggie swerved, and she and her bike nearly collided with a car driving by. She stopped and with her fingers tight around her handle bars stared at the figure sitting on the rocky ledge near Hunter's Hill. She focused on the figure until she recognized the shape of him. It was Daniel, and Daniel was sitting with his legs crossed looking down on Vera's house with such intensity she thought he might be asleep. Something about the way he sat so still made Maggie uncomfortable. She imagined his eyes on her back watching her as she rode toward town.

———

Daniel saw Maggie down below. She looked small, the size of a whistle pig. When she rode toward town, he turned back to watch Miss Vera's house wishing Mr. Treloar would come outside. There was a new fence around her property. He could see all the colors of the rainbow fence, the rainbow fence weaved in and out like the threads of his new sweater. The rainbow fence circled Miss Vera's property, around and around it went over sagebrush near the dirt road and under the branches of the trees on the other side and then around the barn and the other tree, the tree that looked like a lady combing her long hair. The rainbow fence pulsed. It was alive. It was mean. It kept him out.

All he wanted to do was be near her. Miss Vera would protect him from the ghost. Miss Vera had kind eyes. He wanted to tell her he was sorry for scaring her. He wanted to tell her about his dream about the man with the snake boots. He remembered the dream and he was scared. He'd seen him before and now the news said he was dead.

Daniel kept his eyes on Miss Vera's house. The back of his head tingled. If he looked back, he might see the ghost watching him. It lived in the cracks of the earth. He could hear it breath in and out and he could hear the sagebrush tremble when it passed. Daniel wiped his wet cheeks and his nose with the back of his sleeve. He was afraid now, afraid of the thing that had taken over his cave. He knew a human had been inside, going through his things, trying to steal his stuff. He'd heard the voices last night. He'd heard them arguing. He had been surprised when he recognized one of the voices.

His stepfather bellowed, "So where is it then? I'm here with the money and you say somebody stole it!"

"Quit your whining asshole. I know who has it and I'll take care of her. Here's what I've got left. Take it or leave it."

"And what's that stink?"

"Never mind," she told him, "just take the shit and get lost."

Now after all this time, the cave smelled bad. The smell reminded him of when he was little, when his real father had been outside standing by the big garbage can just before he burned the old milk cartons and trash. It would lead to disease; his father had said. We have to purify the garbage. Maybe he should do the same, purify the garbage?

Daniel wanted to get up and run toward the school, but he was afraid to stand up, afraid to turn around and see it watching him. He thought about Mr. Treloar. He remembered something a teacher had told him a long time ago, about not being afraid to talk to the police. Daniel would talk to Mr. Treloar. Mr. Treloar was friends with the police. He would know what to do. Yet he couldn't climb down from the ledge because the rainbow fence would hurt him, and he couldn't stand up and turn around because it would find him. He did not know what to do. He wanted to go back to the school. He wanted Mz. Matthews to come and get him.

—

Andrew woke hearing a voice calling for Ms. Matthews. Vera stirred and pulled away from Andrew. Andrew sat up and looked out the bedroom window. He saw the wood wind chimes moving in the breeze. Beyond the chimes he saw the hill above Vera's house. There was someone on the hill. Andrew climbed out of bed and stepped toward the window. After a moment of intense focus, he recognized the man. Andrew found his blue sweat pants and pullover and a pair of old running shoes. After dressing he walked into the kitchen, opened the sliding door, and stepped outside. He peered up at the silhouette sitting on the ledge above him. The usual baritone had become a bellow as if Daniel had lost all his senses in some primitive fear.

Andrew walked up Opal Road Access. When he reached the boulder signally the ascent to the hill, the bellowing subsided. By the time Andrew reached Daniel the man had his head in his lap and his hands covering his ears. Andrew knelt and touched Daniel's shoulder. Daniel gasped and jerked away.

"It's me, Daniel. Are you hurt?"

Daniel lifted his face. A trail of tears made a path down his dirty cheeks. His nose was dripping onto his pant leg. His eyes were nearly swollen shut, "Come with me Daniel. I'll take you home."

"Is it gone?" Daniel asked wiping the tears away, his eyes, large and frightened searched beyond Andrew's shoulder.

"What's gone? Did you see someone? Is there someone up here?" Andrew stood up and searched the area behind him. He saw the hilltop filled with sagebrush and boulders and the rutted dirt road marking a path between the cliff ledges on either side. There were no cars or people anywhere. There was not so much as a grouse or a butterfly.

Andrew sensed the wrongness in this place. Birds and grouse lived up here. So did other animals: jackrabbits, badgers, snakes, a few stray cows. Even if they were nesting he should have been able to hear the birds chattering to each other or the flapping of wings. It was still too early for all the flies to have died out or the bees to have gone into hibernation.

"Come on. I'll take you back to Ms. Matthews," Andrew said in a soothing voice pulling Daniel up by his arm. Daniel towered over Andrew. Andrew knew Daniel could probably snap him in two, the kid was that strong, yet he wasn't afraid of him. Daniel wasn't the kind of person to hurt anyone. He never had been.

Daniel made a point of walking on Andrew's left side so that Andrew's body blocked the view of the rutted road and most important of all, the cave. Once they descended the hill and were on level ground, Andrew turned toward the house. Daniel jerked away and without a word started running across the meadow toward Jump Creek Road. Andrew watched Daniel jog home, pausing every so often to swipe at his nose. Andrew waited until he saw Daniel slip through the entrance to the Egg before making his way back to Vera's house.

The first thing Andrew saw was Vera by the coffee machine pouring water into the dispenser. She glanced over her shoulder at him and smiled. Andrew sat down in the same chair he had spent the night in and watched as Vera began to fry bacon on the stove. She had changed out of her muddy clothes and had wrapped herself in an old green robe. The green robe made her olive skin glow. All back to normal, he supposed. He debated whether to mention her odd behavior and realized if he did he might ruin the moment.

—

Vera stood on the porch and watched Andrew pull out of the drive and head toward town. She sipped her coffee and surveyed her property with satisfaction. Halloween was over and what she had feared had not happened. No one was hurt. Andrew had told her about finding Daniel on the hillside crying. Vera should have felt sorry for Daniel. She didn't. She wouldn't make him her problem. He was the state's problem now. She went back into the house and looked through the newspaper for a job close to home. Most of the jobs offered were in Boise. She resigned herself to the long drive. She had made up her mind. After calling a few of the listings in the newspaper, Vera showered and dressed for work. She thought about calling in sick and then decided her absence would place an unfair burden on Joann and the others.

When Vera arrived at the school, she entered Joann's classroom without being noticed. Joann and Miss Paterson stood talking in the corner. Vera couldn't hear what they were saying; she assumed they were talking about her mismanagement of Kat. Joann touched Miss Paterson's arm and nodded her head toward Vera. Miss Paterson glanced over her shoulder to sweep her censorious eye over the unworthy one and with a dismissive shrug turned back to Joann. Vera heard Joann ask Miss Paterson, "What time did you make the appointment for?"

"Two o'clock. I'll come round and pick her up," Miss Paterson said without looking in Vera's direction and left the room.

Before Vera had a chance to tidy the classroom, Ms. Matthews entered, "Vera, may I speak to you for a moment?"

"Of course," Vera said unable to think of anything else to say and when she turned glimpsed a look of satisfaction cross Joann's face wondering what she had done to earn the teacher's ire. It was just another example of the capriciousness of people in this type of institution. No one, unless they wanted to risk their jobs, could ever show their true face in a place like this one where everyone had to be so careful.

It must be exhausting for these people to constantly pretend to be civilized, sympathetic, altruistic, and/or wise when realistically there were times when all they wanted to do was pitch a hissy fit or storm out. After only a few days working at the school, smiling like an idiot, and hoping no one would notice how little she knew about children, while on her way home, a driver cut her off. She swerved to avoid him and ended up on the shoulder of the road nearly in the ditch. As her pulse beat wildly, she began to scream and swear and hit the steering wheel like a madwoman.

It had been amazingly therapeutic.

Once the catharsis was over, she felt rather embarrassed at her behavior; yet simultaneously pleased she could remember so many cuss words.

That memory brought a smile to her lips which she wiped off her face once she entered the hall. As she followed Ms. Matthews to her office, a momentary elation shot up her spine with the thought – maybe the director had decided she wasn't equipped to deal with the special needs of these children and she was planning to terminate her employment in the gentlest and kindest way possible. Oh, the modern firing was even nastier than the old-fashioned way people were fired with a bellowing from the boss and a dramatic finger pointing to the door, "You're an idiot, Lee. Never darken this door again. You hear me woman?" Instead Vera would have to sit and squirm for at least fifteen minutes with a long-winded lecture on their appreciation for all her hard work, why her services were no longer required, and their hopes for her future happiness.

Oh please, just rip the band aid off and let me leave with dignity, Vera thought.

She recognized her reaction from similar reactions in the past and promised this time to behave herself. Vera chose the leather chair closest to the window and faced Sarah Matthews with what she hoped appeared to be a detached interest. She could tell nothing from Ms. Matthews' face. How did they do it – these women, how did they smile and give bad news simultaneously? It was a talent for sure.

"I know you've only been here a short while and I really appreciate all your hard work and effort to learn sign language and braille. Really, that is going above and beyond but I am so grateful you're taking the time to learn. I hate to bring this up, but I must be fair to the others and tell you that some people have complained about your handling of Kat. They believe you have potentially put Kat in danger by allowing her to wander freely about the school. I wanted to hear your side of the story."

Vera stood up, "Miss Paterson is absolutely right. I've been thinking a great deal about this school. I admire your work so much and am amazed by the progressiveness of this school compared to the horror stories I've heard about other institutions. But I believe my lack of experience with special needs' children will hold them back from achieving their full potential. I know nothing about autism or the deaf and blind; and just as critically, I have no background in education or child development. I really think it's for the best if I give you my two weeks notice now or if you need me to leave at the end of the day that is perfectly fine with me. You see I came in today thinking I should really give notice but hating to leave you high and dry."

Sarah Matthews looked unhappy, "Your concern is admirable Vera and shows just how much you care about the children. Please reconsider. I'll talk to Miss Paterson. She's just thinking of the welfare of the child. You understand."

"I do. I understand Miss Paterson is a competent nurse and like myself has had little formal training with autistic children which in Paterson's defense, she doesn't need but you need someone with experience not" … she paused and thought to herself – *two childless women playing guessing games* – and instead finished the thought with the word "amateurs."

Vera had vowed to remain calm, but of course, coolness was foreign to her, to her entire family she supposed. She had hoped to find a job before quitting. And she had a speech all composed which included her appreciation of the school's efforts and how great the kids were, and blah, blah, blah. But no, instead she made the implied criticism personal. She regretted using the word "amateurs." Too late now, the words were out in the open, a blatant criticism of Miss. Paterson and herself. Stupid, she thought, why can't you be more like Joann, so cool and confident deflecting all criticism onto someone else? Because I've never been given all the carrots she has – the middle-class life, the lovely home in a safe neighborhood, or the money to go to college.

Sarah didn't seem upset with Vera's announcement. Her reaction was puzzling, "Well, I wish I could choose from a large pool of competent people, but so far that's not the case. Those with the knowledge and expertise to work with autistic children work in large cities and no one is particularly interested in coming all the way out here to work odd shifts. I have just so much money set aside to pay the employees and can't afford to pay an expert."

Then Sarah stood up and pointed at her desk, "I'll tell you something, something in confidence that I haven't told anyone before. Some of these so-called experts are as clueless as the rest of us. They still don't know why some children are born autistic and other children are not. That kind of knowledge is years in the future.

We don't have the luxury to wait for the experts to advise us. We've got to teach and train these children to survive in this world now, not in some utopian future. Some say we should train these children through behavior modification, you know rewards and punishments. The experts do all they can to get these children to behave like normal children. Yet, I believe more is needed, a certain something, a certain strength of character which the children understand at a primitive level. When an adult educator and an autistic child can a find a middle ground, a way to relate to each other, I feel that is a teachable moment, a good beginning. I need people who would rather teach than baby our kids, who recognize these children need to be self-sufficient right away, not tomorrow, not when they are too big and too set in their ways to be independent and productive citizens. Do you understand what I'm trying to say?"

Vera sat down. Sarah relaxed and moved away from her desk, "I have a degree in business and a teaching degree. And I have a younger brother who is blind. I started working as a volunteer at a blind/deaf school when I was in junior high. My best friend is deaf. I know something about blindness and deafness. What I don't know is this thing called autism. I didn't want Kat here. I knew we just didn't have the capability of taking care of an autistic child in this facility.

Most of our Down syndrome children are high functioning and don't need the intense training other facilities provide. But this, this situation with little Kat has me baffled. Until a home can be found for her, I really need you. She misbehaves with the other volunteers and Ms. Paterson, but when she's around you, she actually seeks out your company. No one else has been able to generate the same behaviors. She's driving everyone else crazy. Please reconsider Vera. Please stay with us a little bit longer."

By the time Sarah had finished she was perched on the edge of her desk, so close Vera could see the subtle pink powder on her eyelids and her cheekbones. Vera had the overwhelming urge to run, run right out of the room. She'd been relieved thinking Sarah had called her into the office to let her go. Vera didn't like it when people thrust responsibility on her. She just wanted to live a nice quiet life without complications.

And yet here she was, in this school, involved in the petty jealousies and minor hubris of other people. All these people and their troubles, they made her edgy and uncomfortable. She had enough of her own problems to bear, couldn't they see that? In the past, she used books and lame excuses to separate herself from people. Now this woman was determined to pull her into the vortex, force her to adapt to humanity's imperfections, and even go back into the classroom as if nothing had been said about her conduct.

So, she was supposed to ignore Joann and her excessive tidiness and Miss Paterson's control issues and most especially the exhausted looks of the rest of the staff? Could she do it? Could she ignore the visitors and their pitying looks and not say something snarky? Could she overlook the fact that the kitchen staff worked extra hours without pay? All the good, the bad, and the simply annoying made Vera hypersensitive about how these children demanded so much from everyone. Even normal children can be demanding but these children needed not only constant supervision but every morsel of love the staff could dish out.

An awareness of her own vulnerability creeped along her spine as Vera walked back to Joann's room. She had no control over her situation or others. She'd never had control over her family or friends or the men in her life. Why couldn't she just say no, just once? Most of her adult life had been the avoidance of unpleasantness; and yet unpleasantness knew her address and kept knocking on her door. Why couldn't she have ignored those pleading blue eyes and said no? She was going to regret her promise.

Sarah would talk to Miss Paterson. Sarah wanted her to continue to treat Kat the way she had been for the last few weeks. She would be allowed to do what she thought best for Kat. Within reason, Sarah had cautioned. Yes, Vera thought, and what might within reason be? Vera watched as Miss Paterson entered the school with Denika's coat over her arm. Vera considered whether she should make peace with the nurse. In the past, when she was a feisty teenager and mad at the world, she would have spit in the nurse's eye and challenged her to an all-out hair pulling, nail scratching fight. Over the years, she came to realize with a stomach wrenching certainty her poverty and otherness meant she was the one who would lose and the other jerk, even if wrong, would ultimately win the fight. As an adult, she would have gone up to the woman and made small talk trying to figure out her mood and maybe make a joke or try to explain herself.

This time, she would do nothing.

Not today.

Today she didn't feel like groveling. And why should she? She was sick of being a doormat. She nodded her head acknowledging the nurse's presence and crossed the hall to Joann's classroom door. Once inside the room she relaxed. She supposed the nurse would be wondering why Vera wasn't scurrying out the school door in tears. Won't she be surprised to discover her criticisms had fallen on deaf ears? Oh ho, there you go girl. She'd made a joke. The afternoon felt twenty-four hours long though.

Kat was still the same old Kat avoiding people unless they needed a good slap. Vera suspected she had been charmed into staying at the school by falsehoods. The child didn't look traumatized. Vera made sure not to touch Kat or get too close to her. Surreptitiously she kept an eye on the child as Kat sat amongst the book shelves and pulled the books off the shelves and left them on the floor. After a while, it dawned upon her that Joann was ignoring Kat as if Kat weren't even in the room.

The teacher was concentrating all her attention on the other children in her charge. She read to them. She taught them Braille and American Sign Language and she left Vera the responsibility of supervising and teaching Kat. So far, Vera knew four basic signs: eat, bathroom, sleep, and play. Those four signs had seemed to be enough yesterday; after all, she had been just a glorified babysitter and playground cop then. Now she realized she would need to learn more signs and find out through other teachers where she could sign up for college credit classes in American Sign Language.

Once the children had eaten dinner, Vera rushed outside in the children's wake even beating a few volunteers out the door. She stood near the swings and breathed in the fresh scent of new mown grass closing her eyes for a moment to appreciate the last rays of the sun. The thought depressed Vera, the thought that after all these years of reading, she was reduced to being nothing more than a nanny. As she watched the children play in the sand, she thought about her childhood. She'd never had any concrete goals. She couldn't remember ever thinking about what she might do when she grew up. All she remembered were the do-not-wants: not to be in the fields picking fruit or vegetables ever again; not to move from town to town ever again; not to be stuck with a bunch of screaming kids in a broken-down car; and most especially, not to be at the mercy of a man.

What a joke. The minute she thought she had found the right man – someone rich and successful and a pillar of his tiny community, she discovered she was worse off than she'd ever been as a kid. The only difference between her childhood and her adulthood was that the humiliation and fear happened behind closed doors not out on the streets with the neighbors and police watching. Vera pushed the memory of Arthur away and looked around aware that Kat had disappeared once again.

"Brian. Bring the children to me," Vera called. Brian lifted his head and turned to where he thought Vera stood. His sightless eyes stared off into space. When he simply sat in the sand and did not move, Vera was dismayed. Anxious about Kat, Vera marched toward him and lifted him up out of the sand.

"Brian this is urgent. I need your help," she said to him. An expression crossed his face which at the time Vera misunderstood.

Misty jumped up from the sand and reached out for Vera. Vera led the children toward the school. Denika noticed for the first time that everyone was leaving. Her fat little legs pumping, she made it to the school doors close behind the others. Before Vera could open the doors to escort the children inside, the nurse appeared in the hall.

"Please take the children Miss Paterson. I have to find Kat. She's run off," Vera noticed the woman's disapproving expression and said nothing in her defense. She hurried back outside and began to search for Kat among the bare trees at the furthest end of the school property. It was getting dark. A large figure separated itself from the trees and came towards her. Vera stopped when she recognized Daniel.

"Have you seen Kat, Daniel?"

Vera couldn't see Daniel's face. The sun had sunk below the mountains and the sky without warning had turned a dark gray.

"Daniel, did you hear me? Have you seen Kat?"

"Can you hear it breathing Miss Vera? I'm sure you can hear it breathing. You got the eyes and ears for it."

"I don't know what you're talking about Daniel. This is urgent. We need to find Kat. Have you seen her?"

"It's all around us now. I thought it would stay up in the mountains."

The coach lamps on their black wrought iron poles placed intermittently around the property for effect began to glow. The light cast pools of yellow on the ground. The coach lamps did little to illuminate the rest of the grounds only the playground and the double doors of the school. Everything else was in shadow, a shadow so black, Vera had difficulty telling whether something that looked as if it was crouching was a child or a low growing hedge.

The coach lamp behind Vera began to whine and cast a pale white light. She heard the sizzle of electricity and saw Daniel's face for the first time. She noticed how he trembled. His face was the color of paper. He looked terrified. She should have been frightened. Here he was loaming over her, terrified of the dark, with the mind of a child, a child who could, if he wished, break every bone in her body. Yet she was the one who was calm.

"Go find Ms. Mathews and tell her I'm looking for Kat. Would you do that for me please?"

Vera left him and entered the darkest part of the grounds near the wrought iron fence facing Anderson Pass. She did not have time to cajole Daniel into doing her biding. Kat was like a lighting bug and so much time had gone by already. Vera wondered if she dared call out to Kat. If Kat thought this was some kind of a game, she would run, and if Vera chased after her, Kat might run right out of the grounds and into traffic.

She heard Daniel's heavy footfalls behind her. She spun around anxious and angry, "Do as I say Daniel. Go find Ms. Matthews."

In the dark she heard his voice, wet and terrified, "Don't leave me alone Miss Vera. I'll stay with you. I'll not see it with you."

In the distance, Vera could hear traffic noises, cars driving by, the angry blast of someone's car horn, and then a diesel truck gearing down. She imagined Kat wandering outside in heavy traffic. Several neighborhood dogs began to bark. One howled. Vera flinched at the sound wondering what had alarmed the dogs. She thought about Kat, all alone, so small, wandering through these grounds, perhaps finding a hole somewhere to slip through and escape out into the desert. But there could be no hole. The fence encircled the property; it would be too high for her to climb. Vera thought about the gate, the small gate near the driveway. She started running toward the front, Daniel close on her heels. Kat would be there searching for a way to slip through the iron bars or jiggling the lock to try to open it.

Vera had a stitch in her side by the time she reached the graveled drive. She slowed down and with her hand pressed against her side made herself walk. The coach lamps were more numerous here. Vera could see the borders along the side of the drive, the woodchips that covered the soil, the clumps of clipped evergreen positioned in orderly fashion among dormant flowers with a few hardy rosebushes still flowering. The closer she got to the gate the more relaxed she began to feel. Kat would be there. As if she had said her name aloud, Vera heard Kat scream. Vera ran to the gate and saw Kat with her head stuck between the iron bars. As if she knew Vera was close, Kat screamed again. Vera put her hand on Kat's head.

"Shush now. Calm down," Vera said in a voice she realized was more relieved than calm. "I'm here Kat. Let me help you."

Daniel stood behind them with his hands stuck under his armpits as if he were cold. Vera put three fingers of each hand on the tips of Kat's ears flattening them, so Kat's head could pass through the bars. Once Kat's head was free from its prison, Kat stepped back and swung her arm wide and slapped Vera on the leg, as if she blamed Vera for her predicament.

Vera grabbed the child's hand before she could run away again and led her back to the school. Daniel's larger shadow followed close behind. As Kat was propelled along by Vera's anxiety, the little girl glanced up at the looming figure of Daniel now walking beside them. She began to mumble. Vera thought she heard the word repeated over and over, "Creak, creak, creak."

As if Daniel was an autism linguist, he glared down at the child and said in an injured voice, "No! No swings for you. Bad girl. Bad girl."

When the three of them appeared in the hall, Miss Paterson and Ms. Matthews were standing by the office door. They both turned to watch as Vera, Kat, and Daniel entered the school. Miss

Paterson made an exasperated sound and marched away; the squeak of her shoes echoed down the hall, "Sque ... eek, sque ... eeek," Kat said.

Daniel wiped his nose on his sleeve and said, "She's a bad girl, Mz. Matthews. Bad girl. She got stuck and she gets no swings for a month." He hurried down the hall toward the television room.

Ms. Matthews and Vera exchanged glances. Sarah was the first to laugh. Kat mimicked her laughter. "I'll take Kat up to her room," Vera offered.

"No, you go home and rest. I'll take charge and thank you Vera for listening and understanding."

Before Vera could turn to leave, she felt a pair of arms as strong as a Boa constrictor wrap themselves around her legs. Pinned in the hall on exhibit for the rest of the school to see, Vera stood for a moment in Kat's crushing embrace embarrassed. Vera could see her pink scalp and the fine blonde strands of hair on her small head. She could feel Kat's chin digging into her thigh and Vera realized she and the little girl were afraid.

Ms. Matthews pulled Kat away. Kat's shrill scream pierced Vera's eardrum.

Ms. Matthews glanced at Vera and said, "You see what we have to contend with when you're not around," and watched as Kat wiggled out of Ms. Matthews' grasp and with her usual measured distance she and the adults made their way toward the sound of the television and the children playing inside the room. As if she had the second sight, Ms. Matthews paused to glance over her shoulder and said, "We'll see you tomorrow, yes?"

Vera nodded her head, aware that she hadn't the courage to say no to this woman. Five minutes later she was inside her house and wishing she had had more backbone. She heard Andrew drive up and began to think about what to make for dinner. She wasn't hungry, but now there was someone else in the house she had to consider. She listened as Andrew unlocked the front door and entered the house. She waited for him in the kitchen.

When he dropped his hat on the kitchen countertop and started to put his pistol next to his hat, he saw her face and grabbed his hat and pistol and disappeared down the hall. When he returned to her, he returned without the hat or the gun. She supposed he had set his pistol on the top shelf of the linen cupboard again. She couldn't understand why he carried a concealed weapon. He was supposed to be an artist. Artists didn't run around town wearing concealed weapons in their pants leg. If he had been a fulltime cop, she could have understood. But he wasn't. He was just a temporary grunt like her. The gun disturbed her. She didn't want it in the house and he knew it.

Andrew walked up to her and slid his arms around her. The steaks were frying in the pan and Vera poked one just to be doing something. She felt Andrew's lips on the back of her neck and his hands roaming her waist then her thighs. The room darkened. Vera dropped the fork and leaned into him. His breath warmed her skin. The pressure of his lips sent fire coursing up her legs into her stomach. She dropped the fork and turned.

They adjourned to the bedroom.

The smell of burning steaks followed by the smoke alarm sobered them both up. Andrew ran out of the bedroom naked and switched off the stove returning to her so fast Vera had no time to think about the waste of a good meal.

Chapter Sixteen

A week passed; Vera went to work as usual. Two weeks after Kat got her head stuck in the bars of the gate Vera woke to gray clouds and the threat of rain. The rain poured out of the sky as if all of mankind wept in self-pity and frustration. Andrew wore his yellow slicker over his clothes. Vera watched him run to his Jeep and jump inside. She waited until she could no longer see his taillights, then grabbed her purse and her coat and left the house.

When Andrew asked why Vera was up early and dressed to go out, Vera told him that she had errands to run in Boise. She did not know why she couldn't tell him about her decision to quit the school. She couldn't really understand why herself. All Vera knew was that she couldn't sit around the house and worry about Sarah Matthews showing up to try to talk her into coming back to the school. The days of peaceful solitude were gone. The days when she could lose herself in a book and forget the world outside were gone. The world wanted in and wanted her. If they knew her, the real Vera Lee, the one that lived inside her head and thought thoughts that were evil and wrong; they would be frightened.

The entire day, Vera occupied herself by shopping and driving. She tried on clothes. She fingered merchandize. She read book jackets and listened to people talking. Around five o'clock on her way home, she found herself bumper to bumper with other vehicles heading out of town. Instead of the usual fifty minutes the commute took two hours.

She saw Andrew's jeep parked under the naked catalpa tree. Last week, Vera had woken to find the catalpa stripped of its plate sized leaves, as if during the night some supernatural force had torn the leaves off the branches and flung them to the ground. Not one leaf remained on the branches. On Sunday, Vera had raked up the leaves and shoved them into eight hefty size black bags. Where there had once been shade from the morning sun, now there was a filtering of sunlight between the branches of the tree. Without the leaves to obscure the view, Vera could see from her living room window clear across the street. She could see most of the main road and the Treloar barn. She watched as Andrew's nephew Kit came out of the barn and marched toward his house.

As Vera drove toward her home, reminding herself again to call her home – Rock Wren House, she could see two people inside, a woman standing by Andrew at the window. With a groan, she recognized Sarah Matthews' vehicle. There was no way she could stop and reverse the car and run away. Feeling like a coward, she forced herself to drive forward. This was too much, she thought, her annoyance turning to anger, how dare the woman hound her at home.

Vera slammed on the brakes and put her car in reverse attempting to turn the vehicle back onto the highway. As she tried to rush out into traffic, a vehicle coming up fast honked angrily at her missing her with inches to spare. Vera was forced to stop and check for more cars. When she looked in her rearview mirror, she saw Sarah and Andrew step out onto the porch. With her foot on the accelerator, Vera pushed the Corolla to move faster. Her car didn't like to be hurried. It swayed and bucked. She managed to get control of it and drove away. Her face felt hot. In fact, her entire body was ablaze with embarrassment. What an idiot she was. Of course, Andrew and Sarah would notice her vehicle bolting away as if she were a bank robber fleeing a crime.

Just before McBride Road, Vera looked in her rearview mirror again and spotted Andrew's Jeep getting closer and closer. The vehicle seemed to leap forward without any effort. Vera turned onto McBride road and waited for Andrew to park behind her. She sat in her car noticing for the first time how her fingers shook on the steering wheel. When she heard Andrew approach her car, she dropped her hands in her lap and held them tight against her stomach. Andrew had to knock on her window to get her attention. Vera slid the window down just far enough to hear him.

His silence made her curious. She looked out the window and up at him. She noticed that he was wearing a pair of ragged jeans and an old shirt she had never seen before. His clothes reminded her of a Jackson Pollack painting, a splattering of paint without design or logic but somehow beautiful in its composition. Randomness could be just as breathtaking as careful design, Vera thought, knowing that she should be worried about Andrew's continued silence. Vera climbed out of the Corolla careful not to look him in the eye choosing instead to stare at his clothes and the splashes of yellow, green, blue, and red colors against the background of faded blue jeans and black t-shirt.

"I've been worried about you," she heard him say in a voice she did not recognize. His voice sounded husker as if he had something stuck in his throat. Vera could smell the sage all around her. She heard cows mooing somewhere in the distance. Vera concentrated her attention on the hole in the sleeve of his t-shirt. The hole exposed pink skin. The hole looked out of place with all the other colors. The hole, like a blemish, drew the eye again and again.

She tried to think about Andrew. She tried to concentrate on something that was not quite right about this moment. Vera remembered how Aunt Vista, when Vera did something particularly stupid used to smack her on the head and shout in her ear. Her mother also had the habit of standing real close, close enough Vera could smell the cigarette smoke and beer on her breath. Her mother's face would pinch as if she smelled a bad odor and her lips would contort as if the ugly thoughts could not be contained inside her head any longer.

That other woman, that woman she knew to be her mother, would shake her head, and say, "You're not mine; you're the devil's child." Often when Vera hid in a closet to escape her family or gave away her money or her lunch or let someone take her coat or her clothes or let a bully beat her until her body was one large bruise, her uncles would tease her and call her The Muddy Puddle. They would say, "Here comes the Muddy Puddle, all dirty from the shoes that have stepped on her today."

Vera looked up from the ground and into Andrew's face. He looked as if he had just woken from a bad dream, as if the dream still haunted him.

"You have a hole in your shirt," she said and pointed to the hole.

He glanced down at his sleeve, then into her face, "Yes. I've been working on the spare bedroom next to our room."

"I saw you leave for work this morning," Vera said.

"Yes, I did. I finished the piece early and thought I'd come home and surprise you. I bought paint and rollers and thought I'd have the room prepped and ready before you got home from work."

Vera started to climb back into her car. She heard Andrew say, "Where are you going?"

She paused and looked at him, "I'm going home."

"To your house?"

"Why are you painting the spare room?" she asked him.

"I needed something to do. Physical activity helps me think."

"Are you finished?" she asked.

"Almost," he said.

"I'll help you finish," she told him and climbed in her car.

—

Andrew followed Vera into the house. He had waited until Sarah Matthews drove away before going in search of Vera. Sarah pretended not to notice anything unusual in Vera's hasty departure. He figured Vera had headed south toward Oregon or Nevada. If she had gone through Mintlaw she would have had to slow down for every little intersection and bump and she would know he could easily find her in town. He took US 95 and as he had assumed saw the beige Corolla a few miles ahead. Worried that he might find her little car overturned on the highway, he was so relieved to see the ball of metal putt putting up the steep inclines, annoying other drivers who were forced to creep along behind her or try to pass her on the narrow stretch of road, he stopped being angry. He knew what he'd gotten himself into with this prickly pear of a woman.

Once they were in the privacy of her home, Andrew followed Vera into the bedroom and watched her undress and slip on a pair of old jeans and a sleeveless top. Vera passed him with a shy smile, as if he was a stranger she was meeting for the first time. She walked into the spare bedroom in her bare feet and stood on the news papered floor with her hands on her hips surveying the walls with calm interest. Without comment, she picked up the brush that he had thrown on the floor near the paint can and dipped the tip of the brush bristles into the paint. Andrew pulled a clean roller out of a bag and replaced the old roller. Silently they worked together to finish the room. He rolled the paint onto the wall he had nearly finished; Vera, on the ladder, applied a second coat of paint along the edges where the walls and the ceiling met.

Within an hour they were finished. Vera covered her paint brush in a clear plastic baggy and wrapped a purple band around the handle to lock out the air. Andrew heard her murmur, "Golden pecan." He looked at the color and had to agree that it looked more like golden pecan than yellow. He realized too late that he had bought a matte paint, not a semi-gloss paint. Maybe Vera hadn't noticed his mistake.

As Andrew tapped down the paint lid with a rubber mallet, Vera collected the roller stick and plastic bags and left the room. Andrew carried the paint can outside and put the empty can in a brown paper bag. When Andrew returned to the kitchen, he saw Vera sitting in her rocking chair. The sight chilled him. Then he noticed her tears. He wanted to comfort her but didn't know how. Whenever his mother cried, his father found some excuse to leave the house. Andrew sensed that if he left the house, he might not be able to return.

He'd seen women cry before. Most women didn't just sit there and rock and rock and let the tears fall without making a sound. When he moved toward her and knelt in front of her chair and put his hand on her knee, she looked down at him with surprise. Her surprise made him feel uncomfortable. Why would she be surprised that he was kind? She had yet to tell him the story behind her scar. He wanted her to volunteer the information not force her to tell him. He had done the right thing back there on McBride road.

At first, he'd been furious, embarrassed, and worried the director of the school might think his new girlfriend was certifiably nuts. The time spent following her had given him a chance to calm down and reassess the situation. He had no control over what Ms. Matthews thought about Vera. Neither of them had the expertise to label her crazy anyway. So, by the time he had parked and gotten out of his vehicle, he couldn't think of anything to say. He'd been afraid he would ruin everything by alienating her or saying something really stupid. His silence had saved him.

After a moment or two of sitting silently in a room with a tearful woman, and he not knowing what was going on, time seemed to stretch out and extend into infinity in his mind, Vera wiped the tears off her cheeks and said, "Who's going to be sleeping in the Pecan Room?"

"I don't know. No one I guess. I was thinking about all those books of yours in boxes. I thought you might like some bookshelves so that you can shelve your books properly."

"You do like order don't you," she said in a teasing voice and with a tentative hand tapped him on the shoulder.

He reached out for her hand before she could place it back on the arm of the rocking chair. He kissed the back of her hand and held it to his cheek for a moment, "You can tell me anything Vera, anything at all. I'm listening."

Vera slid off the seat of the rocking chair and knelt beside him. She wrapped her arms around his shoulders and began to kiss his face. He searched for her mouth. An hour later, Andrew awoke to find the other half of the bed empty. He realized that once again she had found a way to avoid the conversation he knew they needed to have if they were ever to move into the next stage of their relationship. He jumped out of bed and went out into the dark hall. He could smell the new paint from the adjoining room and sensed someone inside. The hall light illuminated Vera's body crouched on the floor. She sat naked on the floor with her legs crossed and her arms behind her supporting her weight, "Vera what are you doing?"

She looked up at him and focused for the first time on his face, "I'm thinking about this room. This room would make a wonderful bedroom for a little girl, don't you think?

Panic encased him like an Iron Maiden, "You're thinking about having children?"

Vera stood up and brushed by him, "No, of course not, it's too late for me."

"Don't walk away," Andrew said in a harsher tone then he had intended. He forced himself to remain calm. "I want to talk about this. I want to talk about today also."

Before Vera had a chance to pull on her robe, Andrew led her toward the bed, "Come on; get back into bed with me and let's talk?"

"We don't talk when we're in bed."

"Humor me. I promise we'll just talk. Ok?"

Andrew waited for Vera to make the first move. She stood by the bed considering his request her long neck, erect breasts, slim hips, and long legs distracting him. His response to her nakedness must have made Vera suspicious about his motives. She shrugged as if resigned. Her lack of faith irritated him. He would show her that he was different from the other guys she had known. She slipped under the covers. Andrew lay down beside her and pulled her cold body toward him. He tried to think about something else beside her body and what he would have liked to do just then.

"Why did you run away today? Sarah told me you never showed up for work. She was worried. She thought you might be sick. What's going on, huh?"

Vera rested her head on his chest. Andrew couldn't see her face. Andrew sat up and pushed the pillows behind his back, then lifted Vera up and cradled her in his arms. She buried her face in his chest. He conceded defeat and waited.

After a moment, she turned her head and glanced up at his face, "I can't help them. I don't know anything. I'm just not fit to work with children. They need somebody who knows what they're doing. Not me."

"Sarah thinks differently."

"Sarah needs a babysitter," Vera said with a vehemence that surprised him.

"What about today? What did you do all day?"

"I went to Boise and to the bookstore and drank coffee and watched the people."

"Why didn't you tell me you quit work? I would have understood."

"I can't seem to do anything right," Vera said, again in a voice filled with anger and self-loathing. "I can't even keep a simple, stupid job."

"What do you want to do?"

"I want to read and take care of the farm and fix up my house, maybe grow Christmas trees or flowers and sell them to nurseries."

"And why do you need my permission to do the things you love?" he asked.

"I don't need your permission. It's just different now."

Andrew bent down and kissed her forehead. He sensed beneath the words a truth she wasn't ready to tell him. Even at this moment with their bodies as close as twins in a womb, Vera's thoughts were somewhere else, distant as the space between canyons. He wasn't surprised when she made an excuse to get out of bed; in principle, separating herself from him physically as well as mentally.

—

Maggie sat in front of her desk and stared out her bedroom window. Downstairs she could hear her parents talking in the kitchen. She heard Grandpa Treloar's wheelchair rumble down the hall and hit the strip of metal on the floor separating the hall from the carpeted living room. With the catalpa leaves gone, Maggie had an uninterrupted view of Vera's house. Uncle Andrew was inside the house right now. He and Vera were probably making supper or maybe making love. The thought of the two of them in bed together made the adrenaline surge through her body. Her thoughts were a mixed-up mess of emotions: jealousy, loathing, and desire.

She imagined herself naked sleeping next to Jeremy, imagined them clutched in each other's arms after a night of wild passion. A long time ago, Maggie's mother had caught Maggie masturbating. After that, her mother stopped walking into Maggie's bedroom unannounced. The day her mother had a serious conversation with her about sexuality and adolescent urges Maggie struggled not to show her embarrassment, instead trying to appear mature.

The whole episode had been painful and stupid. Her mother sounded calm and rational and informative, but her eyes never lifted from the page open on her lap, a page which showed diagrams of a woman's vagina and a man's penis. In the end, her mother had handed her the collection of books she'd bought and urged Maggie to read them leaving the bedroom as if the house was on fire.

Stupid, stupid, Maggie thought, *it was stupid to get caught.* Now that she knew her parents had consulted each other and debated over the whole nasty episode, she noticed how careful they were to knock before entering her room; and most of the time these days, they just avoided entering her room at all. Her bedroom had become her place of sanctuary. The episode had created new responsibilities for Maggie; instead of her mother doing all the domestic chores around the house, nowadays, Maggie stripped off her dirty sheets and made her bed. She even cleaned out her closet and put away her clothes. The price for her privacy had been an embarrassing moment she would probably never forget. She could live with that now, because now she enjoyed being alone, enjoyed her solitude: reading, writing, and thinking about boys.

Grandma Margaret Martha Treloar had taught her not to be ashamed of her body. She remembered those long-ago conversations between them. Her grandmother had not been ashamed to look her in the eye. She'd listened to Maggie and nodded her head every so often, her eyes serious and her head tilted to hear the better. Those conversations had been so natural with Maggie asking questions and her grandmother answering the best she could while her light blue eyes rested thoughtfully on Maggie's face.

Her most vivid memory was when her parents left for Spain and she and her brothers went to stay on the Treloar farm for the summer. She must have been about nine or ten. The whole family had come down to Idaho for the reunion, her cousins, aunts, and uncles. She ended up sleeping in the attic with her cousins. She remembered the boys. Some of them must have been teenagers. Her brothers were sleeping in the barn because they had bugged Grandpa Murray until he acquiesced. The twins thought a night out in the barn would be a hoot. Unlike her, they hadn't been stuck up in the attic. She would never forget those boys, those virtual strangers parading in front of her cot pulling out their penises, laughing and stroking themselves, showing off as if their clowning made them men.

Maggie remembered the next morning, the smells in the kitchen, the smells of homemade bread and cookies baking, of her grandmother's shampoo, and the nail polish Aunt Brenda had left on the kitchen table. Maggie remembered she leaned against her grandmother's arm and her grandmother pulled her in close. Maggie liked to touch her grandmother's wedding ring and feel the warmth of her grandmother's fat fingers in her hands. Her grandmother had been reading the Bible. Maggie had said,

"Grandma Mattie, why do boys get to sleep without any pajamas on? I have to sleep with pajamas on. Is it because I'm a girl?"

"Which boys are we talking about Maggie?"

"Oh, you know, just some boys."

"Well pajamas keep you warm in the winter and if you have to run out of the house in the night— to use the outhouse maybe.

"Yuck. There's no outhouse here."

Mattie laughed and hugged her, "No sweetheart, not now, but there used to be before you were born. I'm just explaining reasons why you should always wear your pajamas. They're good for when bugs are around, and they keep them off your legs."

"What's in that book you're reading? Is it a good story?"

"There are a lot of good stories in the Bible, stories about people and places and times long ago. These stories tell you how to live right."

"What about sex? Do people have sex in the Bible?"

"Well, yes, I guess they do. There's a lot of begetting of children in the Bible."

"Do you have to think bad thoughts to have sex?"

"Where do I go from here?" her Grandmother Mattie said aloud, and Maggie had to wait a week before she got an answer to her question. After their conversation, Maggie had been moved into the laundry room across the hall from her grandparent's bedroom. She slept on a cot and had to put up with Murray's snoring and snorting and his occasional nighttime treks to the bathroom off the kitchen. Her grandma liked to sigh at night. She sighed, and the bed springs would squeak; then she'd turn over again and sigh some more. Even though they woke her in the middle of the night sometimes; she felt safe and secure with them so close.

Before her family returned to Minnesota, she and Mattie had their serious talk outside the house while shelling peas for supper. It had been hot all day and unlike her apartment in St. Paul, her grandparents had only a swamp cooler which didn't work all that well. She and Mattie were sitting under the maple tree near the house, Mattie in a chair with a bucket near her feet and Maggie on the blanket watching her baby cousins as they slept.

"Remember that conversation we had awhile back about the Bible?" Mattie asked her.

"Sure Grandma," Maggie said as she uncurled herself from the blanket and sat up to give her grandmother her full attention. "You mean whether sex is dirty?"

"Well, no. Don't you remember; you asked if you have to think bad thoughts to have sex?"

"Oh, yeah, I forgot."

"Let me tell you honey," her grandmother began in a serious tone, "you don't have to think bad thoughts. It's much better if you think good thoughts about the person you're with; but first you have to love the person you're with and know them and trust them."

"How do you know you love them?"

"You'll know."

"But how, I don't understand?"

"Well, if you're ashamed to be with the man; then you don't love him. People who love each other are friends first. And the way to know if you are good friends is if that friend feels sad without you, would never force you to do something you weren't ready to do, keeps your secrets, and defends you against others."

Just as Maggie was going to ask another question, they were interrupted by a baseball hitting the branch of the maple tree and sending leaves and other debris down upon Maggie's head. The twins apologized to Mattie and that ended her conversation with her grandmother. When her grandmother got up from her chair to attend to the babies, she looked down at Maggie and asked, "Well. What do you think about our little talk?"

"Thanks for the information Grandma. I have a lot to think about now."

The others were returning to the house from the game and there was no time to prolong their little talk. But she'd wanted to ask just one more question. She supposed she'd been trying to find the answer to her question ever since. What's the difference between friendship with a girl and friendship with a boy then? It must have something to do with desire. Maggie knew she desired Jeremy. It wasn't just because he was handsome, athletic, and the most popular boy in school. It had to do with something else – something she couldn't quite define.

Jeremy reminded Maggie of the men in her family lean and tall and quiet. Both Jeremy and her uncle were restful to be around. Unlike her father, Jeremy and her uncle were doers not thinkers. She admired and loved her father, but sometimes he just went on and on for hours about his favorite subjects which were numerous; and in her opinion, rather boring. When he'd learned through an innocent remark Maggie made that Grandma Mattie had read stories to her from the Bible, he was upset. He tried to explain his point of view about religion. She listened politely and when he waited for her response said, "I've got a lot to think about now, Dad. Thanks for the information."

It was the same thing she had said to Grandma Mattie.

She missed her Grandma Mattie so much.

—

Daniel polished the best half of his thunderegg, the one with the milky pearl star in the center of the red stone. He polished and paused. Whenever he paused in his work, which was every five minutes or so, he left the shed and walked around to the back to stare beyond the gated yard toward the Owyhee Mountains. He could only see the bits of the hillside from this part of the yard. Yet he could see Miss Vera's house and Andrew Treloar's Jeep parked in the driveway. It was a triangle for him, where he stood was the center, and in the center, he could go in three different directions. Inside the fenced yard, he was in the safety zone. The two remaining points of the triangle— the cave where his treasure was hidden and the house where Miss Vera lived were cut off from him for today. He didn't like the thought of being shut out.

What could he do about it? Ms. Matthews would suggest he think about his problem for a time and perhaps he would come up with a solution. He returned to the shed and polished some more. When he polished or cut or searched for rocks, his body felt light as air. The lightness made him sleepy. He stopped polishing and left the shed and returned to the point of the triangle. It was winter now and cold and few people trespassed on the hill. Only the hunters in autumn messed up the roads and the mountains and the valleys. There were no hunters today. He tried to imagine his cave, tried to remember what was so unpleasant about it now. Perhaps a dirty old skunk had crawled into his cave and died there.

Daniel remembered his father taking him hunting, remembered the long gun and the bullets and the way his legs quivered when the shots rang through the air. His father used to say that you had to be smarter than the animals so as to flush them out. Come spring Daniel would find a way to flush that creature out into the open and he would find it and kill it and make sure it was very, very, dead.

Chapter Seventeen

With her notebook in front of her, Vera sat at the kitchen table, her pencil poised above the sketch she had made of her property. She heard Andrew leave the bathroom and go into the bedroom. She heard drawers being opened. The bed springs squeaked when he sat on the bed to put on his socks. So odd, she thought, to hear someone else moving about in her house. Vera sipped her coffee, then tried to draw a series of miniature trees to the left of the box marked house. She wasn't sure how much land was hers on the right side of the property, so she drew ten trees. Then she paused unable to think any further. Ten trees would take forever to grow to the size she wanted, the size that would provide a wind break and some color in the winter. She heard the heavy tread of his boots on the hardwood floor as he came down the hall and into the kitchen.

He leaned over her shoulder and kissed her on the cheek, "I'll be back before midnight. Don't wait up for me."

When he didn't move from his position behind her chair, she realized he was waiting for her response to his comment and his kiss. It would be better for him if he didn't know what she was thinking.

So, she lifted her head and put on a smile, "I won't. Have fun."

Instead of leaving the house as he had done the previous two Saturdays, he pulled out a chair and sat down to face her. He had put on his favorite blue sweater and wore his tight 501 jeans. She could smell his cologne and aftershave. His hair glistened blue black still wet from a quick shower.

"Why won't you come with me tonight? Alice would love to see you."

"No, I want to work on this project tonight. I'm going into town to buy some pea gravel and paving stones tomorrow and need to know how many I should buy."

Andrew studied the notebook with a thoughtful eye, "What's your real reason for not going with me?"

Vera laid down her pencil and covered the page with her fingers, "Don't look. I'm a terrible artist."

When she felt his hand on her arm, she lifted her head and made herself look at him. He seemed to be studying her face but then again like the police Andrew had a habit of studying faces and decoding reactions. At that moment, she knew she had to tell him the truth. Making excuses had become tiresome.

"George and Alice Metcalf are your friends. You have things in common with them. I don't. I've never been comfortable making small talk. Alice is nice but..."

"The only way to get to know people is to meet them halfway."

"I've met them halfway. For the last two months we've been going over to their house. Every Saturday night we get dressed up and go over to the Metcalfs. Sometimes there are other people there. Most often it's just us. And I end up in the kitchen with Alice. And Alice talks about her irritable bowels. And her kids interrupt me to tell me silly stories that have nothing to do with the topic of conversation. And you spend all your time sitting out in the garage with George drinking beer and talking about work. Is that honest enough for you?" she said. This time she did not mask her annoyance.

From the kitchen window she could see how the moon had spread its milk across the yard. The tips of the grass were covered in a gauzy blanket of dew and the newly stained fence seemed to sparkle. Vera wanted to be out there, in the darkest part of the yard, alone, with objects around her that do not talk back or give her advice or try to change her.

Andrew stood up and walked out of the room. Vera listened as he shut the door quietly behind him. She heard the Jeep start up. She waited for the squeal of tires as Andrew paused on the drive then accelerated onto the black-topped road. She was surprised when she heard the front door open and Andrew reenter the kitchen, surprised enough to turn around and stare at him.

He didn't look upset. Sometimes it was difficult to know what he was thinking. But as far as she could tell, he seemed to have come to a decision. "You've been honest with me, so I'll be honest with you. I've been thinking about you and me and how we've got different ways of thinking," he paused as if he had meant to say something and thought better of it. "You're the kind of person that can be alone and never see a soul for days. I'm not. I like to be around people. I like to talk to people. This is the way I relax. So, if you don't want to come that's fine by me. But whenever I feel the urge, I'm going out. Okay?"

"Sure. Of course," she found herself saying and before she could think of anything else, he left the room again.

As if on cue, once Andrew had left the house and driven away, the doorbell rang. Vera opened the door and smiled at Maggie. Maggie wore a red knitted cap on her head that clashed with her auburn hair. She also had on a down coat and gloves. The wind blew down the hall and pierced cold through Vera's skin, down through the layers right to the bone.

"Boy is it freezing outside!" Maggie said. "And Grandpa grumbled the entire day about how his family always had turkey at Thanksgiving and this year shouldn't be any different and about how eating that fancy stuff made him nauseous. Then when mom said the winters seemed to be colder, he said no such thing and spent an hour telling us how back in 1920 or some such year the cows' hooves froze to the ground."

"You can leave your coat on the couch," Vera said when she had a chance to talk.

"Oh, it's so nice and quiet and peaceful over here. And it smells so good like cinnamon or ginger or something. Are you baking cookies?"

"No," Vera said and shut the door against the cold winter night. Maggie took off her backpack and extracted one of Marquez's books from inside and offered it to Vera. "Dad said he's never read Marquez other than one of his short stories. Thanks for the book Vera. It was so romantic. I never realized that a man could be so devoted to someone all his life. Wow. You think that's true, that someone can be in love with the same woman for fifty years, even if that woman is married to someone else?"

Vera accepted the book and followed Maggie into the kitchen, "I suppose it's possible."

"Fermina doesn't deserve such love. She's an old bat."

"Well, it's a bit more complicated than that Maggie."

"I wish Florentino could have found some worthy person to love, someone like my mother maybe."

"Well."

"Their lives seem so different, you know, different from my life. I mean I've always had mom and dad and my brothers and my uncles and my aunts and my grandparents. I've never been hungry or so poor I couldn't wear nice clothes and things. And the place, the way it's described, it just doesn't sound real, people dying of cholera and people shooting other people, all that death and disease and destruction. It just doesn't seem to be real somehow."

Vera handed Maggie her favorite orange drink and some cookies she'd bought just for her visits. The two were comfortable enough in each other's company now that Vera no longer worried about having to make small talk with her guest; instead, Vera sat down in front of her notebook and contemplated her future landscaping. While Maggie nibbled on a mint chocolate cookie, Vera studied the paper, "There are places just like the ones that Marquez writes about Maggie. All you have to do is watch the news. Someday you might visit those far off places and see how other people live."

Maggie used her cookie to emphasize her point, "You know that book got me thinking about love, about how a man can love a woman. I always thought it was the woman that had such powerful emotions. What do you think?"

Vera shrugged, "It depends on the person I guess."

"What do you mean?"

Vera shut her notebook with a sigh and looked across the table at Maggie, "To tell you the truth when I read that story I just couldn't believe a man would devote his life to loving one woman. But he did. Yet it didn't stop him from making love to other women. He's lifelike in that sense. I mean, I can't relate to it because I've never experienced that sort of feeling before."

"You mean you've never been in love?" Maggie asked. "What about my uncle, don't you love him?

Vera got up from the table and made herself a fresh cup of coffee making sure that her back was to the room so that Maggie couldn't see her flushed cheeks. You are an idiot, Vera thought, talking to Maggie as if she were an adult. She's not. She's just a kid. Vera returned to the table with her coffee; and by the time she reached Maggie, she had her emotions under control.

"Of course, I love Andrew, but only time can tell if I will love him fifty years from now as much as I do today."

"So, you know what love feels like. Can you describe it for me? Is it like loving your parents?"

Vera heard a squawk from the other room followed by the quivering voice of an old man. Maggie jumped up and ran into the living room. She returned holding the small walkie-talkie, pressed a button, and spoke into the mouthpiece, "What's up Grandpa?'

Maggie's grandfather said, "comb om ow."

"I just got here," Maggie grumbled.

Vera and Maggie heard a crash as if a chair had fallen over then heavy boots march across the floor. Maggie's complexion turned three shades of white.

"Something's wrong. I've got to get home. Mom and Dad went to a movie. Grandpa's. He's."

Vera walked with her to the hallway and while Maggie slipped on her coat, Vera fished her parka out of the closet and said, "I'm coming with you."

—

Murray lay on the floor with his cheek pressed to the wood and closed his eyes. He could hear the man running up the stairs, searching the bedrooms. A gust of cold air blew through the room from the open kitchen door. Murray shivered and pretended to sleep. He was a child again listening to his father storming through the house searching for the person that had made him angry. But this stranger was different from his father. Murray heard a wet sound coming from a deep, gravel voice. He heard the voice sniff, snort, gasp, and hiccup.

A thief with a cold, Murray thought, *Or a thief with a nasal problem*. The idea made him want to laugh. He stopped himself in time. Murray's father had always been a quiet man, contained within a world of hot embers that would on occasion strike sparks and those sparks would land on people standing too close. This thief, this intruder was nothing like his father. He was a coward and a moron.

The stranger returned to the kitchen. Murray opened his eyes. I'm not an animal, a frightened whistle pig hiding in a hole. He'd been a strong young man once, just like his grandson Kit and his son Andrew. Murray's arms shook as he lifted himself up. He sat on the floor and rested his back against the counter door beneath the kitchen sink. Murray imagined himself safe between the sink and the kitchen table.

The thief ignored Murray. He could see the man's boots, his big brown boots with the black rubber soles, soles that left black streaks atop Rachel's fancy white vinyl floor as he marched toward the open door. The stranger walked out into the dark. Murray watched him walk down the steps with Kit's hunting rifle slung over his shoulder. He recognized him and called out his name, "aniel!"

The porch light illuminated Daniel for a moment. Daniel glanced back over his shoulder. Murray could see the whites of his eyes and the way he had his mouth wide open as if to scream. Daniel merged with the shadows and Murray could hear him running down the graveled driveway. The wet sounds, the sounds that reminded Murray of a bear with a cold receded and were replaced by the light steps of someone coming toward the front of the house. He heard the front door swing open and the bang as the door hit the opposite wall. He heard the terror in his great granddaughter's voice as she shouted his name. Murray's pride made the moment less painful. He was proud that he met the women sitting up and not lying sprawled on the floor like an injured baby.

—

"It was Daniel," Maggie told Vera. Vera agreed but said nothing. She just sat there at the kitchen table examining her hands without moving or speaking. Vera had helped Maggie to lift Murray back into his wheelchair. The way she did it though seemed odd. Vera had helped Maggie lift Grandpa Murray off the floor with an unpleasant expression on her face as if Murray had soiled himself or something. The rest of the time Vera just sat in the chair and stared at her hands.

Maggie called 911.

The ambulance arrived just as her parents returned from the D & B. The ambulance took Grandpa to the Nampa Hospital and her mother followed the ambulance. Before the ambulance arrived, Maggie asked Vera twice to call Andrew. Vera stared at her in surprise, looked around the kitchen for the phone, and grudgingly called him. Vera sounded as if she were talking to a stranger. Why was she acting so weird?

Upstairs in Grandpa Murray's old bedroom her father was showing Uncle Andrew the broken safe where Grandpa Murray kept his hunting rifles, his forty-five, and his ammunition. Maggie could not understand how Daniel had known about the gun-safe or how he had figured out the combination to the lock. Murray would never have shown someone like Daniel his collection of rifles, much less told him the numbers to open the safe. In Murray's eyes, Daniel was a moron, an unwelcome village idiot.

Maggie heard her father and uncle ascend the stairs and walk down the hall. She heard Andrew say, "Dad wasn't hurt, just frightened. Daniel must have come expressly to get the rifle."

The Mintlaw Police Department had shown up by then and Maggie's father and uncle stood outside near the patrol vehicle and talked for some time. Her parents were too worried about Grandpa Murray to be angry with her for leaving him alone in the house. She couldn't help but wonder whether her presence in the house might have prevented Daniel from breaking in. Would her presence have made any difference at all?

"It would have made no difference. No difference at all," Maggie heard Vera say from the other side of the room.

The hairs on the back of Maggie's neck tingled. Maggie looked at Vera real close, closer than she usually looked at people.

Vera sat there in the bright room with the ceiling fan above her head and the blades rotating and the lights casting shadows on her face with the four bulbs in their matching flower glass cases shining down on Vera's head. The stark light turned Vera's black curls green. With her hair down, Maggie could see a few gray hairs, not really gray more silver the color of tinsel on a Christmas tree.

That was the moment Maggie realized Vera was older than Maggie's own mother. Did Vera's hair color come from a bottle? But she looked so young, young enough to be mistaken for one of her brother's girlfriends. Even Vera's eyebrows were dark and bushy and reminded Maggie of a much younger person. It was the scar on her cheek. The scar made people shy away, the scar kept people from recognizing what Maggie recognized – Vera had the complexion and figure of a twenty-year-old; yet, her eyes were old with wisdom and experience. The expression in her eyes reminded Maggie of her grandmother. Both women radiated an ancient knowledge of the earth and an acceptance of the fragility of life.

For all she knew, Vera could be a hundred years old.

Before Maggie had a chance to say something about Vera responding to Maggie's unspoken thoughts and how nobody in this whole world should be able to do something so supernatural, Andrew returned to the kitchen and touched Vera on the shoulder, "I'll take you home now, come on honey," he said in a voice Maggie had never heard before as if he might have been talking to a frightened stray, as if he were coaxing the stray out of the wild and into a trap for its own good. Vera followed him out the back door and Maggie walked to the kitchen window to watch as he held Vera's arm and guided her down the driveway. She wasn't blind. She wasn't a feeble old lady. Why was he acting so strange as if Vera were some expensive piece of glass?

Maggie forgot Vera as soon as her father entered the kitchen and she noticed the look on his face. It was time for the cross examination. She would do her confessing. He would lecture her on her behavior and then there would be the sentencing. She wanted the whole mess over double quick.

—

Andrew guided Vera toward his vehicle, but Vera jerked out of his hold and started walking toward her house. Andrew called out her name. She ignored him and crossed the road. Andrew sighed and climbed into his vehicle. Vera had reached the porch before he had a chance to pull up and park his car near her Corolla. He entered the house and realized it was empty. He strode to the kitchen and looked around.

She was in the back yard.

He had no time for her strange moods tonight.

Instead of calling out to her, he retrieved his gun from the storage closet, pressed the code to unlock the case, holstered the gun, and wrote a brief note to her before leaving. Steven and the others would be at the school searching for Daniel. Andrew drove toward the school wondering if he had made the most colossal mistake of his life getting involved with Vera Lee. Then he remembered how much she hated guns and the fight they had had over having the gun in her house. He also remembered the first night he'd met her, the night her husband had died. The break-in at the farm tonight must have brought up old memories.

—

Vera avoided the spot where she would one-day plant her barricade of arborvitae and with a clear view below her of the road watched as Andrew drove toward the school. They would not find him there. Vera glanced over her shoulder up at the hill. A good cry right now might make her feel better. She had no room for tears though. Hatred, fear, and passion had jumped out of the cellar hole. It had returned. This new ugliness would pass; yet, she wondered what would be left behind after the wake of destruction. Daniel had the sense to be scared. Andrew and the others lived in a different world. They didn't understand what she and Daniel had always known. There were things out in the dark that were just plain mean and needed killing.

That poor man back there, that poor old man still hanging on to a dream, still wrapped up in fantasies. Touching that poor old man had been like touching a piece of cold stone. His sons, the older ones, the older brothers of Andrew had been eager to get away from the predictability of the old man's dreams. He thought food and shelter and healthy soil enough reason for living. Vera saw the lights below her, the street lights of the small town of Mintlaw, the lamps burning in windows, the headlights of vehicles driving back and forth on Jump Creek Road.

People kept themselves from thinking by making themselves so busy with the trivial. This wasn't the time to be busy. This was the time to pierce through the darkness and see the real danger. As a young child, Vera had faced the ugliness up close and realized that people were most dangerous when they were the most convinced they were right. The world was dangerous because of sanctimonious airheads thinking they knew what was right for the rest of the world.

It took ten minutes to find what she needed from the house. She shut the back door and started hiking up Opal Road Access that would lead her to Daniel. He would be scared. Vera had been scared all her life. It was nothing new to her this feeling that the something that had created the ugliness had also created the rocks and the sagebrush and the mountain peaks. For the first time, Vera realized a truth she had been avoiding for a long time. She unzipped her parka and touched the necklace, thinking what a fool she'd been to hide her childhood in a cookie tin. She would let Daniel touch the stones and remind him that the stones had been here longer than people's hatred, fear, and passion. She wished she had a thunderegg to give him.

———

Daniel rested against the wall of the rock ledge and held the rifle on his lap. He could hear the creatures moving about in the dark. A blast of cold wind swept down the channel between the canyon walls. The wind rushed passed him making his hair stand up. He wanted to push his hair back down, make it stay still, but the wind wanted to play games. Daniel's fingers hurt, and he looked down. His eyes could not see his fingers, but he knew they were holding tight to the rifle, his right hand wrapped around the warm wood of the handle, his left hand wrapped around the cold steel of the pipe.

His father had taught him how to load a rifle and made him stand and not cry when he pulled the trigger and the rifle barked and burned. He remembered the echoes. They sounded as if they came from clear across the valley, from the other side of the highway. He remembered the night the nasty human tried to steal his treasure, the van's headlights had been pointing right at the rabbit-brush hiding his cave, and the headlights illuminated the human carrying the bundle of blankets. Something inside the blankets moaned. No. That can't be right? That must have been a dream. He remembered wishing he'd had a gun. His memory had been a dream, not like this moment, this moment was real.

The ghost was in the cave waiting for him. She might not let him inside. He would flush her out, make her want to come out. She liked dead things. He would find her something dead. His fingers relaxed, and the blood pumped again. He knew about blood. The man in his dream had been hurt, blood on his cheek. He'd been struggling to get away from the other two men. They had made him get in the van. He had been wearing yellow boots. Daniel didn't like the boots. He didn't like snakes either, but he didn't like humans wearing snakeskin. He felt sorry for the man. The man had been crying. He'd been so scared.

Someone else was crying. Was he crying? His father had been in his dream too. His father had been mad at him. He remembered the smell of beer on his father's breath, remembered the trip home as he pretended to be asleep in the back seat of the truck the cool vinyl against his cheek. That was much more real than now. He was so scared. He wished his real dad could tell him what to do.

Then he heard someone moving his way and a familiar voice say, "Daniel, come and see my cat's eye."

He made himself stand up. He pointed his rifle at her.

Miss Vera kept walking toward him. His legs began to tremble. He said a dirty word and she stopped. His words did have power.

"I see what's coming," she said. "You think that by killing me you can make it go away. It won't go away. I know. Believe me I know."

"She likes dead things," he said, mad for admitting the truth.

"You're giving her what she wants."

"I want her out!" he said feeling the spit land on his chin.

"I'll help you get her out. Show me where she's hiding, and I'll help you."

Miss Vera wanted to trick him, he thought, maybe Miss Vera was one of them. Maybe she wanted his treasure.

"I'm not here to trick you Daniel. I just want to help."

Then Daniel saw the shadows behind Miss Vera, shadows that resembled creatures from his night dreams. They stood behind her. They were waiting to drag him into the dark.

Daniel lifted his rifle and cursed at them.

—

Maggie heard the report of a rifle, followed by more until there was silence again. All the while a man screamed, and the screaming echoed through the hills and carried across the valley below. Her father ran to the phone. Maggie ran to the front door. She ignored her father's command to stop and opened the door and rushed outside. The sound had come from Hunter's Hill. Daniel was up there shooting at something that terrified him. There were no lights on at Vera's house. Only the light beside the front door illuminated the porch. Maggie ran past Vera's house. By the time she reached the top of the hill her side ached so much she had to stop.

"Vera," she whispered. There was no sound. She could have been all alone up here. She'd never been up here at night. It was darker than dark. She could not see much in front of her. The hill on her right obscured the moon. Only a lantern's light sitting on the ground allowed her to see the entrance to the cave and some of the brush near her feet. She made herself shout, "Vera!"

Maggie heard footsteps behind her, heard him panting and running in her direction. Maggie walked into the deeper darkness where the moon did not penetrate. She heard something in front of her, a creature frightened out of its wits, crashing about amongst the rocks and brush. She smelled sage, broken sagebrush. A blast of cold wind nearly shoved her off her feet. Then the wind died down and she heard something being dragged across the valley floor, across rocks and dead desert flowers. Before she could move forward, she felt a hand on her arm jerking her back.

"What the hell do you think you're doing?" her father said.

"Daniel's here. He's scared. I think Vera's here too."

Her father stood still and listened. Maggie, even though every limb trembled, wanted to move forward, wanted to find Daniel and Vera.

They stood close together, her father and her, standing by the barricade of boulders, the entrance to the hilltop. The darker shadows on either side of her she recognized as the rocky buttes. The sound had come from her left. Her father wrapped his arm around her shoulder. They stood in the cold darkness and listened. Her trembling must have communicated itself to him because he leaned down and said in her ear, "Go home, Maggie. Let me find Daniel."

Maggie through chattering teeth said, "He doesn't know you Dad. Let me talk to him. He knows me."

Her father grabbed her arm as she tried to pull away and shoved her backwards. His grip hurt, "No! If it is Daniel he's got Murray's rifle and Daniel with a rifle is something different than the Daniel, you know from school. I'm telling you to go home. Do it now Maggie or I swear I'll drag you home and lock you in your bedroom."

Her father hauled her back toward the barricade, his grip closing off the blood supply to her hand. She tried to tell him he was hurting her, but he just kept walking down the hillside with her in tow. Maggie heard the police sirens. Her father changed course and instead of taking her home, he started moving toward Anderson Pass. One of the vehicles turned off the highway onto the field and headed toward them. They stepped aside so as not to get run over. Maggie recognized the Jeep. A police car followed close behind and turned off the main road and headed toward them. Its lights blinded Maggie for a moment.

"Uncle Andrew, I think Vera's up there with Daniel. I heard voices, two people. They were close to the cattle guard."

"How do you know Vera is up there?" he asked glancing toward Vera's house.

"I don't know for sure. I heard a body being dragged across the ground. Hurry, please. Something's wrong."

—

The news that Vera might be hurt made Andrew furious. He was so mad he could barely see what was in front of him; Maggie's pale face looking down at him became a blur. He jerked the car into drive and drove away without a word. He drove faster than he should have up the slope and with only the back wheels touching jumped the ledge and landed on the upper valley floor with a grinding of his undercarriage against rock and trampled sagebrush. His headlights illuminated the old road and the darker shape of the rocky ledge to his left. He pushed down on the pedal, tearing up tender plants and throwing small rocks in his wake. He didn't care. Within seconds he was around the bend. His headlights revealed the barricade and he could go no further. Beyond the barricade, he saw someone spread out on the ground.

He forgot everything in his haste to reach the body. When he got closer he realized that what he had expected hadn't come true. He was still kneeling by the body trying to collect his wits when George ran toward him.

"What you got Andy?" George asked. George's flashlight rested on the face of the man lying on the ground beside Andrew.

"Is he dead?" George asked.

"No," Andrew said standing up, relieved that he could stand.

Andrew and George looked down at Daniel. He had a wound on his forehead. The blood gleamed in the white glow of George's flashlight. Andrew also noticed the deep scratches along his left cheek.

George searched the ground near Daniel's body and Andrew walked back to his patrol car to request an ambulance.

"Did you find the rifle Andy?"

Andrew returned to George's side, "No."

"Who made those scratches on his face?"

"Maggie thought Vera might be up here. She probably came up to find Daniel and persuade him to go home," Andrew said in a relatively calm voice, then couldn't help himself and swore. "Damn it woman. God, she drives me crazy."

"Hold on. Something's wrong here," George said stooping down to examine Daniel. Daniel was out for the night.

When they heard the crack of a branch under a booted foot, both men simultaneously unclipped their holsters and pulled out their guns. George swept the flashlight about until he spotted a figure moving toward them beyond Daniel. Andrew recognized Vera and ran toward her.

Chapter Eighteen

A ndrew stood beside Vera's hospital bed and watched her sleep. The bullet had been removed from her left shoulder. The doctor had said she'd been lucky the shot had missed her heart, a little lower and she would have been dead. Maggie had wanted to come up, but her father had been so furious he'd grounded her for two months. After Daniel's wound had been bandaged, he'd been placed in a jail cell at the Homedale Police Station. Constance Schmidt had been furious with the police for locking her son up with other criminals and insisted Daniel had stolen the gun to hunt rabbits. Her husband remained uncharacteristically quiet. Sarah Matthews insisted on talking to Daniel and was rebuffed. The police, once again blanketed the hilltop with personnel from their divisions searching for Kit's rifle. They found nothing. The rifle had disappeared.

Andrew brushed back a curl from Vera's forehead.

A nurse entered the room, "She needs sleep sir. Don't worry. We'll take good care of her."

Andrew left the room and took the elevator up one floor to his father's room. It seemed as if the entire Treloar clan was at the Nampa Hospital today. Kit had replaced Rachel beside Murray's bed. His father had eaten and seemed more alert. He was also white around the lips with rage.

"I ell ou I ont no ow," Murray said in response to Kit's question.

Kit glanced up and watched Andrew enter the room, "Murray says he doesn't know how Daniel discovered the combination to the gun-safe."

Andrew pulled a chair closer to his father's hospital bed, "Dad, how long have you been using the same combination?"

Murray leaned back against his pillows and stared at the ceiling. It appeared that the ceiling disgusted him as much as the question. Murray twitched the fingers of his good hand. Kit as if he had a telepathic link with his grandfather understood Murray's request and handed him a piece of paper and a pen. Murray with his hand shaking wrote down a date. Andrew picked up the piece of paper from the sheet and read October 10th, 1910.

"Thirty-five years," Andrew said in surprise. "You've been using the same combination all these years? It hasn't changed since I was a kid. How many other people know it?"

Murray pointed at himself.

"Well, Dad, there must be others because Daniel knew it. How did Daniel know the combination?"

"I ont no."

"Has Schmidt ever been in the house? Did you show him your guns?"

Murray shook his head from side to side. Kit shrugged, then stood up and stretched. Andrew patted his father's arm, "I'll be back in a minute Dad."

Kit and Andrew left the room and stood in the corridor speaking in low voices.

"Do you know the significance of the combination Kit?" Andrew asked.

"Yeah, Grandma's birthdate."

"What?" Andrew said and stepped away from the door. "You've got to be kidding? How do you know?"

"Because Murray was concerned about his guns and after his heart attack, he wrote it down for me."

"Did you tell anyone else? Did you leave the number lying around the house?"

Kit looked angry, "No. I destroyed the paper. You think I'd forget Grandma's birthdate?"

"Daniel's not talking, not even to Sarah. When he does say something, he just keeps saying the same thing over and over again, 'She's still in there. She's going to hurt me. I got to get her out.' And until Vera wakes up, I have nothing to work on. We can't find the rifle and we don't know why Daniel stole the rifle or why he was up there."

—

Vera woke. A man was leaning over her bed and his face was so close all she could see was his nose. The doctor peered into her eyes with a pencil light, clicked the light off and straightened. "You are a lucky lady," he said and moved over to the nurse to talk to her. Vera looked around the room and saw Andrew standing by the door watching her. He smiled. She closed her eyes for a moment and looked toward him again. Andrew approached her bed and took her hand. She could feel his calloused palm.

"Where's Daniel?" she asked. "Is he, all right?"

"He's in the Homedale jail."

"He didn't shoot me," Vera said sensing something under the surface, something misunderstood.

"He stole my dad's rifle Vera. We haven't found the rifle, but the evidence is strong that Daniel tried to shoot you."

"He didn't. He was trying to protect me from them."

"From who?"

"The," she paused unable to articulate her thoughts. She couldn't feel her legs or her arms. She seemed to be floating between the hospital room and Hunter's Hill. She tried to remember what she had sensed standing behind her last night. There had been two or three of them, big wild dogs maybe. No, not dogs, maybe coyotes; all she knew for sure was that she sensed fear and danger, "There were two or three. Maybe they were wild dogs or cougars? I don't know. They were behind me. I couldn't see them. I was too frightened to turn around. I could smell a strong odor of musk. Daniel shot at them and hit me by mistake."

Andrew leaned over her bed, "Honey that can't be; we found nothing like what you describe; we found only evidence of you and Daniel where he fell."

When he kissed her forehead, Vera turned her face away from him, "I'm telling you the truth. Daniel wasn't aiming the gun at me. He was scared. He said something strange. He said, 'She likes dead things.' I couldn't help but wonder if maybe he was thinking about Kat's mother. Maybe he imagined Kat's mother haunted him."

"Honey. Just rest now. Don't worry about Daniel. Let the courts take care of this."

Vera tried to sit up. The nurse pushed a button and lifted a portion of the bed to aid her without injuring her shoulder, "Then what happened to the rifle? If I don't have it and Daniel doesn't have it, where is it? Do you think it just walked away by itself?"

"I don't know," Andrew admitted and sank into a chair. "You seem to be the detective, you tell me."

"Daniel was standing in front of a large bush. I walked toward him. There was a ledge behind Daniel. It loomed over us. You know the one that the old road circles around. Somebody must have been hiding there."

"But Daniel shot at you and you were facing the ledge," Andrew said, "so what was behind you?"

"That mound of earth, I think you call it a butte was behind me, the one that's on the other side of the gully; you know the gully where Carolina was dumped? Maybe there was someone hiding on top of the mound? Maybe Daniel saw that person coming toward me? He might have thought the guy was going to hurt me. I don't know."

"He? Why do you say he?" Andrew asked.

Carefully, she settled back on the pillow and shut her eyes, "I don't know, probably for the sake of speeding up the conversation?"

Vera watched Andrew's face. Her story hadn't convinced him of anything. She hadn't wanted to look behind her. The terror on Daniel's face had been enough for her. She'd sensed the presence of a wild animal. She was convinced Daniel hadn't wanted to hurt her, that he'd lifted the rifle to shoot an intruder or maybe frighten away a predator: a big cat or a wild dog. Andrew looked unconvinced.

Chapter Nineteen

M z. Matthews drove Daniel home – back to school, back to his room and his treasures. Before the car stopped Daniel opened the door and jumped out. He could see the corner of the school. He passed the yellow school bus. He waved to the children as they climbed down from the bus. He waved to Mr. Peterson and Mrs. Joann. Mz. Matthews unlocked the shed for him and handed him the extra key.

Daniel walked inside and looked around to make sure everything was as he had left it. He wanted to forget the humans with their uniforms and guns and hard voices. He wanted to forget all he had seen, all he had smelled and heard. It was gone now, the doors closing without hands, the buzzers and beeps, the voice from the microphone, the glass all around them, those other humans on their cots staring at him through prison bars.

He held a stone in his hand, a smooth green and brown piece of picture jasper. He rubbed his thumb and finger along the belly of the stone feeling the ripples through his skin. As he rubbed the stone, he walked behind the shed, so he could see better. He searched for Anderson Pass, there it was, his special way, the way to his treasure. He followed the strip of gravel with his eyes, the gravel winding up the hillside seeming to shoot straight into the sky like the smoke from a bottle rocket. The dirt, the plants, the flowers, they were all brown and gray, only the mountains looked purple.

The wind tried to push him back. He rocked on his heels and laughed. He was home. Miss Vera had told the humans to leave him alone. Miss Vera was Daniel's friend. Maggie's Uncle Andrew had asked about the secret numbers, the numbers 10-10-10. Those numbers were no secret. They were a perfect score.

Daniel returned to the shed and stepped into the warm room. Mz. Matthews had put in a furnace, a green metal furnace a man had bolted to the wall. It was skinny and tall. Behind the furnace was a hole where the hot air came through from an air duct wrapped in its winter coat outside. At the bottom of the furnace was a hole where hot air blew on his legs and circled around him and into the room. She had given him one of the old leather chairs that rocked back and forth. He had a carpet and a color television too.

Daniel walked over to the metal lockers in the corner of the shed near his cot, the lockers that were all his where he kept his new clothes, his new shoes, his paints and colored pencils, his papers, his models, and glue.

"What's an easy number to remember Daniel?" Maggie had asked him.

Daniel turned the knob, first left, then right, then left and opened his locker door. He took out his warmest shirt, the red and black flannel one with the bird on it. He took off his stinky old clothes and put on his new shirt and new pants. No work today. Today was free. He looked at his polisher and the thunderegg waiting on the bench for him. Daniel undressed again and put on his old jeans and an old shirt. He hung up his new clothes and locked his locker. Today, he would finish the thunderegg.

Someone knocked on his door. He went to the door and listened. He opened the door and stepped outside. A cold wind tossed some leaves down the graveled drive. The bus was still parked in the same place waiting to take the children home. He looked to his right and saw the playground. Nobody was outside today. It was too cold. Someone was playing a game on him. He could see through the first-floor windows of the school where Mr. Peterson had his classroom.

He could see Mr. Peterson standing by his desk talking to his students. Daniel waved. Mr. Peterson did not see him. Daniel walked around the shed again searching for the human that had knocked on his door. He saw the bushes and the fence and beyond the fence the trees. There was nobody hiding behind the shed. He went back inside and locked his door.

———

The doctor had released her from the hospital after two days. It had been a relief to go home. She had been worried about insurance. She had no health insurance. The bill would come soon enough, and she wouldn't be able to pay it. The hospital knew the ugly truth. They weren't even going to let her into the emergency room until Rachel Treloar raised holy hell and then some. Andrew hadn't even bothered to ask. He, like most Americans thought everybody had health insurance. And he had been busy trying to figure out what had happened on Hunter's Hill.

For too brief a time, just enough to get a taste of what other people took for granted, less than a year while working in Oregon, she'd had health insurance. And not only health insurance but dental and vision included. It had been wonderful. She'd had a good paying job with benefits at that savings and loan. And then the savings and loan went bust and she was back to part-time temporary zero benefit jobs; most jobs that she could find paid under the table.

Her winnings were almost gone. The Egg paid her very little, not enough to live on.

Vera sat in her kitchen in the dark. All was quiet inside. She was alone and the only sound inside the house was the ticking of the clock and every so often the click of the refrigerator's cooling system. Outside, nature seemed mightily pissed off. Tree limbs rubbed up against the house sounding as if they were scratching at the walls to get in. She could hear the wind rubbing up against the branches coated with an armor of ice. Maybe she would be safer outside? She could jump in her car and drive away. But where would she go?

She listened to the refrigerator hum, the planks in the attic groan, the lathe and plaster walls whisper. In the dark, she could see the hills and valleys of furniture, her rocking chair in the corner, her couch near the window, the coffee table, and the Victorian lamps she'd found at a garage sale. They weren't Tiffany. They had needed considerable renovation. It wasn't that they were cheap. What pleased her about them was that she had taken something ugly and made it beautiful again.

The materials of her world waited in the dark like her. She knows she is the only one breathing, the only one able to hear her heart beat. This skeleton of Vera Lee sits in the dark protected by bones and muscles and fluid. This skeleton might be fragile. She imagines it different, as strong as armor, as strong as frozen mist. She's not alone. She's never been alone.

They would come soon.

No doubt they would come.

She would prepare the house for their arrival.

——

Nearly two days had passed since she'd returned home from the hospital. Andrew had begun to relax his vigil. It just so happened that tomorrow was Saturday and she knew he had plans to party with the Metcalfs, Vera made her decision. She packed up his meager belongings, the odd shirt, sock, comb, and windbreaker he would invariably leave behind, a token that ensured his return and her acceptance of his presence and left his belongings in his suitcase with a note inside. The note had been an afterthought. She had about a hundred dollars in her bank account, the part-time work at the Egg, and only the food Andrew had bought for the week.

She hadn't been hungry enough to eat. And what of tomorrow? Would she be hungry tomorrow? Vera didn't care anymore.

Surprised at how calm she was, she was even tired enough to sleep.

Around midnight she heard Andrew attempt to get into the house with his key and discover his key no longer worked. The locksmith had charged her fifty bucks to change the locks. It had been painful having to give him the little money she had left, painful but imperative. She lay in bed and listened for nearly an hour to him banging on the door and calling her name. The banging reverberated through the walls. The sound traveled into the kitchen and ricochet off metal surfaces. The pounding stopped. Vera could now distinguish between the refrigerator's vibration and the stove's vibration. She'd been afraid he might try to break down the door. No. Not Andrew. She listened to the sound of his Jeep turning over. She heard him drive away. There were no tears.

All morning the phone rang. Vera pulled the cord out of the phone jack. Quiet all day. Toward dusk she heard a scratching on the kitchen bay window. She crept through the dark house and before reaching the window got down on her hands and knees and crawled toward the window seat. Her shoulder still hurt a bit. She ignored the pain. She lifted her head and peeked outside.

A black shape hurled itself against the glass. She screamed and fell backward. Then the dark silhouette shrank to normal size and Vera relaxed her cramped muscles and stood up. With her heart still beating fast, she leaned forward and peered out at the cat pacing back and forth on the outer ledge. At the turn when he must either jump off or walk backward, he would leap down into the wet compost of her empty garden then twist about and leap back onto the ledge. Once on the ledge, he would bump his head against the glass as if caressing her.

She watched him do this strange sentry duty for a few more minutes; then made up her mind. The tingling in her fingers urged her to move. She opened the kitchen door. The big cat shot into the room as if a dog were close behind him. Not knowing quite why, she kept the lights off and carefully made her way to the refrigerator. The refrigerator light illuminated the cat. She froze holding the carton of milk.

Had she just let a bobcat into her house? No. Those ears reminded her of the devil; they were sharp and pointed at the tips sticking straight up on either side of his head with tufts of black hair rising above the lobes like antennae. If he was someone's exotic pet, no wonder they had dumped him on the road. He didn't seem afraid of her. She couldn't say why; yet, she was afraid to turn on the kitchen light to get a better view because she might frighten him.

She poured him a saucer of milk and watched him slurp up the contents. When he leaped onto the table and turned to face her, she knew him. Her knight-in- shining-armor had finally come to her rescue. His green eyes reminded her of her first love – Nicolas. She started laughing and couldn't stop until the tears choked her. She'd forgotten her Uncle Frank's lessons when traveling the backroads at night. The eyes of foxes and raccoons shine with a red light. Felid's eyes shine with a greenish light. Once again, she had leaped to an irrational conclusion. There is no such thing as reincarnation, you dope; she told herself.

As her new house guest watched her carefully, she studied him just as carefully prepared to grab a carving knife if he attacked her. What sort of creature had the ears of a devil and sleek fur of a pampered Siamese? He couldn't be more than thirty pounds. He didn't look like a juvenile. He had to be someone's exotic pet. The big cat impervious to her emotional outburst jumped off the table landing gracefully on her window seat, turning, and turning until he was satisfied with his bed and sank down on her window seat cushion and closed his eyes.

The rational part of Vera figured that some worthless owners too selfish and lazy to take care of their pet had dumped him on the road callously hoping either one of the farmers would take him in or nature's cruel practicality would settle the matter. Was he part Lynx or Ocelot mixed with Siamese? She knew in South America there was a small wild cat that was mild enough to breed with domestic cats. Maybe someone had been successful with this unusual creature.

His eyes weren't really blue. They were more hazel. He was so unusual Vera wondered if the owners had tried to sell him and were prevented by the authorities or the threat of deportation. Maybe they tried to get rid of the evidence before they were fined? She couldn't keep calling him cat. She would have to call him something. She knew a little about Lynxes and since he was from the felis family of small wild cats without the ability to roar, her name for him would have to be appropriate. But she was too tired to think of a good one tonight. She'd call him Felix for now. No. That was too easy and stupid. He looked like royalty. She would call him Rama after the Chakri Rama I of Siam.

When Rama jumped off the window seat and with a hiss took off like a shot into the mud room, Vera knew she had been warned.

It was nearly midnight. Before she could prepare, she had to be sure Rama was safe. A few frantic minutes passed before she heard him. She grabbed the window seat cushion and returned to the mud room. She filled an old tin bucket with water from the farm sink. As she tucked the cushion under her arm, she opened the screen door which led straight to the barn. Rama sniffed the cushion and miraculously followed her out of the house and into the barn. She climbed the steps to the loft.

Hay was no longer kept up here; instead, the Andersons had made the loft into a massive storage unit with individual closets, drawers, and shelves. Vera threw the cushion down in a far corner behind some of her larger unopened boxes, dropped the bucket of water nearby and ran down the stairs shutting the barn door behind her.

Once inside the house, Vera searched her bedroom closet for the portable safe. The tiny key was in her pants pocket. She unlocked the safe and examined the two objects on top of her important documents. She weighed the pros and cons and finally made her decision. Instead of choosing the pepper spray, she chose the tiger's eye necklace. She walked to the spare bedroom and settled herself on the floor in the center of the room rubbing the stone for good luck.

They would come soon.

She'd seen them in town on her way home from the hospital, just that once, an accident she was sure. Two days had passed since then. Seeing them buying beer at the market had been a shock. Her nightmare was now reality. They had been as surprised as she. Bumping into her hadn't been a part of their plan. She was sure they'd wanted to surprise her. Now she hoped to surprise them.

To help her relax, she went in search of her fiddle and began playing a tune her Nonnie composed for Analetta. It was one of the few good moments she could remember from her childhood, Nonnie and her mother playing a duet together. She held the fiddle tight replaying the music and the words in her head and froze in position traitorous thoughts paralyzing her. There was no one left who would miss her if she were gone; no one who would care if she were alive or dead. Not even the people of Mintlaw. In her mind's eye, an image came to her. She saw Rama in the barn. He was curled up on the cushion, his belly full of mouse. Who would take care of him now? Who would know he was locked in the barn? She had to stay alive.

Setting her fiddle on her lap, she shook herself, shaking away the self-pity and fear. Once she felt strong enough, she resumed her former position and began to play. In minor scale with her fingers gently brushing the strings and with the familiar smell of rosin in her nose, she closed her eyes and pictured her Nonnie and Analetta by the campfire, the cedar trees and green hills surrounding and protecting them. She began to sing the song her Nonnie had composed when Vera's mother had been a child, the lullaby her great grandmother called *The Weaver's Skill*.

> Oh, my sweet darling, my sweet stormy Tor.
> Close your eyes darling and dream of the moor.
> 'Tis green and so lovely; 'tis vast and so wide.
> The weaver of dreams she protects - dinna hide.
>
> Your dreams are safe, rest assured in this place.
> Your dreams are entwined in fine Albion lace.
> The lace is so silky; the lace is so strong.
> The weaver of dreams, she will help you along.
>
> Come my sweet darling, come my sweet pea.
> Follow the weaver; oh yes, follow the free.
> Along this bright path, we will glide to the sea.
> The weaver of dreams comes for you and for me.
>
> Hear your dreams call, winding low in this knoll.
> Your dreams are entwined in soft Albion wool.
> The wool is so warm; the wool is so bright.
> The weaver of dreams, she belongs to the night.
>
> Oh, my sweet darling, my sweet little rune.
> Close your eyes darling and capture the moon.
> Your bed is scotch moss and your blanket bluebell.
> The weaver of dreams, yes, she is casting her spell.
>
> Come my sweet darling, come my sweet pea.
> Follow the weaver; oh yes, follow the free.
> Along this bright path, we will glide to the sea.
> The weaver of dreams comes for you and for me.

Vera woke with the morning light warm on her back. Her arm was stiff after sleeping most of the night on the hardwood floor. As she sat up, her arm lay lifeless at her side. She hit the obstinate appendage a couple of times to get the circulation flowing and wiggled her fingers to move the blood down. Once on her feet, she managed to get to the bathroom before she peed all over the floor.

In the kitchen she paused to appreciate the beauty of her home, the way the sunlight streamed through her kitchen window and sparkled on the Irish bowl, the way the sun warmed the surface of her dining room table making the oak gleam with threads of gold. She breathed deep the smell of oak cabinets, dried flowers, nutmeg, cinnamon, and oranges on a blue plate – evidence of life, life in this house. Something inside trembled. She shoved it away, as deep as she could make it go then shuffled over to the window to soak in all that beautiful light.

Feeling a bit braver and wide awake, Vera poured herself a cup of hot coffee and sipped it cautiously as she wandered from window to window searching for them. They must have decided to wait and make sure Andrew had left for good. Vera checked her messages. There were two from Andrew, one from Maggie, and one from Sarah Matthews. Sarah had left news that Daniel had been released from jail and remained in the custody of the school. Maggie wanted to talk. Andrew kept asking why, what's wrong, what did I do?

You're in the way, that's all. I don't want you in the way. I don't want you hurt.

A creak of a loose floorboard sent a sparkler of pain cascading up and down her spine. While her head still tingled, Vera turned in time to see a man walk toward her with a gun pointed at her head. In the last ten years he'd gotten heavier in the jaw and the stomach. His hair was still sleek and black, his eyes dark pebbles of hate. Here was her nightmare come to life.

"Hello, Sweet-Cheeks," he said, staring at the scar on her face with relish.

—

Daniel dropped his thunderegg on the bench. His fingers hurt. His eyes hurt. He wanted to cry. He left the shed and walked back and forth along the fence. He paused once to sniff the air. He thought about his binoculars and ran back to the shed to fetch them. As he swept his binoculars toward the southwest in the general direction of his treasure and Vera's house, objects sprang into life. And when he dropped the binoculars he had to squeeze his eyes to see the same sagebrush. With the binoculars, he could see most everything on the hilltop. He could see Miss Vera's house too. The space between his shed and Miss Vera's house told him nothing new.

The sage and other plants looked as if they'd been dipped in ice and left to stand like statues without voices. Then he saw a stranger. The stranger stood in Miss Vera's backyard eating peanuts or maybe they were seeds. Daniel watched him spit the husks on the ground. The stranger had a body like one of those root beer candy barrels, a short body, big belly, wide shoulders, heavy arms like a wrestler, and funny long skinny legs. The man was staring up at the hill then he dropped his gaze and swerved around to sweep his eyes across the field between Miss Vera's house and the school. He was looking for something or someone, just like Daniel. But he didn't seem to notice Daniel.

When the stranger walked toward Miss Vera's barn, Daniel went back into the shed and closed the door. He shivered. He sat on the edge of his cot and stared at his boots. His mother had bought the boots for his father. She'd given them to Daniel when he was too little to wear them; he was big enough to wear them now. They were hiking boots, boots for hunting, boots for fishing, a man's boots. The skin of them had gone from brown to yellow. They were soft. They fit him perfect. Daniel thought about the man that had worn these boots. He remembered riding in the backseat of a car, smelling tobacco smoke, listening to loud music, only able to see the top of his head. His daddy had a thick neck. He had been strong.

Daniel recognized the voice from the black box by the door. "Daniel, it's time for dinner. Come on in," he heard Mz. Matthews say. Daniel got up from his cot and thought about the man at Miss Vera's house. He wondered if Mr. Treloar was home, if maybe the man was a friend.

"Why aren't you wearing a coat Daniel?" Mz. Matthews asked. "You'll freeze to death."

Daniel looked up and realized he was standing in the food line waiting for it to be his turn to choose the specialty of the house. He put his milk on the red tray and told Chef Debbie, "Hamburger without cheese please." Chef Debbie's hand covered in a clear plastic glove dropped the hamburger on his plate. He said thank you because Mz. Matthews said he should. He got extra fries because he was bigger than anybody else at the school. He waited for the little kids to move aside so he could put his own lettuce and tomato and peaches on his plate. He didn't want mash potatoes today. He passed the children's table and walked toward the big table for the big people. The little girl with the blonde hair saw him and said, "Squeak, squeak."

He ignored her and sat down by Mz. Matthews and Mr. Peterson. They made room for him. After dinner he helped Miss

Pamela with the washing up. He had time to watch television before bed. He walked past the television room and left the school. His stomach hurt. Maybe the peaches were bad?

It was dark outside. Daniel knew his way to the shed in the dark. He walked faster than usual because the wind drove right through his shirt and made his belly sting. He sat in his chair and waited for the pain in his stomach to go away. He rocked back and forth. Someone knocked on his door and he told them to go away. He used all the bad words he knew. The knocking stopped.

Daniel woke from a dream. In his dream, a huge snake had wrapped itself around Miss Vera and he saw the snake squeeze and squeeze the life out of her. Daniel heard her cry out. He rubbed his eyes, wiped his mouth on his sleeve and stood up. Daniel struggled into his clothes and nearly fell face first on the concrete floor. He managed to get his arms in his coat; and as soon as he got outside, he ran as fast as he could across the field to Miss Vera's house without even bothering to make sure the shed door was locked.

—

Vera lay in the bed and waited for her vision to clear. The back of her head hurt where he'd banged it against the headboard. Another man sat on the chair in the corner of the bedroom cracking sunflower seeds and spitting the shells on the floor. Vera thought about the music. This time there was no music, no shower, no quick violence and sudden quiet. This hellish moment might go on for a long time, spread out upon the air in hours rather than seconds.

The brothers enjoyed their work. Now she understood why. Now she understood why Woody had been so afraid of them. She saw Woody all those years ago, pacing the floor and shouting at her. She didn't understand at the time, not until the Foss brothers came looking for him. One day he was gone, skipped town without a word or a warning. She wondered how the Foss brothers had managed to get into her house without her noticing and where they had parked their vehicle. She wondered how long before someone found her body. Woody was dead. Foss had implied Woody was dead and he was responsible.

As he led her into the bedroom (how long ago? Hours ago?) he'd whispered in her ear, "If you don't cooperate with me, I'll do to you what was done to Woody. You understand me?" She hoped he was wrong. Maybe he just wanted to scare her? Ada might have been smarter; she might have had time to get away. Her Aunt Vista used to say – if you sleep with the devil's apprentice, you're bound to wake up in hell. Woody had supplied her with alcohol and drugs.

All those years ago, he'd neglected to tell her that the coke he was cooking wasn't his to use.

Vera believed some people were born soulless. Woody didn't believe much of anything. He thought he could talk his way out of trouble. All the empathy and pity and sacrifice in the world wouldn't make the Foss brothers human. The two in her house, eating her food, using her bathroom, and searching through drawers and closets had no resemblance to humanity nor to the animal kingdom for that matter, because even scorpions and rattle snakes will strike if provoked or when they are protecting their territory, unlike these guys. The Foss brothers get a real kick out of hurting people just for hurting's sake. They get a special thrill if the person is innocent and hasn't done them any wrong.

Had Woody left something behind? *The asshole*, she thought, *I hope you're in hell.* Maybe while he'd been lurking around her place, he had hidden drugs or something else these two morons wanted back? Where? What? Woody was dead. She was sure of it now. Poor, Woody. He'd been such a good kisser but as insightful as a gerbil. Oh God. That part of him she missed. The rest, the slipping off for days without telling her and the coming home with strangers, some smelling so bad she had to fumigate the apartment – no, she didn't miss those days.

But why were the Foss brothers here? It's been fifteen years? She was nothing to them. She looked up and noticed Mark Albert Foss picking a sore on his arm. Obviously, her physical charms were lost on one brother. Maybe they had tortured Woody? Maybe he had implicated her believing that if he accused another he could placate them? Yet, Vera knew these men didn't need a reason to shit on people. That boy, she remembered, the one who boasted about knowing Kung Fu. Everyone had been drunk and laughing and the boy had been weaving around Sim and Mark and punching and kicking the air.

The Foster brothers like a pair of trained pit bulls came from both sides of the poor idiot. Sim had beaten him nearly to death. Everyone had been afraid to tell the police. And Sim had stayed behind when the ambulance showed up while his brother Mark ran off. Sim sat in the only comfortable chair in the house and watched the cops asking the partygoers' questions, his eyes darting about the room with interest making sure no one snitched on him; he acted the part of the innocent witness as the EMTs carried the boy's body away on the gurney. Yes, the Foster brothers enjoyed inflicting pain on people. Most likely he couldn't get it up without cutting a woman or beating a boy senseless.

All those years ago, the terror, her body one big oozing wound, her face twice its size from the beating he'd given her. And the ambulance and the man looking down upon her with pity; and she knew, she knew, she sensed their pity. A neighbor had complained about the noise, thank you dear lord for nosy neighbors.

It wasn't her fault. She'd had to tell the police something. She didn't know their names. She hadn't had time to see the others, only him, the one who tied her to the bed. She'd seen him up close and real, every pore in his face, and every whisker on his jaw. She would never forget the smell of him, the heavy cologne, and his breath stinking of spoiled meat. She had been a coward back then. She'd lied to the police and said it had been dark and she'd kept her eyes closed and begged the man to stop. Woody must have told them where she lived. Woody was dead; Woody had found her, and he had betrayed her once again.

Sim had enjoyed hurting her. Her stomach turned over at the memory. Yet he hadn't killed her. He'd left her as a reminder to Woody about what he was capable of doing. Yet Woody wasn't a part of her life anymore and she didn't do drugs. There was something else she had that he wanted. She wished they would speak, say something that would help her get them gone. Why didn't they ask her questions? Why were they searching her house? She didn't have anything valuable.

She could hear them throwing open cupboard doors and tossing dishes, food, and pans on the floor. They moved into the living room and she heard the protesting screech as several pieces of furniture were pulled away from the walls and chairs from the table. Books fell on the floor and mini-blinds rattled. She suspected one of them the smarter one had closed the house up for the night. Then she heard two sets of footfalls as they moved down the hall. Suddenly the house was quiet. Just barely she realized they were whispering. One of them opened the linen cupboard. Woody hadn't come into her house, so why were they searching her house? They didn't know he hadn't come inside. She would have to tell them.

They entered the bedroom. Vera was prepared having heard their heavy feet on her hardwood floor. Marion Sim Foss strode into the room and up to the bed and with a blank expression banged her head several times against the headboard. He smiled once, his eyes black opaque stones devoid of life. Her stomach tightened as she looked into his eyes. Normal people looked at each other and acknowledged a joint membership in life, an unspoken but understood agreement of a shared humanity. But with Sim she had no idea whether he recognized her humanity or even acknowledged her existence. He smiled because somewhere and at some time in his life he'd been taught to smile; yet, the human gesture meant nothing to him and was as insincere as his words.

She waited for him to speak. Instead he took the chair by her makeup table and turned it around, sat down, and watched her. His brother Mark began to talk. Vera could barely see the room. The back of her head was on fire. She thought she was going to puke. Mark enjoyed retelling Vera the antecedents of his brother's namesake and while Vera endured Mark's rambling monologue, she thought about the word antecedent and strongly suspected Mark slept through most of his schooling and had no idea what antecedent meant, but he kept using the word and mispronouncing it in the process and her suspicions were confirmed that he was an airhead when he forgot the medical term for female castration and had to ask his brother several times to repeat the proper pronunciation of the word.

"You see the anti-seeds surrounding my brother's name go way back. My ma had us at St. John's Hospital and she couldn't figure out what to name us, so she talked to a lady in the bed next to her and the lady told her a story about her great-great grandfather, a famous doctor named J. Marion Sim. Anyway, my ma decided to name my brother after this famous doctor. Marion is the oldest of us. She hoped he would become as famous as that dead doctor. Then Marion decides to look up the name and he finds out what the doctor was famous for and he got a real kick out of that bit of news. Yeah guess what that doctor did? He did a bunch of surgeries on cunts like you. Yeah. Oh, this was years ago, centuries ago in the 19th decade he did these things. He operated on hundreds, thousands of cunts like you, dirty gyp trash like you and he castrated them all. Poetic huh?"

The nightmare continued as Mark kept talking in that hurried excitable way of his, his body unable to stand still. He kept walking around the room. She could see the signs. He was high, high on speed. He kept talking as he walked about the room, "Now Ma liked the name Albert. She said she named me after some prince that married a fat old queen. He must have been a pansy a real man would have beheaded his wife and taken over the throne."

Sim jumped up from the chair, walked over to Mark and beat him about the head, all the while screaming, "I told you not to call me Marion in front of people. Did–I–not–tell–you?"

Once Sim had gained control of his emotions, he sat down on the edge of the bed and looked at the floor, "I know Woody was here. Did he come in the house?"

"No. I wouldn't let him in," she said mimicking his cold calm attitude.

He untied her from the headboard and left the room. She could hear him going through the bathroom then the other two bedrooms throwing open drawers and slamming cupboard doors while Mark sat in Vera's cushioned chair in the bedroom eating sunflower seeds. Marion should have gotten himself a pit bull or a Rottweiler; at least those breeds made more sense than the freak sitting on her chair. Vera sat up and fingered her necklace. Mark glanced at her then down at the bag of sunflower seeds.

"I have to go to the bathroom," she said.

Mark shouted his brother's name. Sim returned and paused on the threshold, "What," he asked impatiently holding a steak knife in his right hand.

"She wants to pee," Mark said.

"So?" Sim said and walked back down the hall as if he could care less. Vera took that as a yes and climbed off the bed. Mark watched her walk out of the room. He followed her to the bathroom and held the door, so she had to pee in front of him. He didn't seem to care whether her underpants were down around her ankles or not. Maybe both brothers only got off when they bound women or made them bleed. The fact they hadn't killed her yet was a constant surprise as the seconds ticked by. She should be grateful.

She flushed the toilet and waited for the man to move. He stepped aside and spit a seed shell into the air. Vera pulled the shell out of her hair and walked into the spare bedroom. She sat in the center of the floor and looked at Mark Foss and then away. He tried to enter the room, then his eyes widened, and he stopped. She turned her head and looked toward the window, the window which faced the fields and beyond the fields the school. From somewhere far away she heard him call out to his brother. She ignored the nasty turd and closed her eyes.

She had been practicing for the last three days, practicing every night while Andrew slept. When Andrew left the house, she would take a nap then start all over again. She lost her sense of place, lost her sense of smell and sight. She could only feel heat. Her body grew warmer and warmer and sweat began trickling down her forehead, down her armpits, between her legs. From faraway she heard someone calling. The voice inside her head spoke to her and reassured her. This time she wasn't alone.

It was difficult to pull back. She swam toward the light and then opened her eyes. The corners of the room were dark, while in the center of the room the moonlight seemed to condense and gather strength and boil into a white froth. The light entered her body. Every nerve tingled, the hairs along her arms and legs and head felt as if they wanted to yank themselves out of her skin and float away.

She sensed a presence to her left.

Sim was sitting on a kitchen chair he had brought into the room and placed in the corner as if he wanted to be able to see the entire room. The window next to him was free of curtains. It was a blank slate. If the overhead light had been on, people would have been able to see them for miles. But the only light came from the hall, a pale-yellow stream of light. It made its way toward her. From the corner of her eye, she knew everything beyond the window was black. No car lights, no street lights, nothing, they were in a sea of dark.

Sim watched her with clinical detachment.

"Are you finished yet?" he asked.

The words she used, she knew would freak out Mark. He hated when people spoke a language he didn't understand. She recited *The Weaver's Skill* the lullaby her great grandmother had created; only instead of singing the lullaby in English, she chose to sing it in Gaelic the way her Nonnie would have liked to have heard it. The foreign words irritate Mark. He rushed into the room and shouted, "Shut up, you, stupid, gypsy cunt."

Sim got up from his chair and shoved Mark out of the room, "She's just getting inside your head, dumbass. Go outside and get my briefcase."

Vera closed her eyes and started the lullaby over again, praying for someone to hear her and make these monsters go away, to leave her house now, to leave her alone for good. She asked her Nonnie for help. She asked Andrew for help. She called out, praying for someone, anyone, to hear her and come to her rescue. When she opened her eyes, she could see Sim moving back into the room. At first, she thought he was headed for the chair in the corner. His back was to the light. She couldn't see his eyes. A tingling from the crown of her head to her eyes warned her. She stood up prepared for the blow. Yet when he struck, and the blow knocked her to the floor, she knew there was someone circling the house searching for a way in.

Sim made satisfied grunts and sighs as he hit her again and again. Waves of pain traveled through the highway of nerves from her head to her toes. She swallowed blood and heard a great buzzing as if thousands of angry bees had burst into the room and were swarming about her head. Death would be good about now. Death will stop the pain.

The overhead light blinded them. Daniel stood on the threshold. She recognized his hiking boots. When he rushed into the room with his heavy arms swinging, she was grateful yet surprised. Of course, she thought, why not? It was a misdirected call that's all, no terrifying demons to send Sim and his brother down to hell, just Daniel to the rescue. She started to laugh. The blood bubbled up in her throat and nearly choked her. She stopped laughing.

Sim in Daniel's mindless path met the full force of Daniel's fist. Sim flew across the room and landed in the corner. She heard the crunch when his head hit the sharp edge of the chair. When Sim didn't move, Vera was relieved. For a breathless moment, she hoped Sim was dead. She was instantly ashamed of herself. Her joy, especially knowing what she believed about death was as bad as Sim's apathy. No one, not even someone as loathsome as Marion Sim Foss should die, at least not in her house.

Vera tried to sit up. Daniel's big hands pulled her to her feet. "Miss Vera's hurt," he said over and over sounding more like a bear with a cold than a man.

Vera padded his arm, "I'll be alright Daniel. Don't cry Daniel."

She made herself stand up. She paused for a moment waiting for the black dots to disappear from her eyes. She forced herself to walk down the hall and saw Mark. Mark had managed to sit up and rest his back against the wall. He must have been near the door when Daniel charged into the house. The force of Daniel's rushing tackle must have knocked Mark out. Mark held his head and moaned.

The door was wide open.

Vera stepped over Mark and closed the door then stepped over him again to get to her kitchen. From a bottom drawer, she pulled out a roll of electrician's tape. She searched the back porch and found the four sections of rolled yellow rope from the old swing set. They were still in the box where she'd left them. On the way to the spare bedroom she located her scissors.

"Help me tie up these bad men Daniel," she told him. Sim was her first priority. With Daniel's assistance, they tied Sim's hands behind his back and secured his ankles.

"Make the knots extra tight Daniel," she told him. Then she cut a section of tape.

"Roll him over Daniel," she said. She covered Sim's mouth with the tape.

Daniel followed her down the hall. Mark had crawled to the front door and was trying to lift himself up using the doorknob for leverage. Daniel grabbed his shoulders and pulled him away from the door. As if he had been a child, Daniel pinned Mark to the floor with one knee.

"Pick him up for me Daniel. We'll take him outside."

Daniel picked Mark up and pinned his arms to his sides and carried him with his legs dangling and his feet uselessly kicking the air. Daniel turned with the man in his arms and grinned. Vera laughed.

"Good job Daniel. No. Wait. We've got to tie him up too. Put him on the floor on his stomach so I can tie him up."

Together she and Daniel trussed up Mark. While Vera finished the knot, Mark stared at her with his small blue eyes. He ignored Daniel completely and just stared at Vera as if he feared Vera more than Daniel. His terror embarrassed her. Daniel had that effect on people, not her. What was the little worm's problem? Did he think they were going to kill him? She wasn't the one that had broken into his home and humiliated him.

Vera pulled on her coat and grabbed her keys, "I'm going to start the car. Wait here."

Daniel called out to her, struggling to get to his feet, "No! Miss Vera. Your car is too small. I'll go get my mom's Suburban."

"You don't have a license! You need a license to drive, Daniel. We'll take my car. We can manage just fine."

"No. They won't fit. I can drive. Mom lets me drive all the time. I know where they hide the spare key," and with a stubborn look he left the house by the front door.

Vera slammed the door shut afraid someone could see Mark Foss tied up like a badly wrapped Christmas package on her hall floor. The door wouldn't lock. Daniel had broken the lock and there was a long-jagged hole in the bottom half of the door where his booted foot must have come right through the wood.

The Harden house was less than a mile away. It seemed to take Daniel forever. She knew she couldn't possibly carry the Foss brothers outside by herself. Forced to wait, she paced the kitchen avoiding the places where the Foss brothers were trussed up. After nearly forty-five minutes Vera figured Daniel had been caught and she was on her own. She was moving toward Mark Foss to drag him out the back way when she heard the heavy throated rumble of the Suburban coming up her drive.

Her relief was mixed with terror that someone would hear the Suburban and see Daniel at the wheel. His mother's odd choice in vehicles passed by the front porch and continued around the house. She ran out the laundry room door and saw Daniel sitting in the driver's seat maneuvering the monster through the narrow space between the farmhouse and the barn. He parked the big red rusty Suburban and left the motor running.

Together she and Daniel managed to carry Sim and Mark Foss to the Suburban. They opened the third door and climbed inside to look around. There were three benches, one in the back, the middle, and the front able to seat at least nine people comfortably. Both the middle and back bench seats were piled with camping gear and boxes. It would have been easier to take out both benches and lay the Foss brothers on the floor, but they had no time to mess with screws and bolts.

Vera began throwing the camping equipment on the floor and said "We can put Mark back here. He's small enough. Then we'll put Sim on the middle bench."

A single outdoor light set near the eaves of the farmhouse near the mud room door might have provided them with more illumination, but Vera didn't want to risk Homeister's dog waking up and warning the neighborhood of intruders. The sound of the Suburban coming up the driveway in the middle of the night should have woken the dog. She rubbed the tiger's eye stone for good luck.

With a heave of his mighty shoulders Daniel lifted Mark Foss up and into the Suburban, dumping him on the newly cleared bench seat in the back. Mark with his mouth taped shut and his right eye beginning to swell looked terrified.

"Pull on his legs so that his head is on the seat," Vera ordered Daniel. "If anyone were to see him from the windows, they might ask questions." Daniel did as she asked, and Mark groaned when the back of his head hit the panel below the window.

Vera climbed out of the Suburban and watched as Daniel knelt on the ground and lifted Sim onto his shoulders. Sim had to have weighed a hundred and eighty pounds, but Daniel carried him as if he'd been a sack of potatoes. By the time Daniel maneuvered the man onto the middle bench seat, they realized Sim Foss had a longer torso than his brother Mark and his legs hung over the bench preventing Daniel from shutting the third door. In an effort to get the door closed, Daniel used his left hand and shoved Sim's legs up so that the man's knees were pressing into his chest. With his right hand he tried to close the door.

When Sim kicked out hitting Daniel in the groin, Daniel turned into something Vera had never seen before. He cried out in angry surprise at the pain and like an enraged beast, leaned into the vehicle and began pounding on Sim, his grunts punctuated by heavy blows down upon the man's stomach, his legs, whatever part of Sim

Daniel could reach. She could hear a muffled wailing from Sim and tugged at Daniel's shoulders trying to pull him out of the Suburban before he killed the man. It was like trying to wrap her arms around a walrus rock, his massive shoulders felt as impenetrable as stone. She grabbed his belt buckle and pulled with all her strength. Nothing happened.

"Stop, Daniel. Please. No more. You're killing him," she hissed afraid the noise the men were making would be heard from the highway. "Please, Daniel. Calm down. It's okay. It's okay. You've got him. He won't hurt you again. Please. Please. No more."

With a strangled cry, Daniel pulled himself out of the vehicle banging his head on the roof in his haste to be free. Vera held his upper arm with both hands. She could feel the muscle convulsing as the adrenaline continued to pulse through his body. He sank to the ground leaning against the panel door sobbing in harsh moans, "I don't like that. I don't like that."

She knew exactly what he meant. It wasn't the pain caused by Sim's heavy boots meeting his groin but Daniel's rage he didn't like. She had felt such rage herself. People like Sim were adrenaline junkies and probably got a kick out of losing control. Unlike Sim, she and Daniel were repulsed by the frenzy of emotions taking over their minds and bodies.

"I know. It feels bad. It feels ugly," Vera assured him kneeling on the ground beside him. "But it's not your fault. He hurt you. You didn't expect that. Let's just sit here for a minute and calm down. We just need to be quiet. We don't want to wake the neighbors."

"No," Daniel said wiping his tears with the back of his sleeve. "The police will come, and I might have to go to jail again."

When all they could hear was the sounds of the night, when Sim no longer moaned, and Daniel had regained his composure, Vera stood up on shaky limbs, "Okay, let's finish this. It's going to be light soon," she told him and helped him to his feet. "Let's go get the ropes and lanterns."

Daniel carried the supplies out to the Suburban and simply dumped them on top of Sim Foss. The Foss brothers were unnaturally quiet. The light on the ceiling of the vehicle illuminated the interior. She could see Sim's eyes gleaming like an animal caught in the glare of headlights on a deserted road. He was afraid of them both. That made her mad. She wasn't like him. She wasn't a monster. She'd never hurt anyone in her life. They were the monsters. They deserved to pay for their crimes and she was going to dish out some good old fashion retribution.

On impulse Vera turned in the driver's seat and leaned over the back so that she could glare into Sim's eyes. Her face inches from his, so close she could smell his rank breath even with the electrician's tape covering his mouth, she searched for the right words. The smell of dead animals and sour milk made her want to puke, but she forced herself to stare him down. The words she spoke came from an unknown place, a buried memory from a time when she was very young. She knew the litany of words because someone had repeated them a dozen times for many days and many nights as she lay in her bed with the firelight flickering from the open door of the trailer.

There had been at least five people sitting around the fire repeating the same curses over and over. Perhaps her Nonnie had been one of them. The repetition and the soft voices had lulled her to sleep. She recognized only a few phrases: *Eu vă trimit diavolului* and *Te blestem*. She learned years later that they had been speaking in Romanian. I send you to the devil and I curse you.

She recited the curse in a mixture of English, Gaelic, and Romanian just to be sure one of those languages would stick to the bastard and come true. When she was finished, she backed out of the Suburban and looked up at the sky. Out here free of city lights, she could see the stars in the winter sky. She sent her wishes out beyond the stars wanting so much to believe her ancestors were right. Part of her, the modern part who had discovered the existentialists and lost her faith wanted to argue with the child raised by her great grandmother and bring up reasons why there were no such things as angels and devils. Way down in the primitive recesses of her soul though, she accepted the old gods. There had to be an offering.

An idea came to her. She ran inside the house and searched the refrigerator. There was nothing worthwhile to offer the god. Then she spied the bananas on the blue dish. She grabbed them and ran back outside and placed them on the floor of the Suburban near her feet. She reentered the house. Vera found a good working flashlight and turned to discover Daniel standing in front of her. He had splashed water on his face. She could see droplets sliding down his chin onto his chest. She led him outside and toward the Suburban.

She opened the passenger door, "Get in Daniel. I'll drive." He managed to squeeze inside the front seat. The equipment they'd brought lay on top of Mark Foss and blocked her view out the rear windshield. Instead of backing up and driving around the house to the road, Vera drove across her backyard and through the gap in the fence. They bumped along the uneven ground until they reached the ditch. The extra weight in the back provided enough traction for the Suburban to climb the ditch and reach Jump Creek Road. Daniel hit his head on the roof of the Suburban and rubbed the top absently all his emotions having been spent in his fury with Sim.

"Sorry Daniel. We're going to have to go the long way around. We'll pass the school and your Mom's house and Prairie Star Estate. Then we'll turn right and head down 95. You watch for Poison Creek Road. See. Here we go. We're passed your Mom's house. Now in a few minutes we'll make the turn. You keep an eye out for Poison Creek Road. I always miss the road."

Once they were on US 95, they should have exhilarated to the posted speed but because she was afraid she would miss the turn, they crawled down the highway at twenty miles an hour. Vera kept looking in the rearview mirror afraid someone would come up behind them and start honking. Her worst nightmare was if they saw light's flashing atop an Owyhee County patrol vehicle signaling them to pull over. How would she explain the two bound men in the Suburban? They were lucky though. No one was on the highway.

"There," Daniel shouted. "Turn there."

Vera turned the Suburban onto the dirt road the vehicle bouncing on the uneven surface, "I would never have expected your Mom to have a vehicle like this. Your Mom doesn't seem like the camping type."

In the dark with just the moonlight to help guide them on the dangerous backcountry road, she could barely see when Daniel turned his head from his contemplation of the view and said, "It's a 1968 Chevrolet Suburban with a 396 cubic-inch big block engine. It belonged to my Dad. We used to go camping in it. Mom didn't like to go much. She didn't like to sleep in a tent or even in the Suburban. The sound of coyotes scared her. Sometimes Dad would take me shooting. I want to tell you a secret," he said as he turned to face her. The front end of the Suburban dipped suddenly and they all heard the front fender hit rock.

Vera backed the Suburban onto the road and together she and Daniel climbed out to look at what they'd hit. From the ledge nearby a small section had broken off and rolled down to land right in the middle of the road. Daniel lifted the rocks in his arms and carried them toward the open passenger door.

"What are you doing Daniel?"

"I'm taking the rocks home," he said tenderly placing them on the floor of the passenger side of the Suburban and climbed onto the bench with a rock in his arms. Once he was inside, he moved to place the rock with the others.

"Be careful, I put the lantern down there to," she warned him forced to use the step to climb into the Suburban. It seemed to take them forever to get to Hunter's Hill from Poison Creek Road. Daniel was the one who saw the entrance to the old rutted road first.

Once they scraped by the narrow opening between two cliffs, she asked Daniel, "Where's the cave? Where should I park?"

"Right here is good," he told her pointing at the cattle guard. She drove over the cattle guard and parked. Her arms and legs were still shaking from the effort not to overturn them or send them flying into a ravine. When she turned off the lights and shut off the engine, the dark and the silence engulfed them. Now she was worried about how she would turn the Suburban around in this tight spot and the dangerous trip home on a narrow track with deep gullies on both sides and treacherous dips in unexpected places. With a squeal of protest from the passenger door, she watched as Daniel climbed out of the vehicle. She followed suit carrying her lantern in front of her so that she wouldn't trip or step on something nasty, something with teeth.

It wasn't easy to drag the two men out of the Suburban, but they managed. The hard part was when she and Daniel had to lift the brothers over the uneven ground and around prickly brush and rocks without tripping. Daniel did most of the heavy lifting. She carried the lantern and lighted the way for him. Once they were by the cave mouth, Daniel lay Mark Foss near the entrance and crawled inside the cave to turn around and pull him through the narrow passageway. The entrance was big enough for Daniel's shoulders, so he had little difficulty pulling them through while Vera kept watch outside in case some early morning hiker decided to climb up Hunter's Hill and catch them by surprise.

How would one explain such a situation to a stranger? Oh, this isn't what you think; we're not kidnapping these two men. We're just pulling a practical joke on them. They'll look back on this night and just laugh and laugh.

"Careful, Daniel," she said when Daniel nearly went head first into the rock face above the cave opening. It was obvious that he was exhausted. Come to think of it, she was exhausted too. With the last of her reserves, she watched as Daniel pulled Sim Foss inside the cave.

Once inside after they had successfully dumped the Foss brothers on the ground, Vera realized an uncomfortable fact, "We can't just leave them here, Daniel. They'll find a way out. Together they can help each other untie their bonds and wriggle free. We've got to make sure they can't get away."

She searched the cave wishing for some good old-fashioned iron rings embedded in the walls or maybe a stalagmite jutting out of the floor which they could hitch the two men to like human bookends. There didn't seem to be anything resembling medieval iron bars or chains or a nice stalagmite the right size which would leave just enough room for the men to sit with their legs sprawled out on the cave floor facing away from each other. Where she stood was big enough for just two people to stand in side by side without touching the walls or bumping their heads on the ceiling.

Daniel moved deeper into the cave, "I know Miss Vera. This will work. See."

Vera stepped over Sim Foss's body ignoring the hate radiating from him like a furnace and walked to where Daniel was standing. He stood in an alcove created by man, much smaller than the main part of the cave. Someone had chipped away at the rock walls leaving long jagged scars from the roof of the cave to the packed dirt floor. It looked as if the unknown craftsman had been purposely widening the cave for his use as a private bed chamber.

Daniel's flashlight illuminated an iron grid rusty in spots from rainwater dripping down from a hole above. The grid was a part of the 21st century but the crevice had taken thousands of years of rain and melting snow constantly dripping down from above to create this jagged incredibly deep abyss. The iron grid was about four feet long and two feet wide bolted in three places to the cave walls and at the final corner bolted to the floor. Someone in her lifetime must have been worried a child or a beloved pet might fall in the deep crevice and be injured, trapped, or killed. The iron bars of the grid were perfect for her purpose.

Once it was all over, Vera feeling filthy inside and out started to crawl toward the entrance. Daniel called out to her in a frantic voice; she looked over her shoulder and saw him nod his head toward an opening which led to another series of caves, "She tried to take my treasure."

"What are you talking about?"

"She's in there. I don't want her near my treasure."

"Who?"

"The ghost?"

"There's no such thing as ghosts. I don't want to talk about ghosts now, Daniel."

"Make her go away, Miss Vera."

"If you're talking about the woman who dumped the body in the gully, she's gone. She's long gone. She won't be stealing your treasures. You did nothing wrong. She's probably finding new victims to abuse and manipulate. Now she and her criminal friends can snort all the coke they want and do all the speed they want and turn into a nest of emaciated skeletons feverishly picking the wallpaper off walls or scrubbing the floors until their skin falls off. I don't care. I just want to be left alone with a brain cell still capable of thinking one beautiful thought at a time."

"She called you by name."

"When? When did you speak to this ghost? I don't understand."

"She shouted out your name. She couldn't see me."

"How did you figure I knew this ghost?"

"She said your name. A stranger wouldn't know your name. I'm telling the truth. She said your name and threatened you, no, she threatened me. She didn't know it was me. She thought I was you."

"I don't understand Daniel. Are we talking about a ghost or a real person?"

"She was a real person, but she changed. She turned into a ghost. I saw her do it."

"Listen. This real person, when she was a real person, she could have looked me up in the phone book. And if not in the phone book, she could have asked around town and found out my name. It's not hard to do. She probably wanted to scare you. She sounds like a liar. If you asked her the time of day, she'd probably lie to you, even though she knew you could walk up to a clock and see the real time. Yes. Those people are called hucksters or con artists. You know what that is? It's someone who pretends to know you, so they can get something from you. I bet she's never said an honest word her whole miserable life. So, shut up about her. We've got more serious problems. We've got to clear our tracks and make sure there's nothing left to find."

"This is bad, Miss Vera. They'll punish us. When you do bad things, you go to jail."

"You won't go to jail Daniel. You didn't do anything wrong. I'm to blame for all this bad luck. It's my curse. I should never have come to this town. I already know what's going to happen to me. There's always a price to pay when you wish someone dead.

Remember that. Don't ever wish someone dead.

My mother told me years ago, you wish someone dead, you curse the person, and you both suffer. The pain comes full circle. It is the justice of the universe. My mother wished someone dead. And years later, I watched my mother die. She was in so much pain. But you, you're not to blame for this. I see nothing but happiness in your future; you'll be happily rock-hunting and rock-polishing. Do you believe me, Daniel?"

He didn't answer. She didn't wait for him instead she crawled out of the cave and marched toward the Suburban prepared to drive the rest of the way without killing them. She could tell that within an hour the sun would be up. They didn't have much time. Vera drove back along Poison Creek Road faster than she had come.

Once at her house, she watched from her porch as the red Suburban crawled along Jump Creek Road at a sedate thirty-five miles an hour and in her head urged Daniel to go faster afraid he would ruin everything with his cautious driving. With profound relief the Suburban finally reached the Harden house turnoff. A few minutes later, when she saw a tall dark silhouette moving toward the gate of the boarding school and thought she saw him lift his arm to wave in her general direction, Vera waved back.

The exchange made Vera want to cry. What had she done to him, this poor man? All this ugliness the Foss brothers had brought here had rubbed off onto him; and yet, he didn't blame her or resent her. It was all her fault. She should have stayed in Vegas.

She turned to go back inside her house glancing uneasily at the hilltop. Her guilt about what they had done conjured another memory. She saw her family around a campfire, a campfire long gone, nearly twenty-five years gone, the firelight in her child's mind seeming to torment the faces staring into the flames making their noses hooked like devils and their eyes black holes; and all the while, as her family sat in a circle chanting in unison, the fire seemed to grow bigger nearly touching the tallest branches of the nearby trees. She recognized a few Gaelic words but that was all, the rest of the words were foreign to her.

When she fell asleep lulled by the steady rhythm of their chanting, she woke believing she'd dreamed the whole thing. It wasn't until many years later that she found the courage to ask her great grandmother if she had dreamed the whole thing. Nonnie had assured her she had not been dreaming. Back then, she'd been a child and as a child accepted the fantasy that if you curse or ill-wish someone, that someone will get sick or have bad luck the rest of his days or maybe even die.

As a child such beliefs seemed perfectly normal most often logical. Of course, words have power, if I swear don't I get a spanking? And then she discovered books and learned about other cultures and other ways of thinking. Yet. What had been bred into her mind at an impressionable age still lurked in dark corners. Part of her still felt a superstitious thrill of excitement mingled with dread at the thought of the power of the Evil Eye and the power of a ritualized family curse. There is something so very ancient and spiritual in the act of joining hands and reciting prayers.

Not only was she struggling between two worlds, the logical part of her also craved some sort of confirmation of the supernatural. It was empowering to think that with a prayer or a curse, she could bring herself good luck or make her enemies suffer. Once in a great while, after praying or cursing, something would happen which would confirm her superstition and push aside any further rational thinking. The practical part of her would say to herself, "Well that's because we haven't figured that one out yet."

Tonight had been a turning point, she'd brushed aside five thousand years of civilization, so she could survive and live another day. Cringing in embarrassment at the memory, she tried to recreate the moment differently. No good. Well, she just hoped her magic trick had worked. Maybe she'd terrified the psychopath enough, he would leave her alone for good?

Probably not. Who was she fooling anyway?

Sim didn't strike her as a person with an overly developed conscience. In fact, as her ancestors would say, he didn't have a soul capable of fearing God's wrath or the Devil's invitation. Just thinking about history and all the monsters like him who had soiled the past with their murders and rapes and genocides made her tiny curse seem silly and stupid. Was she becoming what she hated the most? Just thinking about all those monsters past and present discouraged her. Because once the Foss brothers were behind bars, others like them would rise-up and take their places.

Maybe one day—she wanted so much to believe this—one day, Sim would remember her curse when he was seconds away from being pulled down into hell and he would feel deep pain and regret and maybe compassion for his victims. And if he tried to go religious, thinking Christianity might save him, he might just discover his gods weren't as strong as the one she'd called forth. Idiot, oh you idiot!

Thanks a lot Aunt Vista, Mom, Nonnie, and Uncle Frank. I feel so much better now.

Once inside, Vera knelt on her bedroom floor and began to pick up the shells from Mark's sunflower seeds. She found them all over the bedroom some tucked between the fibers of the carpet. It was oddly soothing to be crawling about the floor searching for the dickhead's sunflower seeds. The search forced her to think about something other than the foul trouble just on the horizon. She knew it was coming. Maybe not today but she could feel the ugliness pressing down on the house. Yes, indeed, there were consequences. Good and bad Karma would find their way to her.

When she was satisfied that all the shells had been removed, she walked to the bathroom and flushed them down the toilet. Ignoring the crazy woman in the bathroom mirror, Vera walked through the rooms picking up trash and straightening overturned furniture. She returned the rope and the tape and the scissors to their proper places. The house was hers again.

Vera woke with sun on her face. The sun's light filtered through the glass and warmed her head and shoulders. It had been a good dream. Then she heard someone in the kitchen. Vera slipped on her jeans and sweater, her socks, and shoes. She walked into the kitchen. Daniel sat at the table eating cereal from a green plastic bowl (which if he had known) belonged to the cat. It was Rama's water bowl. Rama was nowhere in sight. Rama must not mind Daniel's presence then. She joined Daniel at the table. As she sat down to pour a bowl of cereal, Vera realized she'd forgotten the broken front door. She would have to replace the door quickly or there would be questions from her nosy neighbors.

"Do you know how to take a door off its hinges, Daniel?" she asked offering him a glass of milk.

———

At the Treloar farmhouse in his Dad's kitchen, Andrew sat at the table with his cup of coffee growing cold and listened to the laughter and voices swirling around him trying hard not to jump up and run out of the room. It was Dad's birthday and he had promised to come. Ninety years old and his father had had only one woman in his life, Margaret Martha Lucas born in New Orleans in 1910. His mother had loved his father unconditionally, all her sixty-seven years. Someone said his name and he looked up from the contemplation of his coffee into Rachel Treloar's big brown eyes. Kit was a lucky man.

"Hey Mr. Policeman whatever you're thinking about right now will have to wait. Maggie asked you a question Uncle Andrew," Rachel said with a smile pouring him a fresh cup of coffee.

He glanced across the table at his little cousin. Her eyes were intent on his face and she spoke in a rush, "I know this isn't important enough for the Mintlaw police, but I'm worried about Lazy. I saw Jeremy the other day and he was looking for Lazy all over town and even up at Hunter's Hill. I offered to help," she looked down at her hands clutched in her lap then back up into his eyes. "Some kids at school said Lazy is still missing. Is there anything you can do?"

"Has Jeremy called animal control or the Humane Society?"

"I don't know. But isn't the Humane Society in Boise? They can't help us here, can they?"

Unable to look her in the eye, he took a sip of his coffee and nearly burned his tongue. He set the cup down and glanced around the table. His father was sitting at the head of the table in his wheelchair. He had insisted on eating his cake without any help. He was doing his best with his good left hand. The right arm was still giving him trouble. Andrew looked away swept up by an overwhelming sadness. What a rollercoaster ride is life, he thought. He pushed away the sadness concentrating all his attention on Maggie, "I'll see what I can do, Mouse."

"Like what?"

He shrugged, "I don't know. I'll see."

"But what can you do? What can I do?" Maggie asked her eyes refusing to look away from him until she got a definitive answer.

Andrew shoved his chair away from the table and rose to his feet, "Ok. So, let's see, ah, well, I know. I'll make a few phone calls. Hey Dad where's the list of the Owyhee Project members?"

His father looked up from his plate, still determined to get the last piece of cake on the spoon and glanced at him absently, "Where it's always been, right in the cabinet under the telephone nook."

Andrew turned to face the cabinet under the telephone nook. He opened the little doors and peeked inside. There were several yellowed folded pieces of paper stapled together along with pens and pencils. He took the papers out and glanced at the first name on the list. It was Wayne Morrison's number in Oregon. He turned to his father, "Are these numbers current Dad? This paper looks like it's from 1939 when the project began." When there was continued silence from Murray as he sat at the head of the table, Kit tapped his grandfather on the arm. In response, Murray glanced up, his once piercing blue eyes dimmed by cataracts and time.

"What?" he asked impatiently. Kit repeated Andrew's question.

Murray scowled, "Of course it's current. Nobody changes their phone numbers around here. Why should they? What damned difference does it make what your number is anyway? Back in my day, people had only three numbers and sometimes just a party line where everybody had to share. Nowadays you've got to make everything complicated."

While his father continued to rant, Andrew called Wayne Morrison plugging his ear with his finger to be able to hear the voice on the other end. Eventually, he had to take the rotary phone in the hall, "Hold on a minute Wayne," he said to the man on the other end of the line and turned to his father, "It's good to hear your voice Dad. I can understand every word you say now." He turned his attention back to Wayne Morrison, "Hi Wayne. It's Andrew Treloar here. We've got a missing dog and my cousin Maggie is worried about him. I wondered if you've seen a black and white collie that goes by the name Lazy."

The sudden silence in the other room meant his family was waiting to hear Morrison's response to Andrew's question. Wayne Morrison who was probably sitting down to dinner with his family was gracious enough to appear interested in Andrew's question and said, "Don't think so but let me check with the Misses." Andrew waited while Wayne talked to his wife. He came back on the line too quickly which was disappointing. "No sir. We haven't seen a stray collie around here. How about I check with a few of the other fellows and see if they've seen a stray running around."

"Thanks Mr. Morrison, I really appreciate your efforts. I think this might be important. We've had some trouble in this area and I think the missing dog might be connected to what's going on here." He put the receiver back on the phone and turned to face his family. Maggie looked especially disappointed. Murray ignored the drama in the room too busy digging into his ice cream. Andrew returned to his seat and said, "Wayne will check with a few of his neighbors." Maggie looked momentarily relieved. Ah, youth, Andrew thought, always the optimist. They hadn't had time to be jaded by experience.

By the time Murray's presents had been opened and he'd had the celebratory glass of wine with his father, Andrew was ready to go home. He considered stopping by Three Fingers Pub & Grill before heading home sanctimoniously thinking he might ask the guys at the bar if they had seen Lazy. A betraying thought had come to him. Maybe he should just forget all about Vera and find himself a sympathetic ear attached to an attractive female body?

Before he could make his thoughts a reality the phone rang. No one got up from their comfortable spots in the living room except for Maggie who jumped up like a jackrabbit being chased by a hound. Andrew beat her to the telephone nook and answered on the third ring, "Hello Treloar residence. Andrew here," he said into the phone watching as Maggie's bright eyes stared avidly into his face trying to guess the news by his expression.

When she backed up and leaned against the kitchen counter Andrew knew she had read him right. After agreeing to meet with Morrison's neighbor, Andrew set down the phone to look at Maggie. Kit came into the room carrying the wine glasses and set them in the sink and glanced at first Maggie then Andrew.

"That bad huh," his nephew said as he put his arm around Maggie's shoulders, "Hey baby don't cry."

An hour later, Andrew and Jeremy Stubben were in Oregon standing on the road on the edge of Outerkirk Farm near Succor Creek National Park. Stanley Outerkirk had driven them to the area where he periodically deposited his old tires. The prairie vultures had been circling the sky above the graveyard of tires. The flies buzzing around a section of the rubber mound were a clear signal where the collie had been dumped. Whoever had tried to hide him in the tire pile had been in a big hurry and not particularly careful. They only had to lift a few tires off the top of the pile to uncover the poor creature's body. The poisoner, either due to ignorance of the number of scavengers in the Owyhees or his own conviction he'd never be caught had made the dog's discovery that much easier.

Sickened by the sight, Andrew vowed to search for the depraved shit for as long as it took and when he found him, beat him to a bloody pulp. There were no laws against killing animals. But there should be, Andrew thought. When Jeremy confirmed the dog's identity, Andrew turned to the kid and said, "I want an autopsy Jeremy. I want to know how Lazy died. Do you mind? I'll pay for it if you can't."

Andrew glanced at the young man who was busy wiping tears off his face.

"Yeah, Mr. Treloar, that's okay by me. I want to know too," Jeremy said as he followed Andrew to where Outerkirk had lain a blue tarp on the road near the body. Andrew had come prepared. He pulled out his gloves from his coat pocket and lifted the dog's bottom and hind legs while Outerkirk lifted the head and shoulders. They lay him gently on the blue tarp. As far as Andrew could tell, the dog had not been shot. There were no obvious wounds. The body was beginning to decompose though, so he ventured a guess that Lazy had been dead a few days. The veterinarian he had in mind was an old friend and he might be able to get the results of the autopsy back quicker than if he had gone through the usual channels.

The drink at Three Fingers at least helped him to refocus his attention on the crimes happening in his community. Some sick bastard had killed a dog. Why? There were no obvious wounds. Someone had poisoned the dog. Poisoning takes time and premeditation. It also reveals a predilection for sneakiness and callousness. Now who might that be? Woody was dead, so he could scratch him off the list.

Before he could say the name of the woman he was thinking about as his prime suspect, a tall pretty blonde wearing a tight-fitting shirt that outlined her large breasts and exposed her slim belly walked up to his table in the corner of the bar and smiled at him. Was it summer already he asked himself? He smiled back at her. Then she opened her mouth and in a soft voice asked him, "How the fuck are you doing hunky stranger? My, you are one fucking beautiful man. You want to go somewhere and do the nasty with me?"

He was so shocked he just stared for a moment – wondering – did she really think she had a chance in hell with a sewer for a mouth? Maybe other guys less discriminating found her foul mouth attractive, but not him. He gulped down the last of his whiskey and stood up rocking the little table in his haste. She grinned triumphantly and glanced at someone at the other end of the room. It was too dark for him to see who she was looking at and he didn't really give a damn. He shoved past her, "I don't dip into scummy waters," he told her and walked out of the bar.

Andrew sat on his lawn chair wrapped in his parka and blanket and stared at the water flowing by his house. Along the banks of the Snake River the water had hardened into ice, yet the center flowed as always. The Snake River, as far as he knew never froze solid from end to end. The ice he did see along the edges of the river reminded him of how he was feeling inside. What had taken place in his life these last six months had been new, brand new, just like Andrew's pain. Andrew tried to remember that no matter what happened the water kept moving and he, like that pathetic stick tumbling over and over in the fast-flowing river would be taken along for the ride.

He still didn't understand what he'd done to make Vera so mad. As far as he knew she hadn't minded his Saturday nights at the Metcalfs. And since he'd been with her, he hadn't been interested in anyone else. Sure, he looked. He wasn't blind. But he didn't sneak behind her back and she knew it. It was the not knowing that bothered him the most. What had he done?

Her note he had found the night before tucked inside his suitcase under his sweater. He read and reread the note trying to make sense of her cryptic message – *It's not your fault Andrew. I have to keep us both safe. Don't be mad at me. I'm just not good enough for you.*

No amount of beer could rid him of the ache inside his belly. He avoided his family and friends hating to see the pity in their eyes. Today he had had to come out of the house and be among the living for his father's sake. And to make matters worse, the days since she'd thrown him out continued to dawn sublime, so beautiful he knew the landscape and the smells, and the sounds would be imprinted in his memory forever. This is what pain looks like—sun shining down on a world of white and a stick tumbling over and over in an icy cold river.

—

The air was crisp and cold outside. Vera stood beside Daniel and waited for the dawn. She put her hands in the pockets of her parka. Daniel wore only his t-shirt and jeans. Vera walked back into the house and pulled a blanket out of the closet. She handed Daniel the blanket. He grinned a silly grin and made a fuss about covering his shoulders until she wanted to rip it off him and tell him to go home. Then she remembered what he had done for her. She could never repay him enough.

"Show me your treasures Daniel," she asked him, thinking about the ghost he'd mentioned before. He climbed over her fence and made his way up the Access to Hunter's Hill. She followed him taking longer because she used the gate. They reached the cattle guard together. Her heart drummed in her ears. She was so afraid to look to her left, afraid she would see them waiting to ambush her and Daniel. It seemed highly unlikely the Foss brothers could free themselves from their bonds; and besides why would they wait until she and Daniel returned to the hill to get their revenge? No, her discomfort was because her conscience was bothering her. She was no better than them.

It was cold. She could see the ghostly wisps of her breath in the air. Swallowing suddenly seemed impossible. She froze, her body refusing to move and stared at Daniel who paused in surprise and glanced over his shoulder. He frowned. Why was he being so nonchalant about this place so soon after their ordeal? Had he forgotten last night? Did he not remember that the Foss brothers were only a few feet away? Had he forgotten the bad lady, the one everyone assumed was Ada? She tried to remember when he had told her that he didn't want the body near his treasure?

Daniel passed the cave where they had dragged the Foss brothers and stopped a few feet beyond. He turned left crouching on all fours and crawled underneath the sagebrush. Vera made herself move. She owed him. The hardwood sage tore at her coat sleeves. She sensed a hard object ahead of her and ducked her head. It was a part of the cave, the top part, what in a door would be called a lintel. If she'd simply followed Daniel without hesitation, she might have brained herself on that rock lintel. With relief, she saw the soles of Daniel's shoes and ahead of him a light. She followed the shoes crawling on her hands and knees and watched Daniel wiggle himself inside the opening. It took a moment for her to get up the courage to stand. First, she touched the air above her head and when she was confident she wouldn't bang her head, she pushed herself upward.

Once Vera moved further into the cave, she looked up and noticed several pinholes above her where sunlight streamed through the openings. Even with the holes, it was still dim and difficult to see the whole place. The cave was large enough for maybe four people but no more. It stank of urine and wet fur. She supposed coyotes or foxes had used it for shelter. She noticed a backpack near the entrance to the cave. She'd never seen one like it before other than in old World War II movies. It was made of leather canvas and cowhide. She remembered the Germans called them rucksacks.

"Hey, Daniel. Where did you get the old backpack?"

Daniel glanced over his shoulder, shrugged, and in conflict with his pretense of disinterest, his tone suggested defensiveness, "I found it. It's mine now."

"Where did you find it?"

"Around."

"Well it might be important Daniel," she said making a move toward the rucksack.

"No, Miss Vera," he said his voice rising which she recognized as the onset of a temper tantrum. "It's mine. I found it. Someone threw it away. A litterer. Mz. Matthews says people who litter are thoughtless and don't care about the earth."

"I'm not going to take it away from you Daniel. I promise. It might be important though. It might be important because of Kat and her mother's body. It was found so close by. Did you find it in the gully? Was there anything inside, maybe something that could tell us who the rucksack belonged to?"

"No. There was no wallet, just some bags of flour. I threw them away."

She knew she had to remain calm. If Daniel suspected she was in any way upset, he would mirror her behavior tenfold and in this small cramped cave that could be disastrous.

"Where did you throw the bags of flour?"

He pointed at something in the far corner of the cave beyond his pile of rocks, "I threw them down there."

Vera couldn't see into the far corners of the cave from where she stood, at least not enough to know what "down there" meant. She made herself crawl on hands and knees to where Daniel had spread a blue tarp and laid out his thundereggs. She'd never understood the allure of these rocks. Some of them were as big as what she imagined dinosaur eggs would be and they were rough and knobby and in her opinion ugly as sin.

Vera had seen thundereggs at rock shows which had incredibly intricate and beautiful semi-precious stones and agate embedded inside their ugly outer shells. And sometimes the eggs were worth thousands of dollars to collectors. She'd also heard from collectors and local people that the ancient Native Americans believed during thunder storms the mountain spirits from Mount Hood and Mount Jefferson would do battle with each other by hurling these rocks in the sky trying to vanquish their enemies. The ancient people believed thundereggs came from the nests of Thunderbirds.

Still. From the outside, they looked pretty sad to her.

She made herself kneel beside him and pretend an interest she did not feel. He picked one out of the pile to show her. It looked like a lump of coal, only harder. She didn't think it was a thioeregg, but she didn't want to seem ignorant. And besides, if she asked questions, he would go on and on about the damned rocks and she'd end up spending too much time in this claustrophobic smelly place. The rock he handed her sparkled with mica, the flakes falling onto her pant leg as she rolled it between her fingers. She wasn't a geologist. She knew little about rocks. All she knew for sure was that Daniel liked them.

Trying to act as casual as possible, she looked in the direction he had pointed and the first thing she saw made her stiffen with fear. The bones were tucked in a corner as if someone had wanted to hide them away from anyone who might discover the cave by accident. Daniel must have moved the bones as far away from his treasure as he could. They looked human.

As she crawled over to them noticing the skull with a sick heave of her stomach, she saw a deep dark jagged crevice a few feet beyond the bones. Part of her not yet able to grasp the full import of what she was seeing focused on the tear in the earth for a few minutes. How far down does the tear go? She supposed she was trying to postpone the moment when she had to look closely at the skeleton and understand what might have taken place here. She crawled close to the edge of the thin opening and peered down.

In some places the cut in the earth was about three fingers wide and seemed to go on forever down and down into the hill maybe right down to the valley floor. It was too dark to see if the bags were at the bottom. Once she was sure there was no way to retrieve the "evidence" she made herself move toward the skeleton in the corner.

For a panicked moment she thought the body belonged to the person who had dumped Kat's mother in the gully. Maybe she was staring at her skull. Sense returned when her curiosity took over. These bones had been here a long time, long enough for the flesh to be eaten away, also long enough for the hair and other major organs to have been carried away by animals.

"What shall we do with her?" Vera asked.

Daniel looked up and smiled, "She's not bad?"

"No, she's not bad. She's just very old."

"Can she go where the bad people go?"

"No. I'm sorry Daniel. She can't."

"She can stay here then."

As she turned around to crawl back to the larger part of the cave, she saw the blankets. They had been laid near a narrow passageway leading to the other cave. "Where does this passageway go?" she asked somehow knowing what he was going to say and dreading the answer.

"That's where the bad men are sleeping," Daniel said without looking up too engrossed in his specimen.

It was bad enough to know the Foss brothers were right down the passageway from them and could probably hear everything they said but to find two thick gray wool blankets with blue pin stripping stitched around the ends and clinging to the top blanket, a child's sock, one resembling Kat's missing sock, the one she and Andrew noticed on the morning of her discovery made Vera wonder for a sickening moment if her ally during this horrendous time could also be a murderer. She put the evidence together and the ideas running around in her head were not good. Before she panicked and said something stupid, she would need to make her way outside as casually and carefully as possible.

She'd had enough of the cave. She crawled toward the entrance and glanced over her shoulder. Daniel was absorbed in his rocks oblivious to what she was doing. She opened the flap of the rucksack and read the name on the label inside. A wave of nausea swept over her. She had to get out before she threw up and contaminated the scene of the crime. She crawled out of the cave and into the sunshine and began walking rapidly toward her house.

Daniel stayed behind too mesmerized by his treasured rocks.

It was insane to think they could carry this off. Someone would discover the truth. Even in winter, people were crawling all over the Owyhees, camping, fishing, and hiking the trails. And most of the locals used Hunter's Hill as their shortcut.

Hunter's Hill wasn't on her land.

She couldn't run people off with a shotgun.

How could she be such an idiot?

She would go to prison.

Daniel would go to prison.

—

Andrew stood with George Metcalf beside the Lincoln Continental. George slapped a sticker on the back window. "Some people have a lot of nerve, you know, thinking the Owyhee Mountains are their dumping grounds," George said.

The plates had been traced to Los Angeles. The owners had reported the Lincoln stolen a couple of months ago. Andrew watched as Peter Smith hauled the Lincoln away in his truck and accelerated to make enough speed to hit the incline on US 95 heading north toward Homedale. Someone from the Homedale Police Department would check out the interior and find out who had stolen the vehicle. He hoped. Andrew climbed into his Jeep.

George walked up to his window. "You okay buddy?"

"Sure. See you later," he managed to say and followed Peter toward Homedale. He wanted to talk to the Chief of the Homedale Police and see if he couldn't push the investigation into high gear.

—

The cat was again sunning himself by the window. Vera envied the cat's tranquility. The cat could present her with an injured or dead mouse and everyone would shrug and say, "That's what cat's do." But a person who injured or killed another person was a monster. She was a monster. Vera looked beyond the cat and saw Maggie on her bike riding up the drive toward her house.

Vera had her new/old door open before Maggie had time to lift her hand to knock. When Vera had mentioned the need to replace the broken door which Daniel had kicked in on the morning he showed up at her house eating her cereal, he had promptly started working on fixing the door. She was in luck when she found the original door to the farmhouse in the barn and suggested he hang the old door. The nine-panel exterior door made of tiger oak with beveled glass fit neatly into the opening; and as a bonus, the glass allowed beautiful light to stream into her hallway making her house feel warm and cozy. All she had left to do was sand the door then apply one more coat of stain on the surface.

Belatedly Vera realized Maggie looked unhappy. Vera made herself smile. The act of smiling reminded Vera of how glad she was to see Maggie.

"They found Lazy," Maggie started off and quickly finished. "They think he's been poisoned."

"Oh, I'm so sorry, Maggie," Vera said motioning the teenager inside the house.

When Maggie got a good look at Vera's bruises, she stepped back in shock. "That wasn't?" she asked her voice barely able to construct the words.

Vera glanced at herself in the mirror near the door, "No, of course not. Someday, I'll tell you what happened, but not today."

Vera had forgotten about her face. It could have been worse. She could be dead right now. The bruises looked worse than they felt. He hadn't broken any skin and she'd applied plenty of antiseptic cream for the last few days to be sure the small cuts would heal. She'd left off wearing makeup. When she'd tried to hide the bruises with makeup, the ingredients in the tube burned her still tender skin. She'd been an old hand at covering up bruises while married to Arthur Vlasky.

"Come in. I want you to meet my new guest," Vera said.

Maggie entered the house and followed her into the living room.

"This is Chakri Rama the first," Vera said. "I call him Rama for short."

Rama weaved his head back and forth and seemed transported to some other place by the music playing on the stereo. Maggie watched the black cat rock from side to side with his eyes closed and his tongue hanging out. Maggie was transfixed by his devilish ears. She had never seen a cat like him before. He looked so exotic, so unreal. She watched Rama for nearly ten minutes before following Vera into the kitchen.

"Is that a Siamese? I didn't know cats liked music."

"Would you like a soda or something?" Vera asked.

"Sure," Maggie said, her eyes darting about the room and pausing for a moment to glance at Vera. "I'm glad we're still friends."

"So am I," Vera said and handed her a can of black cherry soda. Vera sat across from her and waited for Maggie to come to the point.

"I brought back the book I borrowed last month," Maggie began and pulled the book out of her backpack.

Vera accepted the book and set it on the table beside her, "If you want to read another one I have plenty in the storage room, although it won't be a storage room for long."

"Why?"

"I'm thinking of renting out the two extra rooms."

Maggie leaned forward in surprise, "You mean strangers will be staying here with you?"

"Yes. Why not?"

Maggie leaned back in her chair and just stared at her as if Vera had sprouted wings. Vera reassured her, "I'm not an angel if that's what you're thinking. I'm doing this for money. Well, not all for money. I could find a job I suppose. But somehow this way I can be home working on the house and still have a bit of cash. Even out here, people need a place to stay. I could maybe fix the place up into a Bed & Breakfast. So, that's the situation now. It's just temporary."

"But what about Egg? Don't you want to work there anymore?"

While they had been talking they hadn't noticed Rama enter the kitchen. Vera had a clue when Maggie's eyes lifted as she stared at something over Vera's shoulder. Vera turned in time to see Rama leap off the kitchen countertop and land on her shoulder. She staggered a bit from the weight of him. He was bigger than a Siamese. Rama began rubbing his face against Vera's neck. Vera introduced him to Maggie in a formal way and as if he were human capable of understanding polite introductions, "This is Maggie Treloar. Maggie, this is Chakri Rama the first."

"As in some sort of historical figure maybe?" Maggie asked jokingly.

"He's got the arrogance of a King," Vera said with a snort. "He's part Siamese, I think, and just maybe he could be the reincarnation of the King of Siam. Who knows?"

Maggie lifted her arm in the air and waved and said hello as if she knew the cat understood her. Maybe he did. Rama jumped onto the table and sauntered toward Maggie. Vera pulled out an empty chair next to her and padded the seat inviting Rama to curl up on the cushion. Rama plopped onto the cushion as if he were exhausted which made Maggie giggle.

Maggie finished off her soda and got up, "Well, I'd better be going. Thanks for the loan of the book."

"You can pick out another one if you like."

"No. Better not. I just came over to return the book."

"You didn't," Vera said annoyed with polite insincerities. "You came over to find out why your uncle and I are no longer living together."

Maggie stopped in the act of picking up her backpack, "I guess so."

Vera stood up, "I still like Andrew. I don't know if I love him. I don't know what we've got together. I just wanted some time to myself. He will probably never forgive me, and I understand. But it seemed like a good idea at the time. Things were moving too fast for me. I've been alone for a long time and I sort of like my privacy. Can you understand that?"

Maggie shrugged, "I guess so. But I've never seen him so hurt. He looks like he's been to his best friend's funeral, only the funeral never ends. I want to help if I can."

Vera could find no words to explain the situation. It was better Maggie thought Vera was a rotten bitch than that her uncle was dead by a knife in the back from a murderer. Vera followed Maggie to the door and watched as the young woman slipped on her coat. Vera missed Andrew more than she could say; a pain so deep she thought she would be better off dead. She'd believed by placing Andrew out of danger she could save him. Maybe her scheming had been a mistake. She should have had more confidence in him.

Someone knocked on her front door. Maggie paused in the act of putting on her coat and stood back as Vera brushed past her. Daniel stood on the threshold with a huge grin on his face. Rama had come to meet the visitor. When he saw Daniel, he shot out of the room like a bullet hissing. They could hear him snarling in displeasure in Vera's bedroom down the hall.

Daniel threw out his arms, "I took care of everything. Problem solved."

Vera looked over her shoulder at Maggie. It was too late now. Somehow, she didn't think Maggie would go home quietly. Daniel's excitement vibrated through the room. He was so pleased with himself. Vera felt lightheaded again. She just wanted this mess to be over.

Vera turned to Maggie, "Daniel has something to show us."

He nodded with pleasure and spun around on his heels leaving the house at a fast march. They hurried to catch up with him. He led them up to the top of Hunter's Hill. Daniel, Maggie, and Vera paused on the ridge above the house and stared down at the valley below. Daniel only paused long enough to take a deep refreshing breath of cold air and then left them. When they turned around to face the hilltop they could see him moving quickly down the old road. Vera followed. Maggie followed Vera. When the two females passed the barricade of rocks, they could see Daniel at the other end of the old road near the cattle guard looking down at something in the gully.

Vera let go of Maggie's hand and looked at the young girl with a moment's trepidation wondering why she had allowed her to come with them, "I can't ask you to lie to your parents or your uncle; but as a favor to me, could you please wait a couple of days before saying anything to them. Remember what I said about mysteries beyond our understanding?"

Maggie nodded ascent, "Sure. Don't worry. I won't say anything to anyone unless someone asks me a direct question."

Vera walked up to Daniel and together they stood by the gully and looked down at the two men spread out on the ground below. Vera sensed Maggie moving forward to get a better look standing right next to her as if Maggie was on a school field trip and Vera was her teacher ready to lecture on the flora and fauna of the high desert. Sim and Mark Foss appeared to be sleeping. Two nights in a cave and a few hours in the bitter mountain cold of a gully might kill most people, she supposed, but not these nasty rattlers. She noticed Sim staring up at her with malevolence in his eyes.

"Stay here," she told them and made her way carefully down to him.

If looks could kill, Vera would be dead right there and then. He didn't look so hot and she was pleased. It was time to speak plainly, "Daniel could easily have killed you both. He didn't. I stopped him, remember? Hear me out cockroach. Your time has come. I've said my prayers. You heard the curse. Bad things happen to people who cross me. So, either I set you free and you leave for good or I call the cops and tell them how you broke into my house and beat me up. What's it to be?"

She jerked the electrician's tape off Sim's mouth and noticed the tears with a certain satisfaction. "You, dirty rotten skank," he stuttered his lips cracked and peeling. "I'm going to kill you. But first I'm going to tell the cops everything, all about the body you got stashed in that fucking goddamned cave. We heard the freak. We know he killed her. And now we know you've got our money and our drugs. What do you think the cops are going to do to you, you ugly douchebag?"

"I don't know anything about any money or drugs. Whatever Ada stole from you is her business. Go ask her."

"She's dead you nut job," Sim screamed. "Your brainless boyfriend killed her and dumped her down a hole. I heard everything you said. Remember?"

"Ada isn't dead. I don't know where she is, but she isn't dead."

He looked at her as if she were crazy. Maybe she was but hell would freeze over before she admitted anything to this poisonous rattler. Let him think she was crazy, she didn't care. As far as she knew Ada was hiding from them. When he started shouting, "You told him Ada was a liar. I heard you. Hey, hey up there. You hear me little girl? These two freaks are murderers. They're murderers. And if you know what's good for you, you'll run straight to the cops and tell them everything."

Vera dropped to the ground beside Sim and clamped both of her hands over his mouth pressing down with all the force in her back and shoulders.

"Shut up. Shut up."

When the color drained from his face, she pulled back a bit and relaxed her hold afraid she was suffocating him. Terrified now, she began to whisper in his ear. It must be a good one. It must convince him. All she wanted was for them to walk away and especially for Maggie to see them alive and walking away.

In his ear she said, "Come back to the house tonight at midnight. I know where the money and drugs are hidden. I've known all along. Did you kill Woody? They found Ada's van. They found something in the van. They think a hungry cougar ate part of him. Oh yeah. You didn't know? Don't you read the papers? Or maybe Ada killed Woody? Maybe she left his body in the van for the predators to find? I think Ada's still around somewhere waiting to take her revenge on you. Should I leave you tied up for another night? Hum? It's supposed to get real cold tonight. You want a cougar to find you and take a bite out of your leg?

Or maybe Ada hears you crying and decides to end your misery? So, what's it going to be? Do I let you go now? Yeah? Ok? If I do, you're going to take your brother and go somewhere to collect yourself, maybe clean up and get yourself a meal and a drink then come back at midnight. I'll be waiting. Well? Do you know how to nod and shake your head?"

She held on for a count of thirty while he thought about her offer. When he nodded his head in agreement, she untied the knots around his wrists and legs and tucked the pieces of rope in her jacket pocket. She did the same for Mark. Mark moaned and turned over. Vera sprang back not wanting to be anywhere close to them when they regained their strength and decided they weren't going to wait to punish her. She clawed her way up the gully. Once she felt safe, she turned to watch as Sim struggled to his knees and then attempted to stand. For a few minutes, he swayed from side to side as he regained life in his limbs.

All three of them watched from above as Sim pulled his brother to his feet. Vera stepped back when Sim tried to maneuver up the soft sides of the gully, the murder in his eyes aimed at all of them. Then he had second thoughts, probably remembering the beating he'd gotten from Daniel. He turned and tumbled down the gully on his butt until he reached the bottom near his brother and started making his way in the opposite direction away from them toward the huge willow tree.

Mark followed his brother to where its gigantic roots grew along the slope of the gully. Vera took Maggie's hand and together they walked back to the house. She heard Daniel moving in the opposite direction toward his cave and his treasures, perhaps afraid the Foss brothers might try to steal his precious rocks. She thought about warning him to go home worried the Foss brothers might sneak back and hit him from behind. Then she remembered Daniel's ferocious assault on Sim the other night. Sim might be a psycho, but he wasn't suicidal.

Vera had no doubt the Foss brothers would return to her house. Sim had had two days to think about what he would do to her. She wished she'd killed him when she had the chance.

As soon as Vera got inside, she dialed the police and handed the phone to Maggie, "Ask for your uncle, Maggie. Tell your uncle the Foss brothers were here looking for their drugs and their money. You can tell them everything you saw. I don't care. You decide."

—

Maggie sat on her bike and stared at Jeremy and Jeremy's new girlfriend. She was in Mintlaw to buy more pens and essay books. She had come out of Peterson's Grocery and planned to cross the road to O'Reilly's Ice Cream Shack and buy an ice cream or soda. Jeremy and his new girlfriend hadn't seen her yet, but when they turned to climb into Jeremy's Trooper, the girl would see Maggie. Maggie thought about riding on and pretending she hadn't seen them. Instead she decided to wait at the crosswalk until the light changed. She had every right to be on the street. She wasn't a criminal.

So-what, if Jeremy had a new girlfriend. Maggie knew Tiffany was just an airhead and if Jeremy liked airheads she had misjudged him. The cold winter wind nearly knocked Maggie off her feet as she waited for the street to clear so she could cross. She left the hood of her jacket down, so she could see. Yet, the wind had access to her neck and the cold seemed to seep right down into her bones. The sun came out from behind a cloud for a moment and Maggie drank in the warmth blinking her eyes when the sun's light reflected off someone's chrome bumper.

Maggie noticed from the corner of her eye that Tiffany had climbed into the passenger seat of the Trooper without noticing Maggie. Jeremy didn't noticed Maggie until he'd pulled out onto the street. The light had changed which meant he had to stop at the crosswalk to let Maggie go by. Maggie pushed her bike across the street making sure she took her time. Her legs were trembling as she walked past the Trooper, but she knew Jeremy couldn't tell. She made sure to turn just at the right moment and stare at him. She painted on a smile and said loud enough for everyone to hear, "Hi there Jeremy. How are you?"

Evidently Jeremy had nothing to say. Maggie wasn't surprised. Not until Jeremy had driven away did Maggie relax her stiff shoulders. Someone hailed her, and Maggie turned in time to see Amy riding down the street toward her. "Nice touch, Mags," she said with a grin. "I wish I could be as frosty."

"I wasn't really. If he wasn't such a jerk, he would have heard my teeth chattering. But then he would have figured I was just cold. He's so obtuse."

"Say again?"

"You know. Dim."

"Oh yeah. Obtuse, great word, I like it. What's up?"

"Nothing really, I've just been to the bookmobile. I didn't find anything I liked. I mean I've read practically every book they've got."

"You want to sit down by the river? Some of us are meeting at the park and then going to Stacey's house later."

Maggie looked at her watch and thought she might be able to call her father from Stacey's house, "Sure. That sounds good."

A woman wearing huge purple sunglasses and an ankle length leather coat stopped in front of the girls, "Hola Senoritas. Hablan Espanole?"

Amy looked at Maggie, "What did she say?"

Maggie leaned forward. Maggie wasn't all that tall, but this woman couldn't have been more than four feet four inches in her bare feet. Even wearing winter boots with the high heels, the woman was still shorter than Maggie, the top of her head barely reaching Maggie's neck.

"Ah, no. No hablo Espanole mucho Pero," Maggie said in a sort of panic. She looked around hoping to find someone she knew who could speak English and Spanish. Then she noticed Mrs. Esquivel walking down the street with her daughters in tow.

"Mrs. Esquivel, can you help me please? This lady speaks only Spanish. She's asking us something, but we don't understand."

Mrs. Esquivel wore her usual thick wool plaid jacket and hiking boots. She was almost as tall as she was fat. Rarely did Mrs. Esquivel smile. The world was too serious for smiles. Yet Maggie knew Mrs. Esquivel liked people and enjoyed the local gossip. She just wasn't the smiling type. Mrs. Esquivel sent her daughters off to the diner where they had been heading and approached Maggie and the woman. Amy refused to leave Maggie's side. Mrs. Esquivel and the strange woman spoke for a few minutes, eventually Mrs. Esquivel turned to Maggie.

"She wants to know where she can find her cat. She says he's lost and when she got a call from the pound, they said a lady from Mintlaw called who had found a cat fitting her cat's description and wanted to know if anyone had reported it missing. She said she was on the way to the lady's house to see if the cat is her cat, but she must have gotten the directions mixed up. Do you know who she's talking about?"

"Oh, I know. It must be Rama, Vera's cat. Can you give her directions to Vera Lee's house?"

"You mean the woman with the scar on her face?"

Mrs. Esquivel ignored Maggie's frown and turned back to the stranger to give her directions to Vera's house. Maggie hadn't realized that Mrs. Esquivel knew where Vera lived. After the stranger returned to a black truck and climbed into the passenger seat next to an elderly man, Mrs. Esquivel turned to Maggie with a sweet smile, "It is better for the cat to be with good clean people. That shelter should never have given that woman an animal to care for. A gypsy is more likely to eat one than feed one."

Maggie wanted to defend Vera but had no chance to do so since Mrs. Esquivel made a point of rushing off toward the diner as she spoke and only threw over her shoulder her parting remark. Maggie dumped her bike on the ground and marched toward the door of the diner. She wasn't going to let Mrs. Esquivel have the last word. The diner was busy. Maggie noticed Officer Metcalf sitting at his usual booth and her uncle sitting across from him. Maggie tried to smile when Office Metcalf nodded welcome in her direction.

Instead of heading toward them, Maggie approached the booth where Mrs. Esquivel sat with her daughters. Mrs. Esquivel looked up in surprise when she noticed Maggie hovering above her.

Maggie spoke without thinking, all in a rush before she lost her courage, "You're wrong about Vera. She's a wonderful person and she's done wonderful things for this community. You just don't know the half of what she's done for this place. She's working with the Eggs and helping them to be good students and good citizens and she even caught some dangerous criminals and taught them a lesson they'll never forget. They were drug dealers Mrs. Esquivel, maybe even murderers. They could have sold drugs to your daughters or maybe raped and killed them. There's no knowing what they could have done, so there, Mrs. Esquivel. You shouldn't judge people when you don't know anything about them,"

Maggie was trembling by the time she'd stepped away from the table and left the diner. Maggie stood by her bike and waited for her heart to return to its normal rhythm.

Amy looked back at the diner then Maggie, "I don't know what you said to Mrs. Esquivel but she's getting her coat on and coming out here to give you a piece of her mind. You want to stick around?"

"I'm not going to run away."

Maggie and Amy waited for Mrs. Esquivel to approach. Mrs. Esquivel's complexion had turned a shade lighter than the fake ermine around the collar of her coat. Mrs. Esquivel stopped in front of Maggie and wagged her finger in her face, "Your mother must teach you better manners, young lady. How dare you speak to an older person like me in that way? How dare you. I shall speak to your mother about your rudeness."

Maggie forced herself not to cry, "I have a right to my opinion Mrs. Esquivel and I disagree with yours about Vera Lee. You can go ahead and talk to my parents, but I won't change my mind about Vera. She's a good person."

"She's a gypsy," Mrs. Esquivel spat out. "Gypsies are no good. They'll steal you blind. And worst of all, they bring bad luck."

"You don't know anything about her."

"I know what I know. I know she's a gypsy and that's all I need to know. Now I've wasted enough time on you, young lady. You tell your mother I shall call her sometime today."

Before Maggie had a chance to get on her bike, she saw her Uncle Andrew leave the diner. Mrs. Esquivel passed her uncle with a curt nod. If he'd had a hat on he would have doffed it to Mrs. Esquivel in a gentlemanly salute. By the time he reached her, he'd managed to wipe the smile off his face, "Had a run in with the Dragon Lady, hum?"

"She said Vera's a gypsy and no good. She said gypsies bring bad luck. Is that true?"

"I've heard old folk tales about gypsies bringing bad luck. Don't mind Mrs. Esquivel. She's got her prejudices just like everybody else in the world."

"But you didn't see her face. She looked so serious, just as if Vera were a real witch or something even worse."

"Mrs. Esquivel has had a difficult life, a hard life full of pain and sorrow. I know you haven't lived in Mintlaw very long, so you wouldn't know Mrs. Esquivel's history. She's been raised to believe in good and evil and that people are at the mercy of good and bad luck. Sadly, for her and her family, they have had to deal with a lot of bad luck.

Sometimes people need a reason for their bad luck. So, they rationalize the bad times by thinking someone's put a curse on them. On really bad days even I wonder if I've done something to piss off the devil and wonder if I'm being cursed. Don't worry about Vera. We live in a rational world with laws that protect people. This isn't the dark ages and Mrs. Esquivel isn't going to burn Vera at the stake. Anyway, do you really think Vera cares one-bit what Mrs. Esquivel thinks of her?"

"Well, I won't let anyone trash my friends, Uncle Andrew."

Andrew kissed her forehead, "I'm proud of you Mouse for sticking up for your friends, but you must also respect your elders. You're growing up too fast. Tell your Dad I'll be by some time tonight to talk to him."

Maggie followed Amy down to the river and noticed Mrs. Esquivel's grandson Juan standing next to Stacey. She refused to feel guilty about talking back to Juan's grandmother. Yet, she couldn't help but like Juan. He had always been a good friend and now she was sure his grandmother would forbid him from having anything to do with her.

At the rate she was going, she would lose all her male friends, one by one, first Jeremy, then Juan. In the end she would be a tragic beautiful female shunned by others for being different, for being mysterious and alluring and men would flock to her like moths to a flame. Embarrassed by her daydreams, Maggie made an excuse to hurry home.

———

Delfina Rodriguez and Pablo Desoto sat on the couch with their hands folded and their tender eyes so calm and centered, while in the kitchen Rama paced back and forth, his humming rising in pitch and intensity. Upon entering the house and introducing themselves, Vera noticed how Rama acted as if they were strangers, even though Pablo had been one of Vera's oldest and dearest friends and the woman Delfina was Pablo's married niece. They had come unannounced and Vera had no time to hide her bruises from them.

The atmosphere was growing more uncomfortable by the second and the conversation more stilted. Since opening the door and offering them a seat on her living room couch, Pablo had spoken only once, nodding his head, then smiling warmly. Occasionally he would look at Vera surreptitiously then around the room. Whenever Rama sauntered into the room he would examine the cat with appreciation. All the while, Delfina Rodriquez did most of the talking.

"I explained to the people at the Humane Society that we found Cath during our visit to Las Cruces. Someone must have bred him with a wild cat. We felt sorry for him and we took him in. We tried you know. I think they didn't believe us. Anyway, they said they didn't have the facilities for a wild cat. Maybe they'll find him a home at a zoo. Cath doesn't remember us. I don't understand why. My uncle," Delfina turned to Pablo, "could speak to him if you like? I told the lady I have no room for Cath. I don't make much, you see, just enough to support my children and send a little money home. My husband, he's a soldier. He was injured recently," and as if to clarify the situation Delfina added, "in Grenada. He received a medal you know."

"I'm so sorry," Vera said. "Is he with you? If he's out in your truck, please tell him to come in." While she was urging Delfina to bring him inside the house, she wondered how Delfina's husband could be 'recently injured' when the engagement or invasion or whatever-it-had-been-called at Grenada took place two years ago.

The invasion hadn't lasted long enough to notice. At the time, Vera had been too busy worrying about food and shelter and finding a decent job to watch the news or care about a battle in some place she'd never been or could never afford to be until someone mentioned Grenada at work. Nonnie had said when a country wants to appear tough, especially if the leaders of the country wanted to beat their chests and scare the world – watch out – it means their planning another war.

Delfina shook her head curtly and looked at the floor until she could compose herself again, "No. He's not with us. He's with my parents right now. It isn't just my husband's injuries, we must move, and the apartment doesn't accept pets. Also, I can no longer work and keep my children in daycare. Oregon no longer provides child care assistance, and so we must go and live with my parents in Vegas."

"I'm sorry for your difficulties but Oregon didn't do away with child care assistance," Vera said with real compassion. "The President and the Congress cut many programs that helped the poor. You remember the air traffic controllers? Well they were all fired, fired just because they wanted a living wage and more help to do their jobs. I had a decent job at a savings and loan in Oregon. Then poof, it's gone. I had to leave and find work in Vegas too.

I was lucky enough to meet the Andersons. Before I met them, I worked as a maid at several of the casinos. We met while waiting in line for the smorgasbord dinner, you know, the inexpensive all-you-can-eat dinners. I didn't have any money to gamble (to tell you the truth I really didn't want to gamble) but they gave me a hundred bucks and said go play the machines. I won some money and they sold me this farm. You see? I understand and I'm so sorry you have to move. It's been hard for a lot of people. Please Delfina don't blame yourself for having to live with your parents or for your husband's injuries."

"I don't," Delfina said with a shrug. "My husband received a medal for his service. When he is fully recovered, we're going to buy a home through the GI Bill and will live near my parents. There are plenty of jobs in Vegas. I am proud to be an American. The President just wants us to be self-sufficient.

My family," Delfina continued looking toward Pablo, "we'll be fine. We are hardworking second-generation Latinos. We always bounce back."

"Well, good luck," Vera said as she stood up and moved toward the kitchen. "Then I don't understand why you're here if you're not taking Rama with you?"

"We just wanted to make sure Cath lived in a loving home and that he's happy," Delfina said rising to her feet and stepping toward the kitchen as if to speak to the cat. Rama's purring grew more agitated. She was annoyed her guests continued to call her cat by the name Pablo had given him. If the cat was hers then they should respect her choice in names.

Vera turned her back on them realizing with a sharp stab of regret that Pablo instead of being her favorite uncle had become a stranger. To relieve her disappointment, she spoke to Rama as if he were a person, "It's okay. You're staying here. Don't worry. I won't let them take you to a zoo. I don't think the Humane Society can do that anyway. You want to help me wash dishes?"

Delfina turned to Pablo as if to share the joke with him and when Pablo remained unimpressed, Delfina shrugged. Pablo wasn't entertained or delighted about much of anything lately Vera noticed with concern. Even his exotic cat's playful behavior couldn't get a reaction out of him. The noises from the kitchen stopped. It was a great excuse to get away from the silly woman and the penetrating stares of her old friend. The woman's martyrdom with her clearly stubborn admiration for the myth of American success and her willingness to overlook the facts made Vera furious. She shouldn't be surprised. Children were raised on the American myth that if you worked hard you would be successful. That was what public schools did – brainwashed a new generation; but because Vera lived on the lowest of the rungs of the ladder, looking up, she could see how the whole scheme was rigged.

It looked as if Pablo had given up too. She felt sorry for him.

Rama cocked his head as if were listening to their guests. Vera stopped on the threshold and repeated her question to the cat. The cat ran toward the sink as if washing dishes would save him from imminent torture. Delfina and Pablo were no torturers; maybe naïve, at least Delfina was naïve; and as far as Pablo was concerned, Vera hadn't a clue what was going on behind those brown eyes. He had always been a part of her family and he had been a good friend to Vera many times in the past. She couldn't be mad at him now. Since her Nonnie and mother's deaths he must have been very lonely. The times were different now. He had probably been forced to settle down. It wasn't as easy to travel any more. She hoped he would be happy with his niece and her family but the way Delfina commandeered the conversation made her wonder if this strong-minded woman was pulling the strings and poor Pablo had to follow or be abandoned on the wayside.

Just thinking about the bright-future she might have had in Oregon made Vera sad. She had thought she had reconciled herself to her past misfortune; but, after talking to Delfina and trying to make her understand what had happened, she was discouraged. She had brought up facts, real facts. All someone had to do was call a number and find out what congressional bills had been passed. Although, the way they were worded made them incomprehensible to the average English speaker while nobody seemed to want to make the effort to interpret them to lay people.

Here she was now, thanks to luck and the generosity of the Andersons, the owner of a farm house and ten acres of land. And she did indeed have the Andersons to thank for her good fortune. If Carl Anderson hadn't handed her a hundred bucks that night and said go play one of the machines, she would still be living and working in Vega today. If she had left the casino instead of sitting down to play the machine, she would never have won eighty-five thousand dollars or bought the Anderson Farm or met the Treloar family. And if she hadn't won the money, she might still be working in housekeeping pulling semen stained sheets off beds in a smoke-filled Vegas motel. She shuttered at the memory of spending her free time in that nasty old trailer that smelled of cabbage.

Some might say her luck could have gone in a different direction. And they were right. She used to watch those poor schmucks dumping coin after coin in the machines and getting nothing for their troubles. It was an addiction. And that was why she avoided the machines and the tables. But she also believed in the goodness of certain people. The Andersons were good people. They're goodwill toward her created just the right situation for her to win. Even if she hadn't won, she would still be grateful for their little kindnesses.

Her present situation luckily banished her unhappy memories and with a genuine smile; she gazed in adoration at Rama. He was a beauty with his incredible blue eyes and those devil ears. Cats and their foolish notions, she thought fondly. The suds were nearly gone. Vera turned on the water tap while Rama jumped onto the counter and leaned over the sink. Delfina and Pablo entered the kitchen and stood by the table staring transfixed as the cat fished with his paw in the warm water scooping up suds and tossing them at Vera.

Pablo grinned and stepped closer raising his hand to pet the cat. Rama permitted the old man who had once been his owner (perhaps his creator?) to stroke his soft fur. In a voice so low Vera could barely hear him, he whispered, "Her husband Santiago is suffering in his mind. He has nightmares. He tried to hurt himself."

Delfina who couldn't possibly have heard Pablo, yet she was frowning as she said, "He doesn't seem like the same cat. He seems different."

Vera turned to face the woman and hoped she presented an offhand expression. She shrugged casually and said, "Maybe. I wouldn't know." What was the matter with this woman – did she think Vera was abusing the cat? Delfina doesn't want the cat to go home with her; and Vera suspected she doesn't want Vera to have him either.

Now that they were in the room, she felt duty bound to offer them refreshments. She asked her guests to sit down wondering if Pablo would refuse. He hadn't looked at her openly with his old affection since sitting down on her sofa in the living room. It made her uncomfortable as if she were entertaining two hostile strangers. Delfina and Pablo found seats at the kitchen table and accepted Vera's offer of a cup of coffee with uncomfortable smiles. Now that a decision had been made to accept her offer of refreshment, she could tell, they wanted to be gone.

Rama with beaming face jumped onto the table and sniffed at the coffee cake. Vera cut him a piece and set the plate on the cushioned window seat. Some people might be offended by the sight of a pet eating from a plate near the table. She didn't care. They had found each other and now that Rama was with her, she accepted him as part of her family. And for some odd reason, she felt safer with him in the house. His incredible hearing had warned her once of danger and she expected it would again.

Vera offered Delfina and Pablo a slice of coffee cake. Vera watched the old man and his niece as they sipped their coffee and ate the cake wondering how much Pablo had told his niece about his former life. Rama ignored Pablo. Vera found this whole visit surreal, so much had been left unsaid. Vera had heard from others that cats were more about places than people; although cats could be affectionate when it suited them. With all her senses alert, wondering if she had becoming paranoid after the Foss brothers' experience, Vera spoke only of mundane things, pretending not to care that the person she use to call uncle in the days before Arthur Vlasky had become so cold and impersonal; in fact, he was behaving more like a gadjo. Had she changed so much?

Pablo spoke to his niece in Spanish. Delfina turned toward Vera, "My uncle wishes to use your bathroom. May he?"

Vera felt offended that she would dare translate Pablo's words. Delfina realized her mistake and lifted her hand to her mouth, "I'm so sorry. I forgot you understand Spanish."

Vera shrugged and admitted, "Its okay. I used to remember more but now," and gestured in the general direction of the bathroom telling Pablo, "Es al final del pasillo." Pablo jumped up from his seat bobbing his head and smiling as if she had offered him her life's savings. Such obsequious behavior depressed Vera. Life had either destroyed Pablo's natural self-respect, or he was putting on an act for Delfina's benefit.

The two women sat across from each other and ate coffee cake and smiled politely at each other. Rama, unlike the women, supremely at ease, finished his coffee cake in three bites and started washing his plate. Delfina had barely swallowed her last piece when Rama jumped onto the table and sauntered over to her. She backed away from her plate with her fork in her hand as if she were prepared to stab him if he came any closer and looked at the cat nervously. It had been Vera's impression based on the things Delfina had said that Rama had been a part of the Rodriquez household. Rama swiped at Delfina's plate and sent the plate flying off the table and crashing to the floor.

Vera stopped herself from laughing out loud. Delfina looked frightened. Evidently a sense of humor must run only on one side of the family tree. When Pablo returned to the kitchen, Vera glanced at the clock on the wall and realized he'd been gone nearly fifteen minutes. From the distasteful expression on his face, a look reminiscent of someone who had swallowed a bug, she wondered if he had found her bathroom dirty. After living in cheap hotels and smelly trailers most of her life, she had suddenly become house proud. Anyone could eat off her floor.

He had no right to judge her.

Why was he acting so weird? Her bathroom wasn't the problem.

He found something else distasteful. What? Maybe he'd received a message on his pager? She glanced at the little black device attached to his belt. Since when did Pablo have a pager?

Noticing her uncle for the first time, Delfina stood up. Pablo paused on the threshold and said, "You've been so kind, and I can tell that Cath is safe. We don't want to bother you any further. We have a long drive ahead of us. Thank you for accepting him into your home, Veratina. I am indebted to you."

"I know," she said noting the twinge of surprise and displeasure that crossed Pablo's weathered face. If he thought calling her by her Romani name would soften her up and make her forgive him for his rude behavior, he was wrong. Vera led them to the door thinking all the while—*I must be kind. I must be kind. Pablo took on my burden years ago and now I must follow through and give Rama a second chance.*

When Rama sensed the visitors were leaving for good, he approached the front part of the house for the first time and stood at the window looking out while Vera waited on the porch and politely waved farewell. He and Vera watched until Pablo and Delfina disappeared from view. Some instinct told her she would never see Pablo again. Vera doubted very much that their visit had been on the cat's behalf. There was something else at work here. But what? Their visit must have something to do with the Roma. Was the Roma sending her a message? Was the message not to be so complacent, not to forget them?

Nonnie and her mother Analetta were dead. It couldn't be them. She knew Uncle Frank had passed away a few years back. The only one left. Yes, the message must be from Aunt Vista.

Mrs. Rodriquez wore a well-cut silk pantsuit and matching purse which Vera recognized as handcrafted. Pablo's family had been excellent tailors and Vera guessed either Delfina or someone in her immediate family had made the pantsuit for her. The purse was a cheap plastic knock-off of one of Gucci's designs. Delfina was ambitious. Good for her. Cynically, Vera didn't think she had a gnat's chance in hell here in America, especially during these rough economic times. It would take decades or more for attitudes to change in America.

Pablo had been an old-fashioned traveler, the real thing. Yet Rama had ignored him the entire time he was in Vera's house. It seemed odd that a former pet would ignore the man who raised him from a kitten. Had Rama been a kitten or a cub? Maybe illegally importing exotic animals and interbreeding them had become Pablo's new career? No. She refused to believe the man she had known most of her life, a man who had helped her replace a nest of baby birds in a tree and rescued orphaned turtles in Florida would buy and sell endangered animals.

Vera wondered unhappily if these two had anything to do with the Foss brothers. The idea seemed preposterous, especially the idea of the gentle Pablo having anything to do with drugs and gangs. Delfina didn't seem like the type to run around with monsters like the Foss brothers either. For someone so young, she seemed extremely conservative and conscientious and altogether too ambitious to risk prison for herself or her husband.

Once inside the house, Vera and Rama returned to the kitchen. Vera cleared the table and put away the dishes. Once the dishes were done; she felt restless. As she walked down the hall to put her clean towels in the hall closet, she smelled incense and searched the room suddenly suspicious. Amongst the normal sounds of the house, something was not right. She strode down the hall and threw open the empty spare bedroom door. She had yet to decorate the two windows in the room with curtains. She could still smell the new paint on the walls.

A few days ago, she'd left the window which faced the backyard open a fraction to clear out the paint smell. Belatedly, she realized how foolish she'd been to have forgotten all about the window. As she'd prepared the room for painting, she'd discovered drawings in crayon at the back of the closet. It wasn't a very big room. Back in the 1940s families didn't spend much time in bedrooms the way they do today. The room was big enough for a twin bed, a small dresser, and maybe a bookshelf or toy box. Someday she would furnish the room properly. She couldn't afford to do so now. All her winnings had gone to the purchase of the Anderson Farm. She still owed ten thousand dollars and had a mortgage to pay through a title company.

The open window generated alarm bells in her head. Then she remembered, she had closed and locked the window in the early morning hours after painting the room because a nest of baby birds had been making such a racket. The smell of incense was stronger in this room than the paint smell. She knew she hadn't lit an incense stick in this room. Why would Pablo come in here and bless this room? If he had been blessing the house, he would have gone through all the rooms. For some reason she couldn't quite articulate, she closed the bedroom door and walked over to the tiny closet.

The closet was dark, but the musky smell alerted her senses to an intruder and sent her pulse racing. "Oh no, you old coot, you better not have. Oh, sweet Angel," she said to the room at large. There was a bare light bulb on the ceiling of the closet and dangling from the bulb was a long cord; the cord was close enough for her to pull. Harry was curled up on several baby blankets and at the other end of the closet, Pablo had set a bowl of water on the floor.

Harry came toward Vera sniffing her shoes his bandit-face curious and excited. He rose up on his hind legs and had his front paws together as if in prayer. It was his signal that he was hungry. She hadn't seen him since she left home and married Arthur Vlasky. He had been an orphaned raccoon and she had been too stupid to realize she couldn't raise a raccoon as a traveler. But her mother had given in because Pablo had agreed to help Vera take care of the raccoon.

Vera should have known that Pablo had had a more clandestine reason for his visit. It had been his intention all along to dump Harry on her. *My Angel*," she thought and said aloud, "My little bandit Angel." She crossed over to the window and noticed the screen had been removed and set carefully out of sight against the back wall. While Delfina had kept Vera engaged Pablo pretended to use Vera's bathroom so he could sneak Harry into her house.

Harry's chicken wire cage was on the back porch. The cage fit through the door and surprisingly down the narrow hallway and into the spare bedroom. It was ironic to think that she'd gone to all the trouble of painting the spare bedroom and sanding and staining the hardwood floor just for an eleven-year-old raccoon. It was clear that Pablo Rodriquez had dumped both of his charges off on her.

But why would he do such a thing, why not just ask her to take them? Did he think because she had become a property owner, she was no longer a traveler? Or could his reasons have to do with his age, that he could no longer take care of them alone? It made sense. He was getting old. His niece was willing to take him to Vegas so that he could spend the rest of his remaining days with his brother and his brother's family. There was no diabolical plan to drive her crazy. Again, she was imagining devils where there were none.

For the rest of the morning, the house was chaos as Rama and Harry got to know each other. Rama stayed on the kitchen counters or the top of the refrigerator for most of the day while Harry explored the house room by room. Good times, Vera thought, remembering how she used to follow baby Harry around the trailer making sure that when she saw the clever fellow doing something she valued to offer him a treat as reinforcement. Evidently, Pablo had continued the tradition. Then the significance of the name Pablo had given the cat occurred to her. While married to Vlasky, when Pablo would stop by to see her (probably at the behest of Vera's mother) Arthur would insist Pablo go around to the back door and refuse to allow him to sleep in the house. In Celtic legends Cath fought Arthur. Unfortunately, Arthur won out in the end.

Not in my lifetime, Vera thought, and realized Pablo had sent her a message.

—

Andrew received a call from George Metcalf. After he listened to George grousing about deadbeats, drug addicts, and drunks for twenty minutes, Andrew managed a few times, in-between George's pauses, to make grunting sounds which he hoped sounded sympathetic, yet, his mind was preoccupied with his current project. Once George had gotten tired of moaning and said his goodbyes, Andrew returned to his workshop. He should have yanked the phone out of the jack and locked all the windows and doors and stuck a sign on the front lawn—Do Not Disturb.

During George's tirade he'd mentioned picking up two men walking on US 95. They claimed to be hitchhiking to Nevada and looked as if they'd slept out in the desert. One guy complained of frost bite. George offered to give them a lift to the clinic in Marsing, but they refused. Then George said, "I checked their identifications and discovered they're wanted in Nevada and Utah. I've got a feeling they've got something to do with the stolen Lincoln we found the other day."

Andrew thought about the two men and the Lincoln. He thought about Vera and all the strange coincidences going on lately: Woody, Kat, and the body of Kat's mother. He was afraid the connections would alienate her further from the town. He shook his head, not wanting to go there. The last few days had been a nightmare of wondering and second guessing and wishing. Now he looked at the soaring wing before him, the pieces of scrap metal he'd managed to put together and realized it was turning into something exceptional.

He ran his hand down the cold steel careful to avoid the sharp edges. She's like this wing, cold and beautiful and deadly. Now something inside clicked into place and hope returned. His phone rang again. He gave up and climbed the stairs to his bedroom loft to pick up the phone by his bed. He heard Maggie's voice say, "Uncle Andrew. Vera says she still likes you."

"I told you not to bother her. It's none of your business Maggie," Andrew said.

"But I think she regrets what she did. Guess what?"

"What?" Andrew asked keeping the impatience out of his voice.

"I saw two men up on the hill above Vera's house today. They looked scary. They threatened to kill Vera and me and Daniel. They acted like they were on drugs or something. They were saying crazy stuff. Daniel scared them away. Dad wants to know if you're coming over for supper tonight."

Andrew paused to assimilate all the information his great-niece had given him without getting upset. He stared down at his work, "Not tonight Mouse. I've got to go down to the prison and talk to George."

Maggie's good-bye rang with more cheer than he'd heard in a long time. He realized that he hadn't called her Mouse since the Halloween party.

—

Two more days had passed since Vera had released the Foss brothers. Vera while sitting in her rocking chair in the quiet of her house heard the car approach. She recognized the car and the driver. Before he had a chance to knock, she had the door open. He stood on her porch with an unreadable expression, "I thought you'd want to know that George picked up a couple of guys on US 95 heading for Winnemucca. We've managed to connect them with an old Lincoln Continental we found a few days prior. The Lincoln was reported stolen. Anyway, remember when we found the van, I mean when Maggie and Jeremy discovered it?"

Vera nodded her head unable to speak knowing what was coming.

"Well, there was a body inside, what was left of a body. There was no identification but since it was male, I asked the investigators to check with Woody Kirk's family," Andrew said and paused for her reaction.

When there was one, he frowned and continued, "Anyway, the body was identified as Woody Kirk's and forensics tells us he was shot in the back of the head. There was evidence in the van linking Woody to the Foss brothers, those men I told you about, the ones George stopped on the highway. Mark Foss has been talking and he's been saying some pretty weird stuff. George asked me to come over and talk to you about it. May I come in?"

"Hold on. I've got two new guests. I have to do some wrangling and I'll be right back. I'll explain later," she said as she closed the door in his surprised face and ran to find Harry first. She found him going through her garbage can. Grabbing a banana from the counter she peeled one side and let him sniff the fruit then enticed him with the banana and led him down the hall to the spare bedroom. Once he was inside, she dropped the banana on the floor and scooted out. But Rama was more elusive, and she finally had to give up finding him. She returned to the front door and opened it.

Andrew jumped up from the porch step and paused to scrutinize her face then walked cautiously into her house as if he thought she might have an armed felon just waiting to pounce on him. His hand on his gun holster made her nervous. What if Harry found a way out of the spare bedroom would Andrew shoot him?

Vera closed the front door behind her and followed him into the dark kitchen. He flipped on the overhead light as if he still belonged here, out of habit she supposed. She sat at the kitchen table facing him and waited, "Foss says that his brother Marion Sim came to your house to talk to you about Woody. They said you ordered them to kill Woody."

Andrew leaned forward and held her hand, "Vera. Are they just messing with us or is it true?"

Vera pulled away from him and Andrew let go, "If you check with the Portland Police you'll find I reported having been beaten up and nearly killed by a man. It happened on August 2nd, 1970. The ambulance took me to Good Samaritan Hospital. I told the police that I didn't know the names of the men that came into my apartment with guns and knives. The men demanded to know where Woody Kirk was. Woody Kirk, I learned later had been dealing drugs in my apartment. I worked all day and he did his business in my home while I was at work.

I was a fool back then, a complete idiot to have trusted that skuzzy creep. And I paid for my trust just like I paid for my trust in Arthur Vlasky. When the Foss brothers finally figured out I didn't know where Woody Kirk had gone, they left my apartment. The police artist made a sketch of the man that did this to my face. Do you really think I have the power and influence to persuade these men to kill Woody?"

The silence stretched on for several minutes. She waited, expecting him to react like everyone else had done in her life—with disgust. Of course, a Roma finds its own kind, thieves, and junkies. That was what people thought about her family and by extension herself. No matter how far she ran away from the truth, how much she tried to pretend she was different, people discovered her past and were disgusted.

For years now, she'd been running away. She was tired of pretending to be something different. She should be proud of her heritage. Her mother and her aunt and her uncle and all her cousins were proud of being Roma. They were proud of being survivors, when so many had died in the pogroms and in concentration camps. She was proud of her heritage. She didn't know what she would do if Andrew looked at her the way the gadjos used to look at her and her family.

"Why do you think I asked to come over here to talk to you?" Andrew leaned back in his chair and appeared to be disappointed in her. "I knew something wasn't right. George even laughed when he heard the news. It's ludicrous."

"Then why are you so upset?"

"Damn right I'm upset. These creeps are making trouble for you or trying to make trouble. They did come over to the house, didn't they? What did they want?"

Vera wondered if Daniel had said something or if Maggie had been unable to keep her secret. But another thought surfaced a pleasanter thought than betrayals. Someone might have seen the Foss brothers lurking around her house.

Vera chose to tell Andrew the truth, "They broke into my house and ate my food and made a mess. Then Daniel showed up and when he saw what they were doing, he got mad and knocked them out. We tied them up and took them to the hill by the cattle guard and left them in one of the caves. It was a mistake. I told Daniel it was a mistake. He must have been thinking about it because he came over the next day and told me he'd moved them.

Daniel dumped them in the gully near where the body of Kat's mother was found. Just yesterday we went back, and I untied them and let them go."

Vera stood up and pulled off her shirt. The bruises on her back and shoulder and the side of her jaw were turning yellow. Odd that Andrew hadn't noticed the bruises on her neck and jaw.

"Did they?"

"No!"

Andrew stood up, "May I use your phone?"

"Be my guest," Vera said wondering how Rama would react to Andrew's presence. "I would appreciate if we could do all this in the morning."

"Best not to wait," Andrew told her his face inscrutable.

Then something inside Vera compelled her to check on Kat and she ran to the phone to call Sara Matthews. When the director of the school answered, and Vera learned that Kat had been found trying to slip through the gate of the Egg earlier in the day; Vera interrupted her, "Was there anyone waiting for her on the other side of the gate? Was there a young woman, a Latina with an older man? They were driving a black pickup truck?

"Not that I know of," Sarah said sounding surprised. "No one has come by for Kat. She just tried to slip out the gate on her own. Although there was a phone call from a woman who claimed she was Kat's legal guardian. She never showed up though."

"Did she call herself Ada Aleshire?" Vera asked hoping she was wrong.

"No, I don't think so. I'll check with my secretary to be sure. Why is that name familiar to me?" Sara asked her.

Vera stared at the numbers on her rotary phone, big numbers that had been the Anderson couples handicap. They'd both been blind as bats; and now Vera knew what that metaphor meant to her. She had been blind all along. She'd assumed Daniel had killed Ada and threw her in the cave, perhaps shoving her down the fissure back in the far corner. All along his complaints about the woman haunting his treasures had given her a measure of comfort because if Ada was dead then Vera was safe. Whatever the circumstances, those bones she'd seen in the cave had been there a long time, perhaps thousands of years. They might be an archeologist's career changing discovery, but Daniel's intuition told him something bad still contaminated the hill. And now she thought she knew who had generated Daniel's foreboding.

"Vera, are you still there?"

"What Sarah?" Vera said. "Sorry?"

"Yes. Oh wait. The newspapers, there was a story about a person of interest an Ada Aleshire."

"Ada Aleshire is my sister. It's a long story. Someday I'll tell you all about her, but not now. Please call George Metcalf. He's at the Mintlaw Police Station or he was earlier and tell him she's claiming to be Kat Fletcher's next of kin. Carolina Fletcher's parents died in an auto accident, but I know there are other relatives better able to raise Kat than her. Ada Aleshire is bad-news, Sara. Believe me."

When she dropped the phone back in its cradle and turned to face the room, she saw Andrew's face. He looked furious. Male temper tantrums were nothing new to her. When he continued to stand by the door and stare off into space, it gradually dawned upon her that he wasn't going to fly into a rage and rush her or hit her or scream at her. The fury left his face. She recognized disappointment and his disappointment hurt much more than a slap.

"You knew all along about Kat and her family and you said nothing to me?" he asked her.

"No," she said and took a few steps toward him. "Hold on. I've never met Kat. I've never met Carolina Fletcher. I'd only heard about her second-hand from my sister Ada. Well, to tell you the truth, Ada's my half-sister. We share a mother, but Ada has always identified with her father's family.

She hates my mother's family. She refuses to believe she's Roma too. We grew apart over the years. She hated our life. She hated moving from town to town and being treated like a mongrel. The first time she ran away she was only eight or nine. It was when we were in Florida for the winter. She found her father's brother and tried to live with them. They wouldn't take her. You see her father was in jail. When her father got out of jail, he remarried and had a new family. It nearly killed her.

When she was sixteen, she ran away again, and he took her in for a few months. But she was treated like an outsider. So, when Mom would go get her and return her to us, she would take out her grief and pain on me. She's always been strong and tough and just like her father completely devoid of empathy. I learned a long time ago to be careful around her, that she was dangerous. Even my mother sometimes feared her cold rages. She's very smart and if she thinks you've done her wrong, she'll wait for the right moment and then hurt you good. The last time she took her revenge on me, I nearly died. Not very sisterly is it?

I left home shortly after, not just because of her, but because I wanted to live a normal life. I wanted to settle down and own a home of my own. Unfortunately, I thought marrying Arthur Vlasky would give me that permanency. It didn't. My marriage was the biggest mistake of my life. And Ada and I haven't had anything to do with each other for twenty years. I had no idea Kat was related to Ada. Not when I found her in my backyard.

Maybe Ada has known all along where I live. Woody might have told her. They run with the same type of people. Sim Foss was looking for something Woody stole and Sim made sure to let me know Woody and Ada had been close."

"Does George know about your relationship with Carolina Fletcher?" Andrew asked still standing by the front door.

"I didn't have a relationship with Carolina," Vera reminded him again in a voice she hoped did not quiver. "I'd never met Carolina or Kat until recently. They are Ada's people not mine. Somehow George knew about Woody's connection with Ada though. I suppose you were the one who found that out?"

"I went down to Winnemucca to learn more about Ada Aleshire. The neighbor said she'd seen a man with snakeskin cowboy boots waiting on Aleshire's stoop, your sister's stoop. I figured it must have been Woody," Andrew said as he opened the door. "I wished you'd been honest with me from the beginning. You threw me out because you were ashamed of your past. I get that. But I would have appreciated the truth." With those final words still ringing in her head, he walked out the door and shut it softly behind him.

How could she possibly have told him the truth? He would never have believed her. He would have thought she was nuts. But the signs had been there. The child finds her, or someone dumps the child on her doorstep to implicate her or to send her a warning. Then Carolina Fletcher's body is discovered. And somehow Woody leads the Foss brothers to Vera. It must have been Aunt Vista who told Woody where to find her and he, the skuzzy turd, led the Foss brothers to her. Now Woody is dead, and the Foss brothers are in jail.

Is it some omniscient god's design or just stupid bad luck for them all? And it's not over.

Rama appears out of nowhere which really isn't coincidental since she suspects Pablo dropped off his prized position to the one person he trusted. He trusted her not to mistreat his pet and worried careless children or an overbearing niece might hurt or sell Rama. And then to make sure she gets the message, he appears at her door leaving a gift from the past, as if to say: don't forget me and don't forget where you come from.

And still the hilltop is haunted. The ugliness and fear are not over. Daniel is frightened. He senses something twisted and dangerous still haunting the place. Is it the ghost of Ada Aleshire? Did Vera have something to do with her sister's death? She can't remember. She's sick at the thought that she might have done something that night. At first, she suspected Daniel of carrying Kat down to her house then she began to wonder, after she realized Ada had been nearby, that perhaps her half-sister had set Kat down on the swings to implicate Vera in her crimes.

There was another possibility, the possibility Vera had been sleepwalking again and found the little girl, maybe heard her crying, and carried her down to the house and left her on the porch. If she had been up on the hillside when Daniel was there getting in the way of the litterer's attempts to dispose of her problems could Vera have been there too? No. Not possible. A wave of relief cascaded through her body making her dizzy. She would have had evidence of her trek up the hill. She remembered getting out of bed and running to the window in her bare feet to look out at her swing set. If she'd climbed the Access or walked along the field and up the side of the hill, her feet would have been covered in sand, cheatgrass and so much worse. And, she would have had scratches all over her bare legs.

So maybe Daniel or Ada carried Kat down to her house? It was easy enough to ask Daniel. The thought of her half-sister continuing to cause misery for her and others made her sick inside. Once, a long time ago, when they'd been very young, she and Ada had been close. At the time, they'd had only each other, until the little ones were born. She can't forget that. All the crap that happened to them over the years might have been prevented if her mother hadn't been so obvious about who she loved the most. But her mother isn't to blame for what's going on today.

At some point her children should have grown up and gotten over their miserable unnatural wretched pasts. Other people did. Other people matured and moved on reconciling their past and finding something else to occupy their thoughts. Not her family though. They enjoyed reveling in their misery and piling grudge upon grudge until there was no room for anything else, other than revenge.

Maybe it was fate? Maybe she was destined to be the scapegoat and bear the burden of her family's legacy?

Screw it. Screw fate too.

It dawned on Vera that she hadn't heard Andrew's car start up. Suddenly nervous, she opened the front door and peeked outside. Andrew was sitting on the top step of her porch staring at his father's farmhouse across the road. Vera closed the door, so that Rama wouldn't escape and sat down next to him. The silence made her uncomfortable.

"You knew I was in AA," she told him. "And as a recovering alcoholic, I come with a past. It's not a pretty one. I did some really stupid shit back in the day. Woody and the Foss brothers were a part of that stupidity. So, when Woody showed up, I had a feeling the Foss brothers would be along soon, and I was frightened for you. I didn't want you to get hurt. I didn't want the misery they would bring with them to rub off on you."

"What's your real name?" Andrew asked, "Your Roma name?"

"Vertina Vera Lee Caumlo," she answered feeling the embarrassment burning her cheeks.

"Caumlo?"

"It means handsome one or beautiful one."

For the rest of the time, they sat in silence and waited.

An hour later, George Metcalf and a female police officer from Mintlaw arrived at her door. George and the woman asked her questions. Vera climbed into the back of George's patrol vehicle. From the back seat she watched Andrew as he talked to the deputy. Andrew stood on her porch until the patrol vehicle took her away.

After spending most of the wee hours of the night at the police station, Officer Metcalf dropped Vera off at her front door. Vera had beaten the school bus home. Andrew opened the door. Maggie was in the kitchen feeding Rama. Rama appeared delighted with his new babysitter. Vera found Harry in the back bedroom in his cage. Maggie had found his ball stuffed with live crickets. Maggie followed her to the bedroom and peeked inside, "Uncle Andrew found the ball. I couldn't bring myself to touch it. I know raccoons need to eat too but I'm just not ready to watch him eat live crickets."

Once Maggie headed for the school bus, Vera returned to the kitchen. Andrew washed the dirty dishes while Vera dried them and put them away. Rama talked to them as they worked. Andrew stared at the cat with a puzzled frown. Vera was sure Andrew would eventually get used to the wild cat's eccentric ways. Rama seemed to have accepted Andrew. It had been grueling sitting in the police station for hours and hours forced to reveal every nasty part of her pathetic past to people who had thought of her as just a normal person, a normal white Anglo/Saxon female person, in the American vernacular—a WASP.

Now that she was safely home, Vera wanted so much to sleep, too tired to think straight, too tired, especially, to deal with Andrew's penetrating questions.

Andrew wiped his hands on a dishtowel and turned to face her.

"I guess I'd better be going," he said.

Vera interrupted him before he could say anything else, "I am grateful that you stayed here to watch my cat and Harry of course. That wasn't necessary."

"Actually, Maggie had to come rescue me. She ended up taking Rama home with her. I locked up the place and tried to get into the interrogation room to talk to Metcalf. Funny about your cat though, he didn't seem to care for me. In fact, he went completely ballistic until I got Maggie back here. I'm sorry about the smell. He must have sprayed every piece of furniture in your house."

"Don't worry. He's due to be neutered any day now. Thank you again."

"That's what friends are for Vera. We're still friends?"

They looked at each other. Vera thought she recognized hope in his expression. She didn't know what to say. She nodded and said, "Of course we're friends. We're more than friends. Right now, we're going through a difficult, no, a better word would be horrendous time. Maybe this will be the making of us?" She finished and tried to laugh but had little energy left. Her voice was hoarse from talking all night to the detectives and the sound that came out of her throat was more of a groan.

After Andrew left, Vera lay down on the couch. Rama tried to sit on her feet, "No. Let me sleep." Rama began to sing. Vera stuck her headphones on and sat in the cushioned rocking chair. She closed her eyes and tried to sleep through Turlough O'Carolan's Concerto with Irish harp. The doorbell rang. Vera stumbled toward the door. Maggie stood on the porch.

"It's a half day today. Uncle Andrew said you'd been up all night. I could watch Rama for you," Maggie offered. Vera accepted her offer and stumbled down the hall to her bedroom. She didn't bother to pull the coverlet to the foot of the bed. She listened as Maggie played with the cat. Vera called to Maggie. Maggie stood in the hallway, "You don't have to stay Maggie. Rama is a cat. He can manage fine. Go call one of your friends and have some fun."

"Don't worry, Vera. Get some sleep," Maggie said and turned when Rama began to rub himself against her leg to get her attention. Rama was in ecstasy, his large sapphire eyes seemed to be brighter than usual. Vera wondered which one of them had been sent to purgatory: him or her. Today, she suspected she was the victim of Kali, the dark mother's retribution.

Chapter Twenty

T he doorbell rang. Vera jumped. Were the police coming to take her to prison? What had the Foss brothers told them? She glanced at the clock and realized she'd slept the entire day and night. It was eight o'clock the next morning. Maggie must have locked up the house after spending most of the afternoon with Rama. Knowing Maggie's thoroughness, she would have made sure the animals had plenty of food and water.

As Vera passed the hall, she glanced at the empty guestroom and saw Rama dozing on the floor in a patch of sunlight. Vera wasn't sure he could sleep through the noise a bunch of cops might make in the act of arresting her for kidnapping. Vera opened the door to a strange woman, an extremely large woman with bleached blonde hair cut short near her ears, so short she might have been mistaken for a man from the back. The woman wore a neon orange cotton blouse with short rippled sleeves and a pair of tight fitting beige Capri pants. Vera noticed that she wore sandals and that someone had painted her toenails to match her fingernails, a particularly ghastly shade of purple.

Vera checked the weather again and was reassured to see that it was still winter. All that extra padding must be keeping her warm. Inside the minivan she could see people: two teenage boys sitting on the bench seats behind the driver. They appeared to be smaller clones of the woman. And sitting in the front passenger seat was a scrawny man wearing a cowboy hat and dark glasses. He took off the dark glasses and Vera had the dubious pleasure of seeing his face. His skin reminded her of a dried raisin, a sunburned raisin. Beneath a jutting nose, he had small lips and a poor excuse for a chin.

As he tried to light his cigarette, he sucked on the tip as if it had been a nipple on a baby bottle. For a second, she envied him. She'd quit smoking a year ago. Whenever she passed someone smoking and sniffed the air, her body demanded she run to the store and buy a carton. She shuddered at the sight of his small dark eyes peering at her beneath sparse blonde brows. The urge to have a cigarette vanished.

In less than thirty seconds, Vera took in the sights and sounds and smells. While Vera had been openly assessing the woman and her companions, the woman had been digging through her purse. She pulled out a photograph and in a high-pitched voice, the apparition said, "You must be Miss Lee. I'm Cheri Aleshire and I'm here to collect my great niece. The papers say she's been with you seeings as how this is the place where she was found."

"Your great niece," Vera asked unprepared for that bombshell. Vera knew she must be lying. With every vein in her body surging with blood and her heart pounding through her rib cage, Vera stepped out onto the porch and shut the front door. Trying to keep calm and assess the situation logically, Vera waited. The large woman stepped closer in an attempt to intimidate her.

Vera didn't budge. They eyed each other warily. Aleshire's eyes fell first. This made Vera happy especially because the woman and her family reminded Vera of feral dogs. The children had the same mad look in their eyes, as if they were prepared to surround her and bring her down. She refused to be intimidated This was her home and her property and they had no right to demand anything of her.

"Ms. Matthews the director of the Eagle Gateway School and Mrs. Archer the social worker assigned to Kat Fletcher have yet to contact me about any family members. Until they do, Kat stays with me. You understand as her temporary guardian, I need documentation that proves Kat has been relinquished into your custody," Vera managed to say hoping the woman believed her lie.

She didn't want this creature anywhere near Kat. Vera sensed a commotion in the van and turned in time to see the raisin-skinned cowboy get out of the minivan and walk toward her porch. He must have thought his wife needed added muscle. Vera swallowed a giggle. The man was about Vera's height, five feet two inches tall, maybe an inch taller with no noticeable muscles.

Cheri Aleshire turned toward the man, "I can't get my baby, Emmett. You hear this woman. She says I can't get my baby until she gets a paper that says I have custody. Mz. Archer said nothing about no papers. What am I gonna do?"

"Don't you worry Cheri. I'll handle this woman. She's got no call to keep us from our blood relation. You hear me woman. We got every right to take what's ours," Emmett said as he strode up the stairs. He reminded her of a bandy rooster, a rather dried up undernourished bandy rooster with little to crow about.

A sense of pity overwhelmed her for a moment, pity for his terrible need to be strong for this hideous female. The woman

K McVere

frightened Vera as much as she repulsed her. There was a ruthless streak in Cheri Aleshire. She could think of several unsavory reasons why Cheri Aleshire might want Kat Fletcher in her home: for the money they would get as foster parents or because the Aleshire family feared their blood relations might be raised as Roma.

"When someone can prove to me that you are a blood relation and the courts have given you custody, then and only then, will I give Kat to you. Until then, get off my property before I call the police," Vera finished and turned and stepped into her house. The pathetic rooster stood irresolute beside his woman. Vera locked the door and ran to the kitchen to lock the back door for good measure. Rama lay on the kitchen table drawing circles with his paws.

—

Andrew had been at the Treloar Farm standing by his car when he saw a red Dodge Caravan pull onto Vera's drive. He and Kit had been talking for the last twenty minutes about nothing in particular. He'd promised to come by later for dinner. Yet Andrew didn't feel much like company. He was once again a new man. There was hope for him and Vera. She hadn't exactly given permission for him to move back into the Rock Wren House, but she had said enough to give him hope they had a future together.

A man shouting and banging on Vera's front door caught his attention. He saw a skinny guy wearing a cowboy hat standing on her porch pounding on the front door then move to the bay window. He could hear the man from clear down the valley, "You got no right lady. She's our blood. You bring her out here right now."

Andrew marched up Vera's drive. A large woman in tight fitting Capri pants tried to warn the skinny guy Andrew was heading their way. The cowboy was too worked up to pay attention to her tugs on his arm. Andrew grabbed his bony shoulder and swung him around.

"What do you think you're doing, Mister?" Andrew said.

The blood drained from the cowboy's face. His brown parchment skin turned yellow, "She's got our niece and we got the right to take her home."

"What niece?"

"Katherine Fletcher is my great niece. I'm Emmett Aleshire. This is my wife Cheri. My daughter Ada Aleshire is Carolina Fletcher's cousin. We haven't heard from Ada nor Carolina and we was worried, then a friend said our great niece was found by some folks in Idaho. So, we drove up here from Escondido to see for ourselves. We was told by the newspaper that we could come get our blood relation and take her home. That woman inside there refuses to bring Kat out. She's kidnapped Kat. We're going to call the police, if she don't bring our niece outside pronto."

"Well it looks as if the police are on their way," Andrew said hearing the wail of the police siren in the distance. "I guess Miss Lee had the same idea."

The scrawny man stood firm rather than bolting away in guilty fear. Andrew figured these people must have a legitimate connection with Kat because no one in their right mind would try to kidnap a child with witnesses' present. Unless of course the man was an idiot and didn't know he was headed for trouble. Aleshire looked to be somewhere between an idiot and a concerned family member, well, more self-righteous and perplexed than concerned.

"I just don't get it. Kat is retarded. What's this woman want with a retarded kid huh? Only her blood relations can love her enough to forgive her being retarded. So, what's this woman's problem huh?"

Andrew and the Aleshire family were surprised when the patrol vehicles chose to turn into the Eagle Gateway facility. Vera's door opened. She stepped out onto the porch and stood next to Andrew looking at the police cruiser entering the school grounds.

"She's gone," Vera said to Andrew in a shocked voice. "Sarah must have called the police when she was found missing."

Andrew knew exactly who Vera meant when she said, "She's gone."

"What's she talking about?" Emmett Aleshire demanded pointing his finger at Vera as if accusing her of abducting the child.

"I'll let you know what's going on when I find out. Now step down off the porch Mr. Aleshire," Andrew pulled out his badge from his coat pocket. "This is private property and you are trespassing."

The Aleshires left but not before broadcasting to the entire farming community and probably the residents of Mintlaw several miles away how they felt about being pushed around by snooty cops.

—

Several fruitless hours later, after interviewing the tearful secretary at the boarding school and helping the Homedale Police search the town and the hilltop, Andrew returned to Vera's house. The door was open. Andrew knocked and stepped inside. He saw Mrs. Archer the social worker standing up from the couch just as he entered the hallway. He ignored the woman and found Vera in the kitchen standing by the window hugging her arms to her chest.

He returned to the living room and spoke to the woman, "I didn't expect to see you here Mrs. Archer. How are you?"

"I'm fine, Mr. Treloar. I'm worried about Kat. Where could she be? I just don't understand how Miss Lee could have been so negligent as to leave her at the school."

"Kat doesn't live here. Kat lives at the Eagle Gateway Boarding School."

"Yes, I'm aware of that. But according to the school Vera and Ms. Matthews made arrangements for Kat to stay with her over the holidays. All the children will be placed in temporary homes during Christmas break anyway."

When the doorbell rang Vera crossed the room without looking at either of them and flung the door open. She stepped back and frowned at Sarah Matthews. Sarah entered, "I came to tell you that Daniel is upset and has been asking for you."

"Will you please tell Mrs. Archer that you and I did not arrange an overnight visit for Kat," Vera said.

Sarah walked into the living room and glanced at Andrew and the social worker, "What is this about?"

Mrs. Archer spoke up, "One of your staff called the police, a Mrs. Bitterroot. Kat is missing, and she said a woman came to the school claiming to be Kat's legal guardian. She had papers to prove her claim, a last will and testament, a power of attorney, and a Petition for Guardianship of Person and/or Estate. She showed the petition to Mrs. Bitterroot.

According to Mrs. Bitterroot, the document looked authentic. It had the seal of the state of Washington on it. She made a copy of the petition. It assigned the woman guardianship of Katherine Fletcher. Mrs. Bitterroot called me immediately after. The woman was called Ale something. Wait, let me get my notes," she finished in an irritated voice as she turned to grab her purse from the couch.

"That won't be necessary Mrs. Archer," Andrew said. "I know her name. It's Ada Aleshire."

Mrs. Archer turned to face him, "Yes, I believe you're right. The woman told Mrs. Bitterroot that she and Vera Lee had made plans for Kat to spend the Christmas holidays here. Otherwise, she would have insisted Kat remain at the school until I arrived. I got stuck in traffic in Boise and was delayed twenty minutes."

Sarah glanced at Vera and the look they exchanged made Mrs. Archer's stony expression dissolve, "I see. It was a trick."

"We don't know all the circumstances," Andrew said in defense of Vera. "But I suspect Ada Aleshire had been planning this for some time. She couldn't go back to her house to get a copy of the will or the petition, so she must have gone to Seattle and found the

336

lawyer who drew up the will for her cousin. Why would she want the child now? It's clear she didn't want her when she drugged and dumped her in the desert."

"You can't be sure Ada Aleshire had anything to do with the abandonment of Kat certainly not based on the testimony of Daniel," Ms. Matthews argued. "He never saw the person who was up on Hunter's Hill."

Andrew turned to face Ms. Matthews, "Well, the evidence in the van we found off the highway which is registered to her is pretty conclusive. Kat had been in the van, as well as her mother, and there is plenty of evidence Woodrow Kirk was murdered in that vehicle. We also found DNA from several other people which forensics is still trying to identify."

"When Kat is found," Mrs. Archer said in a passionate, trembling voice, "if she's ever found, she will be placed in a real home, a safer, more secure home. Your staff are obviously too inexperienced for the job of handling children, Ms. Matthews. I should have placed her with a good Christian married couple. They would have had the integrity and responsibility to take care of Kat in the proper way."

Andrew spoke without thinking. The woman's obvious prejudices against Vera made him angry, "You know nothing of the sort, Mrs. Archer. It's obvious you're afraid this mess will backfire on the Department of Social Services. It won't. Ms. Matthews is a responsible administrator and the school is well run. I suggest we concentrate on finding Kat not finding blame."

Andrew approached Vera warily not knowing what to expect. When she turned toward him he noticed the tears and looked away embarrassed for her. She brushed past him without a word. He waited until both Sarah Matthews and the social worker left the house. When he tried to speak to Vera through her closed bedroom door, there was only silence.

At his father's farm, Andrew entered the kitchen and found Rachel basting a turkey. She turned toward him, "Kit's still searching for the lost child. Boy, this is getting old, you know?"

"Yes, I know, but it isn't Vera's fault. I think her first visitors might have had something to do with Kat's disappearance. I was wondering if you noticed their vehicle, maybe if you by some stroke of good fortune jotted down their license plate number," Andrew said.

Rachel grimaced, "You're dreaming bud. I've been here in the kitchen slaving away all morning. Maybe Maggie saw something; go ask her. She's in the living room."

Maggie looked up with an expectant look when he entered the room, "I heard you asking Mom about the vehicle that was at Vera's house earlier. You remember this morning when I was down town and that lady came up to me and she spoke only Spanish. Well, I asked Mrs. Esquivel to interpret and she said those mean things about Vera. You remember?"

"Yes, but I'm only interested in the minivan. Did you see the license plate number?"

"No, I wasn't concentrating on the minivan. The other people visiting Vera were in a black truck, an old rusty truck."

"Wait, you said the woman spoke only Spanish. But that can't be right because Vera told Metcalf that she spoke to the woman for more than two hours. Does Vera know Spanish?"

"I don't know. I don't think so."

Maggie stood up and put her hands in her pockets, "What did those minivan people want with Vera?"

"They're Kat's relatives, seems that man is Kat's grandfather, Emmett Aleshire. They were fine with Kat being at the Egg but as soon as they heard Vera was taking care of Kat, they wanted Kat back," Andrew said.

Maggie smiled, "Hey that might be it. That's why the Aleshires let that guy out before they turned onto Vera's driveway."

"What guy?"

"I was sitting under the honey locust reading when I saw the minivan stop and let a guy out. The guy ran up Opal Road. I thought maybe he'd been a hitchhiker or something. Yet it was weird that he would go so close to Vera's house practically in her backyard."

Andrew jumped up and kissed Maggie's forehead, "Thanks Mouse."

Five minutes later, Andrew arrived on Vera's porch and pounded on the door. Vera threw open the door and scowled up at him.

"I know what happened to Kat. Maggie saw the Aleshires stop and let a guy out of their van before they turned onto your drive. I suspect while Ada Aleshire came to collect Kat at the school, one of the Aleshire clan hid near your house just in case you and Kat slipped out the backdoor.

I think Ada Aleshire got her father involved in this whole mess convincing him somehow that the school was abusing Kat. While they were making a ruckus here, Ada Aleshire was at the school showing her legal documents to Mrs. Bitterroot. I bet they planned to meet up half way to Oregon. It's not too late. We may be able to stop them before they get too far down the road."

Vera looked up at him stunned then made a primeval cry of anguish which shocked and moved him. There was only one thing he could do, and he did it. He put his arms around her and she clung to him. He could feel her trembling. Memories of his son's passing rose to the surface of his mind and he quickly quashed them.

She had seemed so cool and composed an icy maiden quite capable of taking care of herself. He realized now how much pressure she had been under, how much she blamed herself for Kat's disappearance. Within a few hours the Oregon Highway Patrol intercepted the minivan which had been on its way back to California. But when Metcalf relayed his news to Andrew and Andrew stood before Vera to tell her the news, Andrew wished he'd never brought up his suspicions. Fear would replace whatever hope she had had and for himself, he felt ashamed of his reckless ruminations. Sherlock Holmes, he was not.

To Andrew's surprise Vera who had been standing in the hall waiting for him to finish his conversation with the Mintlaw Police strode to the front door. She seemed remote and mildly impatient when he told her what the deputies had found, "I'm sorry. I thought for sure the Aleshires were behind Kat's disappearance. It turns out the reason the guy was on Opal Road was to relieve himself. Emmett Aleshire hasn't heard from his daughter for nearly a year. I thought maybe."

Vera interrupted him, "Go home Andrew. Just go home. I'm tired and you're tired. Let it go for now. We'll find her, no matter what, we'll find her."

Standing on her porch, he stared at her closed door unable to believe his hunch had been wrong. Where was Ada Aleshire now? She could be anywhere. On his way back to the Mintlaw Police Station he knew he had to reach Agent Butlin and find out why they wanted Ada Aleshire so badly. An ugly thought surfaced. It made him sick to think the bitch might get away with everything. The FBI probably promised her immunity; maybe, they planned to put her in a Witness Protection Program if she snitched on her drug sources. If that happened, he and Vera would never find Kat.

—

Daniel dreamed that a snake had wound itself around his body and the snake's mouth was open wide. He could see the flicking tongue and its sharp fangs. The snake closed in until he was so close, Daniel could smell his foul breath. Then the snake spoke in his stepfather's voice, "Get your ass up boy. Now! You hear me boy. Get up." Daniel opened his eyes and saw his step-father's face. The black stubble on Darrell Schmidt's jaws seemed to quiver as if afraid to be embedded in Schmidt's skin. Daniel would hate to be Darrell's beard too. He disliked being so close to him even now. His breath stank of cigarettes and beer. Daniel could smell his sweat and something else, something that reminded him of spray paint from a can.

Schmidt yanked at Daniel's arm and snorted, "Damn it idiot, are you listening to me?"

Daniel sat up and swung his legs off the cot. The cement floor was cold. Daniel knew he didn't have to go home. Mz. Matthews had said the school was his home now.

"Come on Daniel. Your mother needs you. Get dressed. Hurry up. We don't have all night."

After Daniel had dressed he opened the shed door and noticed Mz. Matthews standing nearby with her arms crossed talking to Darrell. She must have let his stepfather into the shed. He heard Darrell tell her he would return Daniel in the afternoon. But when Daniel refused to get into the strange car, Darrell rushed at him waving his arms and spitting as he spoke. Darrell reminded Daniel of a tiny terrier yapping at his feet, "Damned it Daniel, get in the fucking taxi. It's costing me a fortune. Come on. Your momma's sick. She needs you. Come on, we got to get to the hospital."

"Mr. Schmidt, I still don't understand how Mrs. Schmidt is in any condition to visit with Daniel. You said she's had an accident. Can't this wait until the morning and I'll take Daniel to the hospital?"

"No, you can't," Darrell said his face pinched so tight, Daniel thought his eyes would fall inside his skull and get lost in the dark. "Daniel is still in our custody. He's our responsibility and since Candy wants to see her son, then, I'm going to make sure she sees him, pronto."

Daniel looked back and watched Mz. Matthew's standing on the steps of the school. She got smaller and smaller and as the strange car took them further away from the school Daniel began to be afraid. Something was caught in his throat, something that nearly choked him. Darrell slapped his arm, "Stop that noise. It's disgusting. You're not a baby. Your mother needs you. Behave yourself in the hospital, you hear."

Daniel had seen two hospitals in his lifetime. He didn't recognize this one, but he did recognize the woman walking toward him. She was dressed all in white, her uniform was white, and her shoes were white. She was a nurse. She smiled at Daniel. As Daniel and Darrell entered the elevator that would take them up to a higher floor, someone shouted at his stepfather and his stepfather pressed the stop button, so the men could enter. Daniel recognized Andrew Treloar. Andrew Treloar was with a police officer. Daniel's stepfather looked nervous. Daniel waved at the police officer. The police officer smiled back.

He was surprised when Andrew Treloar and the police officer followed them down the hall toward the same door. Darrell paused and looked back at the men. The police officer stepped forward, "You remember me Mr. Schmidt?"

"Yeah, you're George Metcalf. I've seen you at Three Fingers."

"Um hum. I suppose you know why I'm here Mr. Schmidt."

"Ah. No. Not really."

"Will you step over here with me Mr. Schmidt? I'd like to ask you a few questions."

"Candy wants to see Daniel. She's hurt bad. I made a promise to bring him pronto."

Daniel watched as the officer yanked his stepfather away from the door marching him down the hall. He stared at the officer in surprise and watched with a sense of glee as Deputy Metcalf dragged Darrell into the visitor's room. Someone tapped Daniel on the shoulder. He turned and looked into Andrew's face. Mr. Treloar smelled clean like grass warmed by the sun. He looked sad though, "Daniel, you want to see your mother?"

Daniel spun toward the door and pushed it open. Stepping into the room, he saw his mother lying on a hospital bed with a big bandage wrapped around her head and her face, her face looked swollen and sore. She'd cut her lip too. And her arm was in a cast like the one he'd worn only a month ago.

"She's asleep right now, Daniel. But you can sit in this chair and wait. I'll wait with you if you want," Mr. Treloar offered.

"She's hurt. How did she get hurt?" Daniel asked sitting down in the chair Mr. Treloar pulled out for him.

"We're not sure, but Officer Metcalf will find out.'

Daniel slid his chair closer to his mother's bed. He lifted his arm, so he could pat her head and wake her up. He wanted to know what had happened. He wanted to know if the bad men had come back and hurt her.

Mr. Treloar took hold of his arm, "Let her sleep Daniel. We're not supposed to touch her. Okay?"

Daniel dropped his arms into his lap and stared at his mother willing her to wake up and speak to him. When she didn't open her eyes, he looked across the room at Mr. Treloar standing by the window. He remembered that he used to hate Mr. Treloar, that he didn't like him touching Vera. Now he felt sorry for him because Vera liked him better, "Did Darrell hit Mama again and make her cry? Did she run up to the bathroom and lock herself inside until he went to sleep?"

Mr. Treloar turned to face the room. His body blocked Daniel's view of the window, "I'll go get Officer Metcalf, Daniel. You can tell him what you just told me."

Chapter Twenty-One

W ith her book in her lap, Maggie sat under the honey locust. A thump and whack woke her to her surroundings. She looked up just in time to see a pair of canine teeth and a wet hanging tongue before she found herself pinned to the ground by Amos. Amy's black Labrador had a bad habit of jumping on everyone. As Maggie's father liked to say Amos was disobedient and uncouth. Maggie struggled to her feet shoving at Amos and in her most authoritative voice telling him to sit.

He did no such thing. Instead, he left her briefly to escort Amy to the locust. Maggie noticed Amy's wet hair. Pain washed over her when she realized Amy must have been at Jeremy's house. He was the only one with an indoor pool. Amy had gone to the party even though Amy had sworn devotedly to forego the party to show her solidarity with Maggie. Maggie tried to remember that her brain did the feeling, tried to remember what her father said, "If you can think yourself into a funk Mag, you can also think yourself out of one. Thoughts come first. Thoughts determine feelings."

Maggie needed more than ever to control her feelings. She didn't want anyone's pity, least of all Amy's pity. The pain of betrayal was nothing to the gossip and humiliation Maggie would endure if Amy mentioned how upset Maggie was about not being invited to the party. Jeremy's father had recently renovated his home and built a fancy in-door swimming pool. The place also had a bowling alley and two pool tables. There was a custom built changing room and stereo surround and fancy lights for night swimming. All the kids had been talking about the party, at least, all the kids who'd been invited to the party.

Amy leaned her bike against the locust tree and walked toward Maggie. Maggie hoped her face didn't betray her thoughts. She forced a smile. Amy spoke first, "I wanted to tell you before Kris did, you know, about Jeremy's pool party. I mean she wasn't there, but her brother was there, and he would probably say something. I just wanted you to know that I didn't have much fun. I would have had more fun if you'd been there."

This Christmas break had been as dismal as Maggie's frame of mind. There had only been a flurry of snow for one morning and nothing else. The snow would most likely come down once school started again. Today the late afternoon sun still warmed the ground. Maggie could see a few foolish plants poking out of the earth in stupid anticipation of spring. It was four months before spring. Grandpa Murray had been back from the hospital since Lazy had been found, grumpier than usual. She didn't blame him, hospital food tasted awful. He was talking much better now and getting around and everyone thought he would make a complete recovery.

Just then as if her thoughts had been the catalyst, Maggie heard Murray talking on the walkie-talkie, "Who's here Egg?" Murray had started calling her Egg as his way of teasing her, since she worked with the kids at the Eagle Gateway School and he had difficulty pronouncing her name correctly especially her Christian name Margaret Treloar. She glanced at Amy absently forcing a smile she did not feel then spoke into the walkie-talkie, "I'm here Murray. You ready for some lunch now?"

Maggie turned to face Amy, "I've got to go in now Amy. Thanks for stopping by. I'll talk to you later."

"I'll call you tonight after supper. OK?" Amy asked with an uncertain smile.

Maggie nodded agreement and hurried into the house, uncharacteristically grateful that Murray's interruption had also prevented an unpleasant conversation. Maggie found Murray in the living room staring out the window. He turned his wheelchair around smartly and looked over her shoulder in anticipation, "Where's Amy?" he asked. "Is she coming in?"

"Oh, she just stopped by to tell me she'd been swimming."

Murray looked disbelieving then suspicious as if she was teasing him, "Here in Mintlaw? There ain't no pools here. Are you pulling my leg Egg?"

Maggie would rather have talked about something else but knew even with the paralysis on his left side, Murray's brain still worked as sharp as ever, "Jeremy's got an in-door pool. His Dad just finished the renovations on their house."

For a moment Maggie thought she detected anger in Murray's face, anger liked she'd seen last summer before she and Murray had gotten to know each other better. But she couldn't be sure because his expression was back to normal, well, as normal as someone could be that had had two strokes in less than a year.

Maggie spun around and headed for the kitchen. She would make him something spicy. He didn't seem interested in food anymore. He kept saying he wasn't hungry. Even though the doctors wanted him to eat that bland food, she knew Murray liked salsa.

She'd warm up some of the hamburger her mother had used for last night's taco salad and put some on Murray's plate. Maggie glanced at the clock and wondered when her parents would be back from town.

The holidays were the toughest time for Maggie lately; all the parties going on and the feeling of isolation knowing full well she was being deliberately overlooked or ignored were beginning to crush her spirit. It hadn't been so bad last year, last year she'd stayed with Amy and been invited to parties and shopping trips during the Christmas break. Now that Amy and she seemed to have drifted apart, hardly anyone called her anymore. Only Kris called occasionally to chat. Kris was one of the smartest kids in the whole school. Maggie liked her, but she had gotten a taste of what it was like to be with the cool kids and didn't want it to end.

She knew she could learn a lot from Kris yet, how could she carry on a decent conversation when she didn't even understand some of the words Kris used? Sometimes, Maggie had to surreptitiously jot down words Kris used in casual conversation, the word surreptitious having been the first novel word she discovered via Kris' casual conversations. Only after parting, and much later at the supper table, did Maggie ask her Dad how to spell the word surreptitious. Someday, she hoped to understand Kris well enough not to have to look up every other word.

Maggie's parents were pleased with her new friend. Maggie had to be honest, she wasn't brainy and didn't want to be. She struggled to get good grades, while Kris floated through assignments and learned effortlessly. Small compensation was the fact that Kris hated gym and couldn't throw a soft ball if her life depended on it which gave Maggie an edge.

When Maggie heard a heavy crash in the next room and the sound of a wheel spinning, she couldn't move for a few seconds. This time she hadn't been at fault. She knew she wasn't to blame but she was afraid, afraid to go into the living room. At least she remembered to turn off the burner and put the frying pan in the kitchen sink. It took her a second before her legs would obey her.

Ten hours later, after all the chaos had subsided, Maggie realized that her face still felt tight with dried tears and sore from rubbing them away. Even before she'd found Murray on the floor, she'd been crying, feeling sorry for herself because Amy had gone to Jeremy's party. Maggie lay in her bed and stared up at the ceiling listening to the drone of the house, listening to her parents and her uncle talking downstairs, so sober and solemn. Maggie ached inside every time she remembered Murray's face his expression of surprise mixed with fear.

She missed him so much. She would do anything to have him back, back in his wheel chair complaining about the food, about the farm, about everything. Everybody talked about how lucky he had been to go so quickly. This time he'd had a massive heart attack. No pain, they said.

How would they know?

Maggie thought angrily and then slapped a hand over her mouth realizing too late that she'd shouted the question to the four walls. She heard someone's footsteps on the stairs and her father's concerned voice, "Mag, you want to talk now?"

"No, Dad. Just leave me alone. Please."

Maggie rolled over and stared out her window. She could see the full moon in the sky and the locust with its bare branches bending to the wind's will. She could see in her mind's eye Murray's cobalt skin and his eyes wide open. The Murray she knew wasn't there anymore. There was nothing in the body of her great grandfather that she could hold onto. At least she'd had the presence of mind to call the paramedics and her Uncle Andrew. She'd sat on the porch steps outside and urged her parents and uncle to hurry home.

It had only been about a minute or two when she was amazed to see Vera running down the drive toward her. Maggie vaguely remembered Vera wearing a pair of sweat pants, some fluffy blue slippers, and an old wool shirt. Maggie didn't remember going toward her. She just found herself holding onto someone with a heartbeat, someone alive and shivering and hurting for her. Maggie didn't realize how much she'd been crying until she noticed later that Vera's sweater was soaked with tears. Vera stayed long after the paramedics and Andrew arrived, and she was still with Maggie when her parents pulled into the driveway.

It was only when Maggie's mother spoke that Maggie realized she still clung to Vera, "Mag let go of Vera now, honey. Come on, come inside and we'll talk."

Maggie didn't remember what she'd said to her mother to make her mother fall back, nearly tripping over Andrew's feet in her haste. Andrew had been angry, he'd pulled her away from Vera and marched her up the stairs to her room. She could barely remember him saying, "Your mother didn't deserve that. Grow up Maggie. You're not the only one grieving." Thinking about hurting her mother just made the hurt worse.

Maggie couldn't rest, her mind kept going around and around in circles. She jumped off the bed and flung open the door to her room. She wanted to be with the others, even if they hated her now. She wanted to be where there was light and warmth and people.

—

Andrew turned in time to see Maggie standing on the threshold of the kitchen. He was shocked to see the look on his niece's face. She looked like one of those victims of disaster newly aware that the world did not move along predictable lines, that the shear unpredictability of sudden upheaval and violence was more frightening than the violence itself. Gradually the truth dawned upon Andrew; he would never be able to predict the future. People don't live forever. No one is immune from death. His Dad had lived a long life, longer than most, sure, but in the end the hardest part for his father had been living the life of a feeble old man chained to a wheelchair unable to walk his fields and do the hundred odd chores needed to be done around the farm.

Kit opened his arms and Maggie ran to him for a hug. She clung to him for quite a while before she moved. Then she looked at her mother across the table. Andrew got up. It was time to leave. He was an uncomfortable fourth in the room, "Well, I'll head home and make some phone calls. I'll talk to you later."

Just as Kit rose to his feet, Maggie spoke looking at everyone but her mother, "What did I say? I hurt Mom. What did I say to hurt Mom?"

Kit frowned and glanced across the room at Andrew. Rachel was staring at her daughter as if she'd never seen her before. Before Andrew could answer the question, Rachel spoke in a harsh voice, "Now, I know that woman is evil. She's trying to come between me and my child. Maggie, I forbid you to have anything to do with her. You hear me?"

"Whoa wait a minute honey. It couldn't have been that bad. We're all emotional right now. Let's just let things cool down for a few days before we say things we'll regret."

Andrew approached Maggie warily and touched her shoulder, "You want to come outside with me for a spill?"

Maggie looked at her mother. The texture and color of Maggie's skin reminded him of soft suede. No child should be so pale, should have such scars of worry etched along her brow and under her eyes and around her nose. At this moment, the two women could have been sisters with their identical looks of grief and pain. Rachel was in too much pain to rise above her own tender feelings. Andrew had hoped the woman would have pushed aside her own jealousy and come to realize her daughter was in shock and needed her. Rachel was reacting as if Maggie had betrayed her by caring for someone else. Andrew was surprised. Rachel's possessiveness was something unexpected.

Once Andrew stood outside in the crisp air and could look back at the house and the lighted kitchen, he relaxed. Maggie stood beside him, a stiff unnatural creature. He sensed her trembling. He wanted to put his arm around her and comfort her but decided to wait and allow her to come to him. He heard her ask him again, softer this time, the same question she'd asked inside.

Andrew tried to remember the exact words and said, "I heard you say to your mother and these are about the right words – *I don't want to talk anymore. I don't want to talk and talk and talk and forget this feeling. I miss him. I want to remember his face. I want to know he's ok; he's safe and not cold and alone and in the dark. She'll make sure he's ok. She'll go and talk to him and let me know he's ok. That's what Vera can do. So, leave us alone. Just go away and leave us alone.* That's about what you said."

"I said that?" Maggie asked. "Are you sure? That sounds crazy. How can Vera talk to Grandpa Murray? He's dead."

In a whisper he thought he heard her say again, "He's dead," as if the knowledge had finally sunk in. Without a word Maggie ran back into the house. Andrew started toward his car and paused to look up at Rock Wren House. The lights were on. She must be awake. He thought about going to her then changed his mind. It was too early. He would wait. He climbed into his car and drove back to his studio.

—

Vera separated herself from the events of the day. Whenever Kat's face would appear in her mind's eye; she would brush the image away. There was too much pain, pain, and regret. Vera's only solace was the rocking chair and the moonlight streaming through the glass. Rama tried to sit on her lap. After the third attempt, she lifted him into her arms and carried him to the bathroom tossing him inside and shutting the door behind her. She ignored his wailing, behavior which was much more annoying now than when he'd been a man.

A clock ticking away above the refrigerator must have soothed her to sleep. When she woke, she found herself sitting in the chair rocking to-and-fro, clutching her necklace. Then she heard metal tapping against metal. A voice called out, "What the freaking hell are you doing idiot child? Come here, now." Vera hurried to the bathroom door and opened the door a crack. She peeked inside and saw Rama curled up on the terry cloth bathroom rug. She thought about hiding him in Harry's room, changed her mind, and on tiptoe returned to the kitchen listening intently.

When Vera heard the next sound, she bolted from the kitchen and ran out into the moonlit night to stare at the place where the swing set had once been. But there was nothing there. The swings were gone. She heard sounds from the barn and she turned in time to see a woman and a child walking toward her. She waited until the two of them were near the porch and she could see the woman and child more clearly in the moonlight's path.

The shadow that was Ada Aleshire stepped away from the larger shadow of the barn and approached Vera dragging Kat along behind her oblivious to Kat's delicate bones. Ada spoke to Vera in her usual detached superior tone the smoker's rasp more pronounced, "Yes. It's me. And you can see I'm not dead. But this little shit is going to be if you don't hand over my stuff. So where is it?"

"What do you need with Kat?"

Ada sighed and lifted her arm so that Vera could see what she held in her other hand, "I don't have to explain things to you. Just tell me where the asshole hid my stash."

"Not until you tell me why you kidnapped Kat."

"They're teaching her to talk at that school. Someday that's going to be inconvenient for me. I don't have time for your bullshit, gyp girl. Show me or I'll show you something."

Vera turned to face the house and started walking. Ada called out to her, "What the hell are you doing? I know he didn't go in there."

"It's in here. He thought he was so smart," Vera said, her mind rushing ahead of her lies to find the truth. "He showed up at my house when I was digging up the concrete around the old posts." She pointed to the swing-set posts leaning like skinny drunks along the back fence, "I'd been covering up the holes with loose dirt and I was in the process of planting my white cedar tree." Vera pointed at the tree no more than three feet tall sprouting up from the center of the yard like an arm raised in defiance, "That's it there. I had my suspicions he was up to something especially when Woody picked a fight with me."

The lamp by the rocking chair in the corner of the kitchen illuminated only the dining room so that when Vera stepped into the kitchen and passed the refrigerator she had to feel her way toward the kitchen table. Just as she passed the fridge and Ada entered jerking Kat into the room roughly, the presence Vera had sensed gathering strength in the room manifest itself above their heads. Vera saw him just as he leaped into the air. She jumped back in time to avoid his claws and collided with the cupboard.

When Rama landed on Ada's head clawing and hissing and growling, her gun fell and skidded across the floor. Vera ignored the gun. Ada had no time to retrieve her weapon, no time to do anything but desperately pry the wild beast off her. The high-pitched cries of the Siamese and Caracal hybrid in fierce battle with his adversary left Vera stunned, her body frozen in primitive terror and her ears ringing with his growls and high-pitched hissing.

Mixed in with the cacophony of noise from Rama and Ada, Vera heard the slap of the screen door. It wasn't but a moment when Vera realized why the screen door had closed. She'd been so mesmerized by the sight, watching in horror as Ada punched and tore at the cat in equal ferocity, her eyes shut to avoid the needle-sharp claws, her fists striking blows that seldom found their mark. Rama was using his teeth and his claws and his awe-inspiring voice to break the enemy's spirit.

Even though Ada had threatened Vera with a gun and would have had no hesitation in shooting her, her plight sent Vera forward albeit reluctantly. The sensible thing would have been to run. Kat had had the sense to run. But if Vera ran she would never be able to forgive herself if something happened to Rama. She wanted the primeval battle to end. Vera covered her ears against the cat's hissing. She plowed past the combatants with an accompanying screech of her own. She hit the edge of the counter and managed to find the sink basin without mishap and grabbed the sprayer. With all her strength, she yanked the hose. Luckily, she wasn't strong enough to completely remove the hose from the sink basin.

In desperation, she spun around and pointed the hose at the two combatants and pressed the lever. She aimed for Ada, but the stream of cold water hit Rama first. Rama howled and leaped into the air landing on all fours on the dining room table. Her eye caught a glimpse of him as he scrambled away.

In the suddenly quiet room, Vera could hear Ada gasping for air with little bubbly sobs emanating from her throat between the gasps. Vera refused to pity her. She was a cruel greedy woman. She'd never had a moment's empathy for anyone. A woman capable of dumping a child in the mountains deserved no one's pity or compassion. Only a saint could feel sorry for her and Vera was not a saint. Before Ada had time to recover from the cat's attack, she screamed bloody murder and Vera looked down in time to see Harry clawing Ada's leg and opening his mouth to take a bite out of her ankle. Vera called to him, "No Harry. Let go."

Ada grabbed a frying pan off the stove and aimed for Harry's head. Vera screamed, "No," and her terror must have communicated itself to the raccoon. Ada managed only to hit the tip of his tail. Harry streaked out of the kitchen and down the hall. Ada held her bleeding head with one hand and the frying pan with the other. Vera realized quick enough flight would be more prudent. Instead of picking up a weapon such as a large carving knife, Vera cautiously circled the kitchen table and ran out the front door and down the porch steps. She surveyed the night, long enough only to get her bearings before hurling herself down the porch steps.

She could see nothing in the moonless night and desperately searched for a moving shadow about three feet tall. With the full force of her lungs, Vera shouted Kat's name and paused to listen. The ordinary sounds of night greeted her: the creaking of the tree limbs swaying in the breeze, dried leaves on the ground rustling, and in the distance the sound of a car driving away on Jump Creek Road. From the town of Mintlaw, she could hear the wail of a fire truck. Above her head she saw the thin slice of the moon in the cloudy sky. Kat must be close. She was out there somewhere, probably terrified and hiding behind some brush or rock, perhaps even inside the barn. The thought of Kat wandering off into the Owyhees never to be found spurred Vera to move. She searched the barn first but there was no sign of her.

Then Vera thought about the school. Kat would go back to a familiar place, a place she liked. Vera ran down the driveway. A little man with a hammer was busily pounding away inside her skull right between her eyes. The ache made listening difficult. She could hardly distinguish between the rustle of the leaves in the trees and what might have been a little person moving through the cheatgrass. Was that Kat or the wind or some nocturnal creature searching for food? And even without moonlight, the night still offered some hope to the fearful – a good hiding place. There were thousands of possibilities: the tall sage, a boulder or chaparral of bushes and trees, even the odd dip in the ground, a gully, or a ditch.

Oh, for sweet shit's sake; there were so many damned hiding places and no time.

On trembling legs, Vera walked down the incline toward the road searching the ground. Kat could be anywhere. Some of the sagebrush was wide and tall enough to hide a four-year-old. And the trees along the drive, she checked behind each one to be sure. And then she heard a pebble skipping over other pebbles as if a toe had inadvertently touched a stone. Vera knew the game would be played out all night unless she changed her tactics. Instead of chasing after Kat, maybe, she should stop and think. She knew Kat must be close.

If Vera moved forward, she would provoke Kat into moving further away, always keeping a three or four feet distance from her in the mistaken belief they were playing a school game. But this was no time for games. They needed to get away from the house and from the mad woman who used to be her sister, who was probably bleeding all over Vera's kitchen floor right at this very moment and who might just decide to take out her bad temper on Rama or Harry or Kat.

Instead of dashing madly from one end of the road to the other, maybe, it was time to think, to be still as a mouse. Vera sank down on the graveled drive and crossed her legs and bent her head. The gravel hurt her behind, yet she could still feel the warmth radiating off the pebbles from the day's heat. She placed her elbows on her knees and rested her tired head on her hands and waited for Kat to make the next move.

It seemed like eons passed before she sensed someone nearby. Then she heard a rustling in the tall grass. A small shadow separated itself from a clump of bushes. From a few feet away, Vera could see the small figure drawing closer. The shape took form. Kat stopped a hand's breath away from Vera and stared at her, one hand sucking her thumb furiously while the other rubbed a hunk of blonde hair. No words were necessary. Kat hadn't been playing games with Vera. She had used her instincts and hidden from danger.

Vera's relief was enormous. With a silver of hope, Vera rose slowly to her feet so as not to startle the child. She offered her trembling hand to Kat. Time seemed to halt. Vera waited, forcing herself not to make a sound. She sucked in air and expelled it in a sigh wondering what she could do next. As if Kat understood the urgency, she stepped closer, leaned forward, and grasped Vera's hand pulling her away from the house. Under the circumstances, Vera chose to allow Kat to lead them rather than try to fight with Kat about where to go.

Vera would have preferred running down the driveway, crossing the road and heading to the Treloar farm, but instead Kat chose the field of tall dry grass and weeds, which made sense since there was plenty of good hiding places there. But those hiding places were also dangerous. There were snakes and other creatures sleeping in burrows in the field.

And just as dangerous, there were holes, places where someone could trip and maybe break a leg or prickly bushes with their thorns, not to mention the cheatgrass and the irritating bits of them that burrowed into a person's ankles. All these obstacles ran through Vera's mind as Kat led her on a meandering course through the field. Yet as they moved, Vera could tell they were moving east toward the Eagle Gateway School. So rather than fight with Kat over the course of their escape, Vera allowed the child to lead them to safety.

There was a moment when the screen door of Vera's back porch squealed as someone charged through it. The sound startled them both. They froze where they stood and listened to the slapping of the screen door. Hearing someone coming, as one they dropped to the ground and hid behind a clump of tall grasses.

Vera could see the rooftop of her house. The smell of sage surrounded her. She tried hard not to sneeze. Vera waited for Kat to make the first move. The child had an uncanny gift for hiding. In the quiet, Vera heard a sucking sound and realized Kat was busy sucking her thumb. Poor baby, Vera wanted to comfort her but didn't dare in case Kat decided to bolt at her touch. They heard the screen door screech as it opened and closed again, and Vera knew Ada had reentered the house. Vera worried for Rama. Maybe Ada had gone back inside to get her gun? First Vera had to get Kat away from danger then rescue Rama and Harry.

Vera was relieved when Kat chose that moment to stand up and start moving east again. She followed close on Kat's heels. It seemed to take them forever before they were close enough to the road so that they could walk unfettered on the shoulder of the road. Kat began to run, and Vera sprinted after her. Vera thought she heard Kat's voice and the words, "Squeak, Squeak."

Vera was not surprised when peering ahead of Kat, she noticed a large lump motionless on the shoulder of the road. Instead of mistaking the lump for a bear based on its shape and size and the sounds it made, she knew the heavy panting gasps and cries came from a person and she knew the person. As they drew closer to Daniel and stood beside him with Kat looking down at him where he sat on the ground, Vera realized that no ordinary irritant of life would cause him to weep so deeply.

When Kat stepped up to him and put her hand on his shoulder and said, "Squeak, Squeak," Daniel lifted his head and looked at Kat and then Vera.

"She's dead," Vera heard him say. "Mom's dead."

Vera walked up to him and knelt to touch his arm, "I'm so sorry, Daniel. Does Ms. Matthews know?"

"They took him away. He's a bad man. They won't get my treasure. I'm taking it with me.

"Who did they take away Daniel?"

"The bad man, he hurt my Mom."

"Who?"

Kat mimicking Vera leaned down and in a solicitous voice said, "Ou? Ou?"

Daniel ignored Kat and looked at Vera. It hurt just to look at him. He was suffering. She'd never realized how much he loved his mother.

"Who hurt your mother Daniel?"

"Darrell. He's a bad man. He's going to jail forever."

"I'm so sorry Daniel."

"I'm all alone now."

"No, you're not. What about Ms. Matthews? She needs you more than ever now."

"They don't know what to do with me. She'll take my treasure."

"Ms. Matthews won't take your thundereggs."

"Not Mz. Matthews. I mean the ghost."

"Ghosts can't take our things. They can only try to scare us."

"This ghost takes things away from people. She was Darrell's friend. He helped her hide from the police. He was mad when I told Mr. Treloar I dumped the flour down the hole. He called me names. The police are looking for the ghost. She's out here somewhere. She's going to take my treasure."

"I'll make sure she doesn't Daniel. You've got to help me. There's someone bad who wants to hurt Kat. Please take Kat to the school and wake up Ms. Matthews. Can you do that for me Daniel? It's important. Tell her that you found Kat on the road. Please?"

Daniel wiped at his face and glanced in perplexity at Kat who stood above him with her hand on his shoulder. She smiled down at him and said, "Squeak. Squeak."

"I guess that must be your name," Vera said.

"My name is Daniel," Daniel responded in his polite way as if to correct her mistake.

"Will you take her to the school? Please?"

Daniel struggled to stand and with Vera and Kat's help he was on his feet. At first, he just stared at the ground and Vera wondered if he had changed his mind and wanted to leave for good.

Then he pointed at his backpack, "They might take it. I can't let them take it away from me."

"I'll take care of your treasures Daniel. They'll be safe at my house. OK? Please hurry Daniel. Take Kat to the school and remember to wake Ms. Matthews."

Vera knelt to Kat's level and looked at her. Kat looked everywhere but at Vera. Vera told her, "Daniel will take you to the school." Vera searched her face hoping Kat understood. With relief Vera noted that instead of sucking her thumb or rubbing her hair, Kat had chosen to place her hand on Daniel's pant leg as if by holding onto a part of him, she could anchor herself to something familiar.

With reluctance, Daniel handed Vera his backpack. Its weight surprised her. She had expected the backpack to be heavier. She was relieved to know that Daniel's idea of treasure didn't include his massive dinosaur eggs like the ones she'd seen in the shed. Even one of those eggs would have been too heavy for her to carry. These rocks were smaller. While Daniel watched anxiously, Vera drew her arms through the straps and adjusted the straps to fit around her shoulders.

Daniel nodded happily, "Good."

"I'm going back to the house and make sure my cat is safe. Hurry now. Take Kat to the school."

"Kat is here. She's safe."

"No, sorry, I mean my cat. He's a mixed Siamese and something else."

"He's foreign?"

"It's a breed of cat. I'll introduce you to him later. Now do you remember what to do when you get to the school?"

"Wake up Ms. Matthews," Daniel said as he turned on his heels to face east and without further ceremony starting walking away.

"Daniel," Vera called out to him. Daniel paused to look back at her.

"Let Kat walk ahead of you, so you can keep an eye on her and make sure she stays on the shoulder of the road."

"My shoulder?"

"No. I don't want you to carry her, just make sure she doesn't walk in the middle of the road. Keep her on the shoulder of the road, the side of the road, yes, there, where you're standing right now, away from traffic."

"This shoulder?" Daniel asked pointing at the ground between his feet.

"Yes, right there, that is called the shoulder of the road," Vera said, glancing anxiously toward her house wondering if Ada was destroying her house as payback, wondering at herself for spending so much time consoling Daniel and defining a term he should have picked up years ago, while a mad woman caused mayhem and possible murder in her house. The world was full of infinite ironies. She waited another precious minute or two watching as Daniel gently pushed Kat ahead of him; and when Kat stopped in her tracks, Daniel gave her another little push which made Kat giggle. Fortunately, Daniel grew tired of the game and moved ahead. Kat realized the game was over and ran past him and began marching east sensing a strong-minded individual who knew when it was time to go home.

Vera headed in the opposite direction and broke into a run with the backpack full of rocks knocking against each other and against her spine. She made it all the way to the catalpa trees before stopping when she heard a familiar hissing and growling from among the tree branches above her head. She slipped under the low-lying tree limbs and looked up. Then she spotted him midway up the tree clinging to a big limb closest to the trunk. He was too high up for her to fetch. The tree must be thirty feet tall and she just didn't have the energy right now to climb. Besides she'd always hated heights.

"Rama," Vera called to him. "Come down here Rama."

When he continued to hiss and growl, Vera stepped back, "Suit yourself. I'm not climbing up to rescue you. You'll have to find your own way down."

Once Vera had cleared the catalpa and stood in the open, she hesitated staring at her house. Now that there was no one to rescue, she would rather not face Ada alone. Maybe she should wake up the Treloar family and have them deal with her? She couldn't do that to them at this tragic time in their lives though. Murray had died. They were all grieving. Vera would have to take charge of this situation on her own. But then again what was Ada up to in her house? Was she robbing her?

Vera snorted derisively thinking *fat lot of good that will do her*. Then she heard someone in the backyard. Vera slipped behind the protection of the catalpa trunk and waited. When she saw Ada, the insane, nasty monster who had kidnapped Kat and dumped Carolina Fletcher's body like so much garbage and noticed how Ada was walking boldly about the place as if she owned it, Vera felt an unexpected sensation surge through her body, filling her with an energy and power she dimly remembered from long ago.

356

Vera saw Ada pass the barn then bend down and pick up the discarded shovel. The sight of her making herself at home infuriated Vera beyond speech. How dare she act as if the place belonged to her? She was trespassing. She should be running for her life, the arrogant bitch. She saw Ada straighten. And then Ada stood stiff as a statue in the dark holding Vera's shovel, it seemed as if forever. Vera's heart lurched. Could Ada see Vera hiding behind the catalpa? Maybe she was thinking about her next move?

Uneasy now, Vera thought she saw a gun tucked into Ada's waistband. She must be picking up the stuff that might implicate her in Kat's kidnapping. And when would the crazy ass woman get the hell off her property? Vera considered sneaking up on her from behind but changed her mind when she remembered Ada fought dirty. Besides Ada had the advantage, she had a gun and was angry enough to use it.

What astonished Vera the most was the fact that most ordinary people after having been attacked by an angry cat, subsequently bleeding from multiple wounds about the scalp and face would have long since run back to their hidey hole or gone to an emergency room. Not Ada. Ada's single-minded focus had always been admirable but disturbing in its intensity. She was after the "bags of flour" Daniel had found.

But there must have been something else, something even more important than her drugs? Maybe there had been money hidden in the rucksack? Woody might have taken the money and left the drugs. Vera didn't think Woody had ever stolen Ada's rucksack. Ada must have convinced them Woody had taken the drugs and money from her. The Foss brothers would have enjoyed beating a confession out of Woody. Poor Woody, he would have said anything, blamed anyone to be free of the pain.

What the hell did Ada think she was doing? There was an all-points bulletin out on her for kidnapping and here she stayed in Mintlaw searching Vera's property like a demented prospector? Underneath her sweater Vera could feel her tiger's eye necklace laying cold against her skin. She pulled the necklace out and rubbed the stone feeling oddly comforted by its smoothness.

In amazement, Vera watched as Ada calmly retraced her steps and disappeared behind the house. Beyond curious Vera tucked the necklace back inside her sweater and hurried after Ada managing to make her way to the side of the house without tripping. She used the cedar shingled side to guide her in the dark and paused to peer around the corner into the backyard. When Vera saw what Ada was doing, all sense of self-preservation, caution and logic vanished. She burst out into the open and ran at the monstrous creature screaming, "Don't you dare, you crazy, psycho bitch."

Ada spun around startled grasping the narrow trunk of the young cedar tree in her right hand. Vera's momentum carried her straight into Ada's body knocking her down to the ground. Vera rolled off her and without thinking picked up the uprooted tree and stuck it back in the hole she had so recently dug. Unaware of her own danger, yet conscious of movement, Vera shifted avoiding the shovel that whisked past her head. The weight of Daniel's rocks in the backpack shoved her backward until she felt herself falling. She could not stop her backward motion and fell helplessly to the ground, the rocks pressing painfully into her shoulder blades. Frantically she wiggled her way out of the pack and tried to get clear of Ada's malice. Ada lifted the shovel over her shoulders prepared to use it to crush Vera's head.

Vera tried to roll over onto her belly and as she did her leg hit an object in her path. The object happened to be Ada's ankle as she took a step forward for the killing blow. Vera twisted her upper torso to avoid the shovel and kicked out frantically. She felt something thick and hard connect with the side of her foot. Ada lost her balance. She fell forward, and Vera sprang away to avoid being crushed by Ada's weight. The shovel fell. When Vera twisted around, she saw Ada fall forward onto Daniel's backpack. Ada's head hit the rocks inside and Vera heard a snapping of bones. The sound made Vera sick. It seemed to ricochet off the hillside behind her.

Time seemed to stretch on forever as she anxiously waited for Ada to get up. A strange suicidal part of Vera wanted Ada to get up and fight again. Vera waited afraid to breathe. She stared down at her sister and waited for Ada to move or moan or do something. When nothing happened for the longest time, Vera ran to the house and turned on the porch lights. She wanted to be sure. She ran back outside hoping Ada had moved. But she was still lying in the same spot, her head twisted unnaturally.

Vera stood over her. As she surveyed her body, she noticed Daniel's backpack and the truth dawned upon her. It wasn't Daniel's. It had once belonged to Ada and she had lost it up on the hill. It was the leather and canvas World War II reproduction rucksack, the one she had seen in Daniel's cave. Ada would have treasured it; mostly, she would have treasured the thing because the rucksack was a symbol of purity, of Ada's purity.

Someone cried out, a wild cry of despair. It was her, the sound coming from her throat. She couldn't stop. The grief took hold so tight; its talons dug into her heart. She didn't care. It didn't make sense and she didn't care. They had hated each other for so long. And then the memories of when they were children washed over her, how they had had only each other to play with because their family never stayed in one place long enough for them to make friends.

And she remembered those little girls, how they would sit on the curb and pull the fresh tar from the street and make little cakes and their mother would come out of the trailer and march them to the communal pump and wash their hands. They had laughed and shook their wet hands at each other. They had been sisters. They had been family. And now Vera couldn't remember when they had become enemies. It was as if with her death, all the fear, jealousy, and hatred were gone.

A coyote calling woke Vera to the present and she finally had to accept that Ada was dead. Once she accepted the truth, she made her decision. It took a while to remove the clothes from the body, to scrub her clean with soap and water, and finally to wrap her in a cotton sheet from the house. She searched the barn and removed some burlap bags she'd been saving to store her bulbs in. She would place the burlap under the body. Once her sister was prepared for burial, Vera would widen the hole in the ground and make it far bigger than the little cedar tree needed.

Her stomach constricted. The shovel dropped to the ground. She rushed to the garbage cans and opened the closest one. When she was finished, she wiped her chin with the ends of her shirt. The thought of looking out her kitchen window every day and knowing Ada was underneath her cedar tree was too disturbing. Vera would be reminded every morning of her guilt. She couldn't do it. It wouldn't be right. It might have been acceptable in her great grandmother's day but not anymore. She would be breaking a few laws now.

Vera picked up the cedar tree and tenderly replaced it in the hole. She packed the loose earth around the roots. And just to be sure the cedar tree would manage through the night, she walked into her barn and poured a bag of mulch and a bag of small bark together inside her wheel barrow and pushed the wheel barrow back to the tree. With care Vera covered the tree in a protective coat of mulch and made sure the earth was firmly packed. She watered the tree from the well pump.

It wasn't until she sat on the porch step to rest and stared at her sister lying near the cedar tree that Vera knew she couldn't face the police tonight. No more curious reporters and FBI and cops roaming her property and rummaging through her personal belongings. No more publicity and finger pointing. What had happened would look bad no matter how convincing she might be. Vera had one witness to testify on her behave and that witness had a short attention span and few words to express himself and the other witness spoke only two words which meant a good lawyer had a ninety-nine percent chance of convicting Vera for first degree murder. She would go to prison for life or she would die by lethal injection.

By the time she was finished dragging the body into the barn, her arms and legs were trembling with fatigue. The only bright spot in an otherwise horrendous day was finding Harry under her bed still trying to catch the last remaining crickets inside his feeder. And Rama she discovered sleeping on top of her armoire, the armoire she had found at a garage sale, the one she'd spent so many hours sanding and staining and painting. Rama was curled up fast asleep as if he knew the enemy would no longer bother him.

—

The violent pounding on her front door startled Vera awake. Vera lifted her head. Terror ran riot through her brain. She'd been discovered. The police would take her away. Her next thought was: *I'll kill myself first*. Then she heard someone walking around the house to the back. The person began to beat on the glass of the sliding door. She swung her legs off the bed realizing that she was still wearing the jeans and top from the night before. It wasn't until Andrew called her name that all the blood rushed from Vera's head and black dots swam before her eyes.

"I'm coming," she shouted holding onto the wall for support until she could see the floor clearly.

The first thing Andrew said when he saw her was, "Daniel found Kat. She hadn't been kidnapped. She just wandered away. They're both safe and sleeping like the babies they are. Are you okay? Holy shit, what's happened?"

He sank down to the floor beside her and opened his arms. She rested her head on his chest, listening to the beat of his heart as the rhythm went from fast to medium to slow. Then when she heard his heart beating in a slow and even rhythm, she started to talk, "You won't believe me. But I must tell someone. And once I'm done telling you what happened last night, you can decide how we proceed. I have no more energy and clearly no more insight to know what to do." It took her nearly an hour to summarize the events of the night because she kept drifting off to other memories, memories that had nothing to do with the accident but everything to do with her family and Ada and all the miserable events they had shared.

As Andrew and Vera waited for the police, Andrew filled her in on what the police had learned about the Foss brothers, "Utah wants the Foss brothers first. And after Utah, Nevada wants them next. And once they've been convicted in those states, Idaho might get them for their final sentencing. Oh, and Mark admitted that his brother Sim shot Woody in the head.

Darrell Schmidt confessed that he had sheltered Ada Aleshire at his trailer in Jordan Valley. Ada was his supplier of cocaine. Schmidt was the one who stumbled on the van the day after the Foss brothers killed Woody. The brothers had tried to camouflage the van with branches and brush. He told Ada he'd found the van and Ada insisted Schmidt help her take the van to Jordan Valley. She put Woody's body in the freezer and kept the freezer going for the next six months. She wanted to surprise you with a farewell Christmas present—Woody's frozen body on your doorstep. Instead Schmidt got spooked and drove the van to the Oregon Border. Case closed. No more worry about the Foss brothers."

"Whoopee," Vera said in a lackluster voice unable to find the energy to be terrified. "I still don't understand why Ada stuck around Idaho and Oregon for half a year? That doesn't sound like her."

"Evidently, she didn't. Since she'd lost her rucksack with the cocaine and the money, she had to go back to being a mule for her boss. She's been spending the last six months back and forth between the U.S. and Mexico. According to Schmidt, she made a brief detour recently to Seattle to see a lawyer. She was convinced her cousin's kid would eventually learn to talk and tell the authorities about what happened. Schmidt helped that delusion along by telling her how Daniel said Ms. Matthews was the greatest teacher in the world."

They both laughed. It wasn't really funny, but they laughed anyway. Rama came to investigate. Harry showed up shortly after standing on his hind legs and begging for food. Vera jumped to her feet and moved toward the kitchen. Andrew looked up at her and asked, "Will you marry me Veratina Vera Lee Caumlo?"

"Someday I just might, Scrapman."

It felt like déjà vu to be back in the Mintlaw Police Station. Vera went over and over the events of the previous night; and after several hours, she received notification Sarah Matthews had just confirmed Vera's sister Ada Aleshire had been the woman claiming to be Vera's relative and presented a note allegedly from Vera authorizing Ada Aleshire to take Kat out of school. Ada had forged

Vera's signature. No surprise there. The bartender at Three Fingers Rock House also confirmed Ada had booked a room at the motel next door the night before and spent the day asking questions about the Eagle Gateway School claiming to be a relative of one of the students.

Instead of having to spend the night at the police station, Chief Glenjones sent Vera home. It was now late afternoon. When Vera stood under the catalpa tree and stared up into the canopy, she thought she saw something moving but the coloring looked wrong. Once in the house, she sat down in the rocking chair and tried to think. With her head resting on the cushion she rocked back and forth gently. The quiet calmed her nerves. And in the quiet she sensed a presence. It wasn't until he landed on her lap that she was reassured the presence was benign, "How are you getting out of the house, Rama?"

He growled once. *Well as benign as an upset carasiamese can be*, she thought. He curled up on her lap and went to sleep. *All would be well. All is well.*

Vera dreamed of spring.

It was May 1st ,1986. Kat was on the new swing set pumping her legs to get her moving higher and higher, up, and up, into the sky, her eyes closed against the bright sunlight, her expression blissful. Andrew standing by the barbecue opened the lid to examine the steaks sizzling on the grill. When he heard Kat laugh and say, "Creek, Creek," he smiled to himself and took a sip of his beer. With the willow tree behind him, Daniel, on the other side of the swing set was busily securing the net to the remaining pole.

Earlier that day he had helped Vera pour the last of the sand in the box he'd built for Kat in the shade near the willow tree. As he stepped back to look at his work, he forgot about the sandbox and backed into one of the 4 by 4 timbers nearly landing on his butt in the sand. Instinctively, he did a little sidestep dance with his big booted feet, leaned forward with his arms spread like wings and stopped the fall. With a sheepish grin he looked around to see if anyone else had noticed. Nobody had noticed other than herself.

At the picnic table, Maggie and her new boyfriend Juan Esquivel were laying out the plates on the red and white checked plastic tablecloth. Grandma Esquivel won't like that arrangement, Vera thought. Around the corner of Vera's house coming up from the driveway between the house and the barn came Maggie's parents Rachel and Kit. Rachel carried a plate of cookies and Kit carried the potato salad.

Where was she? She couldn't see herself in this dream. Then everyone started moving from side to side as if the ground had shaken itself free from the earth, the way the tablecloth had been shaken to get out the creases, shaken and snapped. The earth beneath her feet shook for real. Vera woke just before her rocking chair fell backward. Rama leaped off her lap and landed safely on the ground. The back of Vera's head hurt where she had hit the slates of the rocking chair. But when she rose up on her feet she realized the dream wasn't over. The world was still shaking. It dawned on her she was experiencing an earthquake. She held onto the heavy kitchen table for support. The earthquake lasted another minute then stopped.

The sudden quiet drove Vera outside. She could see the Treloar Farm. No one was running out to see what had happened. She heard no fire trucks or police sirens. Had she dreamed it all? She ran up the Access and down the rutted road hardly caring that her side hurt. Only when she stood before the cave entrance did she pause in trepidation. And when she brushed aside the prickly limbs of the rabbit-brush and saw the entrance sealed from inside with hundreds of loose rocks, she sank to her knees in thanksgiving. She had not expected this gift. Daniel would be heartbroken. He might even blame her. Her thoughts must have summoned him. Like an apparition from a bad dream, she saw him running toward her, his eyes wild and his mouth open. She backed away and let him see for himself.

He moaned and hit the rocks as if he could push them aside. Then he stood up and looked down at her and for a moment she feared he would blame her. "The ground shook," he said. "Ms. Matthews says it was an earthquake. She says they happen a lot in California. But this isn't California. Did you make it happen?"

Vera could only shake her head and try to step away from him. Something of what she was feeling must have registered. He stepped back, "I don't want to hurt you Miss Vera. You're my friend."

"I know. Go home Daniel. It's been a scary time for us. We've made some mistakes. I should have known better. We can't do anything about the earthquake. It's too dangerous for you to dig for your treasures here. You still have the others at the shed and the police will give you back your little rocks when the time is right."

"They're thundereggs Miss Vera. They're the special ones. I know it. They'll be beautiful inside."

"I'm sure they are," Vera said turning to leave.

Daniel touched her arm. She stopped. "You didn't let me finish my story," he said.

"What story? I don't understand," she told him trying to hide her impatience looking up at him with an uneasy feeling.

"When we were on Poison Creek Road in my Dad's Suburban, you remember, those bad men were in the backseats?"

"I was too busy worrying about running us off the road," she said. "Can't this wait?"

"No," he said emphatically. "I've got to tell you."

She looked around the area. There was nothing she wanted to sit on. She hoped this wouldn't be a long story, "Ok, I'm listening."

"I killed Maggie's grandfather Stewart Treloar."

She crossed her arms and held them close to her chest, "No you didn't."

"How do you know?"

"Where were you when this happened?"

"In the backseat of the Suburban, I heard the shot."

"How old were you?"

He shrugged and looked confused, "I don't know. I was little."

"You didn't kill Stewart Treloar."

"I must have. My father was drunk. He was crying. He kept asking me to get out of the Suburban."

"Come down to the house, Daniel. Andrew should be back with the tacos by now. They'll be plenty for all of us."

"Deputy Stewart asked my father to put down the gun. I heard what my father said; he told Deputy Stewart that kids can be so cruel. Those were his words. He said—I don't want them to hurt my son anymore. You see. I killed Stewart Treloar."

"No. You didn't," Vera told him in a firm voice, stepping forward. "Memories are funny things. Each time we remember something, the memory changes. You feel sad about your father crying. You were in the backseat of the Suburban when you heard the shot. Your father was drunk. You didn't kill Stewart. We'll never know what happened outside the Suburban. It was a long time ago and it's over."

"How do you know it wasn't me?"

"You're about eighteen now. That was eleven years ago. You would have been seven. What kind of a gun was your Dad holding?"

"It was a rifle, a hunting rifle."

"Were you as big as you are now?"

"No. I was small. Mom says. Mom said I was scrawny. That means—

"I know what it means. You heard the shot when you were in the backseat of the Suburban. How could you shoot Stewart Treloar if you were inside the Suburban and your father was outside with the rifle?"

"My father shot Stewart," Daniel said. "I've got to tell Mr. Treloar."

"No. You don't. Andrew is grieving right now Daniel, just like you are about your Mom. He lost his Dad. Let's wait awhile. When the time is right, you can talk to Andrew. Okay?"

He nodded his head in agreement, "Okay."

She looked around, stomped her feet to get them warm and said, "Damned, it's cold out here. Come on down to my house and have a taco."

"No thanks," he said with a smile, the first one she had seen on his face the whole time she'd known him. "I don't like tacos. I got to get back to the school. Mz. Matthews needs me."

As he turned to walk away, she thought of something else and asked, "What do you think you were shooting at the night I was accidently shot?" she asked him, surveying the ledge on the other side of the gully with interest.

She heard him say over his shoulder, "I don't know."

"Was it my sister Ada?"

"No. It was meaner than your sister." She saw him glance at where the cave entrance had been and heard him say, "She's trapped now. She can't hurt anyone anymore."

Vera didn't believe in ghosts. She remembered there had been something behind her, something that smelled wild, maybe a cougar. Only after she was sure Daniel was on his way down the hill and headed across the stretch to school, did she make her way back home. She was glad he hadn't figured out what his father had meant by the words, "I don't want them to hurt my son anymore." It made her more convinced than ever that people who wished they knew the future were batshit crazy.

Who would want to do anything if they knew what was going to happen to them the next day, the next year, or on the day of their death? Not unless one had the power to change it. If Ada had known how she would die would she have changed her behavior? Vera didn't think so. Ada didn't believe in fortune telling. That was one thing she and Ada could agree on. But Aunt Vista and their mother believed in the supernatural. Her mother had used the Ouija board and claimed that Vera would marry a policeman one day. That had been wishful thinking on Analetta's part. It was best not to fool around with Ouija boards and fortune telling or anything to do with the supernatural.

The only thing Vera believed in anymore was making amends for her past mistakes.

Poor, Woody.

Poor, Ada.

Equally as sad was the thought of the bones in Daniel's cave. There would be no grand discovery of the woman guarding Hunter's Hill. She might have been thousands of years old or she might have been only a few decades old. Now, no one would know, at least not in Vera's lifetime.